WIRELESS

ALSO BY JACK O'CONNELL

Box Nine

WIRELESS

JACK O'CONNELL

THE MYSTERIOUS PRESS

Published by Warner Books

A Time Warner Company

Mysterious Press books are published by Warner Books, Inc., 1271 Avenue of the Americas, New York, NY 10020.

A Time Warner Company
The Mysterious Press name and logo are registered trademarks of Warner Books, Inc.

Printed in the United States of America

First printing: November 1993

10 9 8 7 6 5 4 3 2 1

Library of Congress Cataloging-in-Publication Data

O'Connell, Jack.
    Wireless / Jack O'Connell.
        p. cm.
    ISBN 0-89296-546-0
    I. Title.
PS3565.C526W57 1993   92-50895
813'.54—dc20   CIP

Book design: H. Roberts

For my mother
&
in memory of my father

ACKNOWLEDGMENTS

The author is indebted to the following works and wishes to express his gratitude to the authors: *Border Radio,* by Gene Fowler and Bill Crawford; *Radio: A Blast from the Past,* by H. G. Wolff and I. Jacobson; *1991 Passport to World Band Radio; Cambodia: A Book for People Who Find Television Too Slow,* by Brian Fawcett; *Big Secrets,* by William Poundstone; *Worcester's Best,* edited by Elliott B. Knowlton; *Monitoring Times* magazine; and, especially, the *JamCon '84* cassette by Negativland.

I am down on my knees at those wireless knobs.
—Van Morrison

PART ONE

FRIDAY

1.

A good number of the old churches in Quinsigamond have found other uses. These big, dark houses of God have been turned into nightclubs and restaurants, a museum, a weight training salon, and these weird, upscale condos for the city's nouveau riche Europhiles.

There was a big fad that peaked maybe five years back. Developers were grabbing the churches on the point of absolute decay, abandoned monsters whose parishioners had died out or moved on. For a while, every hustler with a real estate license was trying to find a way to target St. Brendan's, Quinsigamond's only cathedral. But the diocese held out, the bishop refused all offers. St. Brendan's was still a legitimate parish, even if the bulk of its worshipers were outpatients from Toth Care Facility, tethered to their pews by a pocketful of lithium.

Now the market's gone bad and more than one builder has filed Chapter 11. St. Brendan's looks like it's outlasted another trend. Speer sits in his car in the church lot and stares up at the structure. *How could they want to desecrate such a thing?*

To Speer, the cathedral is an architectural miracle with only one function—the singular glorification of the one true God. Whoever drafted the plans had to have been divinely inspired. This is the only explanation that makes sense, that offers a justification for the majesty that springs up from a common gravelly lot in the heart of downtown.

The church is almost a hundred and fifty years old, a monument to the tenacity of gray granite. It's a traditional nave-and-transept setup, but its centerpiece is a square tower that rises up in stages of arched windows and concludes with castlelike buttresses at each corner. The tower gives the cathedral the look of a fortress, a bastion of strength that could hold off a lifetime of heresy.

Speer instinctively senses, but has no respect for, the irony of what's happened to this church; the fact that this living artwork and testament to the possibilities of a honed Christian mind should become the stamping ground for the refuse of society. It sickens him these days when he watches the kinds of people who climb the granite stairs to make a visit. There are the dozens of street folk, the deinstitutionalized peasants who live in the alleys and cellar holes off Main Street. There are the drunks and addicts who fixate on some childhood, addlebrained idea of Christ. There are the last remnants of the old neighborhood, the elderly who never moved on and now haunt the cathedral with their walkers and canes. And there are the rapidly growing clans of immigrants, the majority illegal. Speer calls these people *the mutants*. He thinks they're the product of some awful recessive gene that condemned certain countries to a continual backwardness. They are the bottom of the DNA barrel, but nature has seen fit to give them wild breeding abilities, and so they explode beyond their natural boundaries. Every time some petty despot seizes their homeland, they run to America to live the parasite's dream.

They are Hispanic and Indian and, more and more often, any one of a variety of the Asian tribes—Laotian, Vietnamese, a slew of Cambodians. The federal and state governments help them buy the dilapidated tenements packed into the center of town, and then literally dozens move in, five to a bedroom, people sleeping on tables. They bring the aunts, the uncles, the cousins and in-laws over on the next freighter. They raise chickens in the kitchen cabinets and practice unspeakable religious rites on the back porch.

Except for the converts, the ones Father Todorov has gone to great pains to win over. *This is what you want as the future of Catholicism,* Speer thinks, and bites down on his back teeth. He finds the name Todorov particularly suspect. It sounds Russian and they've got their own very insular rite—Russian Orthodox, out of old Constantinople. Speer has read a book on the history of schism in the church. *Splinters from the Rock,* by an ex-Jesuit named Bloom. He couldn't get a handle on where the author's heart lay. But he does know that the modern toleration of heretical thought could be the end of the only true route to God.

There was Todorov just last week allowing a Lutheran minister onto the St. Brendan's altar to read the gospel. A show of ecumenism. A display of understanding. And a two-column photo in the religion section of the *Spy*. Todorov has been pulling down more than his share of press lately. Last summer, when no one was looking and half the chancery was playing golf on Cape Cod, the good father starts up his own radio hour on QSG. *The Word Made Flesh.* His initial broadcast was exactly what Speer expected, an apologia for Liberation Theology and Marxist Clerics. But grudgingly, Speer had to acknowledge the man had classic radio skills, a natural heir to Fulton Sheen, not a trace of an accent, never a stammer or cough, and always building to commercial-time climaxes.

And now Fr. T's latest crusade is the city's mounting gang problem. He explained it on last week's show as a "natural outgrowth of a morally reprehensible foreign policy." Speer was glued to the radio, both disgusted and fascinated by the bizarre progression of the priest's logic, his proposition that American support for "genocidal tyrants around the world" has "bred a violent mind-set" among the "global peasantry, *the fellaheen*." The peasants seek sanctuary in our urban cesspools and "bind into the only form of security they've been allowed to know— the gang system, the tribal rite."

Speer wonders—*where did this guy learn to talk this way?*

So now the priest tries to play big brother to the dozens of immigrant packs attempting to carve out a block or two for themselves in their new home. One day he's down bringing donated food to the Haitian Tonton Loas. The next, it's government cheese to the Castlebar Road Boys, drug-running IRA punks. In the meantime, all this street trash with their coded tattoos and colors are muling skag and doing drive-by clubhouse hits.

Speer thinks that throughout human history, more damage has been done by misguided men than by those with consciously heinous intent. He thinks that maybe the worst sin of all is the sin of confusion. He thinks that on their first day in the seminary, all novitiates should have a quote branded onto their chests, backward, like the ignorant cattle they are. Then each morning they could rise and look in the mirror and read the words that lie on the skin above their heart: *I would not even believe in the Gospels were the Holy Church to forbid it—Francis Xavier.*

Todorov clearly doesn't see the danger of his actions. He views himself as a man with a mission, maybe a destiny to fulfill. The horror is that he's giving these heathen scum some degree of credibility, making the public see them as a genuine collective, an organized force to be dealt with rather than a minor, excisable exception to the rules of order and progress.

Speer knows the gang boys in ways Fr. Todorov never will. He knows them as aberrations, throwbacks to the pack mind of wild dogs, dim-witted, overstimulated, unsure of what they need or want and striking wildly at whatever comes their way.

This is the kind of vile scum Todorov wants to bring into the Church.

To save.

Speer wants to place firm hands on the priest's shoulders and explain slowly, "There is nothing to save. This is basic theology. Look at the faces. Look at the features. Animals. Beasts of the earth. And as such, they have no souls."

Speer puts his hand in his coat pocket, touches the canister, finds two loose Excedrin, pulls them out, and puts them in his mouth. The headache is probably too far gone now, but he dry-swallows the caplets anyway.

Todorov isn't a stupid man. Why can't he see the simple fact that following the fringe, following after the aberration, will always lead down a blind alley? The only explanation for the priest's actions is the sin of vanity, the vice of raging ego. Pride will always make the brain lie to the soul. Todorov wants to be a shepherd so badly he's tending to a flock of serpents.

Speer looks up and sees fewer people exiting the cathedral. He glances to his watch and sees confessions are just about over, so he gets out of the car, crosses the street, and enters through the enormous, castlelike front doors.

He stands in the doorway for a moment and lets his eyes adjust to the dimness. He moves to a small table set next to the St. Vincent de Paul Society collection boxes and picks up a mimeographed flier. It takes him a second to realize it's written in Spanish.

He walks through a second set of double swinging doors into the main body of the cathedral. He slides into the last pew, kneels, folds his hands in prayer, and starts to take inventory. To his left is an elderly couple kneeling in a pew next to the confessional booth. And far to the front, up at the altar, is a large-bodied nun in a reformed habit, folding fresh white linen cloths. Speer scans the whole scene again.

He grew up in churches like this one. Smaller versions, but always built of heavy stone, like the cathedral, always ornate rather than quaint, with long aisles and cold, shadowy choir lofts, and a dark, smoky tinge to the walls where the heating system would push dust and grime upward year after year. Places where every word echoed and threatened to end up unintelligible.

Speer grew up dreaming of overseeing a place like this, four or five curates under his domain, maybe a crowded school staffed by classic disciplinarian nuns, enormous May Processions spilling out into the streets, and local politicians sniffing around each year for a vague endorsement. Three months in the seminary severed any hopes of fulfilling that dream. He found the core dogma of the institution had been subverted. And he knew that once that happens, the cancers of compromise and rationalization spread like an unbroken line of oil fires down the landscape.

Speer left the seminary and signed on with the FBI.

The nun on the altar folds and smooths her last piece of linen and exits into the sacristy. A few moments later the older couple finish praying their penance simultaneously, slide out of the pew, and leave. And Speer is alone with the priest.

There's the sound of a cough and then Todorov appears from the sacristy, a set of keys in his hand, ready to lock up the church now that all the Masses are done.

Speer gives a hesitant voice and says, "Are you leaving, Father?"

Todorov squints down toward the rear of the church, then smiles and says, "Can I help you with something?"

He starts down the aisle toward Speer, and Speer moves his head around sheepishly and motions with one hand toward the confessional booth.

The priest pauses. "Do you want to..." He trails off and mimics the motion with his keys.

"If it's not too much trouble," Speer says.

"Not at all."

Speer waits and allows the priest to enter the box, then moves out of his pew, steps in the adjoining booth, and pulls the heavy curtain closed behind him. He goes down on the cushioned kneeler, waits a beat, and then hears that old sound, that childhood sound of the miniature door, the sliding panel being pushed open to reveal the shadowed face of the priest, in profile, his ear turned to the penitent, obscured behind a heavy mesh.

The sound and the sight take Speer back for a moment, catch him off guard.

Fr. Todorov says, "Go ahead, my brother."

And Speer instinctively begins speaking in a low, rote voice. "Bless me, Father, for I have sinned. It has been—"

Another pause and then an improvisation. "—an awfully long time since my last confession and these are my sins."

He stops. Todorov gives him a good ten seconds, then says, "It's all right, son. Remember why we're here. God has infinite forgiveness."

"You truly believe that, Father?"

Speer can almost see the priest smile on the other side of the mesh. "With all my heart, my friend. That's the root of all my faith."

"But you've made a very broad statement, Father."

"How is that?"

"What I mean is, is forgiveness the same as redemption?"

"I'm not sure I'm—"

"I'm speaking about the unconverted, Father. I'm talking about those outside the Faith. I'm asking you, can they be redeemed?"

"Are you trying to tell me you're not Catholic? Is that—"

"Excuse me, Father, but, in this day and age, what would you mean by Catholic?"

Now Todorov pauses, backs away from the confessional screen, seems to put a hand up to his face.

"Well, very simply, were you ever baptized in the Catholic Church?"

"Is that necessary, Father?"

"Necessary? I'm not sure . . . I'm not sure we're on the same track here. Did you want to make a confession?"

"It's just that I've been following your work, Father. You've been in the *Spy* quite a bit lately. And I'm just wondering what it is you tell the heathens—"

Now Todorov interrupts, his tone turning sharp, his torso leaning back to the screen. "Heathens?"

"The gang boys. The Tonton Loas. The Angkor Hyenas. The Granada Street Popes."

"I'm not sure we're in the right place to—"

"Of course you're right, Father. It's just that your work, what I've read about, the things I've heard—it's all caused me to rethink certain... Well, it has relevance to my confession, you see."

The priest is curious now, maybe on the verge of being flattered. "Go on."

"It's just that, Father, the things I've done... It's very difficult to... I'm very ashamed..."

Todorov is in his element now. His voice turns professional, a brother to his radio voice. "God's brought you here today for a reason, don't you think? We can't change the past, my friend, but we can repent. That's why you're here. There are things you want to tell me, yes?"

"Yes, there are, Father."

"Yes, there are. Now, you take a deep breath and you let the Spirit move you."

"It's very difficult, Father—"

"God will give you the strength. Tell me your story."

Speer begins to whisper in a voice too soft to be heard. Todorov says, "If you could just speak up a bit, my friend."

Speer sees the priest lean his ear toward the screen. The buck knife comes up and slashes the mesh diagonally. Speer's free fist flies through the opening, catches the priest in the eye, breaks open skin. His hand grabs hold of Todorov's throat and pulls the priest's head through, into the penitents' booth. Before the priest can scream, Speer has a full arm around his neck and the blade to his throat.

"I'll have your tongue on the floor before you can make a fucking sound."

The priest starts to let out small, panicky gasps that immediately evolve into a wet gurgle.

"I want you to know what you've done. I want you to realize what your actions have brought you. I hope God can have more mercy on you than I."

Speer brings the knife down, pockets it, and draws from his jacket a small silver metal cylinder about the size of a hip flask.

He holds it up in front of the priest's face, actually touches the man's forehead with it like some kind of quick anointing.

"This is benzine."

He brings the canister up to his mouth, grips the cap with his teeth, unscrews the top, and spits the cap to the floor.

"The Nigerians used to be crazy for this stuff a while back. Warring tribes used to pour it over their captives. Made for an unbelievable sight. A man on fire with this shit—it isn't like he just burns. This is like rocket fuel, okay? You explode."

Todorov makes a single frantic pull backward, a seizurelike move of absolute panic. Speer tightens his grip on the neck and begins to pour the benzine over the top of the priest's head.

"Just like baptism, Father."

He empties the canister and drops it.

"Coincidentally, you know who's big on benzine death these days? That's right. Your own little Hyenas, there. The little Cambodian fuckers. It'll look like you and the Hyenas had a disagreement. But that was bound to happen."

Speer gets ready, takes a breath, then lets another punch fly, connects at the bridge of the priest's nose, hears the bone break. At the same time he releases his hold and Todorov's head shoots backward, back into the confessor's booth.

In a single, graceful motion, Speer swings out of the confessional, grabs his Zippo lighter from his jacket, thumbs up a flame, and tosses the lighter in on top of Todorov. There's an explosive sound of air popping, a gustlike rush of noise that increases in volume and chokes out any scream as the priest's body tumbles sideways out into the church, immediately unrecognizable, a crumbling tower of blue-green flame, an inferno of dizzying incineration of flesh, hair, fabric, and then, in seconds, bone, calcium, muscle, and marrow. It's like staring into the corner of a canvas that depicts the lowest and most brutal level of hell, blown up into a close-up and made animate. Todorov's body stops moving. The curtain of the confessional is transformed into blue flames. The worn carpeting starts to burn below the pile of imploding cleric. The wood of the confessional booth catches. It's a species of burning, a breed of fire that most people never get a chance to see.

But Speer is already in his car and pulling onto Harrington Street, a new Torquemada in a Ford sedan, a rush playing through his body like a pure bolt of speed, as if the glands of some raging god have been planted at the base of his spine. And a small buzz starts up in his ear like a brilliant insect, congratulating him on his step over the line, on his entry into the world of action.

2.

Wireless, despite its name, did not set out to become a meeting place for the city's radio freaks, though its owners, Mr. Ferrie and Mr. Most, were both longtime broadcast buffs. They'd met locally, over at Jonas University, and spent four years together, locked inside the college station, restaging a lot of the pre-television radio gags that had been popular in their parents' era: d.j.'s on the air a week without sleep, ridiculous and endless fake interviews, "Louie, Louie" played for forty-eight hours nonstop.

They took the inevitable step over the line when, a week after the Kent State killings, they ran a mock *War of the Worlds*–type all-day news report concerning the seizure of the campus by fatigue-clad CIA commandos reporting solely to Spiro Agnew, and the subsequent courtyard execution, relayed in graphic blood-spurting detail, of the student newspaper editor, the women's collective coordinator, and two-thirds of the philosophy department.

The dean's office was not amused. Ferrie and Most were suspended for the balance of their final semester and never bothered going back for their degrees. With time on their hands and few employment prospects, they borrowed money from their parents and purchased a condemned 1920s lunch car that was oddly attached to a condemned former factory.

13

Their hope was to round up some hands-off investors and turn the place into Quinsigamond's first cutting-edge, independent, underground radio station. The first prospective financiers didn't stay long after it was revealed that the station would program, in Ferrie's own words, "dramatic readings from the works of Herbert Marcuse—right alongside only the purest R&B." Furthermore, they'd accept no commercial advertising. At this point one possible investor, an uncle of Most's back in Newark, shook his head, confused, and asked, "No advertising? Where do I get my return?"

Ferrie and Most shook their heads back at him and said in unison, both their voices rising in pitch to accent the word's last syllable, "Return?"

As the uncle threw them out of his home, Ferrie made an improvised pitch that they'd sell their blood on a regular basis.

Instead, they scrapped the radio station idea and reopened the diner as a diner. They cleaned the lunch car and fashioned enough Mickey Mouse repairs to placate the licensing board and, surprisingly, during the first month of operation, found they'd stumbled into the right market—blue plate specials for a blue-collar town. Neither was an expert chef, but they borrowed family recipes for meat loaf and chili and turned a modest and, at the time, somewhat embarrassing profit the first year.

Ferrie shocked himself by realizing he had a facility for business. Most uncovered a latent flair for design. They reinvested continually, eventually bought the ruined factory building grafted to their rear. They expanded, renovated the dim mill that had spun a century's worth of machine parts from the sweat of immigrant labor. By the late seventies, the partners drifted onto the dangerous precipice of late-night hipness, and became night-club mavens. They scored a liquor license, contracted live bands, sculpted a hazy-neon back-street motif, suspended huge, original, local artwork on the now-chic exposed-brick walls. And Wireless became a certified hot spot.

Today, people pulling into the crushed-stone parking lot at 10 P.M., letting their headlights play off the unique structure gleaming deep-colored light and literally humming with an electric buzz, have a tendency to indulge in hindsight and state, "The place couldn't miss." But Ferrie and Most would be the first to tell anyone their fortunes rose on the uncontrolled tides of luck and weird social fads.

In their adjoining offices above the dance floor, they keep on the wall, framed in acid-proof matte and imported wood, lit by glareless, recessed lighting, color snapshots of the diner and factory as they existed on the day the partners took title: filthy and falling down, an occasional grave for junkies and derelicts, a nest for urban wild dogs, a fire trap, a blight on the landscape calling out for a John Deere bulldozer. Next to these are shots of the building as it exists today—sandblasted clean, hauled into the future without destroying the feel and look of the past.

In its present, pristine state, something about Wireless looks almost unreal, as if it were the product of Hollywood set designers and special-effects wizards. There's a weird glow that seems to emanate from the diner when you see it from a distance, sitting at the end of the long, dead-end, gravel road. It looks like a streamlined train car designed by men drunk with optimism, crazed with hope for a future of limitless progress where technology paid as much heed to aesthetics as functionality. The diner always seems ready to lurch into motion, to start a frantic but absolutely smooth charge down a set of invisible tracks, powered not by steam or diesel or electricity, but rather by the sheer spectacle and insistence of the neon light that runs in sleek, flowing tubes along the edges of the structure.

The neon is a Halloween orange and it culminates on the roof of the lunch car where deco letters spell out the word *DINER*. Piggyback above the *DINER* sign is a huge deco-style capital letter G that gleams in yellow neon. A lot of the regulars are convinced the G has some special significance, that Ferrie and Most have coded some cryptic meaning into a single letter of the alphabet. But in fact, the G merely stands for the original diner owner's name—Lennie Grimoire. Ferrie and Most could make that fact public and put an end to the rampant speculation and betting. But they live for exactly that air of vagueness and mystery and so the yellow-neon G is allowed to stand for everyone's wildest interpretation.

The front wall of the diner is made of baked porcelain painted a forest green with canary-yellow block letters that read *WIRELESS* and at either end announce *Tables for Ladies*. Above the lettering are an even dozen double-pane windows with gilt trim. The roof is accentuated by a small stainless-steel lip that gives just a touch of overhang and shades the windows.

Inside is all marble and chrome and stainless steel, offset by more neon and wooden paddle fans, deco-tiled floor, polished oak walls, and muted purple and blue spotlights. The lunch car section of the building features the original black-veined marble counter that stretches for fifteen feet with a dozen chrome and Naugahyde stools bolted to the floor behind a long brass foot rail. Behind the stools are a dozen booths with plasticized leather covering over solid-wood frames. The lunch car serves some simple dishes, standard diner food—chili, stews, an occasional goulash. The dishes sit in steam wells and fill the room with a distinctive but unidentifiable aroma.

Where the diner gives way to the interior of the old factory is where Ferrie and Most let their imaginations start to run free. Inside the brick caverns that extend backward behind the lunch car, all rules of design logic were allowed to be broken. There is no grand plan, no underlying theme to the interior of Wireless. Ferrie and Most worked slowly and instinctively in putting their world together. They filled up factory space piecemeal, as the money came in. They rustled the decor from a wide variety of sectors. One week they'd scavenge from flea markets all over New England, the next they'd pay top dollar just for the right to bid at an unannounced auction in a Manhattan gallery. They bought close-out merchandise from salvage companies. They purchased mail-order from weird trade magazines. They bartered and swapped and got involved in drawn-out installment sales on items no one could imagine them needing in the first place.

But the items always fit in with such symmetry and style that now it seems like Ferrie and Most were born masterminds of intricate design and placement. And they've given up on trying to convince anyone otherwise. Who could accept their protestations that everything in Wireless simply gave off a vibration? That it was the items that bagged the owners and not the other way around.

The building is now as crowded as a Victorian china cabinet. There are barber chairs occupied by full human skeletons that were donated by a couple of med school dropouts in exchange for a "regular's" table in the diner. There are three perfectly restored, chrome-festooned Harley-Davidsons impaled through their seats by carousel poles and suspended in midair like some carnival ride for monster children. There's the front end of a 1961 Rolls-Royce Silver Cloud II coupe that appears to have crashed through a sidewall, though closer inspection reveals that the loose bricks and mortar on the hood and floor are cemented in place. Next to this frozen collision is an authentic old fire-engine-red gasoline pump that one regular has customized so that a press of the nozzle dispenses what rumor purports to be a blast of nitrous oxide but what is, in fact, merely pure oxygen.

In the rear of the factory, in a section the regulars call Minnesota, is the billiards room. It includes a high wall of reference books solely devoted to radio. Some of the books are intricate manuals and others are memoirs and nostalgia from the entertainment field, but all chronicle Ferrie and Most's lifelong obsession.

The billiards tables are actually five genuine caskets, sold at cost by an undertaker named Frankie Loftus. A couple of self-styled cabinetmakers went to work on them one day and produced a weird new version of bumper pool complete with sawed-off cues and smaller but denser pool balls. The exposed-brick walls of Minnesota are hung with framed photos of radio legends from bygone days: Major Kord, Cowboy Slim Rinehart, Rose Dawn, Paul Kallinger, and J. C. Bishop.

But most of all, inside Wireless you find radios. They're everywhere. Crosleys, Philcos, Farnsworths, G.E.'s. Running exactly down the center of the factory are a series of floor-to-ceiling brick pillars that serve to buttress the roof. The sturdier waist-high cabinet radios are positioned around these supports like deco altars, as if the nightclub were a cathedral where each priest had his own blessed platform for performing a complex rite. The smaller, rarer models are placed on display shelves, like royal jewels or the bones of saints, underneath arcing acrylic domes. Each booth in Wireless comes equipped with its own radio done up to look like a 1950s chrome-sided, bubble-faced mini-juke.

From the start, Ferrie and Most's shrine to radios and weirdness brought in the crowds—the curious as well as the hard core. They pumped a good cut of their profits back into the machine, kept reinvesting in atmosphere, always giving the customers more of a taste, continually upgrading their tickets to a semi-alien milieu. The process kept paying off.

Though they stumbled into the club-owner life—all tailored Italian suits and a closet just for footwear; imported two-seat cars and annual winter trips to the Caribbean—Ferrie and Most never lost their love for radio. In a prominent corner of Wireless, up on a platform that some regulars call the Shrine, they installed an original, perfect-condition, still-functional forty-one-inch-tall Stewart-Warner cabinet model with the patented Magic Key-board tuner. But despite this beautiful receiver, they could only pick up the same, common commercial broadcasts as anyone else. Until one night when Ferrie went down in the basement to bring up a fresh case of Dewar's, stumbled over some leftover equipment Most had stored there years before, forgot the Scotch, and hauled up a crate of dust-blanketed microphones, amplifiers, turntables, and speakers. He found an empty booth, dumped the stuff on the table, and began hooking up. His enthusiasm caught on immediately and within the hour someone had unplugged the Stewart-Warner and the club owners were sitting opposite each other, their mouths hidden by fat Electrovoice mikes, doing a show that was limited to the interior of Wireless.

But that limited audience was enough to bring back to Ferrie and Most a lost joy. Their improvised interplay had a manic quality to it. They seemed to share one set of brain waves when they were *on the air.* They could finish sentences for each other, come up with brilliant punch lines for on-the-spot jokes. They played rare, sometimes bootleg R&B gems between gabtime. They editorialized, prophesied, lampooned, became passionate in an odd, endearing way.

It was sometimes as if some extra, unnatural current ran between both microphones and into the hands of the men on opposite sides of the booth, some occultish line of mystery that pulled them into sync, meshed their subconscious thoughts, time-shared neurons and synapses, twinned dreams for mutual consumption. The growing cast of regulars at Wireless could feel it, but resisted speaking about it, as if they wanted to guard it, nurture it, and make it into an unspoken cult of electrical storytelling.

But like all cults, word of its existence leaked outside the borders of the diner and mill walls, and the like-minded—radio freaks of one form of another—began to gather. There were the techno-heads, people usually into shortwave and the textbook theories behind its practice. There were the nighthawks, people who only seemed to feel connected to other pockets of humanity when those pockets were perceived at 4 A.M. in a darkened room as detached and very laid-back voices drifting out of a pillow speaker. There were some d.j. groupies, some straight, simple R&B fans, some C.B. folk who loved to listen to the logistical reports of long-distance truckers, some New Wave rejects from the artsy Canal Zone who were into "random radio noise." And there were the jammers.

The Wireless regulars knew of the jammers' existence almost at once, but a strange taboo was in place from the start: you don't rat on jammers. There wasn't much logic behind the dictum. Jammers, by their very nature, represented opposition to, maybe destruction of, the exact medium that gave radio freaks value and meaning in their lives. But logical or not, the jammers were not only tolerated but fully accepted. Possibly they were considered the problemsome black sheep of an already somewhat ostracized family—the prodigal sons and daughters who, though you knew they were going to drain your wallet, break your heart, maybe rupture the very idea of Family that you cherished so much, you helped and protected and endured. Ferrie and Most knew instinctively that logic was not a key strand in the net that bound families—even the most oddly connected and fragile—together.

There was also an appealing aura that jammers seemed to give off when they weren't obsessively concerned about remaining hidden, "deep in average-cover," as Wallace Browning said, in "mole-mode," as G.T. Flynn referred to it. Outside the solitude of their own homes, their hidden jamming stations and disruption rooms, the loosest a jammer could be was at Wireless. When their guards came down, even slightly, they let show just how noble and dangerous and frontline they thought their avocation was. And out of that attitude came a visible surety—not quite a cockiness, but more an assurance of self-worth that was vaguely manifested in their appearance or demeanor. They could throw on their oldest clothing and look hip and pricy. They could preach memorable sermons with the slight turning of eyes and tightening of the mouth. And they seemed to have an edge in the seduction department.

This is close to what Flynn is thinking, standing out in the parking lot, leaning against his car and taking in the beauty of the whole place and peering in a window, watching Hazel cadge drinks from a pair of college-boy d.j.'s with pockets of New York cash.

Is there anyone who knows how old Hazel really is? Best guesses range somewhere around the early twenties, but few of the regulars have ever seen her outside of Wireless and it's hard to get a good look at her face in the dim blue light of the bar.

Hazel was one of the first jammers to start hanging at the bar, right after G.T. and before Wallace, though Wallace doesn't really hang, just uses the place like a 3-D bulletin board. Hazel spends a lot of time teasing the curious newcomers. She allows rumors to spread, sometimes starts them herself. No one except Flynn knows what her day job is, if she has one. Some say hairdresser—based, most likely, on the several different colors and styles she might move through in a given season. Some say stewardess, since she tends to disappear for days at a time and has been seen drinking those tiny nip-bottles of airplane booze in the rest room. If Ferrie and Most know, they're not telling.

Flynn probably knows more about Hazel than anyone else and that's not a lot. He knows she was married once, a teenage romance that didn't last the year. He once heard about a child put up for adoption, a boy that lives somewhere in the county.

A Volvo pulls up in front of him and Flynn smiles, leans to the car window, and says, "I thought you two would've taken home half the gold by now."

Behind the wheel, Wallace Browning rolls his eyes. "We're running late, as usual," he says.

Browning's wife, Olga, leans over and says, "Wish us luck, G.T."

Flynn reaches in the window and grabs Olga's hand. "You two don't need luck, my friend. You've got magic feet." He glances down to the floor, always intrigued by the customized pedals on the Volvo.

Wallace and Olga are both dwarfs. They each stand about three feet tall, but that doesn't prevent them from being two of the most graceful and imaginative ballroom dancers Flynn has ever seen.

Wallace leans his head out the window a bit and whispers, "Did you talk to the problem child yet?"

Flynn sighs and shakes his head, a little annoyed. "I just got here, Wallace. The night is young."

The dwarf makes a mild hissing noise. His voice rises and he says, "Mark my words, G.T. If we don't—"

Flynn cuts him off with a pat on the arm.

"Wallace, leave the situation to me, okay? I'll handle this. There's no need to worry. You two get out of here and have a good time. Win one for your favorite life agent." He shifts his head to see Olga. "Don't let this guy slow you down, Olga. You look gorgeous, by the way."

"We need to talk soon," Wallace mutters, and shifts the car into drive.

"You worry too much," Flynn says, and squeezes Browning's shoulder. Then he steps back and watches the Volvo ease out of the lot.

Whenever he sees Wallace wearing that classic 1940s tuxedo, Flynn can't help thinking the guy looks like some bizarre waiter in a decadent Nazi restaurant, a curiosity hired for the diversion he might provide the easily bored customers.

What must it have been like growing up a dwarf? Flynn wonders. Was it a matter of surviving an endless barrage of repeated, unfunny jokes and taunts? Or was it more a matter of isolation, of being set apart, unincorporated right from the womb, right from day one on the planet, no one pulling you into the breast of the normal, the full-grown?

He leaves the question in the parking lot, turns, and heads for Wireless.

Flynn enters through the diner entrance, stops in the doorway next to Tjun the bouncer, says, "What kind of a night?"

Tjun shrugs. He's an Aborigine, tall, bearded, achingly slender, of indeterminate age, and, supposedly, deadly with a long-blade knife that has a name no one can pronounce. He showed up at Wireless five years ago, responding to a help-wanted ad in the *Spy*. He's been the head bouncer ever since. No one seems to know where he lives. He keeps himself above the social politics of the bar and doesn't even seem too interested in radio in general. When Flynn asked Ferrie about him once, the co-owner went melodramatic and said, "Guy saved my life once and I don't want to say anything else about him." Flynn treats Tjun with a rare respect, never uses his sarcastic brand of humor in the man's presence.

"Hazel and her friends inside?" Flynn asks.

"At the bar," Tjun says in an odd, clipped accent that Flynn loves.

Flynn moves past him, steps into the smoky-blue glow of the room, blinks a few times. Each time he steps inside Wireless, he has to give Ferrie and Most credit for achieving the atmosphere that almost all clubs reach for and the majority look foolish missing. Flynn thinks of it as expensive decadence, a place that can feel foreign even if you've spent a year's worth of nights there, a place where all kinds of verbally coded purchase and sales agreements might take place and payouts feel like they could require three different types of currency. It's even more amazing that the club has this feel when the fact is that most of the regulars are stunningly middle-class and usually short on funds. And yet, there's no denying the room has a tone to it, an envelope of pure mood, a sensory tide produced by no more than two dreamy men with a vision of weird, unstriving hipness and the resurgence of an almost-bygone medium.

Flynn spots Hazel and slides up to the bar between the college boys, clamping an arm across each of their backs, saying, "Guys, I think there's a free pool table around in the back."

The two look at each other as if one should argue, then walk away in a slow double sulk. Flynn moves in close until his arm is touching Hazel and she says, "You really get off on screwing up my fantasies."

"They're babes in the woods, dear. I'm saving you from the law."

Most puts a cognac down in front of Flynn and walks to the other end of the bar without a word.

"Then I guess I owe you."

"Do you work at being a smart-ass? Do you practice when you're alone?"

"I just want to be straight. This would be banter, right? We're bantering?"

"Not even close. I'm just working on not liking you."

"You have to like me, Flynn. I'm one of the fold. That's the rules."

"The rules are," Flynn says, "that there are no rules, my love—"

"Don't call me that."

"Speaking of which, I understand there might be some trouble."

"Meaning?"

"Meaning I got a message on my machine from Wallace in that voice. You know that voice, darling?"

"You've been warned."

"You know I hate playing the mediator schmuck. I hate that crap."

"Who asked you? I never asked for a mediator."

"Why do you always want to stir up trouble?"

There's a beat and then they both burst out laughing. Flynn shakes his head, puts a flat palm up to his forehead, and says, "Look what you've got me saying."

"That," Hazel says, "is an instant classic, G.T. *Stir up trouble.* That won't be forgotten, I promise."

"Look, dearest, heart of my heart, I get the feeling Wallace is going to do a little saber-rattling."

Hazel gives the smile that she knows gets to Flynn. "Well," she says, "you know Wallace. Tiny saber."

"Come on. We don't need these kinds of problems right now."

"Look, Flynn, Wallace is losing it. He's getting more paranoid every day. I don't know how Olga lives with the little bastard. He's lost the point of the whole thing. Little brain's gotten corrupted. What's that quote about ultimate power?"

"Don't know it. Listen, Wallace is just a little uptight about bringing the heat down. He hates press and the *Spy*'s been running these articles on the brothers and all. I think he's just afraid you might escalate things, you know, over the line—"

"Whose line?

"—and ruin it for everyone. You know, for Wallace this is still a lark, a prank kind of thing. He's not into the whole philosophical thing. He just likes the reaction, the way it makes him feel. He doesn't come at it from a—I don't know—a political angle. He's not going to change—"

"And neither am I."

"And neither are you. And I think if we just have a little powwow—"

"Powwow?"

"—upstairs, and try to talk this out, find some agreement—"

"I hate sitting on those orange crates," Hazel says. "I get splinters in my ass."

"—make everyone secure to some extent. Reach a compromise—sorry, sorry, I know how you hate that word, my mistake, not a compromise, but an agreement, an understanding."

"So where is the little toad?"

"That annual dinner-dance thing. Down the Baron."

"He's coming by after?"

"He loves to gloat. He'll probably bring the freaking trophy in with him. Sit it up on the bar."

"He does that," Hazel says, "I swear to God he'll carry it out of here without using his hands."

Flynn looks at Hazel, smiles, and shrugs. "Look, I'm just saying give me a chance here, okay? Think unity."

Hazel makes a face like she's bitten into something rancid, but even with a sour expression there's something about her Flynn finds endearing. Despite all the sneering-punk accessories and the rumors of obscene tattoos and the slightly spiked blond hair that she insists on running a strawberry streak through,

Flynn finds something vulnerable in Hazel. He's sure no one else can see it, that they'd probably laugh him into the parking lot if he mentioned it. But he can't get around it. For all her tough-as-nails rebel act and tomboy-from-hell attitude, he wants to somehow protect her. Maybe from herself. Sometimes he wonders what she'd look like without all the shock makeup. Beneath the eyeliner and occasional nose ring, she's got a sweet, kind of open face—blue-green eyes and smallish features. Her diet of speed and veggie pocket-sandwiches has turned her body into a cadaver-thin reed, but Flynn thinks she has a sensual walk, a kind of languid, careless sway that, were she aware of it, she'd eliminate immediately.

Somebody yells, "G.T.," from somewhere deeper in the bar and Flynn says, "I've got to make the rounds. Just think about what I've said, okay?"

Hazel reaches over and pinches his cheek, then disappears into the crowd. Flynn heads for Minnesota. He enters the billiards room to a hail of calls and whistles, then endures several minutes of back-slapping and arm punching. Someone slides a drink into his hand and finally the room settles back down and turns its collective attention to the antique Philco radio. Flynn listens for just a second, then asks, "Who'd they go after tonight?"

In unison, several voices yell, "WQSG," as if it were a cheer of some kind.

"QSG," Flynn says, then glances at his watch. "Jesus, the boys are cutting it close tonight."

From the speaker of the Philco issues the hottest broadcast in Quinsigamond this season—the O'Zebedee Brothers' Outlaw Network, radio pirates extraordinaire, myth creatures of the airwaves, an urban legend without rival in this town.

And as if the brothers could somehow sense the growing tension in Minnesota, they start to confront the crowd's main concern:

...and a glance to the digital in the dash tells us that about now all the radio rats huddled down under the big neon *G* are starting to sweat just a little as it begins to look like their allegiances could be tested. But listen up and lighten up, subcitizens, 'cause James and John are fellow devotees of the one and only erotic empress herself. And we promise we will never come between you and Veronica. So rest at ease, the goddess will embrace your ears on schedule . . .

3.

It's not until after she's parked in the deserted mall garage that Ronnie realizes she never turned on the radio, that she drove from her apartment to the radio station in silence. She likes to put herself on, joke with herself, so she sits in the Jeep and starts acting out a five-second tragedy, her head down on top of her hands as they grip the steering wheel. *Where's my loyalty,* she pretends to think, *where's my devotion?* She brings her head up, laughing, her own best audience. She grabs her old Girl Scout knapsack and says out loud, "Ronnie, why are you wasting your time in this city?"

She climbs out of the jeep, slams the door so that it echoes the length of the cement garage, walks down the exit ramp toward the small quadrangle of Astroturf between the garage and the mall. She loves stopping in the quadrangle at this time of night, the place eerie and filled with this smoky mist she never sees anywhere else. She likes to stop midway across the fake grass, look back at the wall of the garage, seven stories of cement levels with windowlike symmetrical squares cut in everywhere. She likes to stand there, enclosed, caught inside this pocket of air between the parking garage and the glass rear wall of the mall. It makes her feel like she's the only character in some forgotten French or Italian art film from decades back. She wishes she spoke a foreign language so she could ad-lib a scene. Something

28

about *an invading army just miles away. She's the broken-down servant girl, abused beyond description, the sole carrier of information that could hold off the enemy. Her warrior lover is waiting here on these foggy moors. He's bleeding from behind the ear, deep red oozing into the ragged cotton cloth he's wrapped around his neck like a bandanna. She runs the last few yards toward him, throws herself into his arms. They both fall to the wet ground. Mud covers their legs. It begins to rain. The wind picks up, gets even worse. He looks down at her, his vision obscuring. He says only, "My brave one." She stares back up at him, one foot over the borderline of delirium. Her red lips quiver, part. She says, "We, we . . ." He waits, desperate for her news. She draws in a breath, tries again. "We . . .'ll be right back after a word from our sponsor."*

She moves up to the glass elevator affixed to the mall wall and says, "Girl, what is wrong with your brain?"

The elevator door opens and she enters and turns around to look out on the quad as she rises. She reaches under the olive-green flap of the knapsack, digs down into the canvas folds, pulls out with one hand an antique silver hip flask. She screws off the flask top and swallows a warm mouthful of mescal. She secures the flask, resacks it, and turns toward the inner wall just as the elevator arrives at the third floor. Once again, a master of timing.

She steps out onto the slippery Spanish-tile floor, lets her eyes adjust to the dimmed after-hours lighting of the mall. This is the only time she can stomach the mall, and thankfully ten-to-two has always been her shift since she came to the station. Sometimes, after she turns the mike over to Sonny, who does the two-to-six occult show, she goes window shopping. Security doesn't seem to mind. She passes them on their rounds, makes risqué comments that they love, scratches the German shepherd behind the ears.

Ronnie knows every store in the mall, but she's never purchased a thing here. She buys everything mail-order, through catalogues. She wishes she could get her groceries this way. She doesn't know what it is about the mall in daylight, when the stores are open for business, that repels her. She's never stopped to analyze it, find a meaning that could alter things. She just takes it as a given that she can only accept the mall when it's closed, a retail ghost town. Last month, peering into the display window of Lear Jeweler's, she thought of herself as the vampire browser—she walks by night, skulks through the shadows of the Orange Julius kiosk, swoops past the crypt of the shoeshine bench.

Down the enclosed alley from the elevator, Wayne, the engineer, is playing catch, bouncing a red rubber ball off the cement wall that leads up to the studio. This is not a good sign. Beyond him, inside the huge plate-glass window that lets shoppers look in on the daytime announcers hard at work, like they were as interesting as pizza flippers, she can see Vinnie, the station manager, and Ray, the Nazi who mans the six-to-ten shift. They're having another mini-fit, flailing arms and screaming at each other. The broadcast booth is soundproof and this turns their raging into a silent comedy, an Abbott and Costello bit set in the not-so-golden age of radio.

"Would this be a good night to call in sick?" she says, starting to approach Wayne.

He goes into his baseball routine. He makes exaggerated moves with his body, somehow jumps and leaps in slow motion, turns on his cigar-scarred, hysterical, play-by-play voice. "What a shot . . . the Wayne-man can kiss this one . . . No, no sir, no siree, it's off the left-field wall . . . the runner is barreling around second . . . Mr. W fields it and fires for home . . . the runner is sliding . . . Wilcox takes position . . ."

He fires the rubber ball at her. She doesn't stop, doesn't break her stride. She punches her right arm upward, all confidence, and rips the ball out of its trajectory.

Wayne's voice surges upward in pitch and volume. "She's got him, she's nailed him, she's put the game away. The crowd goes insane . . ." He cuts into the garbled hiss of a capacity mob pumped up on immediate victory and does a solo version of the Wave.

"You missed your calling," she says, moving up next to him, keeping an eye on the histrionics in the broadcast booth.

"The Voice of Baseball?"

"Terrorist. You've got that kind of ego."

"And to think I was going to spring for the number four at Tiananmen Takeout."

"Uh-uh. No more midnight buffets, Wayne. I'm turning into Ms. MSG."

"Microphone's Saving Grace."

"Stop being funny. What's the story with Schultzie and Klink?"

"Uh-oh, I guess someone didn't have the station tuned in on the drive to work."

"I can't listen to Ray anymore. Throws my whole mood. Ruins my show."

"You used to be amused and now you're just disgusted."

"Yeah, something like that. We've been hit again?"

"They're still at it. We're still off the air."

"For Christ sake, Wayne, I'm on in twenty minutes."

"That's what I told them. Nothing to worry about."

"There's nothing you can do?"

"These guys get better every day. I'm a hack compared to some of them."

"You tried everything?"

"All I know is it's coming from the east side."

"Vinnie's not going to make it."

"You should have been here when Federman called."

"Oh, Jesus."

"I told Vinnie. I said, 'Vinnie, we'll be clear by ten. Ronnie's on at ten and she's their goddess.'"

"You charmer. Here we go, I'm blushing."

"What? *Es verdad,* darling. They've hit every shift at the station, at least twice, except for ten-to-two. The Ronnie shift. Sweetheart of the subset."

"Seriously, every shift?"

"They've hit Ray six times this month. Jesus, do they hate Ray."

"So they've got taste on top of brains."

"Speaking of taste, old pal..."

"Honest to God, Wayne, I can't do Chinese tonight. Maybe nachos, later on. Did you fix the microwave?"

"I'm not talking Velveeta here, you know. I'm feeling pretty worn down tonight. Doing a lot of overtime. This could be a long night for your favorite tech-man."

"Mr. Coffee broken?"

"Studio coffee? On my stomach?"

"Jesus, you're a leech. Why don't you ever bring the booze?"

"C'mon. You're the big breadwinner around here. What do you say?"

"I say let's see if we get our signal back up—"

"Guaranteed, fifteen minutes."

"Yeah, well, you talk to me then."

"So you're saying it's conditional? Your generosity to a friend is conditional? This is an either/or thing?"

Ronnie gives him a tight smile, throws the rubber ball into the air over his head, and starts to walk toward the studio door. Ray is breaking things, snapping pencils in two as she enters the broadcast booth. Vinnie has fallen into a silent depression. This always happens after a call from Mr. Federman.

"So, Raymie," she says, dumping her knapsack onto the board, "the whole city shut you off tonight. What the hell did you say?"

Ray takes a breath and sits back in his chair, puts on his low, in-control voice. "That's right, Wilcox, push some buttons. Brilliant move. Annoy me some more."

She squints down at him, moves over to the-lump-called-Vinnie, and starts to massage his shoulders. "Relax, Raymond. Pull yourself together. Your status as a professional is on the line here."

"Make some jokes, girl—"

"That's bitch-goddess to you, Ray."

"—be funny, be a wise-ass."

"That's what they pay me for, remember?"

"Shock-jock shrink with the whore's mouth."

"It's a weird world, Ray. You have to know your market. There're a lot more lovesick depressives out there than paranoid Nazis. That's what I try to tell Federman over lunch. '*That's* the reason for Raymond's numbers, Mr. F.' So far he buys it."

Ray loses his grip, goes for the bait like a dim trout. "You want to throw the numbers at me, you little bitch, you want to start in?"

"People," Vinnie manages to say.

"Love to start in, Ray. I'm amazed these east-siders could jam your show. No one else seems to know it exists."

"My freaking numbers would be fine if I had a little consistency, if I weren't off the freaking air twice a week because some little delinquents are allowed—"

"Here we go, here it is. We've got to keep the little bastards out of the Radio Shacks, right? That's the answer, right?"

"Listen, the next time you're out with Federman, if you've ever been out with Federman—"

"Twice a week, Ray, just like these interruptions."

He's boiling over. He knocks a metal clipboard to the floor. "You tell Federman, the son of a bitch, that maybe the problem with the ratings book is because he's screwed with the station's whole identity. We're freaking schizophrenic. We're confusing the goddamn audience. He lines up my political reportage—"

"Political reportage," she repeats in a deep and put-on voice. "C'mon, Raymie, you're a reactionary hack with a good voice. You're Morton Downey with a head injury."

"Followed by your bedroom filth, followed by the satanist crap from that fairy with the earring—"

"His name's Sonny, Ray. He told me he loves your show."

"Followed by that moronic excuse for humor during commute time. Collect call to the Vatican. There's something original."

"Well, we can't all book acclaimed Holocaust revisionists, Ray."

"Did you even listen to that show?"

"Sorry, Ray. I was eating sushi in Little Asia. With Federman."

"Bullshit you were with Federman."

"Whatever you say, Ray. Vinnie, pal, you okay?"

"I don't know why they're singling us out," Vinnie says. He's dressed in a navy polyester suit that's too big in some places and too small in others.

"They don't single us out," Ronnie says. "They're hitting other stations."

"They're hitting us the most," Vinnie whines.

Ray gets up and walks out of the booth. Ronnie slides into his chair and says, "We're all-talk. We're a better target. For Christ sake, Vinnie, some of the metal music stations wouldn't even know they were being jammed."

"I wish you wouldn't go after Ray like that."

"Aw, Mom, he hit me first."

"Do you really have lunch with Federman?"

"Vinnie, you wouldn't believe it. Man's got an appetite that won't quit."

"You're not making my night any easier, Ronnie."

"Sorry, Vin. Get on the floor and I'll change everything."

"I hate it when you do that."

"Give me a break, Vinnie. They write me a check every week 'cause I do that."

"Federman called. He was all over me."

"This isn't your fault."

"He called me incompetent."

"He likes to yell. He thinks that's the thing to do. He's basically a very insecure man."

"He said he was calling the FCC and Mayor Welby."

"Welby won't take his call."

"I just can't believe they can't track these kids."

"Who says they're kids?"

"I don't know. I don't know why I called them kids."

The red rubber ball comes flying through the air over their heads, smashes against the plate-glass window without breaking

it, and bounces once, down onto the board and then out into the
hallway. It's accompanied by Ray letting out a throat-rupturing
scream. "You leave your goddamn toys at home."

Ronnie shakes her head and pulls her chair up to the board.
She turns up the in-booth volume and Vinnie makes a wincing
sound. The speakers give out a second of high-pitch squeal,
stabilize, and then reveal a man's voice, this deep, smooth, 4
A.M. voice:

Ouch, sorry about that. Brother John is asleep at the dials. And it
looks like it's almost time for the beauty of the band-spread, the
Cassandra of coitus, the sweet sister of all serial subcasters, our
Ms. Ronnie. Kick this engine over, driver, the O'Zebedee Brothers
best be mobile before those anal Fed-men follow our frequency. To
Raymond, the fascist in short pants, don't bother to thank us for
these little vacations. Till next time, friends, remember, our mission
is transmission. Jam high and jam wide.

The booth fills up with white noise and Ray rushes in and
goes for the headphones. Ronnie grabs them first and slides them
around her neck saying, "Sorry, Ray, it's ten o'clock. I'm on the
air."

. . . What you're telling me is that you need some certainty that she's
fulfilled.

I just wish there was some signal, some way to know for sure.
Women don't have to worry—

We're about to argue, darling.

No, I don't mean—

I'm fairly certain I know just what you mean.

Don't be like that, Ronnie, don't—

Listen. Take a second here and listen. I'm about to do you a favor.

I'm about to share something with you. Certainty is the enemy of sensual ecstasy. Say that to yourself. I'll repeat it for you. Certainty is the enemy of sensual ecstasy. Our pleasure always derives from our plunge into the unknown, the risk, the daring. The excitement comes from *not* knowing how far things can go, what levels of experience might be reached, the possibility, each and every time, that some ceiling might be broken through, that we might just get beyond known sensation, surpass anything our imagination has come up with.

You're saying doubt is good?

Not doubt. Listen to me. Uncertainty. Risk. Unknown territory. Unrevealed wisdom. Are you listening to me?

Yeah, yes. Yes.

But you can't see me. There's a good chance you don't even know what I look like. That's the beauty of this medium. One of the few that can still retain mystery. Mystery. That's an enticing word. I love that word. I don't know who you are or where you are or what you look like. You don't know anything about me beyond the sound of my voice. Are you lying in a bed right now?

I'm in the kitchen.

You shouldn't have told me. Turn off the lights. Get down on the floor.

Down on the floor?

Just stop talking. Just listen to me. Give up on this need to be certain of everything, looking for hidden signals everywhere.

Okay, I'm on the—

Knock it off. I mean it. Stop telling me. Do you know what I look like? Have you ever seen a picture?

I don't—

Answer me.

No. I don't know what you look like.

All right, then. Now, you just try to keep quiet for a second. It's been a different night for me. My engineer went home sick. Normally he's my partner here. He's a tremendous help to me. But tonight I'm left all alone here in the studio. But that's all right. I can easily adjust. The animal that survives is the one that can adapt. You have to always remember that. So it's a different night, an unknown. So maybe that accounts for what I've done.

What you've done . . .

Quiet. Now, I don't know if you've ever seen our studios or been down here, but our broadcast booth is located behind a great big picture window that looks out on the East Corridor of the mall. I guess the idea is that shoppers can come by and watch the announcers broadcast, see how radio works. Personally, I think this is a mistake. I think you're taking something away from the people rather than giving something. You're removing the image in their heads, the faces and bodies they've hung on these floating voices. I think it's a mistake. But I've adapted. My particular show is on after the mall closes up. So the only audience I have is an occasional security guard and his dog as they walk their patrol. The guard might stop for a second. He might stare at me a little absentmindedly, scratching the dog's ear as it hangs close to his leg. Then he'll nod and move on. This is fine with me. I'm really more or less ambivalent about his presence. I'm normally too tuned into the caller. I'm in the loop of the call, you know. I'm in the process, building something, letting one word lead to the next. Pulling the anonymous voice out of itself and splattering it out over fifty thousand watts to all the unseen ears listening in six states. That's what my engineer and I *do* here. We create little happenings. We construct new environments, on the spot, instantaneously, no blueprints, no plans, no permits. But my engineer is out sick tonight. So I'm alone here in the studio. And it's a peaceful place. Everyone should have this serene kind of place. The lights are dim, easy on the eyes. The booth is soundproof so there're no harsh noises or distractions. And it's warm. Actually, too warm. I began to find it uncomfortable after a while. Do you know what I did, caller? Don't answer. Keep still. First I removed my blazer. I hung it on the back of my chair. And I felt a little better. I kicked off my shoes, let my feet out of the vise, okay? And then I just kept going with it. It felt wonderful and I kept going. I unbuttoned my blouse, and folded it and put it on the floor next to my chair. And I pulled my camisole over my head and let it fall on top of my blouse. And then I just pulled down the zipper of my skirt, lifted out of the seat a little, and slid it off down my legs. And I ended up naked, alone here in the broadcast booth, taking calls, and nobody knowing, until now, what was happening. And then, you'll love this part, caller—don't say a word—I was putting on a public service announcement, about fifteen minutes back, remember, the Emergency Systems Test? And I looked up from the board, and there was Mr. Security Guard and his shepherd, right outside the booth, staring in the window at me, mouth just hanging open slightly. I burst out laughing and I waved, and after a second, he just went on his way, went on to the rest of his checkpoints and all—

Are you still naked?

Yes, I am. When I finish with you I'll get dressed again. The point is, I had no idea this would occur when I came to work tonight. And certainly the guard didn't know. The dog didn't know. It was just this momentary occurrence. Won't happen again in a lifetime, probably. But it did happen tonight. You just never know. It jumps out at you. You have to go with it. Shake up the routine. Shake down the system. That's where the juice comes from, caller. That's where life heats up. It's that little mystery-charge that makes breathing worthwhile. You've got to stop looking for these signals to confirm everything for you. You're looking for sureties that just aren't there. You bought into this religion that says logic exists, that one and one will always equal two. And I'm sorry, but I can't say that's the case. That guard tonight had his math shaken, okay? And if you ask me, it was for the better.

So you're naked right now?

Okay, there's no helping some people. I'm pulling your plug, caller. Give your girlfriend a flare gun for Christmas. Maybe that'll help you out. This is *Libido Liveline* and we'll be back after these messages.

4.

Detective Shaw is on her knees. She's leaning against the wooden railing of the choir loft, all her weight on her elbows. She's looking out into the enclosed cavern of St. Brendan's, trying to remember how long ago it was when a structure like this one could invoke feelings of both security and doom, majesty and abomination, and a vague, hazy kind of awe.

She thinks that maybe a lot of these feelings were products of perspective, the overwhelming smallness of the child set so harshly against the enormity of the cathedral, the bishop's own church, with its ceilings that rose up so high that looking at them, striving to make out the biblical icons depicted in their curves, brought on vertigo and even quick belts of frightening nausea.

Now St. Brendan's just looks overly ornate, an example of misplaced economic priorities and fashions that will never come back. Maybe, more than anything, the church is a lesson in the cost of stasis, the bland, cold fact of obsolescence.

The choir loft door makes a whining sound and Hannah turns to see an elderly Oriental man shuffling toward the immense organ.

She stands and shakes her head.

"Dr. Cheng," she says, "you didn't have to climb all the way up here."

"Detective Shaw," he says, his voice a raspy whisper, his eyes closing and his head bowing slightly.

The old man takes her hand in his, comes forward, and plants a subtle, fatherly kiss on her cheek. They settle down onto the organ bench and Dr. Cheng slowly begins to unbutton a black Burberry overcoat and loosen a paisley silk scarf from around his neck. Hannah sees that, as always, underneath, he wears a simple black cassock, a coolie-type cotton gown that's completely out of step with his wealth and status. She knows that parked down in the street, somewhere behind the cruisers and the M.E.'s car, is the doctor's chauffeured Rolls-Royce. And she knows that if anyone can steer her down the right road after Fr. Todorov's killer, it's the unofficial emperor of Little Asia.

From below comes the flash of the cameras documenting the charred confessional booth and the hushed murmur of the chancery's director of communications conferring with a reporter from the *Spy*'s city desk.

Hannah reaches over and touches Dr. Cheng's arm. "I want to thank you for taking my call. It wasn't necessary for you to drive down here. I could've come to you."

"It's better this way," Dr. Cheng says.

Hannah nods and fingers some white keys on the organ.

"Meaning you don't want me down Little Asia anymore?"

Dr. Cheng lets out a rough, wheezy breath.

"The landscape is changing, Hannah. You know this. Ever since our mutual friend left. Things are deteriorating more and more. I can feel the ground crumbling under my feet."

Hannah looks up at him, tries to smile, and manages a shrug.

Their mutual friend is Lenore Thomas, already a dark myth in Bangkok Park. Lenore was the original strong-arm goddess, a woman with the will of Stalin and a tongue like a razor. When Hannah applied to work narcotics, Lenore was the one who backed her, then showed her the trade. And though more often than not Hannah fell victim to Lenore's bullying wit, she also fell under Lenore's spell, came to view her as something beyond a role model, something more like a wildly complex Zen master, a *roshi* of not simply narc detail, but the landscapes of power and force and persuasion and dominance.

It was no secret to Hannah that Lenore had a bone-deep amphetamine habit, but it did seem inconceivable that any chemical could outmaneuver the woman. Lenore was just too savvy, too smart and instinctive and obsessively disciplined. But about a year back, Lenore got involved in an unsanctioned bust down in St. James Cemetery. To this day internal affairs has blanketed the details, but the entire department knows something went utterly wrong that night. A fellow officer and a department liaison were killed and the king of Bangkok Park, a Latino named Cortez, disappeared with an undetermined cache of what the rumormongers simply call *product*.

And after a week talking into a tape recorder in Mayor Welby's office, Lenore also disappeared. The official word was a leave of absence and an extended stay at a detox clinic in Vermont. But Shaw will never buy this. It just doesn't wash with what she knows about Lenore Thomas.

In Lenore's wake, Hannah was immediately transferred to homicide. And for the past year she's lived with an emptiness that only seems to increase. It's as if her teacher vanished before she could impart the final and most important set of instructions. To fight this feeling, Hannah has tried to make herself into Lenore's ghost. It's not an easy transformation. Their personalities and techniques were never similar. But as Lenore always said, *You can probably will the dead to life if you want it badly enough.* So for the past six months Hannah's been haunting the streets of Bangkok Park, kicking informant ass, schmoozing with the hookers and pimps, growing more comfortable with the nuances of casual brutality.

Dr. Cheng finally removes his leather gloves and says, "How is her brother's asthma?"

Hannah's developed a habit of checking in on Lenore's

brother, Ike. "Much better," she says. "I think that mandrake root compress you put together really did the trick."

There's a few seconds of silence.

Dr. Cheng looks down at her hand resting on the organ keys and says, "Don't read more into my words than is intended, Hannah."

Then he gets up and slowly walks to the balcony railing and looks down at the small pockets of homicide cops and lab men sealing plastic bags and drinking takeout coffee. He crosses his arms over his chest and says, "Our relationship is still secure. My presence here makes that certain. I've come to think of you as one of my own, Hannah."

"A bastard daughter," she says, and gives him a smile.

He squints as if embarrassed by her language and says, "Perhaps a long-lost niece."

Dr. Cheng is the last testament to the first wave of Asian immigrants to make Bangkok Park their home. Hannah has no idea if he's a licensed medical doctor, but she's aware that he's spent sixty-plus years ministering to the health of his people with herb remedies and acupuncture. She has no idea how old he is, but she knows he arrived in Quinsigamond sometime after the Volstead Act, in his early twenties and with more money in his pocket than his fellow travelers. She's never known the specifics of his Tong connections, but she knows that by the end of World War II, he had some kind of interest in all the bigger businesses in the Little Asia end of Bangkok Park.

Hannah sees Dr. Cheng as a classic example of the neighborhood mayor, a man never officially elected to a position of authority, but who controls the flow of money down his block, who can secure jobs and housing, who can keep the peace and take care of the helpless.

On his tax forms, Dr. Cheng is listed as a merchant, and it's true that for the past half-century he's owned and overseen the operation of Dr. Cheng's Herbarium, a tiny hole in the wall on the corner of Verlin Ave, that continues to offer exotic balms and oils and medicinal teas to the consumers of Little Asia. He's always lived in the small apartment above the business, alone except for a long line of valets that are all rumored to come from the same family.

Dr. Cheng has no immediate family of his own. He never married and has no children that anyone knows of. But he's filled his upper management positions with various distant cousins and loosely adopted kin. Today the doctor is diversified into everything from frozen yogurt franchises to a controlling interest in WOXS, New England's only all-Asian radio station. But Hannah knows that it's an empire forged long ago in the bowels of a dozen or more early Bangkok Park tenements. And that the doctor's only overhead costs were thin mattresses, bamboo pipes, and the importation costs on the best opium run out of Shanghai.

Hannah gets a kick out of their relationship, a bond between a white female narcotics cop and the granddaddy of the biggest ring of classic opium dens in the Northeast. She finds a similarity to their brain patterns. She finds they share parallel notions of will and power. She thinks that possibly they both war against radical egos that could obscure their judgment and rationality.

Dr. Cheng has lived a life pretty much unconnected to the surface brand of hypocritical ethics and morality they peddle in the City Council chambers. He's so much wiser than the hack pols who've seemingly charted the course of this city. He's allowed them to think they've controlled his destiny. Three generations of Quinsigamond ruling class have pocketed the doctor's kickbacks and gone to sleep assured of their stability and superiority, all the while oblivious to another hidden but enormous picture, a wildly complex system of covert economics that slowly carved a secret face on the surface of the city, and more important, that excavated raw earth until there came to exist an underground more intricate and enigmatic than anything on the outer skin of the municipality.

Every ethnic group in Quinsigamond has its own neighborhood mayor. Some are cut-and-dried wise guys from a long line of mob families. Others appear to run a cleaner show than the City Council and control their streets like a closely held corporation. But every one of them understands the basic, primal facts that supply and demand is God's own rule and there's more darkness in the human heart than light.

The Italians have the legendary Gennaro Pecci. The blacks have the Reverend Hartley James, longtime king of the north-side projects. The Jews have always had the Singer brothers, first Shel and now Meyer. The Irish still have "the Mortician," Willy "Bud" Loftus. The Latinos, until recently, had the mysterious Mr. Cortez. The new arrivals—the Haitians, the Jamaicans, the small pocket of Turks over on Smyrna—all have candidates jockeying for position, sorting each other out with cut throats and car bombs. But no one has ruled longer, with more fore-sight or discretion or financial brilliance, than the ancient Dr. Cheng.

Hannah gets up and follows the old man to the railing. There's still a heavy smell in the air—charred wood and flesh. She puts a hand on the doctor's shoulder and says, "Things have been a little crazy for a couple of years. It'll get back to normal soon."

Dr. Cheng seems to be having trouble breathing tonight. It bothers Hannah that he's starting to look his age. Just a year ago, when she first set out to know him, when she started buying ginseng twice a week down at the Herbarium, he still seemed like he was in his prime.

Without looking at her, he says quietly, "In the past, Hannah, I always found a way to enforce a balance, to make the neighborhood work for all. You can't imagine what had to be overcome. There was a mentality to reshape."

He turns and leans his backside against the railing, which makes Hannah nervous.

"I had to will a radical notion into every individual head. That we were now a new breed, that we were collective Asians rather than separate, nationalist tribes. History had to be obliterated in the name of survival, and then in the name of progress. I hated doing this, but there was no other way. And I was never completely successful—I never thought I would be—but I managed, always, to give the appearance of unity. The image. And often, this was enough."

I've always thought what you managed was stunning," Hannah says.

Dr. Cheng reaches out, squeezes her hand again. "You have no shame, flattering an old man with lies." He pauses and looks down to his feet. "Six months ago, Chak, the Cambodian, eliminates Mo, the Laotian. War among the tribes. We're spilling our own blood now. The Singer brothers once told me an old Yiddish saying. It translates roughly, but the point survives: *One stupid person can throw a stone so deep into the river that ten wise men will never find it.*"

Hannah lets a moment pass and then says, "Anything you can tell me about the priest, Doc?"

He acts as if he hasn't heard her.

"What I've accomplished," he says, "is unraveling week by week. No one knows better than you what's happening to Bangkok. My control is eroding. Agreements are not being honored. Treaties are not being acknowledged. Tribes are battling over nickel-and-dime nonsense. Territories challenged for the sake of an additional street, another half-block of fire-bombed tenements..."

"Doctor," Hannah tries.

"Gennaro Pecci wouldn't take my call last week, Hannah. What am I to think? There are rumors about the Loftus family."

Hannah stays quiet, stares down at the floor.

"And among my own... They're all thinking of themselves as villagers again. The Cambodians have let it be known they have no confidence in the doctor. The gangs are loose cannons ready to plow the old way into the ground."

He struggles up from the railing and half turns, extends his thin arms outward as if to present himself to Hannah.

"What can this old man do for you?"

Hannah stands, and before she can control herself, she steps into him, gives him a full, long hug, feels, even through the Burberry, how frail he's gotten.

Then she releases him and before either can signify embarrassment, she head-motions to the floor beneath the choir loft and says, "Did the gangs do that, Doctor? Did the Hyenas set fire to the priest?"

He raises his thin eyebrows and says, "Do you think so?"

Hannah bites on her lip. "Todorov has been grabbing a lot of press by nosing into the gangs. He's spent time in Bangkok lately. You just said how loose these kids are. Todorov says the wrong word to a couple of seventeen-year-old Hyenas juiced on PCP and meth. He ends up in the middle of a bilingual argument. Next thing you know, the poor bastard is toast."

Dr. Cheng takes air in through his nose and says, "Keep going."

Hannah stares at him, then nods. "Okay. We've got a precedent for the benzine. We know that three months back, the Hyenas blew a bodega in a raid on the Popes. Our lab guys were drooling telling us it was benzine."

"Yes."

"But no matter how juiced they are, the Hyenas have to answer to your boy Uncle Chak—"

Dr. Cheng shakes his head. "He's not my boy, Hannah. Chak doesn't even come to the monthly summits anymore. He's preaching a sermon of Cambodian purity."

She nods. She feels bad for the old man. The topography of his world is changing as quickly as he says and no amount of reassurance from her can hide the truth.

"Still," Hannah says, "I don't see the percentage. If Chak wants to be a long-term player, and we know he does, he's not going to sanction random violence. Especially not outside of the Park. Whacking the crusading priest doesn't ensure your stability. This kind of thing is going to be on the front page of the *Spy* for weeks. You know Welby and Bendix and the Council are going to have to make some noise and slap someone hard."

Dr. Cheng walks back to the organ and toes a foot pedal distractedly.

He says, "Chak would sooner have the Hyenas attack me than this Father Todorov."

"Then the Hyenas simply lost their heads or acted on their own for reasons we can only guess—"

"In which case we'll know by tomorrow. Chak will need to send a signal that he can police his own territory. He'll round up a few of their low-level soldiers, whether they were involved with the priest or not. He'll leave them hanging by their feet from the streetlamps on Voegelin Avenue."

"Then again," Hannah says, "if the Hyenas didn't torch Todorov—"

"Then perhaps someone wants us to believe that they did."

"That's your theory?" Hannah says, only partially a question.

Dr. Cheng doesn't respond.

Hannah turns back toward the railing and looks out at a life-sized Christ figure suspended by metal chains from the ceiling, hanging on a silver metal cross over the marble altar below. Even from this distance she can make out the silver beads that represent droplets of blood from the hands and feet, from the wound in the side, from the crown of thorns biting into the rim of the head. It's a particularly gruesome crucifix, a haunting monument to an endless and unjustified agony.

She wonders for a second if Fr. Todorov had a chance to glimpse the dying metal Christ in the air above him before the priest's heart exploded from shock and incalculable pain.

She turns away. There's no test the lab techs can run to answer her question. No way to analyze the seared eyeball, to dip it in some beaker of chemicals and reveal a trace image of a crucified redeemer.

Hannah waits a few seconds, then moves over to Dr.

Cheng, pulls his coat closed over his chest, and takes him by the arm. She starts to steer him to the exit, walking slowly, listening, uncomfortably, to the old man's wheeze.

At the top of the spiral stairway, Dr. Cheng turns to her and says, "Did I tell you Gennaro Pecci wouldn't take my call?"

5.

DeForest Road looks like someone's chronic dream of suburbia. In fact, it's located completely within the city, ten minutes from the heart of downtown. It's just that this cookie-cutter design seems so familiar—row on row of identically sized lots, graced with tract houses, three-bedroom ranches in pastel colors, lined up, a lesson in uniformity.

Crouched low in the shrubbery, Speer chews on nicotine gum and thinks the whole street could be the exterior set of an endless situation comedy. Clean-cut kids hysterically agonizing over the new dent in Dad's bumper. The zany neighbor with the get-rich-quick scheme. The door-to-door salesman hawking an explosive vacuum cleaner. A millennium of story lines about familial high jinks in the land of God.

If anyone spots him, Speer will take the offensive, flash the badge, bark from behind clenched teeth, roll the eyes of the weary protector. *DEA, dickhead, get lost, there's a crack house right here on Primrose Lane.* Let the bastard go home and wonder which neighbor is the invader, which fellow traveler has breached the system. Why do they value it so much? Why do they give their lives over to streets and houses like this? Why do they break their backs to dig into the bosom of a dreamy laugh track only they can hear?

Speer spits out the gum and inserts another piece, lets his

saliva turn it moist before he starts to chew. He knows he should have the answer, that the answer should be instinctual, not open to analysis or recall, but simply felt and understood, a reflex, an instantaneous response. The answer should be primal. And the fact that it isn't is the key to what's wrong with Speer's whole life.

They want these streets, these houses, these nests of *family life,* for a sense of order. Speer should feel this more directly than any of the residents around him. He's a guardian of order, an overseer. That's what the Bureau was all about. That's what Mr. Hoover's life was all about. These days they try to taint his name, say he had aberrant desires and that he used the Bureau for his own political ends. Beyond being untrue, this has nothing to do with the fact that there are basic rules that must be upheld and enforced. And they're more precious in the field of communication than anywhere else, as far as Speer is concerned.

And yet, he's not a part of that network of family life. He's been married twice. Both unions lasted less than a year and the last one involved a modicum of violence. Neither marriage produced children. For the past six months, Speer has lived in a basement apartment that holds just the faintest trace of a sweet and sour sewer aroma. Speer's parents are both dead. He has a brother somewhere in the wilds of Manitoba that he hasn't seen or spoken with in five years.

There are acquaintances, faces that come to him from the set routines of daily life—a waitress, a mechanic, the guy who sells the *Spy* at the newsstand. But for quite a while now, there have been no friends, and certainly no romance. He's become a moving recluse, a mobile hermit. A man who defines himself purely by his job.

So, it's nights like this that keep Speer going, that provide him with a synthetic replacement for the meaning that he assumes is found on streets like this one, in houses like these little ranches. A year ago, the job was a moderate consolation. Tonight it's everything. It's the reason to make the bed, drink the coffee, launder the shirts, brush the teeth, pull air into the lungs.

A funny thing about the lungs: Speer quit smoking the day before the last wife, Margie, bolted town with his '78 Monte Carlo and the whole of their passbook account. If he was going to go back to the unfiltered Camels, it would have been in that crucial five minutes after he read the note she left on the back of an envelope on the kitchen table. Instead, he turned his withdrawal into one more test of will, and in his weaker moments, he played one of those silent, cosmic-wager games. He told himself that if he got through one more day without a smoke, Margie would change her mind and come home. Now he's hooked on the nicotine gum.

He walks out of the bushes, crosses the street at a normal, unhurried pace, moves into the backyard, and pulls from his pocket a glass cutter and suction cup. He squeezes in behind an azalea bush, finds the kitchen window, uses his elbow to smash in one of the panes, then reaches inside the dark of the kitchen, unlatches the lock, and slides the window open.

He pulls himself inside and there's this weird, short drop to the sink that he didn't expect. The seat of his pants gets wet from a small pool of soapy water. He swings his legs off the counter, lowers himself to the floor, and immediately pulls a long-handled flashlight from his coat and snaps it on. He plays the beam around the room twice and the kitchen seems like a stage that's been abandoned by actors. Speer cups a hand over his mouth, focuses the beam on the kitchen set, lets out a shocked and hand-obscured "Son of a bitch."

He walks over to the table and stoops slightly to touch one of the chairs. It's like a set piece for the Snow White story. It's a miniature, a kid's play set. But it's top quality. Nothing plastic or veneer. Heavy, solid wood. He lifts a miniature chair with one hand, guesses at the weight. The kitchen table is only about two feet off the ground. Then he notices that the knickknacks on the walls—the spice rack, the framed needlepoint saying—are all hung at about his belt level. Waist level.

Speer tilts his head back on his neck like he was inspecting the ceiling. He whispers, "Son of a bitch was telling the truth," then moves into the living room.

There are two recessed, built-in bookcases on either side of a brick fireplace. He shines a light on them both, then moves to the right-hand shelf and pulls out a photo album, a big white wedding album. He flips open to the first page, lets out a laugh, throws his arms out to the sides, and says, "Midgets. Fucking midgets," as if he'd just come to understand a joke he heard yesterday.

He walks in a slow circle around the room, drumming on his leg with the flashlight, mumbling, "I love this. Goddamn wonderful life. Never a dull moment. Tremendous. Midgets."

It takes a minute to resign himself to this new element in the night. He assures himself nothing has changed but the scenery, that there's no reason to alter the procedures, that if anything, this will make the interrogation not only easier but possibly humorous and a little refreshing.

He moves into a hall off the living room, follows it to the master bedroom. It's the same story—miniature bedroom set, low to the ground, little doll-like bureau and dresser. He opens the closets and inspects the clothing. He expects something garish, overly colorful, and it's a second before he realizes this is from a lifetime of seeing circus dwarfs perform in red satin tuxes and ballooning clown shoes and patchwork checkerboard pants. But all the outfits in the closet are just smaller versions of everyday suits, slacks, shirts, dresses, shoes, and ties. He feels a little let down by this, a little angry, and he pulls the hanger pole from its socket and lets the whole wardrobe fall to the floor.

He goes to the dresser, pulls each drawer out of the unit, and dumps the contents into a pile on the bed. With one hand, he does a lazy sift through underwear and socks and handkerchiefs and some jewelry. He pockets a gold tie clip with an inlaid emerald and moves out to find the basement door.

The cellar is a genuine museum piece, a classic 1960s rec

room, all thin, imitation-walnut paneling and red shag carpet, acoustic tile ceiling and recessed yellow-bulb lighting. There's a pine wet bar at one end of the room with a glossy black Formica top and a half dozen wooden stools with matching black vinyl seat covers. Set up on the bartop is a row of shot glasses decorated with red-ink cartoon figures and little non sequiturs in quotes. Behind the bar, red and green Christmas tree lights trim a set of shelves that rest on gold-plated brackets. Lining the shelves are two rows of tall, bulky trophies, traditional jobs, big engraved wooden bases with silver side columns supporting silver and gold figures mounted on top. The figures, little humans, men and women, are posed in a variety of dance routines—tango, waltz, tap, jazz.

Next to the bar there's a big, boxy RCA cabinet stereo that must have gone out of production a quarter-century ago. There's a plaid wool couch and matching easy chairs, a wrought-iron coffee table with glass top, enormous pop-art ashtrays with corners that wing out at a ridiculous length. There's a small fireplace against another wall and hung over it is a huge framed poster that gives detailed square-dancing instructions. Leaning against the brick of the fireplace is a miniature set of golf clubs in a lime-green bag. There are dusty red Lava Lites, mismatched end tables covered with bright plastic drink coasters, and a line of hanging plastic multicolored beads to wall off the furnace, oil tank, and water main.

But the real eye-catcher in the room, the only thing that might just be of genuine value, is a classic Philco radio. It's the kind of big, glossy, stand-up model that was so popular just before World War II. Speer walks over to it, stares at it with his hands in his pockets. He remembers his grandmother had a similar radio when he was a child. He guesses it's now residing up in Manitoba with the rest of the family legacy.

He turns it on, and, though he actually expects it, he's a little disturbed that the music that fills the room dates from the same time period as the machine itself, a scratchy mono-recorded rendition of "Bye, Bye, Blackbird." Speer starts to whistle along to the tune, then begins a graceful dance of the hips and shoulders, sort of a sweeping, skating move with hands still planted in pockets. He does this until the song ends, then smiles at himself and moves to the bar to fix himself a drink.

The room makes him want a martini, and all the ingredients are available, even a movie-type ribbed-glass shaker with silver cap. He wishes a mambo would come on the radio so he could do the drink justice. He makes a pitcher's worth of drinks, pours the first one into a glass that reads *One more for the road*. And then he spots it—one of those personal putting greens, a four-foot strip of foamy green carpet with a brown plastic electric ball-returner waiting at the end. He immediately carries his drink over to the fireplace, places it on the mantel, and grabs a putter and two Spaldings from the golf bag. He drops the balls to the edge of the green and spends a full minute finding the right grip on the putter. He drops into a stance, lines up, draws back slowly, then gives the ball an easy smack. It misses the white circle that signifies a hole, but rolls into the return socket and gets fired back at him with a pleasing, amplified click-sound.

He loves it. Why doesn't he own one of these mothers? What a wonderful gift this would make. He grabs his glass, takes a quick sip, lines up a second shot, and putts. This time the ball rolls off the green halfway down the carpet and bounces off the baseboard. Speer responds by flinging the mini-club through the air. It crashes into the wall behind the bar, knocks a trophy to the floor. He takes a breath, moves to the bar, finds the club, picks it up, and lets loose on the remaining trophies, taking wild, unaimed cuts, severing gold and silver dancers from their platforms, gouging wood, cracking columns, until finally all the shelves are cleared.

He picks up the martini shaker, moves to the couch, and starts to sit down when professional intuition kicks in. He gets hold of himself, straightens his tie, brushes down the lapels of his suit, and calmly steps over to the fireplace. He crouches down, makes a fist, pauses, then knocks on the brick fire wall.

"Bingo," he says, and presses with both hands, first one side of the bricks, then the other. The fire wall turns on a hinge and opens a small passage into another room.

Speer gets down on hands and knees and squeezes through with some difficulty. On the other side, he sits on the floor, annoyed with himself for leaving the flashlight behind. He moves a hand into the air, touches a hanging string, and pulls on it. An overhead bulb clicks on.

He's inside some sort of small vault, maybe five by five by five, windowless. The walls and ceiling are all blueboard. The floor is unfinished plywood. There are two secretary's typing chairs, swiveled down to their lowest point. He seats himself in one and rolls forward to a homemade, mix-and-match broadcast board. There are transformers, boosters, monitors, an array of microphones and loose speakers, a turntable, cart machines for prerecorded tape loops, and a stack of labeled carts that read *applause, wheezing laughter, raspberry, thunder, whistle, lion roar, sneeze, Chinese gong, car crash #1, car crash #2, fire alarm, breaking glass, monsoon, gunshot, balloon pop, foghorn, slamming door, telephone ring, Tarzan yell, typewriter,* and *bomb drop—whistle & blast.* Nailed to the rear wall is a yellowed photo of Harry Houdini.

Speer looks over the board, begins hitting unlabeled toggle switches until the meters light up and then needles swing up into view. He takes an index card and pen from his suitcoat pocket, finds a volume knob, and gingerly turns it to the right. From the speakers comes a sultry female voice saying, "You've got to learn to appreciate your inherent carnality." He points the pen to the frequency indicator, then transcribes a set of numbers onto the card.

He turns his attention to a large reel-to-reel recorder with a flashing red button labeled *timer.* He hits the rewind toggle and the tapes spin backward on their axles. He hits *stop* and then *play.*

"Here we go," Speer whispers aloud.

The woman's voice is replaced by a squeal of feedback, then the static cuts out completely, and after a second of dead air, a laid-back voice announces:

You're welcome. Don't mention it. We here at anarchy central agree wholeheartedly. "All-talk radio," my ass. What they're handing out here is all babble. Straight from the puppet's mouth. I'm not saying I got anything better. I'm just saying we're here to knock them on their asses for a while. So, tell your friends. The rumors are true. *We're ba-a-a-ck.*

Speer smiles and says, "So am I, dickhead."

6.

...Well, you've been even more libidinously confused than normal tonight. I see my services are needed now more than ever. But the hour is late and my tongue is tired. So, until next time, this is Veronica Wilcox, the diva of deviant delights, saying, fuel the fantasy and keep in touch.

As the close-out theme rises, the regulars in Minnesota immediately start their critiquing of *Libido Liveline*. Flynn starts to file through bodies, moving out of the crowd, either nodding his head in agreement with their assessments or giving a warm and noncommittal laugh. He won't argue with even the most ludicrous of criticisms. He'll simply pat the commentator on the back and move on to more lucid company.

Flynn doesn't like antagonism. He doesn't see what it accomplishes, finds it reductive and time-consuming. As a result, he ends up spending a large chunk of all his time in Wireless playing the healer, soothing hurt feelings and trying to build shaky treaties between overly sensitive and cliquish people.

A regular named Frank St. Claire starts to rewind the requisite tape they've made of the show and Flynn knows this means the heavy-duty analysis is about to start. They'll be huddled over the reel-to-reel beyond closing time, replaying the show inch by inch, jotting down notes and thumbing through cross-referenced index cards, debating every word of advice that's fallen from the lips of *the goddess*. This is the core cult of *Libido Liveline* fans, the die-hards, the people who just can't get enough, whose daily meaning and reason for moving and drawing breath has filtered down to a local radio show.

G.T. squeezes a last few arms on his way to the barber chair. He's not into the obsessive dissection. As a matter of fact, though he'd never admit it to the fanatics, he's not even that interested in what Ronnie Wilcox has to say. It's simply her voice that gets to him. For all he knows, he'd get the same sweet charge, the same addictive chill, just listening to her read from the phone book.

He mounts his throne, the antique, handle-pump, brass-trimmed barber chair that's located in a dim, cavelike niche in the rear of the bar. It's from this post that he plays big daddy every night, dispensing love advice, floating loans of up to a C-note and occasionally beyond, reinterpreting a painful quarrel between two edgy friends, confiscating car keys for the overindulgent and offering rides home to all parts of the city. Each night, it's as if a visit to Flynn's barber chair is an essential part of the Wireless experience. Newcomers sheepishly approach and shake hands and mumble nicknames. Acquaintances swing by on their way to the rest rooms, dropping the latest radio joke or asking a pop fashion opinion. Novice radio-heads solicit quick quotes on antique sets, while the longtime aficionados settle in for ten-minute debates about recent FCC legislation. The punks come by for a free beer. The tech-heads want a pat on the back for their latest innovations. The amorous seek out an introduction to a newfound prospect. And the simply lonely want any kind of exchange, the basic interplay of human voices.

Flynn supplies it all, every night, and quietly, demurely, revels in it. He's the main player of Wireless, maybe more essential than either Ferrie or Most. Tonight's no exception to the tradition. Over the course of a half hour he sees most of the congregation. Hazel cruises by to ask if she can borrow his car

next week and he smiles and assures her *mi Saab es su Saab.*
Jimmy Donato hits him up for a twenty to lay on an upcoming
round of nine ball and Flynn slides him a crisp, new bill. Jojo
Mehlman needs some bolstering over the brutal divorce he's
wading through and Flynn goes to work, assuring a quick
resolution and predicting lines of new women by spring. Norris
Christianson has a need to recount the graphic details of his
recent proctosigmoidoscopy and Flynn nods gravely and sympa-
thizes over the strange ways of the lower digestive tract. Everybody seems to have a problem tonight. Laurie Geneva is convinced
her new husband the dentist is *slamming that bitch hygienist* and
Flynn assures her Graham would never do this. Nina Texier,
lead guitarist for the industrial-funk band Grammatology, has
sprained her wrist and Flynn recommends a specialist who owes
him a favor and won't charge her. A three-hundred-pound bald
guy, known only as Dix, relays his recent problems with the
licensing commission and Flynn promises he'll make a call to
Counselor Donaghue.

For the next half hour, they come like pilgrims to the barber
chair, some edgy and some smashed and some angry, but most
just anxious for five minutes of G.T.'s time. Does it ever bother
him that no one comes *offering* a favor? Flynn knows that's not
the nature of the game. It's not the posture he's assumed and
besides, he doesn't need any favors. He's more than content just
being able to pass them out.

As Dix waddles away, Flynn smiles to see the next visitor is
one of his favorites. Gabe is probably also the youngest regular at
Wireless, maybe about fifteen years old. In the beginning, Ferrie
got a little nervous when he found the underage kid next to
Flynn at the bar. But Flynn calmed him down by hinting at
friends on the liquor board and Gabe has now become not only a
regular but one of Hazel's inner circle. On this score, Flynn feels
a bit ambiguous. Hazel's people are young and it's good Gabe
can hang with people close to his own age. But some part of

G.T. wanted to keep the kid pure, shield him, at least for a short while, from the political feuding of the jammers.

Like Hazel and himself, Flynn knows Gabe doesn't have much in the line of family. He's a mulatto out of someplace on the border of the Canal Zone. And, unfortunately, when he gets the least bit excited, he's overtaken by a siege of stuttering. Lately, though, Flynn's noticed that the boy's speech seems to improve when he's around Hazel. And for that reason alone, he can't bring himself to discourage the enormous case of infatuation he's seen build up over the past couple of months. Gabe's got it bad for Hazel, a classic case of puppy love, a schoolboy crush of painful scope.

Flynn studies him now, slouched in the adjoining chair, ignoring the slick skateboarding magazine that Flynn brought him. The kid's staring across the room to where Hazel is holding court with her muscle-boy, Eddie, and two new faces, possibly new recruits to the clique.

"Another Moxie?" Flynn asks, but Gabe shakes him off without looking over.

Finally he says, "I ga-ga-gotta take a piss," and slides out of the chair.

Gabe has to wait ten minutes before the men's room is completely empty. Then he stands in front of the wall mirror, brings his face close until his nose is just about touching the glass, and slowly, methodically, begins to make a series of exaggerated shapes with his mouth, rounding it into a huge "O," pulling in the lower lip and clamping it with his teeth. He only gets a minute or so before someone comes in, then he exits and drifts through the crowd for a while.

Gabe wishes he could line everyone up, the whole jammer circle. Both factions. Even Wallace Browning and the old boys. Even Billy J, the little midget shithead. He wishes he could take on Flynn's voice and relaxed confidence. He wishes he could mimic Hazel's attitude and her courage. He'd even take Wallace's knowledge of jamming history and the wisdom that comes with it. And he wishes he could put all these attributes together into a single lecture, one full-blown, attention-freezing speech of a lifetime.

He'd wake the jammers up. He'd speak slowly, but with force. And he'd never once stutter. He'd speak until they came to, until they saw the simplicity of his words. Until they gave up their chokeholds on all these specific, particular ideas, all this political and philosophical crap, all this art shit, and just started to think about the group, the people who sit elbow-to-elbow every night at Wireless. The crowd that he once heard Flynn call *the family*.

But Gabe's only fifteen years old and he's too confused to even begin understanding why everything feels like it's falling apart at Wireless. He feels he shouldn't be in this position, that as the youngest jammer, he should be exempt from the infighting. He should be cared for, looked after a little. He knows Hazel would be annoyed at thoughts like this. Maybe more than annoyed, more like ashamed. But this is how he genuinely feels, that a sense of place and belonging has to count more than a sense of independence. At least at fifteen, when every hormone in his body is pushing and prodding him and five times a day he feels like his head could tear loose from his shoulders and launch itself into orbit.

When Gabe was five years old, his old man left for a two-week hunting trip and never came home. The hunting buddy turned out to be a waitress named Denise. Gabe's ma filed for divorce a year later and had to go back to night work as a projectionist at Herzog's Erotic Palace. Gabe was raised by a string of impatient cousins and, now and then, hired sitters.

He tries not to think much about his father these days. He tries not to think about what a normal childhood might have been like. He tries to focus on Wireless—how he can learn from Flynn. How he can be of help to Hazel. He knows his feelings for Hazel are, at best, unrealistic. But how do you turn off a crush of this magnitude? How do you simply will yourself not to care?

Gabe looks across the room to Flynn, still seated in the brass and red leather confessional, whispering calming words into the ear of a weeping young woman.

A regular named Chatman comes up behind Flynn and says into his ear, "Ferrie wants to see you in the basement," then moves away quickly.

Flynn wades through the crowd to the front of the club, slides behind the bar, unlocks the cellar door, and starts down the stairs into the dim and musty air below. Immediately, the environment changes. The walls at his side are now rough and bulging natural boulders mortared together and caked with a century's worth of silt and soot. The stairs beneath his feet are an ancient, creaky wood. And even the air seems to come from some decay-plagued era that everyone's forgotten.

Coming off the bottom step, Flynn plants his foot in a pool of cold water and lets out a fast, overly loud, "Shit."

From somewhere deeper in the basement, Ferrie yells, "It's flooded a little."

"Timely advice," Flynn mutters.

"Who's there?" Ferrie calls.

"Thought police," Flynn yells. "We've got your mother. Come out slowly."

"Señor Flynn," Ferrie yells back. "I'm down with the antiques."

Flynn doesn't know how the man can spend so much time in this cellar. Every time Most sends him down for a crate of vodka, he disappears for an hour. Flynn thinks of the cellar as an enormous tomb, a dank mausoleum that seems to fill with water every time it rains. The cellar is divided into dozens of chambers or "vaults," as Ferrie tends to call them. There's a wide center aisle that runs from the front of the factory to the back, unobstructed, then dead-ends into a woodshed area that spans the width of the building. Off this center aisle are small rooms, little storage areas partitioned by scrap wood and sometimes chicken wire. Most of these storage chambers are empty, but a few are still crammed to capacity with crates and cartons and naked bales of rolled wire, ancient stock and supplies abandoned by the factory's owners when the place went under.

Flynn moves to the first vault and looks in. Under the glare of a mesh-caged light bulb, hanging from a hook in the rafter above, sits Ferrie behind a long redwood picnic table. He's seated in an old-fashioned wooden swivel chair that tilts to one side. His feet are propped up on a slotted crate to keep them out of the puddle of water beneath the table. Behind him, mounted on the wall, is a large Peg-Board fitted with old fuse boxes and newer circuit breakers—the electrical wiring for the whole building. The table itself is covered with an eclectic selection of antique radios. Flynn spots Philcos and Farnsworths, Crosleys and Stewart-Warners, and at least one old Fairbanks-Morse that he'd guess dates from the late thirties.

Flynn tiptoes deeper into the room until he finds a dry mound of earth to stand on. Then he just digs his hands into his pants pockets and smiles at Ferrie.

Ferrie has a cheap red plastic fishing tackle box open in his lap. It's filled not with lures but with small hand tools, tweezers and small pliers and wire strippers. A half dozen other tools are scattered on the picnic table around the old radios. And, unbelievably, in the midst of a hundred years' worth of dirt and soot, there's a spray can of Lemon Pledge furniture polish and a thick chamois buffing cloth.

Flynn puts his hand to his forehead and says, "Ferr, if you love these units so much, why do you leave them down here in this rat hole?"

Ferrie stares at him for a few seconds and finally, in a whisper, says, "Usually no one but me comes down here."

"Yeah, with good reason."

"It's not so bad when you get used to it. Pretty peaceful, really."

"That's the last word I'd go for. I hate it down here."

"Rough on the suits?"

"We had a basement like this where I grew up. I was in it all the time. It took in water, just like this place. God, the smell down here..."

"Why'd you go in the basement if you hated it?" Ferrie asks.

Flynn ignores him. "I heard you wanted to see me. Good news or bad? I already talked to Hazel. I put out the fire—"

"Good news. Interesting news."

"You got another lead for me? That liquor salesman was a dog, you know. I bought the geek a steak down at Winchester's, he tells me over dessert he's looking for cheap term but no one will write him 'cause this genetic heart thing—"

"Forget business, G.T. She's in here. Tonight."

"She?"

Ferrie gives up a self-satisfied nod.

"Who's in here tonight?"

Ferrie closes his mouth, lets a smile cut larger across his face.

Flynn comes upright, furrows his brows, gives a "get out of here" mock-annoyed grin.

"Five minutes ago. Most was behind the bar. Woman comes in. Not a regular. Never seen her before. Very stylish. A presence. She orders a mescal. Bang. The voice. Most almost falls over. She gives him a look—*don't give me away, help me out here.* He swears to me it's her."

Flynn's heart speeds up. "Where is she?" he says.

Ferrie shrugs. "Took the drink and blended into the crowd. Most is already starting to doubt himself. You know how that happens. You're sure of something and then five minutes later you're not."

"What direction did she go in?"

"She just went into the crowd. You don't know what she looks like, do you? I've seen a photo, but the die-hards all say it's a decoy—"

"Most give you a description?"

"I didn't ask. It was the voice that killed him, you know?"

"I know."

Flynn starts out of the chamber and up the stairs.

"What?" Ferrie yells after him. "You're going to talk to every woman in here?"

7.

The Volvo pulls up under the winged portico of the Baron Quinsigamond, and two carhops, a man and a woman, jump into action. They pull open doors, give a small bow with the head, and offer an arm to help Olga and Wallace extract themselves from the front seat.

Olga straightens the crocheted shawl around her shoulders and smiles up at the young Hispanic woman, presses a five into her hand, and takes from her the pink parking stub for validation. She walks around the front of the car and takes Wallace's arm, brings her mouth to his ear, and says, "We're going to break some records tonight. I can feel it."

They enter the hotel lobby with the saunter of self-imposed nobility. The Baron is already a decade old, but has lost none of its impressiveness. It's got that top-of-the-franchise feel to it. None of the old Mickey Mouse stuff that used to pass for traveler accommodations here in Quinsigamond. This place has the big open lobby with the hanging crystal chandelier, the rooftop revolving restaurant, the health club and pool. And most of all, the beautiful, crushed-velvet, mauve uniforms worn by the staff. Wallace thinks, *You know you're in a big-money place when the bellboy's thighs whistle.*

A tall, bony-faced woman in a black satin evening gown says, "Mr. and Mrs. Browning, we've been expecting you."

67

She takes each of them by the hand, smiles down at them.

"Just like the president and secretary to be late," Wallace says.

Olga does a practiced eye roll. "Don't listen to him, Magda. Wallace likes to make an entrance."

Magda gives a just-as-practiced laugh and says, "I think you'll find everything you requested. I can tell you the ice sculpture is a big hit. Table One has been asking for you. Now, if you need anything at all, just ask for Aldo or myself."

"I'm sure it's all perfect," Olga says.

"Did the drummer make it?" Wallace asks. "They said yesterday there could be a problem with the drummer."

Magda puts a hand on his shoulder. "He's been punctuating all of Mr. Dixon's jokes."

Wallace brings a hand up to his forehead like a migraine's just exploded over the eyes. "Oh my God, honey, we'd better get in there. Dixon is trying to play emcee again."

"Have a wonderful night," Magda says, then lowers her voice. "You're the odds-on favorite to bring home the gold."

Olga takes Wallace's arm and they walk through the lobby and veer left into the Duchess Ballroom. Hanging over the entryway is a crimson banner that reads:

Q.L.P.L. 19

And underneath, the explanation:

Quinsigamond Little People's Lodge 19
Eighth Annual Dinner Dance

They stop in the entryway, directly underneath the banner, survey the room, and let the crowd observe their arrival.

"Oh, honey, Magda outdid herself this year," Olga says softly.

"You pay for the best..." Wallace responds, and starts to wave at the crowd.

From the other side of the room, a voice yells, "Our fearless leader made it."

Wallace cups his hands around his mouth and yells back, "No more of the punch for Dixon," then gives a "yer out" sign with thumb and swinging arm. There's some laughter and a rim-shot drumbeat. Assured of the room's attention, Wallace takes Olga's arm and they start to move through the crowd toward the head table, patting backs and grabbing extended hands along the way.

The room is a sight. All the chrome and gold plating has been polished immaculate. The bandstand is lit professionally with multicolored spots for the slow numbers. There's an ice sculpture, a huge four-foot swan, neck turned as if in the midst of a vision. They've remembered the fresh-cut flowers, the hundreds of helium balloons, the crepe paper and streamers. There's the train of gleaming aluminum Sterno carts for the endless buffet. And, thank God, Magda was able to rent enough of the special-order tables and chairs, custom-designed for formal dwarf functions.

Now Magda just has to pray that Wallace triumphs at the dance contest. She can only hope the band, the locally famous Les Roberts Quintet, will supply the tunes he likes, the ones that allow him to show his best moves. The odds are that Wallace and Olga will walk out with the night's biggest trophy. They usually do. If not, she knows Olga already appreciates the extra effort. But Wallace is another story. Three and a half feet of tough customer.

She watches him as he moves toward the head table, an instinctive politician, a crowd handler, an image pro. His stature is inconsequential. He knows how to maneuver within the heart of the mob. He knows when to go with the joke and when to plunge into soulful earnestness. He knows when to smile, when to roll the eyes, when to grimace, and when to drop the salty tear to the cheekbone. And like all creatures who know how to use these tools to optimum advantage, Wallace is, at his core, a cold and ruthless device, a machine for goal attainment.

He reaches Table One, seats Olga, then lingers for a moment behind his own chair, an arm stretched upward to recognize someone supposedly toward the rear of the room. Then he settles in at the table with a greeting for each of his dinner companions.

"So, Al," he says, "will we be having some fun tonight?"

"Don't we always, Wallace," Al says. "I just hope you and the missus cleared some room in the trunk for all the metal you'll be hauling out of here tonight."

The table laughs its agreement and approval and Wallace nods and says, "I put on the lucky shoes. The feet have no excuse."

There's a second chorus of laughter and Wallace feels a hand on his shoulder. Before he can turn to greet his visitor, he sees the fright on Olga's face and knows it's Billy J. These younger kids have no sense of timing or manners. He was just getting the table off the ground.

Wallace pushes his chair back and says, "Excuse me for just a sec. Kitchen problem, I'm sure."

Billy J works as a busboy at the Baron. He's dressed in a double-breasted white cotton busing jacket decorated with fading gravy stains. Wallace takes Billy J by the elbow, gives a squeeze that he hopes will leave a bruise in the morning, and moves the youngest member of his inner circle over near the bandstand where they can talk privately.

"You've got all the polish of a carnival act, you little putz."

Billy J puts on the hurt eyes and swallows down the last of his drink.

"I've been trying to call you all day," he says.

"Olga and I were practicing. We never take calls when we're practicing."

"Jeez, Fred and Ginger here—"

"Okay, Mr. Smart Mouth, what's the big emergency that you have to pull me away from dinner?"

"I was down Wireless last night—"

"Something new?"

"Hazel was in. We got talking—"

"A regular miracle."

"Hey, you want to know?"

"Come on, come on."

"You want to know?"

"Yes, Billy, I want to know."

"Hazel says, and I told you this would happen, you go back two months, I told you this. She says, they're going to break, they're going to splinter off. They want nothing to do with us, Wallace."

Wallace looks down at his shoes, custom-made in the Philippines, just now at that perfect holding pattern between broken in and wearing out. He shakes his head slightly, lets just enough of a smile spread over his lips so that it looks like an unsuccessful attempt to suppress his amusement.

"What," Billy says, "this is funny to you?"

"First of all," Wallace says in a lowered voice, "this is not the time nor the place and you should know that by now. More importantly, and once again, you speak without thinking. You open your mouth and dump everything out, without bothering to think. I don't know why I make an effort with you—"

Billy is stunned and his face shows it. "I don't get it," he says. "This doesn't bother you? This news doesn't upset you?"

He cups Billy around the back of the neck. "I pray that someday before I die, just once, you'll learn to look for a bigger picture. You think that'll ever happen?"

"I just don't get it."

"Think now, Billy. What are we at heart? You and I?"

Billy's terrified of a wrong answer and his fear makes it difficult to concentrate. He decides he has to go with the obvious and says, "Dwarfs."

Wallace gives him a sharp, open-palmed slap to the cheek, so fast he hopes that even if any of the guests witnessed it, they'll spend the night questioning their vision.

"You infuriate me, you little bastard."

Billy cowers, hangs his head, wishes the band would start playing.

"We're anarchists, you schmuck. Remember that word, Billy? Did you read even one of the books I bought for you?"

Billy prays he's not required to answer.

"Anarchists don't wear uniforms, Billy. Anarchists can't worry about splinter groups. We *are* a splinter group, for Christ sake. We're antiunity, we're antiregulatory. We're goddamn anarchists."

"Listen," Billy says, avoiding eye contact. "There are more strangers down Wireless every week. Everybody's getting nervous. Nobody knows who could be what, okay? The *Spy* says the FCC's all pissed off. You think we need a bunch of people all hot to blow things up? You think we need them out there bringing heat down on us?"

"Now, you lower your voice right now, mister. There're a lot of friends here who would not think too much of our little hobby. Now, I will deal with Hazel and her people. That's not your problem. I will square Hazel and company away. But I want you to burn this into your memory, Billy: don't you ever, ever, never again, approach me at an affair like this to discuss anything to do with jamming. Do you understand me, Billy?"

Olga's concerned. She's half-turned in her chair, head-motioning for Wallace to return. But surprisingly, Billy's a little stubborn. He says, "I just think we got some problems starting up here."

Wallace leans in toward him and says, "Son, you wouldn't know a problem if it pulled out a sword and sliced off your ear."

8.

Flynn heads for the rear of Wireless, beyond the pool tables. He realizes the best course of action is a logical one, something planned and systematic—divide the room into geometric blocks and eliminate them one by one, a steady pace, a thorough search. All he'd have to hear would be *hello;* even *get lost* could confirm or deny. His ears could play polygraph. He'd know the truth the second the sound penetrated down the canal, impacted on the drum, one syllable, even in the midst of this bar din, the brain could tell him—*Veronica.*

But, as always, his body won't cooperate. It insists on being erratic, patternless. His eyes spot possible women by their likely age, but they won't stay focused on the subject long enough for his intuition to react one way or another. He ends up randomly moving in big sweeping circles, only occasionally singling some-one out, pumping them for a response, a word, a way to know. He hears *Fuck off, Hello again, Flynn, Excuse me,* and *I'm with someone.* He starts coming up from behind, placing his hand on shoulders and the backs of necks. Mostly, he gets glares or con-fused looks. He turns down a single offer to dance.

He's about to head back to the bar, grill Most for any piece of information—eye color, length of hair, height—but he's stopped by the voice as he passes his antique barber chair against the wall.

She says, "You look lost."

What he's hit with is something very close to fear. He looks down to his feet for a second, suddenly not sure he wants to know what she looks like. The classic pilgrim, willing to search for years, but terrified to end the pilgrimage.

Like leaping into ice water, he makes himself do it without thinking. He brings his head up, stares directly at her face. It's hard to say that she's just what he's imagined, since he's imagined a wide variety of possibilities. But she is beautiful. That part of the projection isn't compromised at all. Her hair is shorter than he'd expected, darker. She's a bit smaller-boned than her voice indicates, but not delicate. Her eyes are deep blue—he'd pictured them brown or green. Her skin is as pale as he'd thought. He's always imagined her inside, artificially lit, and though he's never thought about this before, he knows now, in this instant, this is because he often hears the voice late at night, at home, enclosed himself, wrapped up under a blanket in the dentist's chair.

He widens his angle, takes in the full body, wonders if there's any significance to the fact that she's in his barber chair, tilted back, almost the same angle he falls into when listening to her show. He likes the way she's dressed, the short black suede skirt and the white silk blouse. It's a style he's pictured, sensual and hip and completely fitting.

"Some nights," he says, "you just can't get on track."

She reaches over, pats the seat of an empty chair next to her. The pilgrim's chair. He hesitates, then climbs in, lets his hand fall down to touch the tilt lever, but refrains from pulling, stays upright.

"So," she says, "know where I can get a secure annuity? Maybe some exceptional life with a reducing premium? I'm a nonsmoker."

It works. He's caught off guard and he lets his face show it. He recovers with a forced laugh and says, "I'm at a disadvantage here—"

She cuts him off. "C'mon, G.T. I thought we'd save some

time by not lying to each other. This place closes in less than an hour."

He shrugs. "Yeah, well, the inner core can stay as long as they want."

"The inner core? Is that what you are?"

"One of many. Can I ask how you know me?"

"I don't want to get too specific. I've got a lot of fans, you know? Lot of teenage boys, little hackers, up all night in their bedrooms, just my voice and the light from their P.C.'s It's weird. It gets so there's this language, this verbal shorthand between you and your hard-core listeners. You just refer to something, ask a question, and bang—they're calling the station with more than you want to know."

"You asked about me? On the air? I'm a pretty constant listener, you know—"

"Oh, I can imagine."

"And I never heard any mention—"

"I've got an inner core, too. Lots of ways to communicate in this town."

"You know, Ronnie, you wanted to buy life insurance, all you had to do was look in the yellow pages."

"And if I want to find out who's been knocking my station off the air? What directory do I look in then?"

He flinches, genuinely surprised by the comment. "That's how I came up? You think *I've* been jamming QSG? Some kid gave you my name as the jammer?"

"So, this would be a denial?"

"Who told you this? Who gave you my name?"

"Oh, c'mon, please, Mr. Flynn—"

He lets his head fall back in the chair till he's looking at the tin-plated ceiling. He lets out a low whistle, shakes his head slightly.

"I've wanted to meet you for a year now. You know that?"

"Yeah, you fit the fan demographics."

"I'm not a fan—"

"You say it like it's an insult..."

"There's a certain mentality—"

"As opposed to jammers?"

"Mizz, I don't know what you're referring to. I don't know the meaning of that word."

"You come here for the ambience? You're into nuclear deco?"

"I'm just another blues fan."

"Oh, a music lover—"

"Exactly."

"But my show's all-talk."

"I make exceptions. And you've sort of got a bluesy style."

"You know, Flynn, I'm not a radio cop or something. I just wanted to ask why, see if we could work out an arrangement."

"An arrangement?"

"I'm not here to nail you or something. You know that, right?"

"I'm not the guy. I'm not the person you're interested in."

"Would there be any chance you'd know who I should talk to?"

He stares at her for a while until she breaks a nervous smile, then he gets out of the chair, takes a step away, and says, "This figures."

She leans forward, reaches out, and takes his coat sleeve.

"You're leaving?"

He stops, bounces slightly on the balls of his feet, steps back in toward her.

"I wait a year, keep myself from finding out about you. Concentrate on the voice—"

"You and fifty thousand others. According to last week's book, anyway."

"—keep you in the dream. But it won't work. My luck. The dream has to mug me. From behind. In my own bar." He takes a breath, lowers his voice, but retains the testiness. "I didn't knock out your pathetic station. And I don't know who did. And if I did know, I wouldn't tell you. End of story."

"Honor among thieves. How trite."

"Who's a thief?" Flynn asks. "What was stolen?"

"Airtime."

"How do you own *airtime*?"

"What do you mean, how do you own it? You purchase it. You buy a license. You sign a contract. Hey, Mr. Life Insurance, you familiar with these terms?"

"See, you can't trust the voice. It never works. I took you to be smarter than this."

"Moving right along. Is this the part where we start to insult each other? Tell me when to throw my drink."

"Okay, fine. What can I say? I'm not your man. You got bad information. Hazard of our age."

"I'm just curious, you know," Ronnie says. "I mean, what's the big attraction? Why would someone want to waste their time jamming radio stations?"

Flynn shrugs and shakes his head. "I can only speculate."

"Please do."

"My guess is there's probably a lot of different motivations. Some of them probably feel powerless and frustrated and some-how they stumbled on this little hobby to compensate. You know, hit the big boys. Others are probably just old-time practical jokers. And then I'd guess there are the egos, right? They do it 'cause they can. 'Cause it's complicated and technical, and they know how. I don't know."

She nods, lifts her drink to mock-toast him, gulps down the rest of the mescal, hands him the empty glass.

"Last question. I'll frame it hypothetically since you're not familiar with the people involved. If you *were* a jammer, why would you spare my show? What's so special about *Libido Liveline*?"

"You've got an army of horny adolescents at your heels and you're asking me that question?"

"I need a more worldly opinion, someone closer to my own perceptions. A peer."

"You're making a lot of assumptions there—"

"Yeah, yeah, yeah. Just answer the question. Take a stab."

Flynn shrugs. "For Christ sake, you heard the guy yourself. I'd take what he said at face value. He finds everything else on your station babble. That means he must find some value to your show."

"I guess," Ronnie says, "that's what I'm looking for. How he defines that value."

"You'd have to find the guy and ask him. And I can't help you in that department, whether you believe me or not."

Ronnie lifts her arms up over her head in a slow stretch. Flynn wishes he had a drink, then wishes that he'd never left the house tonight, that he'd told Wallace and Hazel to settle their own differences.

Her hands come down, run through her hair. She gives a smile and says, "Forget it," and then adds, "Want to go for a ride?"

They end up at the airport, the old one, abandoned but undemolished for a decade now. They sit in Ronnie's Jeep, passing her flask of mescal back and forth like a slow-motion Ping-Pong game. As they talk, they stare out at the ghost-town terminal, every window shattered, all doors missing. The landing strips are a gritty museum of frost heaves and potholes, brown weed shooting up through every cracked parcel of cement. In the deserted section of parking lot where they drink, dozens of giant spikish halogen lamps have all been dented in near the base, like someone with a drivable wreck and a lot of undirected hostility has rammed them at cruising speed, caused them to bend over as if eternally racked by shooting ulcer pain.

Flynn knows he's getting more drunk than he intended, but that it's necessary if the night is to progress somewhere, if some percentage of his fantasy can be brought back.

The booze doesn't seem to hit Ronnie. Her voice stays constant, changeless in tone and volume. This could be a by-product of her profession, Flynn thinks, but it's more likely she's got a high tolerance from some steady practice. She's been telling him stories from her youth, vignettes sort of, little glimpses that may have a point or lesson that he's missing. She's let him in on her mother's many husbands, her bizarre teenage crush on Walter Cronkite, and, most of all, her required research into the intricacies of human sexuality in all its varied masks.

"The thing is," she says, pausing to take the flask from him and fire a double, "I realized early on, I just instinctively understood, the need for specialization. You want to take a guess how many straight talk shows there are out there? Answer—too many. And it's been that way for a long time. They come and go. It gets boring fast. You know this. I'm not telling you anything new. So you have to zero in. You have to find the collective pulse and tap it, give it the jolt it's waiting for. Whether it knows it or not. Okay, you can go politics, like old Ray at the station. Do I need to say more? Listen to Ray. No humor. No sensitivity. Literal-minded. No feeling for the audience. You end up exclusively with the fanatics. I know what you're thinking. No fanatics like the ones you find in Libidoland. Okay, true to a point. But what I've found is that your fanatics in this department, and *only* in this department, cut across the whole spectrum. Race, creed, age. Economic, geographic, sociopolitical. The whole shebang. We're all fanatics, Flynn. *You* are a fanatic, Mr. Flynn. We're all pioneers, willing or not."

Flynn shakes his head, holds back a laugh. "I'm sorry. I know you're the expert here, but your thinking is dated. No one's obsessed with sex anymore—"

"Hold up. Stop. You're confused. You're misreading symptoms. Our obsession's gone back underground, below the skin. We're back to the age of suppression. It's cyclical, like everything else in history. We're into appearance again. Governmental mores. It's an epidemic mentality. Combined with backlash. You just have to take my word on this."

"Well, like you say, Ray's been getting bumped regularly, but you seem sacred."

"My show. My show seems sacred."

Flynn smiles. "Same difference, right?"

"I don't think so. The show is more than just me. There has to be an exchange, an interplay. A caller. It's essential. Old story. The whole is greater than the sum of the parts. It's the big picture that the brothers like."

"The brothers?"

She holds her mouth over the nozzle of the flask, gives him an impatient look, refuses to speak.

"What?" he says.

"Please. Let's say you *are* just the neighborhood life insurance guy. Let's say that. You don't read the *Spy*? You didn't notice the little article about the patron saints of the city's jammers? Why does this have to be such a bitch?"

He takes the flask from her, decides that maybe drunk is the best way to go at this point. He goes to upend it, then says, "We're out."

"More in the glove box."

He pulls out a fresh pint, cracks the seal, offers her the first hit, which she takes.

"Okay, fine," he says, "yes, I read the article. First off, it was pretty ill informed—"

"Correct my misconceptions."

He ignores the interruption. "The point is, and you should know this better than anyone, right? The beauty of radio is the anonymity. Anybody can broadcast. And anybody can call themselves James and John—"

"Weren't you listening tonight? They came right out and said 'O'Zebedee.'"

"Anybody can call themselves O'Zebedee."

"You're saying someone's framing them. That it's not the real thing."

He sighs, takes back the bottle. "I'm not even saying that, really. I guess I'm saying that's one possibility."

"What's your opinion?"

He waits awhile before saying, "My opinion is that maybe we should head back to the bar."

She slouches down in her seat. "I was going to give you a tour of the terminal."

He looks out at the decayed building. "You make a habit of coming up here?"

"When I need to think."

"Could be a little dangerous, couldn't it?"

"I've never had a problem. It's a great place. It's like walking around in a dream."

"You're nuts. There are probably rats in there."

She laughs. "There are no rats."

"I've got a better idea," Flynn says, and reaches to the dash and turns on the radio. But instead of tuning in QSG, he slides down the band until he comes to some subdued, bluesy sax music, just an old-fashioned kind of tenor melody with a strong bass line, no strings or orchestra crap. Very simple. Two people in a dark room, hunched into their instruments.

They both sit back in silence for a few minutes. The tune goes on and on and finally Ronnie says, in spite of herself, "This is great," and then, coming forward, adds, "I've got an even better idea."

She rolls her window all the way down, turns the volume up slightly, snaps on the headlights, then pulls up the door latch and climbs outside. Flynn watches her motion to him through the windshield, gets out of the Jeep, and joins her in the shine of the headlights. She faces him, bites down on a smile, takes him by the wrists, and directs his hands around her waist. She starts to dance, this slow, unstructured sway, mostly hip movement. He goes along with it and they fall into the rhythm of the song, pick up some pace, join their bodies closer together. They begin to experiment, laughing slightly, more surprised than embarrassed.

She leans into him, brings her head up near his ear, and says, "It's true, you know, you concentrate on the music and it just gets easier."

He indulges himself, gives her a mobile hug, runs a hand up into her hair.

"It's weird," he says, "in the headlights."

"We could use some fog."

"Maybe a little rain. Little drizzle."

She rests her head against his shoulder. He turns her and she looks out at the landing strip. The Jeep's headlights screen their shadows onto the tarmac, elongated giants swaying, long waves of spectral nomads blowing over the desert. Some wind starts up, moves scrap along the lot, makes a gushing noise through the terminal that adds something to the saxophone.

She says, "I used to watch that movie all the time when I was young. Sidney Poitier and Lulu. Remember the scene where they danced? I always wanted to dance like that."

"With Poitier?"

"Or someone like him."

Flynn leans in, puts his lips to her neck.

"But this is pretty good. This is okay."

She begins to slow-dance him backward in the direction of the Jeep until he's backed against the hood and the dancing fades into a tight, full-body embrace. His mouth moves around her neck, sucking and licking, and he feels her buck a little, her back arch out and her arms press into him. The pace of their hands and mouths speeds up as if their fingers and lips can't decide where to land. She's pushing into him, his back is against the grille, the Jeep taking his weight, his ass sliding down toward the bumper. He's in a crouched, almost-sitting position, slightly below her. Ronnie shifts position, moves her legs outside his. She reaches down, starts to rub him, and hears his breathing immediately go shallow, almost as if she's hurt him. She hesitates and he says, "No," in a clipped, too-high pitch. She starts to fumble with his belt buckle and zipper, too anxious. He runs his hands up her thighs, lifting her skirt, coming around and squeezing her behind. He rises up slightly off the bumper and she manages to pull his pants free with a series of clumsy yanks. He pushes his face into the crook of her neck, slides into her, and the noises begin, clogged moans from an adamantly sealed mouth. She rocks backward, holding onto his shoulders, finds a rhythm, a midtempo wave that can build. His arms are locked around her waist and she can feel his feet sliding a bit in the gravel. She starts to blow out quick breaths, trying for control, typical, not wanting to give away any sound. It goes on like this for a couple of minutes, Flynn getting slightly louder, easing his head back finally, his eyes closed, his bottom lip held down by his upper teeth.

Then he shocks her by jumping up into a standing position, still managing to stay in her, bear-hugging her below her belt line. He's frantic, dipping at his waist until her legs, locked around his back, tilt to the sky. It's like some old 1950s soda-shop dance move, poodle skirts sent sailing to a Buddy Holly tune. He does it again and again, bending, bowing in a sweeping plunge, then reversing, coming upright, actually tilting back-ward a bit.

Ronnie locks in, tightens her legs around him, closes her eyes, holds close to his chest. And begins a low-throated, rum-bling moan, a keening kind of suppressed wail. She catches herself, goes into some shallow breaths, but it doesn't matter, he's drowning her out with this final series of dreamlike yips, a speedy litany of identical monotones that sounds like an Oriental parrot.

When he finishes, he maneuvers a slow fall to the ground and they lie there for a while, still interlocked and breathing heavy just underneath the smoky beams of the headlights.

After a while, when he catches his breath, Flynn says, "So, would I make it on *Libido Liveline*?"

Ronnie laughs and runs a hand over his face, feels the sweat cooling in the November air.

"I'll tell you, Flynn," she says, "you're going to need some private practice."

9.

Wallace pulls the Volvo into the garage and as the door comes down behind them, Olga says, "It just wasn't our night, honey. It wasn't meant to be."

He shakes off her consolation. "Entirely my fault. I couldn't concentrate." He cuts the engine and adds, "Though, God knows, the band's been better."

They enter the house and start to turn on lights. Olga knows she won't feel the full brunt of Wallace's disappointment until tomorrow. Overnight, the excuses and bitterness will breed, multiply like cancer cells, colonize the whole of his brain and larynx. And in a way, she's grateful for the short reprieve. She's just too tired tonight to comfort him, to agree with his assessment of the poor drumming and song selection.

Wallace undoes his tie and says, "Let's just check on the taping and then get some sleep."

Olga follows him down into the basement. They both cry out at the same time when they see the pile of demolished trophies at the foot of the stairs.

A voice comes back at them, a broken echo, "Somehow I don't think I'm in Kansas anymore."

They stare at each other. Olga waits for directions—should she run, call the police, find a weapon of some kind?

"Fred, Ginger, get your tiny little asses down here."

Wallace closes his eyes for a long second and when he opens them it looks as if he'll cry. Instead, he starts down the rest of the stairs and his wife follows, stepping over a mound of broken male and female dancers, silver and gold arms, legs, heads strewn into a mismatched grave, a figurine pyre waiting for a temperature that can melt metal.

Speer is lounging on the couch, half-drunk, reclining down its length, head on an embroidered pillow, shoes kicked off and legs inclined upward resting on the back. His Smith & Wesson is on the coffee table as natural as a bowl of hard candies, as if he were daring someone to make a grab for it. Olga and Wallace come around the corner and stand in front of him.

"Hey, hey," he yells, "circus is in town."

Wallace hopes Olga will stay quiet, but like she reads his mind and willfully opposes it, she blurts out, "Who are you?"

Speer comes upright on the couch and says, "You know exactly who I am. You've been waiting for me since day one. Jesus, you are adorable, aren't you? Kind of like a puppy. In the mall, you know. Just want to take it home."

"Some identification?" Wallace says, trying to pull the attention onto himself.

Speer smiles, picks up his gun, holds it in the air like a badge. "Here's my identification, shithead."

He stands up, partly to show them his height, and motions toward the bar. "Sorry about the mess there. Little accident. Small tremor. You guys must be on a fault line."

They stay silent, stare at him, expressionless.

"I've got to guess that you were out dancing up a storm. Huh? Am I right? I just want to ask you, you know, before we get the party started here, what's the story with the dancing anyway? I mean, size-wise and all, is it harder or easier? I've got no idea. Being so low to the ground and all. Is it easier? Is that how you score all the gold? Or do you pull a lot of sympathy votes? Pity the dwarfs, you know?"

"Are you from the police department?" Wallace asks, desperate to sound calm. "Do you have a name?"

"Son," Speer says, even though Wallace has two decades on him, "we haven't started the question-and-answer part of the evening yet. And when we do, you'll be in the answer section. Right now, we're still getting acquainted. So, could you do me a favor and turn on that beauty over there. The Philco G25-P. Nineteen forty-one, right? Gorgeous machine, there. Hope you've got that baby insured."

Wallace hesitates, then moves to the radio and turns it on. "April in Paris" begins to play. Speer closes his eyes, lets a big boyish grin break on his face, and starts to sway a bit, hands out in front of him like he was ready to climb an invisible ladder.

"What a song. What a wonderful piece of music. Melodious, you know. Not like the crap today. And I'm speaking as a relatively young man. I see a common denominator in today's music. Not the preprogrammed electronics. Not the satanic lyrics. Nope. Lack of melody. Bottom line is a pervasive lack of melody. Drives me crazy."

He opens his eyes, stops swaying. "Getting back to dancing. I'm genuinely curious. You've got such small extremities. Is this a hindrance or a help?"

He pauses, staring at them, smile gone.

"I suppose," he says, nodding to himself, "it really depends on who your partner is. By that I mean—fellow dwarf or not. Do you two dance exclusively with one another? You ever tried it with a normal-sized person?"

He moves away from the couch and next to Olga. Wallace remains next to the radio.

He puts an arm around Olga's shoulder, gestures toward her with his head, says to Wallace, in this mock whisper, "Hey, little guy, you mind if I give her a whirl here? Just take a second."

Wallace's heart starts to pump. He looks around the room, says, "Look, we both know why you're here—"

Speer cuts him off. "Thanks, pal. Return the favor someday."

He scoops Olga up with one arm, turns her until she's facing him, maneuvers her into an awkward waltz stance, an arm around her waist, hand in hand, out to the side a bit. Her shoes dangle two feet above the floor.

"Ooh, you're heftier than you look, dear. Now relax and I'll lead."

He starts a strange semiwaltz toward the center of the room, turns it into a sloppy tango, humming music that doesn't match what the radio plays.

"Please put her down," Wallace says, helpless, fading toward a whine, frantic for a plan, a course of action.

Speer ignores him and says, "This is really wonderful. Really different. I like this. You tell me if I'm squeezing too tight. Wouldn't want to snap the spine. You know, I'm not sure I could go back to a full-sized partner now. You've spoiled me, Olga."

Her eyes are closed. She's fighting both tears and a rage that tells her from where she's hanging she could get off a perfect pointed-toe into his groin, bring him right to the ground. She hopes that Wallace would be ready to act, to grab a golf club and cave in his skull, shatter the bridge of his nose, break a kneecap. But she can't help knowing the guy's a cop. And everything she's feared since the day she married Wallace has suddenly come true. Finally, tonight, in the safety of their rec room, every bad daydream has been made flesh.

He brings his mouth close to her ear like they were at some eternal high school prom. She anticipates the moistness before it actually comes. And then it comes. His tongue dips in toward her eustachian tube, a quick lick and then a whisper, "What do you say you and I ditch this guy and head out to my car?"

The tears win out and start to stream.

"You want money?" Wallace yells. "I got money. You want to bring me in, then let's go."

Speer stops dancing, releases Olga, and she falls to the floor like a heavy, lifeless doll. A look grows on Speer's face, an annoyed, rigid-lipped squint.

"Change partners," he says, steps over to Wallace and picks

him up in a rougher grip. They start to do something resembling a samba and Speer asks, "This a rented tux?"

Wallace can't answer. Olga stays on the ground, pulls herself into a corner, and weeps.

"Now, Mr. Browning," Speer says, dipping, "there are a lot of ways we can do this. And not all of them have to involve losing the deposit on this tux. Not all of them have to involve me taking pretty Olga away with me. Now, I don't want to bust you. I'd be a goddamn laughingstock bringing in munchkins-gone-bad, you know? And I don't want your fucking money. I'll tell you, that was insulting. That was not a wise thing to say. I always picture you people as being more polite or something. I don't know why."

He does a sudden, off-balance spin, then lifts Wallace and places him on the fireplace mantel.

"What I want is for the three of us to have a long conversation about your private little broadcast booth behind the fireplace there. And I want some names—"

"We'll tell you," Olga yells. "Whatever you want."

Wallace gives her a confused, maybe pained, look, and Olga's fear bolts into a surge of anger. She screams, "Don't you dare look at me like that."

Wallace puts his hands up over his ears and bites in on his bottom lip. He looks like an oversized pop-art statue, a roadside souvenir that somehow went horribly wrong during the creation process.

Speer's got them both, turned them against one another. It took less time than he anticipated and he's more than a little proud of this. He lets his pleasure show by easing the act a bit, smiling, holding up his hands in a joint stop sign to both husband and wife.

"Kids, kids, kids," he says, "we don't have to be this way. There's no need for this behavior. That's what I've been trying to make clear to you all along. I just need a little cooperation. Now, what do you say?"

He saunters to the fireplace, lifts Wallace, and deposits him on the floor.

"Mr. B, you're an old pro in this department. I took a little tour of your studio there behind the fireplace. Little cramped. From my perspective anyway. But there's enough evidence behind that wall to take this life away. Take old DeForest Road away. You've been here over twenty years. Mortgage is almost paid off, right? We can take away the house, the job, the savings. You're a CPA, right? Upstanding member of the community and all, right? You're on committees. You've got friends. This little—" he pretends he's reaching for a correct word—"hobby of yours would surprise them all quite a bit, don't you think?"

He steps back, offers Olga a hand up without looking at her. She accepts it and gets to her feet.

"Let's calm down here a second. Let's catch our breath. Sit down on the couch there, the two of you. Next to each other."

They comply and he begins a slow pace in front of them, an act he hopes shows just a hint of patience, reasonableness. He stops now and then at the fireplace mantel, leans against it, strikes the pose of a 1950s TV dad, a young Robert Young, a slightly hipper Hugh Beaumont. He gives the tone that he's rehearsed in the runny mirror of his basement apartment for over a month:

"Okay. I think the three of us need to accept certain givens. Things are not the same right now as they were yesterday. Yesterday your lives had not yet changed. Wallace, you were working on some small company's tax problems. Olga, you were baking a bundt cake, clearing up last-minute details with Magda down at the Baron. Am I right? Have I done my homework? Okay, overnight things change. *That* is the nature of life. We don't like it. As creatures, as animals, we don't like change. Particularly this type of change. Nightmarish change. And your nightmare has a name. Its name is Agent Speer. I'm your nightmare. I'm sorry, but that's how it's worked out. The currents of fate brought us together. Nothing either of us can do about that.

"Now, Wallace. You have a problem. You're not alone in this. Thousands of Americans across the country have the same affliction. I view it as a disease, though I really don't know if, at this point, the AMA would back me up. But I've spent some time studying the phenomenon. I'm not some novice jumping into the fray at the last minute. My knowledge has evolved. You people show the same symptoms as an addict, as an abuser. You're compulsive. Lousy cure percentage, even with help. Help that you don't want. No matter what the cost to family and friends around you. I don't know if Mr. Phil Donahue has ever done one of his shows on your affliction, but he ought to. It'd be a genuine public service. To my mind anyway.

"Right now, you're saying, 'What's the big deal? What have I done that's so wrong?' And I want you to know that I understand that type of thought. You've been honing it, refining it for so long it's got a thick sheen over it. But, Wallace, the truth is the truth. At some point, you have to climb up on the step stool and look in the mirror and admit to yourself. You have to look in the mirror, into you own eyes, no one else's, and say, *God save me, I'm a jammer.*

"There. I said the J-word. As you're both well aware, there are very specific laws in this country regarding the transmission and content of radio signals. There are licensing requirements and financial obligations. Papers to be filed. Inspections. Legal documentation. Bonds. The Federal Communications Commission oversees this entire enterprise. It's an enormous responsibility. There's so much to be considered.

"The air around us is bursting with radio waves. There's only one way to prevent absolute chaos. And that's to rely on mutually agreed-upon laws and regulations, standards and practices. There's a complex system that's been in existence for a long, long time. It's grown as culture and technology have changed. The system has evolved with the times.

"Mr. and Mrs. B, I think you'd agree with me that in any system there are bugs. There are inherent, annoying snags. I think *bugs* is the perfect word. Perfectly descriptive. Maybe it's part of the nature of things. God's design, a wrench in the works just to keep us on our toes, keep us from stagnating. Or maybe it's so we can appreciate normalcy when we manage to glimpse it. I don't know. I know, very simply, that I've been given a job to do. My job is your nightmare. I am an officer of the federal government. I'm a federal cop. My jurisdiction is coast-to-coast. My specialty is search and destroy. Search and destroy bugs in the system of public communications. I'm an exterminator. And you, Wallace, and you, Olga, you are the cockroaches."

He goes for the long pause, lets the weight of his words settle down on top of them, push them a little deeper into the couch.

"Specifically," Wallace says, voice on the edge of cracking, "what is it you want from me?"

"Specifically," Speer says, almost a mimic, but not quite, "I want you to assist me in any and all ways necessary to bring my investigation to an efficient conclusion."

"You want me to be an informer," Wallace says.

"I dislike the connotation of the word."

"You want me to supply you with a list of my associates."

"Fellow jammers, yeah. That would be a start. I'll also want their addresses, occupations, where they spend their time, where they purchase their equipment. That sort of thing."

"And if I don't assist you?"

Speer pulls in some air, blows it out, shrugs. He takes a handkerchief from a back pocket and blows his nose, refolds the rag, and repockets it.

"Excuse me. Pollen count is murder today."

"You'll ruin us," Olga puts in. "You'll arrest us, humiliate us. You'll supply the stations with any information they need for a lawsuit."

Speer stares down at his wing tips, gives a sheepish grin and a hesitant nod. He says, "Look, you're bright people. You've both been around the block a few times. You don't need me to explain to you how this life works. You've got an above-average imagination. You can envision the consequences. Do you really need me to make a list for you?"

He waits just a second and then, "Of course not. Game's over. The good guys have won. Say to yourselves, 'It was fun while it lasted.' Then do what's necessary. Protect your way of life, for God's sake. Look, Wallace, you're the patriarch, as far as I can see. My files say you've been at this since the beginning, early fifties, am I right? These younger jammers, they look up to you. I'll bet you're practically a legend in this town, in your little cult. A figure of respect among these people, am I right?

"You've seen the whole parade, okay? You started out a young man, solo, maybe even before you met Olga. You started small-time—prank stuff. Maybe you vandalized a small transmitter with a baseball bat. Maybe you knocked out power in the basement of a station building. But the years went by and things got more and more complicated. Technology took the express train, right? And you kept up. You did the work. You kept pace, got to know the new equipment as it came along. Then you start actually broadcasting yourself. Ham. C.B. You get more refined. You get a reputation. You're knocking the official stuff off the air more and more often. And you even pick up an M.O.— you're the *sound-effects guy*. That's your label, your tag. You knock their signals down with a Spike Jones routine, shotgun bangs, raspberries, Chinese gongs. The younger people love it. Becomes a cult kind of thing. More kids get involved, they seek you out somehow, there's a network evolving, a way for you to stay safe but branch out, form a little rebel community. And the beauty is, and this is always the beauty, right? The beauty is it's all done in deep cover. On the surface, all of you guys carry on quote, normal, unquote, lives, right? Anyone can be a secret jammer. Your milkman, your kid's kindergarten teacher, the candy store owner. Like the gays way back. Like the drug people sometimes. The communists after World War II. It's a Jekyll-Hyde kind of thing. And that's what makes it exciting. Am I right?"

Wallace just stares at him.

Speer holds his hands out palms-up.

"Now, I'm not bargain hunting here. I'm ready to be prudent but fair. Basically, as I see it, the more you tell me, the more insulated I can make you. At some point I could even see a way for this to not only secure you from any personal harm but, in fact, profit you to some degree. There's no reason we can't all benefit from this relationship. Believe me, no one wants a smooth, quiet ride more than I do."

Olga and Wallace look at each other. She reaches over and takes his hand in both of hers.

It's Wallace's turn to start weeping. His eyes moisten, salt up, start to drip.

Speer takes a cardboard notebook from the breast pocket of his coat. It's got a spiral wire binding across the top, like a mini dictation pad. He thumb-clicks a long ballpoint and scribbles something. He can't manage to suppress the smugness that's spreading on his face.

He moves over, sits down next to Wallace on the couch, and says, "Who knocked QSG off the air tonight?"

But he's tried to reel his fish just a bit too early. Wallace balls his fists and presses them to his eyes. When he takes them away, desperation has been replaced by outrage. His tongue comes stuttering out of his mouth and licks across his bottom lip, and though his voice has a quaking rhythm, his words are low and clear.

He says, "Up yours, pigboy."

There's a classic paralyzed second, then Speer explodes, grabs Wallace by his shirtfront, and yanks him off the couch and onto the floor. He removes a leather blackjack from his jacket pocket, takes a step toward Wallace, stops, blows air out his nose, reaches back without looking, and backhands Olga in the head.

She's knocked sideways on the couch and Wallace starts to yell. But it's too late. Speer has turned full-body to face the woman. She's stunned, sprawled sideways like a small side of pink beef on a cutting table. Speer goes to work with an old-time bell-ringing motion, right arm pulling downward in alternating cross-arcs. The slap-sound of lead-weighted leather impacting against Olga's body is horrible: first a high, cracking snap into skin, then a more dulled, unreverberating thud into bone.

All the screams come from Wallace. Olga is hunched into a shocked silence, her face pushed into the cushion. Wallace has crawled to Speer's feet and latched onto his legs, trying to pull him away. But it's a futile move. Speer is pumped and ready to do anything. A line of blood has started to flow from Olga's visible ear.

Speer interrupts the whipping to bring up a leg and stomp at Wallace with his wing tips. He lands two heel blows dead center to the dwarf's chest, follows them up with a kick that lifts and sails Wallace back to the fireplace.

The dwarf lands on his back, his vision blurring, trying to suck air. And suddenly Speer is above him, holding a limp, unconscious Olga around the waist like a doll.

Speer's teeth are bared and he spits on Wallace. He's on the verge of hyperventilating. When his voice comes it's more a rasp than a scream. He says, "You fuck, look what you've done."

Then he drops Olga to the floor and grabs hold of her dangling arm by the wrist. He stares, unblinking, at Wallace, and begins to turn the arm until a snapping sound fills up the space between the two men. And a random, undersized bone rips loose from its connections and bursts through the skin.

10.

For close to a century, the P&C Abattoir was a functioning slaughterhouse run by a French family named Perec. It's been shut down for well over two decades and there's probably no one left in the Park who can even remember the last Perec, the small bachelor with the bushy crown of silver hair and the pencil mustache, who was called simply "the Frenchman" and wore the same brown trench coat to work through all the seasons and carried his lunch of an onion and a wedge of cheese in a crumpled white pastry bag.

Now everyone on West Street just calls the two-story brick mill house "the abattoir," as if this were a generic name for all empty brick arcs, or as if the sound of the word implied something more exotic and maybe sexual, a Latino dream of Gallic brothels, the floors stained forever with perfumes and talc rather than fifty years' worth of steer blood and the sand of band-sawed bones.

Hannah has her gun out, gripped in her right hand, held down by her thigh. She approaches the building by the rear alley and comes up the fire escape to the second-floor entrance. The old steel door is ajar the way Iguaran promised it would be.

She steps into a loft-office area, a place that once processed paperwork, filled orders for a gross of steaks, a thousand center-cut roasts, ten thousand pounds of ground chuck. The office is empty now except for a large gunmetal desk pushed against a wall and missing all its drawers. There's a sun-faded, oversized calendar still hanging from an opposite wall, nailed into the bricks with a large rusted spike and announcing, perpetually, that it's May 1972.

Moving across the loft to a wrought-iron balcony, Hannah looks down to see three figures clustered in a far corner below. The only light is a white beam that fans out to shine on a far wall. Stray wisps of smoke drift through the light. There's a familiar ticking sound echoing through the brick cavern and it's a second before Hannah realizes it's the sound of a movie projector. She pivots and is able to make out the images playing against the bricks—a grainy shot of rats scrambling out of the hold of a ship, first one, then a few, then a swarm, crawling over each other, seemingly frantic. It's a film she's seen before, a silent black-and-white classic—*Nosferatu*. German, she remembers. Around 1922, she thinks. The first adaptation of *Dracula*.

She moves to the narrow iron stairway and descends into what was once the largest meat processing plant in town. She can recall walking with her father once, just before the abattoir closed. They passed one of the front loading ports just as a delivery truck had pulled away and the huge metal roll-down door was still open. It was late fall and the air held a hard chill. White steam hung around her father's mouth as he spoke to her, holding her hand, keeping her close. But the talk ceased as they passed the loading door and both took in the scene: a man in a heavy-looking white smock, stained everywhere with rust-colored blotches, a green rubber garden hose held with both hands, a jet of water spurting from the nozzle down onto the concrete floor. The man was hosing away steer blood, and the water from the hose was hot, and as it mixed with the cold November air, gusts of steam flew everywhere, making vision into some hyper-real dream, some trace memory that seemed to be climbing back to the here and now. The concrete floor was sloped slightly, like a movie theater, and there was a round, grate-covered drain set into the lowest point and the blood and water eased into an ongoing whirlpool around the edge of the drain. And beyond the drain, where the flooring rose back to level, there were racks of metal frames fitted with thick steel hooks, huge, mutant fishing hooks out of your most troubling nightmares. And, of course, hanging from these industrial hooks were sides of beef, almost-whole steers, headless and hideless but with legs intact, the run of their powerful bodies completely evident, totally recognizable for what they once were and looking enormous. They hung in a uniform row, like pressed suits in a walk-in closet.

Hannah remembers her father pulling her past the loading door, but not before a burst of nausea exploded through her stomach and something like a mix of fear and pity and guilt and confusion broke on her neck and arms and legs. She remembers her father tried to start talking again, to pick up their conversation as if it had never been interrupted. And Hannah loved him for his effort, but resented him for not realizing its futility, for not accepting that there was no way to steal back the vision she'd just been given. And trying to was something like a loving insult.

She advances toward the three figures. A small table lamp is turned on and things become clearer. She sees a large man sprawled on a ratty, black leather couch. He's beefy-looking but not fat or flabby, a full face with a conspicuous dark mole angled out below his right nostril and above his bushy Zapata mustache. She'd place him in his mid-forties. Traces of gray filter through his closely cropped dark hair. His eyebrows are still completely black and very thick, his forehead lined with permanent creases. He's got deep, purplish circles under his eyes that might betray a tendency to insomnia or maybe a vitamin deficiency, but the eyes themselves are stunningly vivid, even in this poor light, completely alive and focused on her. Her first impression is of a patriarchal presence that has somehow solidified before its time. He projects the bearing of a wise grandfather without the number of years to account for it. And he dresses young—a stylish black V-neck sweater, the sleeves pushed up on his arms, and a pair of gray pleated pants with cuffed legs.

There's a small monkey, like an organ grinder's monkey, lying prone on the man's shoulder, asleep and nuzzling near his neck. There's an old-fashioned black round-topped doctor's bag on the couch next to him, open, revealing dozens of plastic vials. He's chewing on the end of a red felt-tip pen. Open in his lap is a newspaper Hannah's not familiar with—*Pacific Rim Journal*. Various sections of newsprint are corralled with red circles.

Next to the man is a small, dark woman wearing royal-blue spandex bicycle pants and a leather bra with intricate stitching that looks somewhat like a harness. The outfit shows off an assortment of perfectly toned muscles. Her face is all cheekbones and lips. Hannah thinks the woman could make a fortune as a model, a pouty, postmodern mannequin sneering at a camera lens while seated on the hood of some glitzy sports car. She has a waterfall of black wiry hair that's been pulled back and tied into a loose ponytail. Her function seems to have something to do with the silver IV pole next to the couch. The pole supports a clear plastic bag that hangs from a small S-shaped hook. The bag is filled with a brownish solution that's dripping at scheduled intervals into a plastic vein that, in turn, is plugged into the man's arm.

Sitting behind the couch is the projectionist, a younger, leaner version of the patriarch. He's hunched on a stool, working with a rag, silently cleaning a sawed-off shotgun that rests next to the movie projector on a rickety wooden worktable. He's handsome in a threatening, predatory kind of way—huge eyes, brown to the point of blackness, a square jaw, clean-shaven, an alertness to his bearing. His hair looks like it may have once been as wiry as the woman's, but he seems to have had it straightened, an old-time conk job. There's a short, fat scar on the side of his neck.

Spray-painted on the wall behind the worktable are huge block letters of neon scarlet that spell out *Welcome to the Last Wave*. Hannah thinks it's like a message you'd read entering the fun-house ride at some malign traveling carnival.

The man caps the felt pen, slides it behind his right ear,

takes a breath, and says, "Thank you for dropping by, Detective Shaw."

Hannah gives a formal nod and says, "Thanks for having me, Mr. Iguaran." She head-motions toward the graffiti and adds, "You've got to find yourself a new designer."

Iguaran makes a slight shrug. "At this moment in the Park's history, having the ability to process graffiti is handier than having a fax machine. But that will change. Please," he says, gesturing to the couch, "have a seat."

Hannah looks at the projectionist and says, "Thanks, but I'll stand."

Iguaran nods. "However you feel comfortable. Would you like a drink?"

She gestures to the IV flow. "Thanks, but chemo isn't on my diet these days."

"Platelets and washed cells," Iguaran says with a huge grin as if he's just shown her snapshots of his children. "From the wombs of newborn lambs. Or is it the uterus? Imported from Switzerland. They breed them on a compound outside of Guarda. Costs me a fortune. And then there are the courier charges. Your FDA can be so provincial."

"I'm sure."

"But I must say I've never felt better. I've got the reflexes of a twenty-year-old. Though I do get chills when I pass by angora."

Hannah can't suppress a smile and says, "Well, there are side effects to every cocktail."

Iguaran takes some air in through a clogged nose and says, "Forgive my rudeness." He extends a hand to the woman and says, "This is Ursula, my administrative assistant. And this," turning his head to look at the projectionist, "is my son, Nabo."

Hannah nods to both of them without saying a word and they respond in kind. There's some awkward silence, then Hannah makes an exaggerated turn from side to side and says, "So the abattoir is your place now."

"We passed papers a month ago. Still haven't completely moved in."

"I thought you just liked a primitive look."

Iguaran slaps his leg, too hard. "I was hoping you'd have a sense of humor. You haven't disappointed me. Wonderful. Very good." He looks up toward the ceiling and says, "I bought it for the space. Plenty of room to move around here. Very spacious for a starter home—"

"Meaning you're already planning another move?" Hannah interrupts. "To the Hotel Penumbra, maybe?"

Iguaran juts out his jaw and gives a slow-motion headshake that says *no*. "You Yankees," he says, "always so anxious to get straight to business."

"I'm not a Yankee," Hannah says, quietly but definitively.

Iguaran shrugs again and mumbles, "Have it your way," then picks his voice up and continues. "I have no interest in acquiring the Penumbra. For me, it will always hold the spirit of Cortez. A man has to put his own character onto a building. You wait two years, maybe eighteen months. Then come back to the abattoir. It will be the country of Iguaran. Besides, the word is the Loftus boys are looking at the Penumbra."

Now Hannah shakes her head, "I don't think so. Where's the Irish margin? Their population base in the Park is minimal except for the Castlebar Road Boys. And they're real uneasy about that connection. Old man Loftus is too legitimate to step back into the Park. And the kids are too eccentric. They don't want the crudities enough. They don't revel in it. They're media-heads—"

Iguaran smiles like a smug lawyer or chess player and cuts her off. "I would agree." He pauses, his mouth still open, clear that there's more to come, stopping just for effect until it seems like the silence of the huge building will take shape, metamorphose into some jungle monster from the collective imagination of the whole third world, and come at this white woman who holds a badge and a gun. Finally, Iguaran says, "So you see I'm the logical choice to fill the vacuum."

This is what Hannah expected but still feared to hear. She says, "Uncle Chak would disagree with that conclusion."

"Please," Iguaran says, mock-offended, "let's not turn this conversation into a farce. The Cambodian is totally regressive. Chak is a tribal mentality in a global net. He's encouraging his men to speak Khmer, for God's sake. Tell me something, Detective. If Dr. Cheng himself were forced to choose between me and Chak, racial allegiances standing, who do you think he'd pick?"

Hannah lifts her eyebrows, adamant. "I think the point is, Iguaran, Dr. Cheng is still very much in the picture."

"If you truly believe that, you're not fit to walk Lenore's streets, are you?"

Hannah hesitates at the mention of the name, then comes back with, "They're not Lenore's streets anymore, are they?"

Iguaran slaps his thigh again as if he's scored a point. "Exactly, Detective Shaw. My point exactly. They're open streets at the moment. The Park is wide open. There's a window right now. A time frame when moves can be made, the system retooled. Cortez was one player in a vast and constantly evolving machine. He had his skills, a very distinct style, but in crucial ways he was ill equipped."

"My reading," Hannah interrupts, "is that Cortez left the Park of his own volition."

Iguaran waves a hand, concedes the point. "Whatever. He is gone. I am here—"

"Along with Dr. Cheng and Uncle Chak and Sylvain the Haitian and Peker the Turk and—"

Iguaran comes forward on the couch, clearly annoyed. "But *I* know the market. I understand the mind of the customer. The product, the service, they're immaterial. The customer wants the bells and the whistles to be continually louder and longer-lasting. And he wants delivery now. Always now. Immediately is not soon enough. I understand distribution, division of territories, the commission incentive. I understand management. The fragility of the carrot and the stick. When to prune and weed and when to overlook the marbling of fat. I understand the nuances of postindustrial commerce, Detective. I understand the polysystem itself. Do you know why, Detective?"

"I think I'm about to be told."

Iguaran settles back down and starts to tap lightly at the plastic tubing running into his arm. "Because I know, to the core of my brain I know, that there is an animal in the human heart. In every single throbbing heart on this planet, there is a perpetually hungry creature that's motivated by the most primal of instincts. And that beast, Detective, is never satiated."

There's a second of silence and then Hannah says, "You're a real visionary, Iggy."

Iguaran crosses his legs. "The coming months will show you the truth."

"I'm always looking to be educated."

Hannah can tell he's not completely sure how to play her. He wants an ally, but he needs a certain level of respect at this crucial stage. He's calculating how much to push and how much to take. He's instinctive, like Cortez and like Dr. Cheng. Like all the neighborhood mayors. But he's also rabidly ambitious. If Cortez didn't want to rule the Park enough, it's possible Iguaran wants it too much.

He runs a tongue around his lips, then says, "You mock me, Detective Shaw. But we're already hooking into our resources. We're tying into monetary funds and banking networks that transcend ideas of history. Of ideology. There is no more good versus evil, Detective. There is only the connected versus the unconnected. And this is why I'll never understand you or your predecessor. You jokingly call me a visionary. But you appear to be a blind woman. You are a mystery, Detective. You are intelligent. You are strong. You appear to be realistic. Why do you willfully choose to remain on the losing side? It simply makes no sense."

Hannah approaches and sits down next to Iguaran on the couch, clearly annoying Ursula, who glares and tugs down on the hem of the leather bra.

"I'm kind of a genetic mutant," Hannah says. "Just one of those freaks that screw up all the stats."

Iguaran gives a small laugh that echoes lightly, then he turns his attention to the movie as if some alarm has sounded and ended their meeting.

"But I'm not really the issue here, am I?" Hannah says, and stops for a long pause to show her change of tone and attitude. The introductions are over and it's time to get down to some understanding. "Let's assume I've looked over the recent events in Bangkok and let's assume that basically, you and I concur on most of the major conclusions. Cortez is not coming home. Dr. Cheng does not have the leash on his people the way he once did. The Irish and the Jews and the Italians have gentrified themselves so they've all got at least one foot in the mainstream. And the rest, the newcomers, the Jamaicans and the Haitians and the Turks and the rest—they don't yet have the numbers or the experience or the organization."

Iguaran continues to stare out at the movie, but he says, "I'm listening."

"Look, Iguaran," she says, "both you and I know things are about to happen. There was a balance for a long time down here. You people ran Latino Town and Cheng ran Little Asia and Reverend James took the Projects and everything north. Little pockets of upstarts came and went but the disputes were always worked out before business could be damaged. Okay, fine. But now it's gone. The old order is running down. Contrary to what you might think, I'm not blind. And I think you and I are both looking for a new balance. I'm saying the two of us have some mutual goals."

Finally, he looks back at her and in a bland voice says, "You're saying we're both pragmatists . . ."

She stares at his eyes. "And I'm saying we both know there's no such thing as a free lunch."

Iguaran gives away a smile and glances over his shoulder at Nabo, as if he wants his son to pay close attention to a lesson in progress. He says, "Very true. That's the only belief allowed in this part of town. We're both devotees of the barter system."

"I'm looking for some information."

Iguaran waits a long beat, then begins to nod his head slightly and in a much lower voice says, "The priest's murder."

"What do you know?"

"I know my people had nothing to do with it. I hope we can agree on this point. We had no quarrel with Father Todorov. We're Catholics, for God's sake. And even if, for some hidden reason, we *did* have a grudge against the priest, now wouldn't be the time for a move. Would it, Detective?"

Hannah sighs and turns to look at the movie. After a minutes she turns back and says, "I don't think the Popes did it. But I think it's possible they could find out who did. If you asked them to."

Now Iguaran fights a smile. "We may be able to ask around. Look for any new faces. Check into any deviant behavior..."

He lets his words drift off and Hannah says, "I'm prepared to offer some future concessions."

"Give me twelve hours, my friend. If there's anything worth knowing, I'll have it by then." He gives an abrupt nod, turns to Ursula, and snaps, *"Quita la aguja."*

And it's clear to Hannah that their meeting has adjourned. She turns awkwardly and heads for the stairs, glancing at *Nosferatu* as she walks. A young man in period dress is reading from an oversized book. Hannah knows the book is the log of the captain of the *Demeter*, the ship that brings Dracula to England. The captain's entry flashes up on the bricks:

18 May 1838

Passed Gibralta—Panic on board
Three men dead already—mate out of his mind
Rats in the hold—I fear the plague

Up in the office loft, she takes one last look down at Iguaran. It's as if she's waiting for a feeling to hit her, something comforting but without a name, some corollary to instinct that could assure her that a year down the road she'll have formed a delicate accommodation with this Colombian patriarch, a well-tuned give-and-take that would allow them both not only crucial information but also a margin of ease where they could share loose counsel.

The desire bothers her because it feels like a betrayal of Dr. Cheng. Because it's a coded way of acknowledging or even affirming the thought that maybe Cheng won't be around in six months. And that maybe it's time to start forming new relationships.

She watches as Ursula removes the IV needle from Iguaran's arm and applies a round, flesh-colored Band-Aid to the wound. She tries to study Iguaran's face as he gestures for his son to approach and then starts whispering in the young man's ear. She doesn't feel any kind of connection. Not even the vague stirrings of chemistry that could result in a future connection, a moment when she could caution him that the best evolutions are always the slowest, the ones that subtly give the organism plenty of time to assimilate in its new form, to get comfortable and natural enough within its new self to pay full attention to its environment.

She'd like to envision a coming era when she could inject this kind of warning. But right now, all she feels is the certainty that it's just not her job.

11.

As you cross through the intersection of Voegelin Street and Watson Street and unofficially enter into the outer perimeter of Bangkok Park, you pass under the shadow of a huge, abandoned billboard mounted long ago atop the old Habermas factory. Over the course of the past decade, the advertisement for fire safety has faded and chipped into a dull, sun-bleached rectangle of white. Now none of the original picture or words remain. In their place, on the white background, an anonymous artist has painted, in a Day-Glo shade of green, a detailed rendering of an apelike creature. It's a fierce animal and there's an unnatural intelligence in its face, along with a humanlike expression of rage. Underneath the beast is a foreign inscription that the locals know is written in Khmer. In smaller letters beneath this, in English, is printed a rough translation: *Hyenas Rule.*

Hazel glances briefly up at the billboard, catches herself, lowers her eyes back to the sidewalk, and picks up her pace. She's wearing a pair of black stretch jeans and a blue sleeveless T-shirt with the words *You're Guilty* stenciled in black across the front. She's getting a lot of looks from all the drunks as she walks by their stoops. Eddie had wanted to come with her, but she refused. It would have been nice to have brought in two sets of eyes and Eddie's biceps and attitude, but she couldn't let him think she needed an escort into what she hopes will be

106

their new home. It was bad enough that Eddie had to make the connection for her.

He plays nine ball every now and then at a dump on the Canal-Bangkok border, a place called the Play Penh Social Club. It's one of the few halls that still keep a room in the back strictly for billiards. And as Eddie has said to her more than once, "You know how much those jarheads go for billiards." After the Play Penh closed up one night, Eddie paid twenty bucks to a guy named Tho for a five-minute conversation. It was clear from Tho's lack of colors or tattoos that he wasn't a Hyena, but he had a cousin who was a lieutenant to Loke, the Hyenas' current CEO. For another twenty, Tho promised to set something up.

So now Hazel's headed for a tiny brick storefront with a hand-painted sign nailed over the entrance that reads *The Angkor Arcade*. She glances at her watch to make sure she's on time and knocks on the dented steel door twice with hard flat-palmed raps. A full minute goes by, then the door is opened by a skinny Oriental kid wearing a black T-shirt and a pair of filthy white dishwasher's pants. He's got long, silky bangs that fall in a rigid line just barely above his eyes. He stands in the doorway, expressionless, looking her over. There's no muscle on him and Hazel would bet she could take him down to the floor with a fast knee and a boot to the ankle, but she's the intruder here and no matter how rude things get, no matter how much attitude gets thrown at her, she's got to stay quiet and respectful. Maybe more than anywhere else, in Bangkok Park beggars cannot be choosers.

"I'm here to see Loke," she finally says to the skinny kid. "I've got an appointment."

His eyes are locked on her breasts and she lets it go and waits and after a minute, without looking up to her face, the kid says, "Get inside."

It's dark in the clubhouse and she blinks a few times to help her vision adjust. The place is smaller than she'd expected. Years ago it was a neighborhood spa and there's still a small marble lunch counter at the rear of the room with built-in silver soda-water dispensers. Hazel keeps her head steady but lets her eyes move in a circle. Things become clearer.

There's a small billiards table in the center of the room with a trio of hooded green lamps suspended over it. Mounted on the right wall is a series of cue holders filled with a display of unmatched sticks. There's an old Asteroids video game in a corner with its power cord unplugged and dangling before the black screen. Running along the left wall are three Naugahyde booths and scarred wooden tables. A single Hyena sits in each booth, slouched sideways, back against the wall, legs propped up on the seat. They're dressed in their standard gear—black stretch muscle shirts, white cotton gi pants, and sandals that look like they're made of hemp. And they're nothing like the doorman. They're all pumped up, definitions of upper-body strength. Their hair is cropped close to their scalps. Hazel would judge them to be eighteen or nineteen years old. One of them has a set of nun-chucks draped around his neck like a fighter's towel.

They stare at her without saying a word and she tries to keep herself from acknowledging that she could be in some serious trouble. But this is the price she needs to pay and there's always danger in moving to a new world.

Behind the lunch counter, a set of swinging double doors suddenly opens and a tall Hyena steps through and stands with his hands on his hips. He barks a command in Khmer at the doorman, and the kid jumps into action, moving behind Hazel and putting his hands on her shoulders. She starts to flinch and then realizes he means to frisk her, so she makes herself stand rigid as hands run over her body, pausing way too long on her ass and breasts.

After rifling her pockets, the doorman steps away from her and nods. The Hyena behind the counter motions for her to walk toward him. She moves slowly, trying not to betray the growing suspicion that this meeting probably won't get her much beyond robbed and humiliated.

She steps behind the lunch counter and the Hyena points to the swinging doors. She ends up in a small paneled corridor with a single door halfway down. She looks for a rear entrance, but doesn't see one, so she steps up to the door and knocks.

A voice from within yells, "It's open."

Inside, behind a teak platform desk, sits Loke, the head of the Angkor Hyenas. He's tilted back in a deep green leather swivel chair that's trimmed with nailheads. On the desk is a white cordless phone, a foreign newspaper, and a blank yellow legal pad.

Loke's head is tilted slightly to the side and he has his hands clasped together and resting on his stomach. He's wearing a variation on the Hyena colors. He's got on the sandals and gi pants, but his torso is covered with a white cotton V-neck sweater that bears a small Yale University insignia.

He looks older than the ones outside, maybe in his early twenties. His hair is longer than his soldiers' and he's got it slicked straight back with styling gel. On the back of his right hand, Hazel spots a tattoo of the same Hyena from the Habermas factory billboard.

"Have a seat," he says in a low and friendly voice, and he indicates two matching, low-slung black leather chairs positioned before his desk.

Hazel sinks into one and glances around. Loke's office is much brighter than the outer clubhouse. The decor shocks her. The place has a clean and ordered feel to it. Three walls are painted white and the fourth is lined with black metal utility cabinets all padlocked closed. On the wall behind Loke are two matted and framed maps—one of Quinsigamond and the other of Cambodia. Between them is a framed calligraphied quotation that reads:

> *Preserve Them—No Profit*
> *Eliminate Them—No Loss*
> *We will burn the old grass*
> *and the new will grow*

"Shall I call you Hazel?" Loke asks, sitting up, smiling.

Hazel nods. "Everyone does."

"Would you like a drink, Hazel? Glass of wine?"

She shakes her head. His voice is clear and almost unaccented. His diction is crisp, maybe a little overprecise.

Hazel knows she should state her case simply and quietly, accept the verdict, and get out. But something about Loke's manner tempts her to improvise.

"You're not what I expected," she says.

He lets a smile break and says, "For a warlord," giving the phrase a mock seriousness.

"Do you really use words like that?"

He shrugs. "Only in the old pulps," he says, and gestures over his shoulder with a thumb. Behind him is a small teak bookcase that matches the desk. Hazel leans to the side and sees a line of slim paperbacks with gaudy-colored spines and titles running down them like *Teen-Age Mafia* and *The Black Leather Barbarians*.

"I've got all the classics. *Rumble. The Royal Vultures. The Amboy Dukes.*"

On the shelf below the paperbacks is what looks like a small set of encyclopedias or identically bound textbooks. In gold leaf down the spines is the title *The Tuol Sleng Manual*.

"The first thing you're going to need to know," Loke says, "if we can work out"—he pauses, looks up at the ceiling—"an arrangement, is that most of your ideas about the various organizations here in Bangkok are wrong."

Hazel nods and says, "My people and I are all ready to learn."

Loke leans back in the chair again.

"How many people are there?"

"About a dozen."

Loke shakes his head. "I'm going to need an exact figure."

Hazel nods. "I can give you individual names and addresses. Backgrounds. Whatever."

"And everyone wants to emigrate?"

"It's unanimous."

There are a few seconds of silence. Loke picks up a fat Mont Blanc pen that sits on the legal pad and scratches a few notes. Then he puts the pen back down and says, "Once you come over the border, you don't go back."

"I know that," Hazel says.

"I need to say it anyway. I need to go through the motions here. I need to give the speech."

He takes a breath and continues, suddenly seeming a bit annoyed. "The Canal Zone is not Bangkok Park. It never will be. You want to emigrate, fine. We'll discuss terms. But know that the mortality rate here is higher than in Haiti. And know that when players change that fast, there's little stability. Your status and your loyalties can be altered in an instant. And your time is taken up with things a good deal more serious than fucking up radio stations—"

She cuts him off, points to his sweater, and says, "Did you actually go to Yale?"

He stares at her with an absolutely blank expression and she thinks he's about to whistle for his lieutenant, but instead he smiles and says, "Jesus, haven't you got some balls." He picks up the pen again and says, "I did three years. Never took a diploma. Annoyed the shit out of the family. They took me in the business. But the boss says I've got to pay some dues in middle management before I can eat at the grown-ups' table, so..." He trails off and extends a hand palm-up as if his surroundings explained the rest.

"The boss," Hazel says, "would be your father?"

Loke shakes his head. "My Uncle Chak. Mother's brother. Owns the Plain Jar Cafe. He's the bank for our people. He's trying to buy up the Goulden Ave block. He hands out housing, jobs. Got a half brother back in Phnom Penh. You can imagine."

Hazel leans forward over her knees. "You think it's a good idea to tell strangers your genealogy?"

Loke gives the now-familiar smile. "We've done the research, Hazel. You're not exactly informer material. And you know that if we even see you with the wrong people you'll be gang-fucked, set on fire, and served as the lunch special down the Plain Jar.''

He says this as if he were relaying the score of a boring ball game.

Loke goes on. "We've got over sixty full-member Hyenas. Mainly we're errand boys and supplemental muscle for Uncle Chak's company. Though I'd never say that to any of my boys. We handle all the merchant payments down Voegelin and Grassman. We do security for the O dens and whorehouses in our cut of the Park. We move some smack around Goulden. But mainly we're linemen. We watch the border for the Popes."

"The Colombians," Hazel says.

Loke nods. "Scumbags. Which brings us to the question—"

"Why did I come to you instead of them?"

"So why?"

"If you've checked, you know I'm pretty well plugged in down the Zone. I've got all these little tech-hoods jumping through hoops for me. They're into the Registry of Deeds mainframe on a regular basis. Since Cortez vanished, the Colombians are scrambling. There's no one holding it together. Rayuela Realty Trust is going Chapter 11 any day. Didn't take a genius to know that if you wanted to emigrate, Uncle Chak was the man to see."

"You think you can afford the"—again he pauses—"licensing fees?"

"Tell me what you need."

Loke bites on his lip and seems to drift into thought. He pushes the sleeves of his sweater up on his arms and slowly gets out of his chair. He walks around the desk and comes to a stop behind Hazel.

When his voice comes, it's lower.

"There's the entrance fee itself. It's based on a per-person setup." He places a hand on her shoulder. "Maybe I'll see what I can do about a discount in this case."

She tries not to let him feel her muscles tighten under his palm.

"You'll have to clear whatever franchises you want to work through me. We'll want forty percent of your gross the first twelve months. We'll renegotiate after that. You'll have some start-up costs at first and we're not out to make you starve."

He starts to rub at her neck lightly.

"What else?" she asks, keeping an even voice.

He slides a hand inside her T-shirt, takes hold of her right breast, runs his thumb over her nipple. She lets out a heavy breath but stays quiet.

"All organizations," Loke says, his own breath audible, "have some initiation rites."

He pushes himself up against the back of her chair, starts to run his free hand through her hair.

"Rites," Hazel repeats.

"We're going to have to see a demonstration of some sort," he says. "Show us you mean business. Show us some skills."

"It's taken care of," Hazel says. "We've already picked someplace to hit."

"Then there's only one more piece of business," Loke says, taking his hand from her hair and grabbing the back of her T-shirt, pulling her out of the chair and down onto the floor. She rolls onto her back and he gets on his knees, straddling her at her waist.

"You have any problems taking a Hyena?" he says, starting to pull off his Yale sweater.

Hazel shakes her head.

"Very good," Loke says. "You're going to love this neighborhood."

12.

Speer's apartment is at the southern end of Bangkok Park, down off Brinkley Boulevard, a one-room studio in the basement of a five-story red brick monster built in the early twenties. Because of the building's location and the position of the apartment's two tiny rectangular windows, very little sunlight ever makes it inside. Speer thinks it would be the perfect place to raise mushrooms.

He pays two fifty a month to the super, who everyone calls Corny, an Armenian guy of indeterminate age who wears a purple eye patch and never speaks except to say *gaddahm welfare state*. The rent does not include heat, but the apartment gets the benefit of the two enormous cast-iron furnaces on the other side of the interior wall. Once or twice a week, always in the middle of the night, one of the furnaces will start an awful banging and thrashing, often punctuated with an excruciating series of pauses to deceive the tenants into thinking it's always about to stop. Speer doesn't mind the racket anymore. He's almost ready to admit to himself that he welcomes it as a signal that things haven't changed, that he's still where he was when he went to sleep. Usually the banging pulls him out of a nightmare.

The apartment came semifurnished with a single metal-frame bed, an aluminum patio table that Speer uses as a desk, a wicker rocking chair painted kelly green, a five-drawer bureau with cardboard backing, a mini, dorm-style refrigerator, and a gas stove. To this he added a wall mirror that he hung over the bureau, the original Mr. Coffee he and Margie had received as a wedding gift, his collection of bound back issues of *Ham Man Digest,* and his radio equipment: a Kenwood R-5000 receiver, a Tascam recorder, and a set of Koss Pro 75 headphones.

Two weeks after he moved in, Speer gave Corny fifty dollars to allow a Dymek antenna to be bolted to the chimney up on the roof. He secured the coaxial lead to a drainpipe that ran down the corner of the building, then brought the wire in through the sidewalk-level window. Now, on a good day, he can monitor as far away as Nigeria. But Speer isn't interested in most of the chat and babble found around the dial. He usually zeros in on a handful of frequencies. He listens for sounds that the hobbyists ignore. He strains to pull in the obscure and unclear.

Right now, for instance, it's 4 A.M. and he's sitting on the red Naugahyde seat of a metal stool and delicately turning the tuner knob on his Kenwood. Open flat on the kitchen table is a spiral-bound notebook, a standard 8½ × 11 schoolboy job, college-ruled and a red-line margin down the left side of each page. On the front cover, on the appropriate line, Speer has printed his name in block letters with a black felt-tip pen. On the inside of the front cover, running down in a neat column, is a series of numbers:

Frqcy (KHz)	
3060	Spnsh
3090	Sp
4642	Frnch
4770	Grmn
10450	Krn
14947	Gr
23120	Gr

Speer wears a starched T-shirt, the pants to one of his suits, and felt moccasins on his feet. From a water glass on the table he takes a pen, a Papermate metal roller fine-point. He picks it up as if it were a knife, maybe a scalpel, as if he could injure himself by mishandling it. He uncaps the pen and places it on the notebook page, reaches up, and turns on the radio. He spins the tuning knob with the side of his index finger, stops at the desired frequency, adjusts volume and squelch, then sits motionless for a moment as a voice enters the room from the speaker. It's a female voice with a heavy Spanish accent. He finds it impossible to determine the speaker's age. He tries to prevent his mind from forming a picture of the woman. He wants to concentrate solely on the voice, the words that come to his ears.

Only they're not words. They're numbers. In Spanish. She speaks them in a bland, uninterested manner. She keeps a mechanical, absolutely controlled rhythm, the same spacing between breaths, the same tone: *"Atención grupo número cuarenta y nueve...51512...12152...32085...28911...11211...61208 ...Atención grupo número sesenta y dos...03151...08201...02611 ...08129...22519..."*

Speer closes his eyes for a moment, listens to the numbers, tries to prevent himself from speculating or analyzing. He just wants this Spanish voice to wash over him like a kind of primal music. He wants to put himself into a mood, create an atmosphere.

And when he feels he's come as close as he'll get, he uncaps his pen and in a practiced, legible, no-nonsense script he writes:

4 A.M.

Dear Margie,

What is a man to do? I'm no stranger to discipline. I have attempted to be as ordered and precise with my life as is reasonable. I have attempted to be prudent. As you know, my methodology has always been to review all available options and select the most promising. I often said to you, "We can only work with the available facts." I have steadfastly acknowledged that there will always be certain parcels of information that we aren't privy to. No matter how much skill or intuition a man possesses, there will be events he can't alter. I've always felt that understanding this was one of the chief signals of maturity. I've always felt I had an unalterable grasp of this fact.

Were I acting in a professional manner, applying all I've learned to this turn my life has taken, there are questions I would ask. This is how I would begin. I would start with broad, general questions. Later, based on the answers I'd obtained, I'd narrow in. I'd select the most promising avenues. Try to verify evidence. Try to establish patterns and trails. See what led to what. This is sometimes called "tracking" and I like to think of the word in the way an outdoorsman would, in literal terms—following markings to trace the route of your prey.

I think you know, Margie, that if I wanted to, I could track you down. You're an intelligent woman, and though I was limited in the degree to which I could discuss my work, certainly you're aware of the tools at my disposal, the networks of information, the breadth of data I can access, the amount of manpower that would be willing to do a favor for a fellow agent. I'm reasonably sure that it would take no more than a week to ten days to locate the city you're in, who you're with, where you're staying, where you've been, and on and on. Ad infinitum.

At the moment, for complex reasons of my own, I've chosen not to take this route. Ultimately, I'm not sure what the benefit would be to either of us. As adults, we each make choices, take actions, accept the consequences. Thinking about this last week, I realized that my goal in seeking you out, my true goal, would be simply to explain my feelings, to talk to you. Right now, at this moment, I can see where you'd find tremendous irony in this. Perhaps that's typical in the reality of any marriage. But if what I want to do is enumerate my feelings, convey to you what's happened to me since your departure, I can do that here, in the safety of this room. Someday these words may get to you. By conventional means or other.

This is a journal of my heart, Margie. Please don't laugh so bitterly. I'm aware how trite this sounds, how trite it looks to me now, in ink, on the page. But I won't cross it out. I won't begin again. Because that would imply an attempt to alter the past, to change history. And we both know what a childish, futile wish that is. We can only chart what is to come (and some would even argue against this).

If you know me, then you know I align myself on the side of free will rather than fate, that we have the definitive say in how our future lives will go.

You should know that I have stopped using amphetamines. Two days after you left, I took all the vials and poured them into the toilet, got on my knees, and pulled the lever. I will admit to you that I experienced a somewhat painful withdrawal for forty-eight hours. But I've purified myself with an ongoing regime of weak tea and club soda. (I've also been taking extended steam baths at the Y.)

I have also purchased a few paperbacks concerning spousal abuse and its treatment. I recall the incident last spring when I discovered a book of this type in your drawer, but, again, this is the unalterable past. I've read over a hundred pages in Dr. H. L. Helms's *Dark Glasses and Rouge*.

Possibly these signs of change mean little or nothing to you, Margie. Perhaps you believe there is no hope for me and that everything was entirely my fault. I will concede this.

But, for your part, what you must do, what any notion of justice would insist that you do, is acknowledge, right now, wherever you are, in whatever miserable second-rate motel room or trailer park, that you've broken my heart. The triteness of that phrase only makes the pain greater, larger, and more relentless. I am a changed man, Margie. You would see this if you came back. I can control the behavior that terrified you. I can eliminate the drug usage. I can participate in an open, rational exchange of ideas.

Alter my future, Margie. I'm waiting.

Send me a message.

13.

Ronnie steps inside the apartment, turns off the alarm, and begins to undress in the dark. She has that strange tired but excited sensation, kind of a sweet fatigue, like when she drinks too-potent cappuccino on top of too-cheap mescal, that slow but giddy war within the nervous system that makes her almost stupid the entire next day.

It's not that she'd take back the airport dance with Flynn. She's glad it happened and she hopes it happens again. But she *has* screwed with her normal postshow routine and that always leaves her a little concerned, as if she's messing with a system that's taken years to fine-tune and once broken, might never heal.

So, though she's only got an hour till dawn, she wants to squeeze in at least some of the ritual. She dumps her clothes in the bathroom hamper, takes her short kimono from the hook on the back of the door, and slides it on. She goes to the sink and throws some cold water on her face, dries off, and jogs into the kitchen, where she grabs a pint of ice cream from the freezer and a pint of mescal from the liquor cabinet.

Then it's out to the balcony, seventeen stories above Main Street. The air is really too cold now for the kimono, but it reminds her of the summer, when every night, from two-thirty till dawn, she took her watch over the city, still hard-core, still the cutting-edge night-owl and still-young Voice of Quin-sigamond.

Ronnie's apartment building is the gray-faced, concrete Heptagon that shoots up twenty-one stories at the west end of Main Street. The first three floors were once owned and occupied by Westblitz Savings and Loan, but about a year ago the Feds walked in one Monday morning, seized the books, sent home the staff, and directed a vanload of bulky young men weighed down with elaborate toolbelts to change all the locks and alarms. A week later the *Spy* reported that the S&L's president and two senior V.P.'s were thought to be in either Antigua or southern France, that the institution's assets were frozen pending a lengthy audit and analysis, and that the trust which owned the Heptagon, which housed Westblitz, had filed for bankruptcy protection.

Outside of Westblitz, the trust had managed to rent only three of the luxury apartments that made up the remaining eighteen floors of the building. In a registered letter, the court had informed Ronnie they'd release her from the lease she'd signed when she'd moved in. Her two neighbors took the opportunity to cut their losses and run. But Ronnie saw no reason for another disruptive move, so now she's the sole occupant of over 350,000 square feet of downtown Quinsigamond real estate. And as such, she's taken it upon herself to rename the building. She now insists on calling the Heptagon *Solitary,* after a sleazy women's-prison movie she saw on cable late one night.

After the last tenant moved out of Solitary, Ronnie took to exploring the building. One morning, as dawn began to break, she found she still couldn't sleep and decided to head out to a convenience store and buy a newspaper. But she hit the wrong button in the elevator and instead of the doors sliding open to reveal the garage, they parted on the hallway of the fourth floor. And on impulse, Ronnie stepped off and started to walk around. There wasn't much to see. She tried the door to every apartment, but they were all locked. She got bored, forgot about the newspaper, went back up to seventeen, and took a bath and listened to the radio.

But the next morning, at dawn, she did the same thing, this time exploring the seventh floor and this time finding an open apartment. It was bare and still had an unfinished feel to it. The electrical outlets were missing faceplates and the carpeting was dusted with dozens of those stray fabric strands left after installation. But Ronnie spent a half hour in the apartment, enjoying the feeling that she wasn't supposed to be there, savoring this imagined danger of being discovered.

The next night, for reasons she refused to analyze, Ronnie brought her sleeping bag down to the seventh floor and napped in the bare unit until 8 A.M.

Since then, she's discovered another half dozen open doors. She's slept in each of them at least once. But she's made a rule that she'll only play squatter once a week and so far she's managed to obey herself.

She's been in the building for over a year, which for Ronnie is a long stay. She rented it over the phone, long-distance, telling the broker her only requirements were "to be up high and have thick walls." The height requirement was more for radio reception than view, but now, out on the balcony, seventeen floors over the street, she appreciates the perspective. It's not that she's treated to some stunning panorama each morning at two-thirty, coming home from the station, shedding her clothes and washing her face, throwing on her favorite white silk kimono and sprawling on the plastic-weave lounge chair she bought mail-order, snacking on "Cappuccino Commotion" Häagen-Dazs or microwave popcorn washed down with mescal and orange juice. It's that at this height everything down in the street can seem like a distant film, some grainy B-flick thrown up on a weathered drive-in screen, something she could glimpse from a highway and pass on by. From this height, every action down on Main Street is void of the bulk of its sounds and smells, from the visceral impact of a real encounter. Living on the seventeenth floor is like continuing her radio show throughout the context of the rest of her life. The individuals that she watches in that hour after she returns from QSG are like embodied voices of her callers, their faces still hidden, their crises and obsessions and bizarre traumas all reduced to a distant summation. There's all the qualities of the true confession, from boredom to physical danger, with none of the consequences of real interaction. She sometimes thinks of Main Street, between the hours of three and five, as her own enormous wide-screen TV, the biggest cathode-ray tube in the city. And the ability of her head to pivot on her spine is a deft remote control that allows her to flip from the gay pickup lines that roll in and out of the bus terminal to the homeless scavengers forever sifting through the Dumpsters outside the public library to the twin sisters who alternate tricks behind Kepler and Gleick's All-Night Billiard Hall.

This downscale voyeurism has turned into something of a ritual over the past six months and Ronnie wonders what she'll do when winter hits and she's forced to lock up the sliders that lead to the balcony. The summer was wonderful. She'd finish *Libido Liveline* at two, then pack all her gear into her worn, faded-green Girl Scout knapsack, kiss Wayne on the forehead, usually leaving bright red lipmarks, and hand over the airwaves to *Sonny Botkin's Pagan Confidential*. During the summer months, she kept the top off the Jeep and sometimes she'd jump up on the interstate before heading home, pick up the speed a little, and let the rush of warm wind drum on her body and head. When she felt fully decompressed, she'd head for Main Street and Solitary. She'd pull the Jeep into her empty underground garage and keep her thumb on the red button of her Mace tube while she waited for the express elevator. Then she'd ride up to her floor singing aloud to the Muzak versions of Supremes hits that played on a tape loop every night.

Ronnie doesn't know where her habit of renaming things comes from. Technically, and as far as the post office is concerned, she lives in apartment 1707. But in the privacy of her own quirky brain, she insists on calling her place apartment 3-G, after the classic comic strip that she only vaguely remembers from her childhood. Wasn't it three gals in the big city, all roommates, all young and cartoon-glamorous and ready for new romance at every turn? All summer, Ronnie got a kick out of pretending her roommates were on lengthy modeling assignments in Europe. The vision of Lu Ann and Margo quarreling with a thin, slightly fascistic fashion photographer against the backdrop of spurting Roman fountains contrasted beautifully with the gritty Quinsigamond landscape below the balcony. It was like mixing the sweetness of the gourmet ice cream with the saltiness of the microwave popcorn—it shouldn't have worked, but for Ronnie it did.

Now she settles herself into the chaise lounge, scans the sky for traces of any sunlight, sees none, and is thankful she hasn't completely blown the ceremony. She looks back over her shoulder into the dark of her apartment and instantly wonders what Flynn would make of her place. Would he be turned off by the lack of any feminine homeyness? Something about him feels a little old-fashioned, just a hint of anachronism about the guy.

Ronnie's apartment is a spacious two-bedroom, two-bath "luxury" unit with a galley kitchen and a huge living/dining area that opens onto the balcony. It costs most of her salary, but she's never been very concerned with savings plans or exotic vacations. Her idea of traveling is to make a job change every year or two and relocate to another part of the country, then dig in for a while, shock and build a virgin audience, and when she hits her peak and the national syndication people come sniffing around, pack the bags again and pull out the trade journals and the road atlas.

Vinnie, the QSG station manager, was shocked by her résumé and ratings sheets. "I don't get it," he'd said to her in their first interview. "These numbers, you're a station saver, you're a radio messiah. You could head to New York or Atlanta, name your price, let the big sales guys rent your voice coast-to-coast."

Ronnie gave him her most libidinous smile and said, "I'd rather keep a low profile."

And Vinnie gave his chronic, world-weary sigh and said, "You've come to the right station."

A week later Ronnie signed the lease for 3-G, called a local rental franchise, and furnished the place in a day. Her only aesthetic requirement was neutral colors, neither too masculine nor too feminine. When the moving men left after delivery she had an earth-toned hotel room, all muted angles and practicality. This was exactly what she'd been after, a setting where she could go to sleep each night and dream that she was in an airport Ramada and due to board a flight at the terminal next door.

Her one oddball, nonrented modification was a huge antique bookcase she bought a week after moving in. Her first Sunday in town, she overpaid a Russian émigré down at the refugee flea market in the train lot on Ironhouse Ave. It was an ornate monster, old and battered and painted a flat black, but hand-tooled with a curving, scrolled headpiece and little pointed spires rising at the top. She had to pay again to have it hauled to the apartment, but it was her one concession to personalization—she loaded it with the contents of her steamer trunk.

Ronnie is a tape-head. She considers her condition a benign affliction. She purchases blank cassettes, through the mail and in bulk quantities. Then she scans the band wave and records hundreds of diverse noises, music, talk shows, news reports, station jingles, EBS tests. Before she moves out of a city, she spends a week sorting through her latest collection. She keeps what she judges to be the top ten percent, though she doesn't have a system for qualitative judgment. It's more of an instinctual, instantaneous choice. Then she simply throws the rest of the tapes in trash bags and leaves them in a closet of the vacated apartment. *Disposable sound-crap,* she calls it. She puts the keepers in the steamer trunk and brings them with her to the next job. She thinks of the cassettes as her version of a photo album, a coded record of all her journeys, an audio cipher of all the highway crisscrossing she's done for a decade now.

Ronnie never tapes her own show and it amuses her a little that she's already forgotten a couple of her titles. There was *Sensual Sessions* in Cleveland and *The Carnal Response* in Santa Fe, but for some reason Toronto is a blur. She can remember how boxy the broadcast booth was and she still has an occasional fantasy about Yves, her engineer that season. But the name of the show itself has escaped her.

Ronnie has already stayed in Quinsigamond longer than any of her other stops. That fact both bothers and consoles her. Back in June, she'd thought that by Christmas she'd give Vinnie her notice and start sorting her tapes. On Labor Day—a muggy, bad-air holiday that found the city looking as if it had evacuated for the nuclear strike of her childhood daydreams—Ronnie shocked herself by deciding, out on the balcony, about 4 A.M., to work on until spring.

She knows she should have been getting the itch by now, the signals that begin warning of an oncoming move. But it hasn't happened. She's migratorily "late," and this should be causing worry and frustration. This time around, something's different. It could be her age or a change in body chemistry, but this time she's got an odd, instinctual hunch that what's delaying her departure is the city itself. It's almost as if she clicked with this dying mill town in a way that's never happened before. And of course it's pathetically ironic that the one place where she's starting to feel she could actually remain is on its way out, decaying into a harsh powder of warring people and evaporating industries. If she can see these signs, then why isn't she making the normal moves, setting the process in motion again? Why isn't she checking the trades and sorting her cassettes? Why isn't she phoning the modeling agencies?

In the past, before she'd leave each city, Ronnie would drop some money on an expensive quirk. She'd begin by visiting a local modeling agency, paging through their layout books until she spotted a woman of approximately her own age who gave off a subtle leer. It was always something in the face, something about the positioning of the eyes and the lips. And it would have to be mildly hidden, visible only peripherally beneath a layer of disinterest, a lingerie catalogue model as opposed to a *Playboy* centerfold.

When she'd find the right look, Ronnie would pay for some photographs, black-and-white portraits, soft-focus head shots, the hair and lipstick perfect, the skin smooth and often translucent. Finally, before packing up the Jeep and moving on, she'd have the photographer print up a hundred eight-by-tens. Then, once she was established in her new city, plugging into the repressed community psyche and starting to make some waves, invariably the letters would start to roll in, a new batch of fans requesting a photo of Ronnie Wilcox. She'd dig out her stack of head shots, sign her name across the bottom with a red felt marker, and send back a glossy of some anonymous model from a thousand miles away. And as long as Ronnie stayed in that particular city, this coolly seductive visage, this countenance radiating airbrushed carnality, would always be her image.

Ronnie pulls a plastic spoon from the pocket of her robe and starts in on the ice cream. She knows she'll be freezing in about three minutes, but it's a price she's willing to pay. While she eats she starts to wonder about what Flynn would think of her fake publicity stills and this leads her to wonder: if she put a photo of herself next to a photo of the faux Ronnie, which one would Flynn choose? The subliminal nymph or the real road-woman? To be scientific, she should insert a control in the experiment, maybe some perfect suburban homemaker drawn from cooking or station wagon ads. Maybe that's what would really hammer his button. He's what, thirty-five, thirty-six, ripe for that settling-down mode, primed to marry the hardworking dream woman, ten years his junior, bored with her career now and ready to start pumping out a couple offspring for the breadwinner.

Suddenly, she can picture Flynn in some too-green field, pitching a whiffle ball, underhand, to a six-year-old version of himself.

She puts the pint of Häagen-Dazs down and uncaps the mescal. *Get a grip, girl,* she thinks, *you just met this bastard.*

Ronnie never knew her father. Classic abandonment story. All her mother would say was he was "in sales" and was "too handsome to be trusted." He left one weekend, supposedly to put a deposit on a vacation rental. Instead, he cashed out the checking account, gassed up the Chevy Impala, and never came home. Ronnie was born five weeks later.

Her mother went to work as a skittish waitress willing to date the first generous tip she saw and Ronnie grew up watching the woman slide from being badly disappointed in a series of stupid and abusive men to being genuinely unbalanced. In between there were a lot of moves and two quick, horror-story marriages.

At one point between these marriages, for a short time when Ronnie was about twelve, she and her mother ended up living in a trailer park outside of Gainesville, Florida. It was here that Mother got into the habit of leaving the radio on all night. At first it drove Ronnie crazy, all these Bible Belt preachers yelling about repenting before the fires of eternal damnation consumed your evil flesh. She wanted to hear the Top Forty, pop music for the young. They reached a compromise when they found a strange AM station that was broadcasting old-fashioned radio plays. They'd lie in the dark, in the mini bunk beds, Ronnie on top, and listen to intriguing voice productions like *The Invisible Man* or *The Tell-Tale Heart.* Over the course of several weeks there were romances and detective dramas, love stories, and O. Henry adaptations.

Then one night, the narrator's voice announced the station's final production. He said there'd been a format change. From the top bunk in the trailer, Ronnie thought she heard her mother start to weep. She asked if everything was all right, but her mother didn't answer. So she closed her eyes and began to listen to *The Diary of Anne Frank*.

In the twenty years that have passed since that night, Ronnie knows she has never been so moved and torn up and generally *affected* by any book or movie or song or painting or relationship. Over the course of two hours, in a pitch-black trailer, in stifling Florida, it was as if this young victim, this girl called Anne, with her intelligent voice and perfect words, had stood next to the bunk and whispered her story into Ronnie's ear. Ronnie could see every aspect of it, the family, the movement into the attic, the others—Mr. and Mrs. Van Daan and young Peter, Miep bringing supplies to the hiding place. Ronnie balled the ends of the worn sheet that covered her legs and felt everything alongside Anne. Terror, frustration, anger, infatuation. But mostly terror, agonizing fear when a noise sounded below the attic floor, crippling worry when the food rations shrank with each merciful delivery from Miep. That night in Florida, Ronnie's trailer became Anne Frank's attic.

And for the next five or six years, as her mother's condition worsened and they continued to move around America, Ronnie began to daydream, to fantasize a very elaborate, ritualized invention where she and her mother, like Anne and the Frank family, were pursued by heinous, deranged, Nazi-like men in dark uniforms and leather boots that came high up their shins. But, unlike Anne, Ronnie stayed mobile, always a step ahead of these murderous soldiers, always leading her mother to narrow escape in a new town, always using intelligence and an emotionless savvy to maneuver around the elaborate traps and roadblocks and ambushes.

The fantasies ended when Ronnie turned eighteen and her mother slid into the fully delusional. They were living near a distant cousin in upstate New York. The cousin helped place Mother in something like a nursing home where she died of a massive embolism after six months.

Ronnie doesn't like to think about the fact that there might have been some degree of relief mixed in with her pain that day.

There turned out to be a surprise death benefit from an old life policy her mother had purchased when she was born. It was only ten grand, but it got Ronnie through two years of a junior college, where she stumbled upon the campus radio station. Her freshman year, she pushed until she got a night slot spinning late-seventies disco. And each night in that makeshift studio, fitting on the taped-up headphones and adjusting her meters, muting the Gibb brothers' voices from the studio speakers and maybe smoking a joint in the dimness and the quiet, she'd approach a feeling that was something like the night in Gainesville, Florida, when Anne Frank's ghost stood next to her and taught her how to be wise and strong and practical, how to survive.

In that junior college studio, Ronnie came to realize that it was possible to present yourself simply and solely as a voice. Pure voice. A ghost with no bodily presence in this world.

Sitting in that Mickey Mouse broadcasting booth, while most of the campus was studying or partying or screwing or sleeping, Ronnie dredged up the last remnants of her mother's face and decided three things, three primary commandments that guide her life to this day:

Never put your faith in someone simply because you've slept with them.

Never lie to yourself.

Never stop moving.

Exactly, she thinks now. *Never stop moving.*

She gets up from the lounge, tightens the belt of her robe, walks to the railing, and looks down over Main Street. All the night cliques are out, a half dozen nighthawk subcultures prowling around the alleys off Main, trying to move quickly in the darkness, to wrap up their transactions before dawn. The gay hustlers and the runaway whores. The Toth clinic outpatients and the beeper-packing crack clerks. Ronnie feels like she's watching an enormous ant farm, filled on a cruel whim with a random mixture of life-forms, who may or may not be suited to this artificial environment. And she wonders about the varying extent of their awareness. Are they conscious of their own motivations? Or are they instinctively driven by the last and best commandment, *Never stop moving*?

So why are you still sitting here in Solitary?

And why are you starting to screw around with a guy you could end up liking?

14.

It's four-thirty in the morning and all Hannah can think about is eating the remains of the takeout carbonara that's sitting in her refrigerator. She knows she won't bother to heat it. She'll wolf it straight out of the carton, wash it down with the last of the Chablis. On the drive home she realized, in an instantaneous and almost shocking way, just how hungry she was. Crossing Hoffman Square she flashed on the carbonara, pictured it sitting on the fridge shelf like a forgotten Christmas gift that turned out to be exactly what she'd wanted. As she pulled in behind the house and killed the engine she sat in the car for an extra few seconds, thinking about the sad fact that even if there was some mate, some devoted insomniac lover, waiting on the other side of her apartment door, some caring and thoughtful individual who'd spent the last hour preparing something hot and delicious and nourishing, she'd still want the cold carbonara. She wonders if this is a sign she should always stay single.

She scoops her mail off the top stair where Mrs. Acker leaves it every afternoon and lets herself into her apartment, the middle unit of an old wood-frame three-decker opposite St. Matthias Hospital. She's lived in the same place for over five years now. Mrs. Acker lives on the first floor with a Rottweiler named Franz, after her late husband. The top floor has been empty since Mr. Bradbury died last spring.

Hannah loves the apartment, a spacious two-bedroom with all-natural wood, antique brass fixtures everywhere, and eleven-foot-high ceilings. The rent is more than reasonable and she's got a full-sized kitchen and this enormous old bathtub with claw legs. Sometimes she considers approaching Mrs. Acker about eventually buying the place. Maybe they could work out some sort of arrangement, an agreed-upon price, or at least something like a right of first refusal. It'd be a sensible investment and the rents would make the mortgage workable.

She steps into the kitchen, locks the door behind her, flips on the fluorescent ceiling light, and slides off her jeans jacket. She throws the jacket over the back of a kitchen chair, pulls open the refrigerator, and takes out an empty Gallo bottle. She drops the bottle in the trash, pulls out a beer, and twists off the cap. She squats down in front of the refrigerator and searches for the carbonara. But it's nowhere to be found. She opens the crisper and the meat keeper, shoves aside the orange juice carton and a half dozen yogurt containers and the Tupperware that she knows is filled with a week-old, decaying salad, but there's no pasta anywhere.

"I'm losing it," she whispers to herself, pulls out a blueberry yogurt, then puts it back and opens the freezer. She pulls down a pint of fudge swirl gourmet ice cream, yanks off the lid, and throws it in the trash next to the wine bottle as a sign of total commitment.

She grabs a soup spoon from the drawer and goes to work, standing the whole time at the counter, leafing halfheartedly through the mail. There's a music club offer, her Visa statement, her electric bill, a lingerie catalogue, a donation request from some cancer society, a donation request from some children's relief society, and Mr. Bradbury's *Reader's Digest*. Since the old man died, Mrs. Acker has been giving Hannah all his magazines.

There's also a medium-sized padded manila mailer. Hannah's name and address are printed in black block letters in the very center of the package. There's no return address and there's no stamp or cancellation mark.

Hannah puts her spoon in her mouth and tears open the package. She pulls out a notebook. A common drugstore notebook, the kind a kid would take to school. It's got a brown cardboard cover and spiral binding down the side. The cover says "Saint Ignatius" in Gothic lettering.

An odd, cold feeling starts up in her stomach. She puts the soup spoon down on the countertop and opens to the first page of the notebook. Her eyes fall on the handwriting. She immediately grabs the envelope again and turns it over, looking for something more. But there's nothing beyond her name and address. No markings. No sign of origin.

She looks back to the words printed on the first page and there's no way to deny the fact that this is Lenore Thomas's notebook. The writing is smaller than normal for Lenore, but it's unmistakable—the abundance of ink, the rigidity of angles on certain letters, the deep imprint that results from too much pressure exerted on the nub of the pen.

Hannah lets her thumb fan through a run of pages. Lenore has crammed as much writing as possible into the notebook. And not just writing. There are lists of unattached words, crude graphs, even a rough sketch or two. And hundreds of arrows pointing from one passage—or proper name or dollar amount or quotation—to another. It's like the nighttime jottings of an obsessive scientist plagued by a difficult theory. Or the diary of a half-mad monk looking for an absolute proof of the Divine. Or the work journal of a drug-whacked poet plotting a unified field theory in the gorgeous words of a newly invented language.

She opens randomly to some middle page and sees a whirlpool of words, written and printed in a slightly circular pattern, tied together only by the arrow marks Lenore has drawn between them. Some of the words Hannah understands. Others she instinctively doesn't want to. But the look of the page holds her, and it occurs to her that, maybe, rather than read the page normally, she'd have better luck deciphering it by viewing it as a picture.

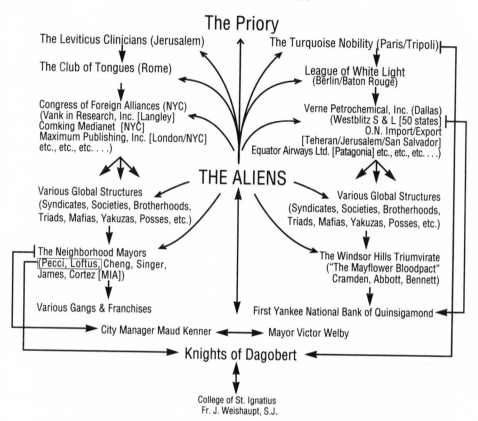

The Priory

The Leviticus Clinicians (Jerusalem)

The Club of Tongues (Rome)

Congress of Foreign Alliances (NYC)
(Vank in Research, Inc. [Langley]
Comking Medianet [NYC]
Maximum Publishing, Inc. [London/NYC]
etc., etc., etc. . . .)

The Turquoise Nobility (Paris/Tripoli)

League of White Light
(Berlin/Baton Rouge)

Verne Petrochemical, Inc. (Dallas)
(Westblitz S & L [50 states]
O.N. Import/Export
[Teheran/Jerusalem/San Salvador]
Equator Airways Ltd. [Patagonia] etc., etc., etc. . . .)

THE ALIENS

Various Global Structures
(Syndicates, Societies, Brotherhoods,
Triads, Mafias, Yakuzas, Posses, etc.)

The Neighborhood Mayors
(Pecci, Loftus, Cheng, Singer,
James, Cortez [MIA])

Various Gangs & Franchises

Various Global Structures
(Syndicates, Societies, Brotherhoods,
Triads, Mafias, Yakuzas, Posses, etc.)

The Windsor Hills Triumvirate
("The Mayflower Bloodpact"
Cramden, Abbott, Bennett)

First Yankee National Bank of Quinsigamond

City Manager Maud Kenner ⟷ Mayor Victor Welby

Knights of Dagobert

College of St. Ignatius
Fr. J. Weishaupt, S.J.

Hannah flips to the last page and sees that Lenore has written *End of Notebook One*.

Meaning, Hannah muses, there must be more to come.

But goddamn it, Lenore, I don't want any more. I want you to leave me alone. I don't want your mannerisms and I don't want your gestures and I don't want your attitudes. And I don't want your voice. I do not want your voice. But it keeps happening. It started out innocently. I'd be down Bangkok and I'd be scared and I'd try to think of exactly how you'd move and exactly what you'd say. And it got easier and easier. And it got results. But now it's like I have this parasite inside of me. Feeding off of me. And it's growing and I'm getting smaller. I don't want to be your ghost, Lenore. Leave me alone, Lenore. I don't want your voice. I don't.

She closes the notebook, then opens it again near the rear, just pages from the end. She runs her hand over the writing.

There's a slight skim-coat of some kind of grainy dust, as if the notebook had been dropped on a beach of red sand.

She brushes the dust away and it sticks to her palm. She brings her palm to her nose, smells nothing, brings it to her mouth, and licks at her skin, then, without thinking, she takes the notebook under her arm and walks into her bedroom. Without putting on a light, she goes to her closet, opens the door, reaches up to a high shelf, and pulls down a brown gunmetal strongbox. She reaches into her pants pocket and takes out a key, turns the lock, and opens the box. She reaches behind to her belt holster, draws out her Magnum, and places it inside. Then she slides Lenore's notebook underneath the gun, relocks the box, and puts it back on the closet shelf.

She stands for a second before the closet door. Then she moves to her bureau and looks at herself in the mirror. She leans in, pulls down the skin at the corners of her eyes, and mutters, "I've got to get more sleep."

She turns on the digital clock radio on the bureau and the room fills up with music, an old tune that used to be a favorite of Lenore's. She sticks her tongue out to her mirror image and tries to inspect it as Warren Zevon sings:

> ...in walks the village idiot
> and his face is all aglow
> he's been up all night listening to
> Mohammed's radio...

She places a hand over her mouth and when she swallows, there's an ache all the way down her throat. She remembers she's out of aspirin, then she starts back toward the kitchen, hoping there's another bottle of wine in the cabinet. And trying to ignore the feeling that's already started to grow in her stomach.

15.

WQSG is running a 7 A.M. traffic update—advice on how to maneuver around a three-car pileup at the Hoffman Square Rotary—when they're hit. First there's the three standard bursts of static followed by the signature trumpet blast. It could be a loop from an old Sphere bootleg. The rumor down the Canal Zone is that the brothers are fans.

Then QSG is history and O'ZBON comes alive.

Aloha. Shalom. Buenos días. And sorry for the interruption, but the only traffic problems you need worry about are the locations of the roadblocks between truth and deception, the blockades between illusion and reality, the police horses separating belonging from isolation. And that's what we're here for.

Brother John speaks the gospel truth, friends. I want to start off the day by grabbing the broadcast bull by his antennae-horns, as it were. Juan and I have heard down the pipe that there's some dispute going 'round as to the authenticity of these transmissions. I had a feeling this might happen. If *mon frère* cares to remember, I mentioned just such a possibility during our sojourn up and down Route 66 a couple years back, during the St. Ti Jean Pilgrimage that my obsessive bro insisted upon. I think we were in Denver, trying to catch a little overdue Z-time in a trailer parked down on Laramie Street. It was hot and we'd chugged way too much joe from the endless thermos and came to review the fond memories of our breakthrough days back in the old hometown. My question was, should the heat ever back down to temperate and we cruise northeast like some mutant Irish salmon, would the apostles embrace us all over again? Or would it be rerun season and we end up stuck in that episode of *Post-Easter Blues* with special guest star Doubting Thomas? Well, Johnny-boy puts down his much-thumbed copy of *Flashes of Moriarty* to castigate yours truly over blaspheming the faithful. He says that if we headed back to the Q-town hills, within forty-eight hours word'd be blasting through the Canal Zone that the brothers were back in town and Radio Free Subterranea was about to queue up. I let the issue lie and dipped back into an old P. A. Taylor mystery. But lo and behold, a few years roll by, we slide from the headlines, the FCC turns its worry beads on the morning drivetime shock-jocks, and the coast starts to look clear for a homecoming. We make some arrangements, alert kin, and prepare security. And start the long haul out of May-he-ko—that's right, who guessed correctly?—and make the Quinsigamond borders by the end of last month. It takes a week to retool and upgrade the old equipment, but finally we make the big comeback broadcast.

[*Pause*]

And what's the first feedback we hear? "It's not them, man." "Couldn't be the O'Zebedees." "No way. They're still tending bar in Dublin. These guys are a weak imitation." Fine. Break my heart some more, you little ingrates. What is it you need to be sure? Would you like to press your hand into our old cart-deck? How about probe our microphone ports with your fingers? Would that do the trick?

Whoa, boy, calm it down. Here, take mine, it's decaf. Hello, friends, Brother John, back again. As you can hear, you've done some momentous upsetting in the heart of the boy wonder. I've tried to salve the wounds with ancient adages—no man's a prophet in his own market share. But though he proclaims otherwise, I think your suspiciousness genuinely surprised him. He expected more from the hard core, as the saying goes. My own feeling is, you stay on top of the mountain by giving the people what they want. So if it's proof you need, we'll try to come up with some irrefutable evidence that we're the one and only, genuine, original saboteurs. Until we can think of something airtight, however, I'm going to have to ask you to try to have faith. It's the honest-to-Marconi James and John, no matter what your ears tell you.

Yo, hermano, the timer says we just passed our safety margin.

That means it's time to recede into the caverns from which we came. Keep the ears peeled 'cause we'll be back. And until then, *Hic Calix.*

PART TWO

SATURDAY

16.

Normally, the small bathroom off Flynn's office is a little sanctuary, a solitary free zone where he can steal five minutes from the day and browse through his collection of rare old *Shadow* magazines. Today, it's more like a holding cell or an isolation booth from some upscale, impossible game show.

He leans the weight of his body against the black lacquered sink, stares at his Cartier watch. He can feel a sweat breaking under the Bill Blass suit and, though he knows it will do no good, he taps on the top of the Grundig, slaps at its side like it was a clogged parking meter.

"Bound to happen," he whispers. "Should have known."

The Grundig is an antique. Flynn rescued it from a flea market seven years ago. He has it mounted on a shelf over the toilet. He keeps the original handbook in a sealed Baggie under the radio. The handbook is entirely in German, a language Flynn can neither speak nor read.

"Son of a bitch, come on," he whispers.

He comes forward, leans over the toilet, presses his ear to the mesh that covers the speaker. A squeal of interference sounds and he steps back awkwardly. There's a few seconds of static and then:

...and for those among the faithful who worship the voice of the goddess, the brothers will try to vamoose by ten...

Flynn lets out a lungful of nervous air, comes forward again, plants a kiss on the mesh, and laughs at himself. He runs some cold water over his hands, splashes some on his face, dries off with a towel, and looks at himself in the mirror. Thin traces of pink vein run through his eyes. He's gotten maybe two hours of sleep. He's definitely not at the top of his form for the coming pitch. The phone call from Wallace came at 3 A.M., just as he was climbing into bed. He couldn't catch all the words. The dwarf's voice was high and frantic, something about meeting him at the hospital, something about Olga's accident and questions from the police. He'd driven to St. Matthias dressed in sweats and slippers and only been allowed into Olga's room for a few seconds. She looked so tiny in the mechanical bed, swimming in the pale blue johnny and the frayed sheets. She was wrapped like a fragile, shrunken mummy and medicated into a sleep that Flynn hoped was beyond pain. In the corridor he'd paced with Wallace and tried to get the story straight. The Brownings had come home from their dance. They'd both had a few drinks. Olga had gone down to the rec room for some reason, tripped on the first stair, and fallen the rest of the way. Everything else out of Wallace's mouth was a jumble—words about the look on the doctor's face in the E.R., a visit with some young cop with a clipboard and a series of endless questions. He kept looking up at Flynn, wringing his hands, saying, in that awful cracking voice, "She'll be all right, won't she, G.T.?" When the sun started to come up, Flynn finally talked Wallace into going home. He looked away as the dwarf climbed up on a metal stool to kiss his wife's bandage-swathed cheek, then followed after Wallace in the Saab till his friend was safely back home. He'd gotten back to his own place by six, sprawled in the dentist's chair for a couple hours, taken a hot shower, and swilled some black coffee.

Now he shakes his head and opens the medicine cabinet,

takes out the Visine and shakes drops into each eye, towels off again, and looks in the mirror a last time.

"Okay, G.T.," he says, "time to make some coin."

He runs through a series of deep breaths, squares his shoulders back, flattens down a rumple in the front of the suit, tightens his tie. He brings his hands up so they block his face in the mirror, interlocks the fingers, and cracks the knuckles elaborately.

Then he clears his throat, takes a last breath, forms his mouth into a humble smile, and exits the bathroom.

Mr. and Mrs. Miller are seated in front of his desk, sunk deep into the buttery leather chairs Flynn had special-ordered from Europe. The rest of his office, his whole building for that matter, is authentically Victorian. Five years back, when he first purchased the property, he hired a pricy decorator and paid through the nose to bring the whole place back to its original 1875 look. The hand-cut sign hanging out front that reads

G.T. Flynn CFP, CLU
Life Insurance
and
Estate Planning

was modeled on a genuine Yankee shingle on display in the city's historical society archives.

But Flynn had to pull an annoying compromise when it came to the customer chairs. He split with the decorator over this issue. He couldn't make her see that the chairs were part of a larger, intricate process, a ritual or ceremony, a subtle but complex therapy. He couldn't convey to her that the chairs were an essential cog in the wheel of the coin, a strut that sat next to Flynn's voice, eye contact, the lighting of the room, and, most of all, the words, the individual signifiers that linked together in a logic chain and formed something larger—a picture, an image, a 3-D full-color hologram of total security and peace of mind. He needed the clientele to sink down into that expensive leather until they felt almost weightless, or better, until they felt like they were floating in saline, womb-rooted again, protected from the horrible glare of air-breathing life.

He stops in the doorway to make the judgment call. They look ready, he decides, so he starts to walk to the desk, lets them see he's relaxed, unhurried, unpressured, as if he were walking toward a summertime hammock on a farmhouse porch.

He takes his seat behind the antique, hand-scrolled Chippendale desk and says, "Sorry about the interruption." He smiles and nods his head.

There have been times, instances set up just like this, when his voice box failed him and his first crucial, tone-setting words came out in a squawk or, worse, a phlegmy, throat-clogged rasp. Now he's superstitious about the first words. He keeps an old-time atomizer in the bathroom medicine cabinet and a jar of honey in the mini-fridge.

"Well, Mr. and Mrs. Miller—let me ask, do you mind if I call you Bob and Carol?"

The man shakes his head and the woman says, "We call him Bo at home."

Flynn smiles, addresses the man, "Should I call you Bo? You tell me."

Bo shrugs and mumbles, "Fine."

The guy is uncomfortable, not someone used to this kind of meeting. Flynn is going to have to change that, adjust some of the pitch up front, make things familiar.

"Well, you can both call me G.T. My high school catcher hung that on me and it stuck."

"Played ball?" Bo asks.

"Oh, yeah," Flynn says, low voice, breaking eye contact momentarily as if embarrassed. "All the way through college." He flinches but manages to hide it. "Anyway, I think you'll both find there are no formalities in this office. Now, before we begin, can I get either one of you a refreshment? Cup of coffee or tea? Bo, I got a cold one back there, if you'd like."

Bo shakes him off and Carol says, "We're all set right now."

"Okay, great, just let me know if you change your mind. Now"—he slides open a drawer and brings a manila folder up onto the desktop—"I've had a chance to look over your informational sheets here. I hope they weren't too much of a bear to fill out."

"They were no problem," Bo says.

Bo could be tough. If things get too bad, he'll refocus all his energy and pitch directly to Carol.

"That's great. I'm telling you, some of the forms these days, I don't know, the banks are the worst. Couple years back I went in for a car loan. Simple car loan, okay? It was like a trip to a blind dentist. You needed a degree from MIT just to fill out page one."

"You looked over our papers?" Bo asks.

Flynn looks up from the desk, stares into Bo's eyes. *You can't cajole this guy.* He lets the smile drift off his lips. *You can't friendly this guy into signing the papers.* He looks back down to the desk, takes a second, closes the folder. He looks up at Carol, over to Bo, back to Carol again. He changes strategy, fades into the tone of a legendary grammar school principal.

"Says here you have three children?"

"Three girls," Carol says.

"Three girls, that's wonderful. Terrific. You wouldn't have a photo by any chance?"

It's a dangerous play. Used to be a standard, but in this day and age, when you've got molesters pictured on the front page every other night, it's risky. They could question your motives, get a little queasy.

Carol goes into her handbag, takes out the wallet, slips a color shot from a plastic sleeve, and hands it across the desk to him. Flynn starts a long, unblinking stare at the picture, like he's trying to translate an ancient language. Then he starts to nod and asks, without looking up, without directing himself to either one of them, in a purposefully unfriendly voice, "How'd you two meet?"

Neither one was prepared for that question. They were both expecting something about the kids, a question about the girls' ages, what schools they attended.

Bo says, "I, I . . . ," and Carol jumps in with, "High school. We were in the same class—"

Flynn cuts her off, his voice sucked clean of emotion, "So you'd both be the same age?"

"Bo's a few months—"

"Approximately the same age? Born the same year?"

"The same year, yes, nineteen—"

"Any other dependents?"

There's a pause. He assumes they're looking at each other, one of them trying to come up with the nerve to just walk out. But he continues staring at the photo until Bo says, "Just the girls. Just the ones in the picture there."

Flynn's been waiting for Bo's voice and it comes out just right—tentative, too unsure for anger or action. A little helpless.

In front of Flynn, at the top of the desk, is a heavy brass pen holder, an antique, a long flat base with the Flynn family crest engraved on it and two floutlike stems that jut up and can pivot on a secured ball bearing. He reaches out and grabs the piece, turns it around with one hand so that the two Mont Blancs point out toward Bo and Carol. Then, delicately, he places the picture of the three girls in front, leans it against the pens like a small easel, so the faces of the children beam up at the parents.

He comes forward in his seat, rests his weight on his arms and elbows, seems to push his upper body toward them.

In a low voice, the voice of some anguished last-century minister, he says, "I want five minutes of your time to tell you a story. You're not beholden to me at all. If there's some reason you're no longer interested in my services, then you're free to go. I don't require an explanation or an apology. But I'd like to give you this story to keep. A little token of this night. Okay? No matter what happens after you leave, if we never see one another again, all right, I want you to hear this story. Will you do that?"

They do what he wants. They nod rather than answer.

He takes a deep breath, like an Olympic swimmer about to leap from his pedestal. And he begins.

"All right, then. This is about a man with a lot of ambition. Great tenacity. What you and I would most likely consider a good man. He makes a family early in life, cares for them to the best of his ability. I look at you. I study the two of you. I see you understand this man's motivations. You share his sense of what is and is not important in this life. Let's name the things. Let's say them and judge them. Fame? No, I don't think so. Luxury? No, unnecessary. Status? No, empty, subjective. Power? No. Travel? Adventure? Simple no. Family?..." A slight pause. "Okay, all right. Family. Correct? Kin. Blood. The love and caring of man, woman, child. Yes? I think so. You have to choose what to make an effort for. You're given so many years. You don't even know how many. It's a gamble. The average man gets what? What is it today? I'm no actuary, but it's coming in around seventy-two years. Little more for the women. That's the average. Do you get more? Less? There's only one person who knows that. He's not telling. Not on this earth, he's not. So you make the choice. Whether you know it or not, you weigh the alternatives. The different avenues of this lifetime. Independence, self-interest, no worry. You're young at some point. You say, 'I could be in the Caribbean, I could sail chartered catamarans, live in a shack, sleep in the sun half the day.' You say, maybe, 'Vegas, Learn to be a blackjack dealer. Different showgirl every night,' huh? You say, 'I'm a beautiful young girl, fresh out of high school, I'll go to New York, take the stage by storm, champagne and flowers in the dressing room,' huh? I don't think so. You made the choices. Like the man in the story, you took the route—husband, wife, family. You found the job. You found the house. You raced to the hospital, four A.M., the contractions coming faster, the water breaking on the cart into maternity, the pain. You brought her home. Look at the picture there, people, you brought the little girl home. It begins. Number two, number three. Days pass, you clean the house, you buy the used cars, you go to parents' night. Hamburger Helper twice a week, so what? The guys from high school, all getting together, going fishing, beautiful lake, upstate New York—uh-uh, no can do, sorry, guys. You get the legal pad out, late at night, April, tax time, Carson's in the background, your mate's asleep in the easy chair, you can hear the breathing. You've walked down the hall, looked in their bedroom, checked to make sure the covers are pulled up, no bad dreams or stomachaches. You go back to the legal pad. You start a list, things that will come up, no question, orthodontist bills, piano lessons, maybe a second car when the first one gets the license, God help us. You play with numbers. You rearrange things, try to figure the best case and the worst. The promotion comes through. The promotion does not come through. You go in, talk to the others at work, get some feedback. They're not experts, granted, but they're honest working people, like yourself. They've got kids of their own. They're struggling like everyone else. Everyone's got an opinion. There doesn't seem to be any consensus. Some go with payroll savings. All well and good. Secure. Certainly secure, no question. But the time against the return, who knows what's right? Others stick with a passbook. They can see the interest accrue in black and white. Some have the brother-in-law who'll pick the stocks, the investments. They've got faith. He's family and he's done okay for himself. Still others buy long chains of lottery tickets on Wednesdays and Saturdays. Who knows? It keeps coming back to that—who knows? And you know the question is only going to get louder. 'Cause after the braces and the Yamaha upright and the eight-year-old Cutlass Supreme that eats too much gas, after those comes college, the all-time backbreaker. What? Twenty grand a year? By then, could be fifty grand a year. But you don't care. You know you have to do it. No other choice. 'Cause outside of marrying a prince, she'll be flipping burgers sixty-plus hours a week. Now you say, this is in the future, mister, this is abstract, this is a lot of theorizing, speculating, sky-is-falling crap. Okay, fair enough. Let's pull it down to earth for you. Let's ground the conversation, put it squarely in the here and now. I told you this was a story. I'll add now, just to make certain, clarify in case any doubt exists, this is a true story. This is factual. Historical. I told you about a good man, like yourselves. Family man. Chose those same avenues. Lived responsibly. Sacrificed. Did everything right to the best of his ability. But there was one ability lacking. Small but crucial ability. You know, right? You know already. *Foresight.* Can't have enough of it. But you can't purchase it. You can't go to school for it. It's part of your nature or it isn't. The particular man we're talking about, the hero, you might say, of our story here, went the passbook route. Okay. You can see it. You can picture him, can't you, gets off shift, stops by the local branch on the way home, dumps, what, ten, fifteen percent into the little blue passbook inside the scratched-up plastic envelope. The teller runs the book through the machine. The man sort of bounces on the balls of his feet, trying to listen to the sound of the machine as it calculates and then prints out this month's interest on the little white page. The teller hands him back the book, he steps to the side, lets the next customer move ahead. He opens to the current page and stares, reassures himself they've given him his due. Then one day, on the way home from the bank, the man, forty-seven years old and hasn't been out sick from work in over two years, he has a coronary. Massive heart attack. Car crashes into a telephone pole over on Chin Avenue. But he's dead before the impact. He's dead behind the wheel. That's it. No need for the jaws of life. No need for the EMTs and those electroshock paddles there. He's gone. Forty-seven. Dead."

Flynn takes the first real break, allows himself a long, audible breath. It's a necessary risk. The worry is that he won't find exactly the same voice tone, that the set of the face might change. But he knows he's got them. They're rigid in their seats. No amount of buttery, imported Italian leather can comfort these two now. He drops his eyes, for just the briefest second, down to the desk, closes them slowly, bites his top lip, and reopens the eyes.

"You want to take the guess?" he asks. "Either one of you? 'Cause you're right. The guy in the story was my old man."

The second pause, this time just heavy breathing.

"Excuse my language, but forty-seven goddamn years old. Yeah, I'm still a little bitter. And I'm sorry for that. But I was just ten years old at the time. And my brothers and sisters were even younger. And, I'm sorry, but unless it's happened to you, you can't, you don't..."

He takes a minute, pauses, then starts again. "Here's the point. The story doesn't end there. Not by a long shot. There's burial insurance, okay, and there's that passbook savings account. But at forty-seven you haven't built up too big a pension. And you've got a mortgage that's not even half paid off."

Fourth pause. The briefest so far.

"My mom went back to work, but we still had to sell the house, moving in with some relatives who tried their hardest not to resent us. I'm not trying to say we were the Job family or anything. I'm sure you could match me story for story. There are plenty of people out there who've been dealt worse. Deformities. Lingering diseases. Mental illness. No question. But this isn't my point. I'm not bartering for sympathy. The past is the past. Let it go. Look ahead. Fine. I did okay. You can see that. There are visible signs of that all around you right now, as we speak. But let me tell you something, and if you think I'm blowing my own horn, so be it. I'm the exception, not the rule. I worked hard. And let's say it, I got some lucky breaks. I'm the first to admit this. You can't purchase luck. I crawled out of the hole that was left when my old man's heart blew up. Others in my family, God help them, haven't been so lucky. You know what I'm saying. Every extended family can tell the same stories. The lost jobs, the drugs, the failed marriages. It's a tough life. We agree. I try to help out as best I can. And not just with the money stick, if you follow. I've got a sister, and I don't want to get too personal here, but we think she's in Florida. I say 'think' because we don't know. Last heard from her six months ago. My mother's heart. You can imagine. Okay, enough about me and mine. The thing is, we could not, capital C, capital N, could not have prevented our father's death. No way. When it's time, it's time. But with a little foresight, things could have been very, very different in the wake of that death. A little planning and maybe we could have kept the house. Maybe we could have paid for a few college educations. I delivered pizza till four A.M., four years, just to get through State. Maybe, with a little adequate planning, some of my siblings could've gotten some counseling before it was too late. Here are the questions: Could the old man have afforded some life insurance? Well, he afforded the pass-book, right? Huh? There are always options. You can't cut the whole life, bang, go with the term. There's never been more flexibility. Never been more possibilities to provide for a family."

The last pause. A long look from his face to hers.

"Bo. Carol. You made some choices. You made some sacrifices. You're on your way down the road of your life. Do me this favor. Do me one favor, all right? Tonight. Eleven o'clock tonight. The local news is going on, okay? Walk away from the set. Get up out of the chair and walk down the corridor. Together. I'm serious. Literally *do* this. You stop at the bedrooms. You look in the door. Study those little faces, sound asleep, total faith that Mom and Dad have everything under control. Okay? Look hard. Then you picture those faces about ten, fifteen years down the road. And now here's the hard part. Mom, or Dad, or, God forbid, both, are gone. They're not there anymore to keep things under control. And you, and I mean both of you, ask these questions: Where are they living? Where are they sleeping at night? Who's buying their clothes? Their Christmas presents? Who's going to put them through school? Pay for the weddings? Tough questions? Yes. Absolutely. But they need answers. Those little girls, sound asleep in that dim room, need those questions answered. By you two. You're the only ones."

A shrug. A raising of the eyebrows.

"What's the answer, Carol? What do you say, Bo?"

There they are, two puddles of anxiety, two terrified gobs of flesh, sweating onto the leather arms of the chairs, looking at each other, choked throats, swelling tongues.

Bo actually says it: "I don't know."

Flynn finally sits back in his chair and heaves an almost genuine sigh. "I know you don't. That's why I'm here."

It's another half hour to the signatures at the bottom of the policy. Flynn reads from the preprinted form about the required AIDS test. Carol writes out the check, a rectangle of paper decorated with beagle puppies. Bo gives the name of their family doctor and makes a mild joke about the urine specimen.

At the front door, Carol actually gives Flynn a hug and Bo bursts out in a thrilled laugh. He pumps Flynn's hand, thanks him earnestly. Flynn walks them both to the sidewalk, a hand on each of their backs. He beseeches them to bring the girls by someday, promises Bo a pair of complimentary Red Sox tickets, stands waving, smiling, as they drive away in a Ford wagon.

Back inside, Flynn locks the doors and starts to shut down the office. He's meticulous about this, making sure each light is out, each monitor shut off. He sets the alarm, then exits up the spiral staircase to his apartment. He's anxious to get into his study. Though his office and apartment are entirely Victorian, his study is strictly contemporary—all high-tech minimalist done in blacks and whites. Flynn loves the idea that no one looking at the outside of the building could imagine the study's interior. One just doesn't lead to the other.

He removes his suitcoat, goes to the bathroom, and splashes cold water on his face again. He dries off, looking in the mirror, thinking that maybe it's true, in some alternate universe or some dream life, maybe it's true that his father died at a young age, that he has troubled brothers and sisters, that fate dealt his family a rough hand. But in this conscious life, Flynn was still raised by an army of meat-fisted, ancient nuns at The Galilee Home for Boys.

It's been a good night. The Millers weren't a huge sale, but Flynn would rather a consistent number of medium-sized policies anyway, a couple a week, middle-class folk who'll never restructure the package, never borrow against the pot, always pay the premium a month before it's due. And the only thing they'll want in return is the free calendar, at Christmastime, with enormous, hyper-clear photos of selected national parks. *I'm telling you, Carol, we've got to get to Yosemite.*

Flynn undresses, hangs up his suit carefully, no creases, pocket flaps out. He changes into the gray cotton pants he picked up in Japan last year and a black-on-black sweater with just the slightest hint of turtleneck. He goes to the refrigerator, pours himself a Gatorade from a glass pitcher, moves to the answering machine, and hits the flashing button.

Hello, Flynn, it's Hazel. I think we've got some problems. I'll talk to you tonight.

G.T., it's Wallace. Just wanted to let you know I've spoken with the doctors and Olga's condition is stable. Sorry about last night. See you at Wireless. And G.T., could we keep the whole accident to ourselves?

He heads for the study, unlocks the reinforced sliding doors, rolls them back into the wall, leaves the lights off. He likes the kind of shadows he can get in this room, the way natural light will play off the ugly industrial-metal shelving that covers all the spare wall space. The study is soundproof. The floor is covered with a special, hard-to-get carpeting that the importer promised would "soak up eighty to ninety percent of your basic foot-level sound." The carpet is odd-feeling under his feet. It makes the floor seem to dip in places as you cross the room. It's a bland industrial gray, unpatterned. So far, Flynn thinks the importer told the truth.

At the far end of the room, in place of a desk, Flynn has an antique dentist's chair complete with accompanying instrument pedestal, a big cold turret with jointed arms of drill, water gun, suction tube, fluorescent lights. There's a round, swing-over tray attached to the pedestal and he uses this as a desktop. It suits his needs perfectly.

The rest of the room looks a lot like a small electronics warehouse. The rows of bolted-together metal racks give a hard-to-name glow to the room, an earthtone of some kind, partly dull green, partly gray-brown. The shelves are filled with stacks of boxy, matte-black hardware—world-band receivers, amps, equalizers, boosters, and recorders. Lined up on the shelf closest to the dentist's chair are three Otari MTR-12 reel-to-reel recorders. On the shelf below them is an Icom IC-9000 receiver stacked atop a Japan Radio backup unit.

Flynn moves to the first reel-to-reel, hits the rewind toggle, waits a beat, hits the play toggle, and folds his arms across his chest. From the Bose speaker issues his own voice:

"—you took the route—husband, wife, family. You found the job. You found the house. You raced to the hospital, four A.M., the contractions coming faster, the water breaking on the cart into maternity, the pain. You brought her home. Look at the picture there, people, you brought the little girl home. It begins. Number two, number three. Days pass, you clean the house, you buy the used cars, you go to parents' night. Hamburger Helper twice a week, so what?—"

Flynn massages his forehead with the tips of his fingers, then runs his hands back through his hair until he links his fingers behind his head. He does a minute of deep breathing, but images from last night at the airport start to flood, so he grabs the cordless phone off the swing tray and quickly punches in some numbers.

When Ferrie answers, Flynn says, "Open up the museum and tell the crybabies to sit down. I'm coming in to solve the whole feud."

17.

Ronnie knows there are things she should be doing. There's two weeks' worth of laundry sitting in the hamper and she hasn't given the apartment a cleaning in at least that long. She should get the Jeep washed, do some banking, shop for a few groceries.

Instead she continues to lie on her stomach in the unmade bed, lazily eating the last of a bowl of Wheaties and washing the soggy flakes down with a generous Bloody Mary. The radio is tuned to some station out of Boston, one of those yuppie jobs that play soft jazz on the weekend mornings, music that starts out sort of relaxing and after an hour turns cloying. Ronnie doesn't care. She just wants some white noise. And she definitely doesn't want to hear WQSG.

It's 10 A.M. on a Saturday. She's looking at a self-help quiz in a magazine someone had left at the station. It's one of those glossy fashion rags that run fifty pages of photos showing hundred-pound models with thick lips and sculpted bodies, followed by an article on "Why You Have a Poor Self-image."

The quiz is entitled "Do I Fear Intimacy?" and it's illustrated with a black-and-white, shadowy photo of a man and a woman, both with wavy hair covering their shoulders. Both have wildly pronounced cheekbones. The couple is standing in some indistinct, urban alleyway. The man has his head inclined toward the woman. And she's holding him at bay with her arm extended straight out and the palm of her hand pushing at his chest.

Ronnie stares at the photo for a few minutes before reading the first question. She thinks maybe there's a way to determine why the couple is in an inner-city alley. There isn't, so she grabs a felt marker from the nightstand and begins testing herself.

At first, the questions are pretty straightforward. You can see how they relate to the problem of intimacy. But halfway through the quiz they're suddenly hitting her with "How often do you eat fast food?" and "How many times a month do you go to the movies?"

This line of questioning annoys Ronnie, but she persists and at the end she tallies her score and checks it against the score key. She rates in the bottom category, summed up with the explanation: "You are an island unto yourself. Your failure to share your life and open your heart to even your closest of lovers is deeply rooted in your past. Therapy beckons. Don't give up hope. With time, patience, and hard work you can overcome your clammish ways and learn to share life and love with a giving partner."

She throws the magazine against the wall and guzzles the last of the Bloody Mary. Then she rolls onto the edge of the bed, comes upright into a sitting position, runs her hands through her hair, looks at her watch, and says out loud, "I think we need to get some air."

A half hour later, she's showered, dressed in jeans, a red cotton sweater, and her oldest, favorite Keds. She steers the Jeep down Ziesing Ave and cranks up the volume on the radio as Chrissie Hynde belts out the end of "Thin Line Between Love and Hate," then she pulls into the curb in front of a storefront that sports an enormous orange neon sign on the roof that blinks the words

Shockwave Riders
A Fantastic Fiction Bookshop

Ziesing Ave has become known as Bookstore Boulevard over the past couple of years. In addition to Shockwave, there's Ephraim Beck's, which specializes in mystery literature, Doc Kerrigan's, which has the best poetry stock west of Boston, and Alexandria, which comprises two full floors of the old Streeter Mill and is filled to bursting with tens of thousands of used, unsorted, unpriced volumes.

Ronnie cuts the engine but sits in the Jeep for a minute studying the store. She's never been inside, but drives past it several times a week and always gets a little jolt, a quick aesthetic buzz that she's never bothered to analyze. Now, for the first time, she looks closer at the building and sees the extent of effort that went into its design.

The owner, Toby Odets, is a scion of one of the city's oldest families and he dumped a good chunk of his trust fund into the renovation of a standard wood-frame, brick façade box of a store. Toby was determined to make the structure reflect the concerns of his stock and trade and he spared no expense in transforming the three thousand square feet of raw space into some kind of gleaming, immaculate jet age that never existed. He drew up the design himself, stealing liberally from Streamline Moderne and the Googie School, but straining it all through the sieve of his unique sensibility until it came out looking like a lost movie set from some high-budget 1950s drive-in space opera.

Toby started with the roof and erected a stainless-steel pylon, a sleek useless antennalike tower that was encircled by seven equidistant loops of different-colored neon. These circles of light flashed on and off in sequential order, bottom to top. At the lip of the roof he placed the neon Shockwave sign, then fashioned a soaring delta-wing canopy that shot out at its base and hung over the sidewalk like the streamlined fin of a comic book rocket. The edges of the wing were outfitted with a string of marquee-style blinking bulbs, alternating reds and whites.

Extending from the front wall of the shop at a sharp angle to the sidewalk, Toby bolted mock-steel girders adorned with huge, functionless bolts and random-sized portholes. The two display windows were exaggerated bubbles of Plexiglas that dissolved into a stainless-steel fronting with all the corners rounded away.

Like walking into an antique spaceship, Ronnie thinks. *I should have worn my steel-cone bra.*

She looks at her watch, gets out of the Jeep, and moves inside. The interior of the shop is no less striking than the outside. The ceiling is high, maybe a full twelve feet, and it's composed of some kind of chrome or aluminum, some reflective metal, worked into a series of concentric circles that culminates in a good-sized, multipointed, crystal-looking star that hangs dead center like a Martian chandelier. The walls are done in black and white deco tile and they're covered with artwork taken from dozens of 1930s science fiction pulps, classic stuff from names like Earl K. Bergey and Frank R. Paul and Howard V. Brown. There are pictures of bullet-shaped spaceships with gaping holes torn through them by an asteroid storm. There's a future city of glass, built in ascending tiers, being shattered by a massive tidal wave. There are flying insects as big as Buicks doing battle with laser-cannon-equipped sailors of tomorrow. The art is all framed by tubes of red neon. Ronnie thinks Toby Odets's electric bill must be backbreaking.

She starts to wander the aisles. The display racks are sloping metal frames that mimic the I-beam design outside. A sign mounted on the rear wall announces *100,000 Volumes Always in Stock.* The Infinity speakers on the wall fill the room with Throbbing Gristle's *Second Annual Report.* The store is busy for a Saturday morning. There are a half dozen teenagers decked out in skateboard attire mulling over the comic book racks. There's a flock of college students swinging their bulging nylon knapsacks over their shoulders as they rummage in the used-paperback section. There's an elderly couple scanning the new releases.

Ronnie starts down a random aisle, stops in the middle, picks up a paperback, and starts to thumb through it. After a minute, a skateboarder moves up next to her and starts paging through a fat anthology. He doesn't appear to have much interest in the book. He keeps lifting his head and looking over his shoulder. The kid's mulatto with a tight head of curly hair. He's wearing a peach-colored T-shirt with the sleeves cut off. On the front is a cartoon of a skateboarder, suspended in the air, flying through a gap that's been cut in a barbed-wire fence. Underneath the picture are the words *Rupture the Linkage.*

"I didn't th-think you'd sh-show," the kid stutters without looking at Ronnie.

She can't help but smile at him.

"I'll assume you're Gabe," she says.

He clenches his teeth and whispers, "You w-want to keep it d-down a little."

Ronnie folds her arms across her chest and says, "What, is it bad form to be seen with an old broad?"

Gabe moves farther down the aisle and she looks around, then follows him.

"Hey, kid," Ronnie says to his back, "you contacted me, remember?"

He turns around and gives a version of a solemn nod.

"First off," she asks, "how'd you get my number? It's unlisted."

"Oh, p-please," he says, as if she's just told him a bad joke, then he smiles and says, "I can't believe you c-c-came."

"I wouldn't have. I almost didn't. You mentioned Flynn."

He nods again and says, "We should p-probably keep moving, you know?"

Ronnie lets out a sigh. "Jesus, you people are born paranoid. How old are you anyway?"

Gabe head-motions her toward a stairway. "C-c'mon," he says, "I don't think anyone's in the b-b-basement."

They descend a narrow black spiral staircase into a low-ceilinged cellar filled with rows of silver aluminum picnic tables. The tables are, in turn, lined with red plastic milk crates that hold runs of old magazines with names like *Wonder Stories*

Quarterly and *Astounding Science-Fiction*. Gabe picks an aisle and starts halfheartedly flipping through the magazines. Ronnie moves next to him and does the same.

"You know, I don't have all day," she says.

"I really ap-appreciate that you came. I didn't think you w-would."

"What about Flynn? You said you had to tell me something about Flynn."

Gabe seems torn, like he needs to talk and at the same time he's bound not to. He takes a breath and blurts out, "Fl-Flynn isn't the one hitting your station, l-lady, okay? It's not him."

Ronnie gives him a forced smile, shrugs, then mutters, "If you say so, kid—"

Gabe interrupts her and says, "L-look, there's a lot of talk down W-W-W—"

"Wireless?" she says.

He nods quickly. "People s-say you were in there last night. People heard the voice, all right? They s-say you left with Flynn—"

"And what if I did?" She cuts him off with the same challenging finality that never fails on *Libido Liveline*.

Gabe moves his head side to side and stammers, "Look, if you're trying to n-n-nail Flynn—"

"Who said that?"

She's got him on the run. And he knows asking to meet her was a bad idea, that he should always clear everything, every goddamn move, through Hazel.

Ronnie lets him hang for just the right amount of time, then turns her body toward him and relaxes her posture a little. She allows a glance at the spiral staircase, lowers her voice, and says, "All right, now calm down. I just want to make a point with you here. You people, you jammers, you seem so sensitive about being judged the wrong way, about how the newspapers write about you, about your goddamn image..."

Gabe is staring up at her trying not to look nervous. Ronnie lets her voice soften a little more. "We meet for the first time, right? And you want me to just take it on faith, on your word, on this teenage-skateboard-punk word, right, that you're all innocent of jamming QSG. That it's the mythical O'Zebedee Brothers who've come back into town and attacked my station. Flynn's got nothing to do with it. He can't control these guys. Doesn't even know who they are —"

"But that's the tr-truth," Gabe says, too loud.

"Quiet down," Ronnie says. "Okay, let's assume it is. Maybe I believe you. Maybe I believed it from Flynn and there was no need for you to even call me..."

She pauses, steps forward, and gives Gabe a soft push to the chest with her fingertips. He thinks she might be teasing him but there's no smile on her face.

Her voice gets even lower and she says, "But you're asking for a lot, kid. You're asking that I believe the words of a bunch of strangers. And you're asking that I believe these particular strangers never lie to each other."

"What's that s-supposed to mean?" Gabe asks.

"It means," Ronnie says, "how the hell do you know that Flynn isn't behind the jams? How do you know Flynn isn't playing O'ZBON? He sure as hell has the equipment and the brains, right?"

"Oh, c-c'mon," Gabe says, shaking his head.

"Yeah, fine," Ronnie says, giving an annoyed smile. "You're convinced. To doubt each other means the whole thing starts to fall apart. But this is what pisses me off, kid. Like I just said, maybe I really do believe Flynn. And beyond that, maybe I don't care whether it's him or not. No one's jamming *my* show. Whoever it is keeps hitting Ray Todd, the station scumbag. I think it's a riot, okay?"

"Then what's the pr-problem?"

"The problem," Ronnie says, "is that you're all presumptuous bastards. You get hold of my phone number somehow. You call me up at the crack of dawn. You ask me to meet you here on Venus, right? And I show up like an idiot. And you want to ask me to lay off big daddy Flynn, the fat wallet behind the whole Wireless cult—"

"It's not a ca-ca-cult."

"Shut up for a second and let me finish. I understand. Flynn's the center cog. Flynn's the one you need to keep it going. He does all the favors. He wipes all the noses and gives all the pep talks. He's the voice of reason. I can see it. He's slick. I like the guy. A lot."

She pauses for Gabe to say something. He seems to think for a second, to weigh something. Then he says, "You d-don't know how it is. W-Wireless is deeper than you think, all right? It's like, not everyone is at the sa-same level. There are different, I don't know, sa-sa-circles. Different groups. Things are ch-changing. We've g-got... W-w-we..."

He seems to be having some problem choosing his words. "We've got d-d-different people supplying different info to different groups. There's a lot of fighting right now, okay? There are these hackers who aren't exactly inside yet. They keep spreading rumors. And no one knows for sure, but everyone feels like something b-big is coming at us."

"The problem is," Ronnie says, speaking slowly, "I don't like you assuming *I'm* the enemy. For people so concerned with image, you're pretty careless how you look at others—"

"Nobody na-knows I ca-called you. I da-did it myself. They'd be ba-ba-bullshit."

"I don't like you assuming I'm some sleazy errand boy who'd rat out you people for the employer. I don't like you assuming I'd play up to Flynn just to find out his secrets and turn him in. I think it sucks. You don't like the accusations coming your way, but you've got no problem asking me down here to call me a liar and a phony and an informer—"

"N-n-no. No wa-way. That wa-wasn't—"

"You piss me off, you know that?"

"La-la-look, I da-didn't ma-mean—"

"You're over your goddamn head, junior. I'm the last person in the world you should get angry."

"Pa-pa-please," he says, and he sounds sufficiently contrite, so Ronnie stops and breathes and looks him up and down.

After an awkward minute, Gabe says, "I da-didn't know what to do. Everybody's so ta-tense. I didn't want Fa-Fa-Fa..." and he trails off.

"Yes," she prods.

Gabe shrugs. "I don't want to la-lose Flynn," he says, and turns back to the magazines.

Ronnie stares at him a second longer, then turns to the bin in front of her and slowly starts to flip through the old pulps.

"How old are you, Gabe?" she asks.

"Fa-Fa-Fifteen," he says without looking up.

There's a few seconds of silence, then Ronnie says, "I'm not some cop for QSG, I swear to you."

Gabe nods and says, "And Fa-Flynn isn't the one hitting the st-station."

Ronnie raises her eyebrows and suddenly, without thinking, gives Gabe a playful punch on the arm.

"The thing is," she says, "we both have to take it on faith."

18.

The Anarchy Museum was the brainchild of a Canal Zone artist and radio freak known only as Throttle who has since disappeared. It's housed in what once passed for a workers' lunch room on the second floor of Wireless. It's in the rear of the building, partitioned from a storeroom loaded with liquor cases and broken radio housings that Ferrie can't bear to part with. The Anarchy Museum was completely underwritten by G.T. Flynn.

The permanent exhibit is a half-finished mishmash. No one knows what Throttle's final plan for the museum was and so it's left in this half-completed state, waiting for his unlikely return. The room is filled with what the creator termed evidence of disorder, turmoil, lawlessness, and general chaos. The brick walls are hung with caricatures of terrorists, of both the political and the artistic kind. There are display cases filled with broken china soup tureens that contain the black ashes of the King James Bible, the compact edition of *The Oxford English Dictionary, Robert's Rules of Order, Black's Law Dictionary, Hoyle's Rules of Games,* and *A Layman's Guide to F.C.C. Regulation,* by Brink Johnson.

And there's an enormous, spinnable Wheel of Chance mounted on a sidewall, a big wooden roulette-style wheel that makes that nervous ticking sound whenever anyone gives it a spin. Flynn

166

paid a carnival barker a ridiculous sum of money for the thing, then scratched the roof of the Saab transporting it to the club.

These days, the jammers are the only ones who go into the museum. They've claimed it as an unofficial clubhouse. Lately the room has seen nothing but loud and spiteful feuding. Flynn thinks he can change that this morning. He's whistling as he walks into the Anarchy Museum, carrying two dozen fresh Danish from the best bakery in town. He realizes he should bring a more sober tone to these proceedings, act semidour and contemplative. But he feels like he's ten years younger and six inches taller. He's wearing his favorite gray-pin double-breasted suit and the new Bally loafers. He spent the morning at the barber's, then stopped by the florist on his way to the meeting. He had a dozen roses sent to Ronnie with a card that read: *To Lulu, With Love, Sir Syd.*

He thinks it's possible his upbeat attitude could be helpful, that his general demeanor could be more harmonizing than any speech he could make. Isn't it always best to lead by example? He could just let them all take in his mood, drink it up. He could get a firm arm around Wallace's shoulder, another around Hazel's, bear-hug them into understanding, walk them a full, bouncing circle around the museum like some choreographed trio from a forties movie—*For Christ's sake, people, look how sweet life can be. Twenty-four hours back, I'm busting my hump like everyone else, kissing surly ass and hawking policies no one wants to buy. And then, bang—the voice of my dreams takes me waltzing in the fog at the top of the city...*

No, he can't get too specific about things. He can't actually tell about Ronnie. Not yet. The general mood is enough. It's simple. Just let them know that joy is still possible in this life.

But now, looking at their faces, divided into two distinct sections on opposite sides of the room, he's almost deflated. He picks out Wallace Browning's face and their eyes meet. Wallace looks like a mess, his face gone a papery shade of gray, his eyes narrowed to veiny slits. But in classic Wallace fashion, he doesn't want Olga's accident discussed in public. So Flynn will abide by his wishes and not say a word in front of the others.

Flynn's eyes appraise the rest of the sullen crowd. He wants to walk back outside, yell over his shoulder, *I'm part of something else now.* They're both pathetic, he thinks. Both camps. Wallace and the old boys, chauvinists, know-it-alls, segregationists. And Hazel and her New Wave brats, cold, more and more humorless, superior in their imagined decadence. Does this always have to happen when a movement grows? When a family gets larger?

The museum is filled with smoke, cigars from Wallace and company, imported Gitanes, and maybe a joint or two from the kids. Ferrie and Most wouldn't appreciate this. But Flynn won't mention it. Why start things off more negative than they already are? In a sense, this is just another sales call, and the emphasis has to be upbeat. He has to keep his voice full of possibility and enjoyment. Unfortunately, Flynn's coming down with the sales-man's worst enemy. He's losing faith in his product. And he's losing his ability to hide that fact.

There's only one fallback when this happens: let the words take over. Just keep talking until something comes to you. Let your subconscious steer you toward a current you can't yet see.

So Flynn brings his hands together in an air-snapping crack that's made louder by the acoustics of the old factory and jolts both groups from their muttering daydreams.

"Okay," he almost hollers, tossing his suit jacket over the arm of a bronze Madonna clothed in jungle fatigues. He's all motion, kinetic energy. He loosens his tie and unfastens the collar button of his shirt, then starts to roll up his sleeves like an aggressive seminar leader about to kick off a weekend course in some new self-help discipline.

He picks a point midway between both groups, a show of impartiality. He puts his hands on his hips, turns his head slowly from side to side, letting the crowd think he's surveying them, picking out faces and doing obscure calculations in his brain. He wishes he had a long-handled microphone to hold onto, make pointing motions with.

"First of all," he starts, "I want to thank each one of you for agreeing to come here today. I know in some cases it meant missing work. And I think that just shows how committed we all feel to our little family here. And I use the word *family*." He pauses, nods, raises his voice. "Family, that's right. I see your faces. Some of you don't like my terminology..."

He pivots on one foot, lets his body sway loosely from side to side, then actually turns his back on them, hoping he's taking the right tack. He sucks in a huge pocket of air, then screams out, top of his lungs, "Well, tough shit."

He comes back around, catches the shocked faces. He's won at least some minimal ground, a momentary advantage. The thing now is to capitalize on it. They were all expecting Mr. Conciliatory, all appeasement and pleadings. He knew going in that the whole thing would be dead in five minutes if he came out soft and begged for compromise. He's got to slap their faces and appeal strictly to the fear that brought them to Wireless in the first place, the chronic terror that they just don't belong to something. He's got to threaten them with breakdown, with the total dismantling of this thin subculture, make them flash on a previous life void of connections and a shared purpose.

And the first volley looks like it's worked. Wallace's gang looks white, like small pains are starting in their barreled chests and they all forgot their nitro medicine back at the house. Hazel's clique suddenly seems younger, like stunned children blasted by the first stinging lick of a fire hose.

"You heard me."

He lets his volume drop a bit. He's learned from studying the cable preachers that continuous shouting loses its effectiveness within the first five minutes. "Every one of you heard me, goddamn it. I'm here today for one reason. To let off a little personal steam before I walk. You are all a bunch of spoiled goddamn little brats who should have your asses kicked red by the real world.

"You know what I'm thinking? I'm thinking that, regardless of your age"—a look to Wallace—"you really don't have a clue

what you've involved yourselves in here. It's an old story,
people. You don't miss it till it's gone. And then it's too late.
When I use the word *family,* I couldn't be more exact in my
thoughts. I use it after much thought. After sitting up alone all
night in my office wondering what I can say to all of you,
wondering how I can save something that I've given my heart
and soul to, given all my goddamn faith to."

Hazel opens her mouth to speak and he jumps over to
her. "You shut up right now," he yells. "This is my shot. When
I leave, you bastards can bitch at each other all you want."

He spots a visual aid next to Hazel, reaches down, and pulls
Gabe up to his feet. The kid is about fifteen, sixteen years old, all
birdlike hair and acne, awkward bones, embarrassed by his own
presence.

Flynn throws an arm across Gabe's shoulder. He can feel the
boy shaking.

"Look here. Our newest family member. Well, we've set a
fine example, haven't we? We've just convinced this one how
understanding and accepting we can be, right? How we take care
of our own? How we work it out inside? Yeah, nice goddamn
job. Should be real proud."

He gives Gabe a shove back toward his seat and starts to
pace between the two camps.

"You know, people, we weren't the first jammers in the
world"—again, a disappointed eye for Wallace, who flinches and
stares down at the floor—"not by a long shot. And most likely,
we won't be the last. So maybe in some larger scheme of things,
we just won't matter that much. That's probably the case. That's
the thing we all seem to fear, try to keep hidden. That's the big
goddamn secret, right? That in the end, we just don't matter.

"I think every one of us ends up here for the same reason.
Fine. Argue with me till one of us drops. My mind is made up.
We all end up here because we're lacking something. Because we
want to belong to something. You know, you could jam in the
privacy of your own home, down in your basement, up in your
attic. Maybe you could get up on top of one of the big hills in

your car. Stay mobile. But it doesn't work out that way. We all end up here. 'Cause we want to be together. 'Cause whether we admit it to ourselves or not, we feel better when we're with each other.

"Have you checked out how cold it is out there lately? Or have you been too busy fighting with each other? Huh? I'm going to say this once. Simple declarative sentence. It's the only truth I know these days. So consider yourself warned. You don't want to listen to me—the hell with you. You don't care enough to save this thing—screw it. Let it fall apart. Here's the sentence: *All we've got is each other.* There you go. You think differently, you're nuts. I know the truth. You've all lost sight of the reasons you came here in the first place. And you're going to pay for that unless you wake up fast."

He pauses, looks down, puts hands in pockets, lets the voice start to come back just a hair toward friendly. "There is nothing here that can't be worked out. There are no problems that cannot be mediated. I'm willing to be the middleman. I'm willing to be the sounding board. For God's sake, use me."

He looks up. They all know the speech is over, but no one knows what to say. He stares at the faces, egging them toward a comment, baiting them with a smirk that gives off more sadness than self-satisfaction. And that's why he knows none of them will bite. He lets the silence build for a second before he pulls his jacket from the Madonna's arm, then he raises his hand toward his head, gives something like a weary salute, and turns to the exit.

He gets about five steps and Hazel lets out, "Okay. All right. You've made your point."

He turns, stares at her.

She shrugs and says, "So what now?"

"That's not up to me," he says, not wanting to cash in too early, almost believing in his own willingness to walk out the door.

"Let's say we're willing to agree to make an effort. To open some discussions and see where it leads."

"That's a start," he says, giving some approval with a nod.

"I thought that's what we came here for in the first place."

It comes from Wallace. Flynn would have bet at the start that it would be Wallace, good old mentor, last of the old regime, the dwarf with the vision, who'd give him a problem.

Flynn rolls with it. He says, "Then let's not waste any more time."

He redeposits the jacket on the arm, and establishes a new position sitting down on an abandoned old RCA TV, a big cherry cabinet model. The picture tube has been removed and someone has built a diorama inside—a stunning scene of natural disaster, a mud slide drowning a tiny town.

Flynn folds his hands in his lap and tries for a second wind.

"Now, the way I see it is we've got two opposing philosophies. Let's start off by agreeing that there's nothing wrong with this. It's healthy, good for the whole body. Keeps us on our toes, keeps the blood flowing through the brain. I think we have to look at this almost from an Eastern perspective. Yin and Yang. A balance. Personally, I don't see a problem."

He runs his hand through his hair, thinks for a second, and gives up a risky smile toward Hazel.

"The *problem*," emphasizing the word, "comes when we start to translate a philosophy from the head to the street, so to speak. When words become actions. Which, correct me if I'm wrong here, is what Hazel and her people would like to do."

He pauses to give a chance for objection.

"I think Hazel would like to see some evolution. We've spent some time at the bar together and I don't think I'm out of line saying that she smells some stagnation within the family. And this bothers her a great deal since the reason she became involved at the start was for the charge, the rush, you know, the thrill of being on the other side of the fence. But I shouldn't speak for her. I'm putting words in her mouth. Hazel, just tell me, tell us, if you could, okay, why you first wandered into Wireless."

She's not prepared and Flynn knows it. It disarms her a little and all she can do is take the question on, try for a straightforward answer.

"Jesus, I don't, uh—"

Flynn jumps into the breach. "Repeat what you said last week. Remember when we were talking last week? Back near the pool tables?"

"Well, I, uh—"

"She said, 'I hooked up with you people 'cause I thought you knew the truth.' Right, Hazel?"

She gives this confused nod.

"And I asked her what the truth was, 'cause let's admit it, I'm a little dim sometimes. And she said, 'You see that their idea of order is just an illusion—"

Hazel interrupts with, "I said 'just bullshit.' Their idea of order is just bullshit."

"Okay, my mistake, like I said." He taps his forehead with his index finger. "Now, Wallace—" he shifts his behind slightly on the set until he's angled toward the old boys—"what I want to ask you is, is there anything about that statement you disagree with?"

Wallace is silent, sucking nervously on a fat stogie.

Flynn continues before the lack of a response can seem like a challenge.

"You, Wallace, my mentor, the guy who charted my course from day one, the guy who showed me how to take apart and put back together my first mail-away crystal set."

He slides off the RCA, shuffles over to Wallace while nodding to himself, and places a hand on the dwarf's shoulder while grinning over at Hazel.

In a lowered voice: "The man who once said to a very green prankster, 'The problem is there's no logic or order to anything and everyone wants you to believe that there is.'"

Pause.

"Do you remember saying that, Wallace? One spring night, about twenty years back, I'd run from Galilee for the tenth time. We met in an aisle at that old store on Hollis—University Radio.

We got to talking. And you brought me back to DeForest Road. You and your wife, Olga, showed some kindness to a kid without a home. Had him to dinner. She served Swedish meatballs, Wallace. The radio was tuned to old WSTR all through the meal. You were wearing a maroon sweater vest. You remember any of that, Wallace? Because I do. I remember every second of that dinner. Of that whole night. 'Cause my life changed that night, my friend."

He tries to be casual as he takes his hand from Wallace's shoulder and starts his stroll across the room toward the opposite team. He comes to a stop in front of Hazel, extends his two hands palms-up. She flinches, looks quickly at the person next to her, and, not knowing what else to do, puts her hands in his. He continues to talk in the same deep, self-loving voice of a professional storyteller.

"That night, the wonderful Swedish meatball dinner, the spätzle, the coffee afterward, and your words, Wallace," though he's staring into Hazel's eyes, "especially your words. That was what was going through my mind three years ago. Back on the day I found a young woman, a little scared, rabbity, outside in the parking lot, trying to figure out how to go inside, what to say to Tjun at the door. She was a runaway. Remember that, Hazel? Remember the dinner I got you down at the Rib Room? I do. You had the chili and three plates of soda bread just out of the oven. And milk. It was pouring that night. You remember sleeping on my couch? I played you some old Bob and Ray tapes? Right?"

He drops his hands, steps back, says to the crowd in general, "Anybody see a little pattern there? Huh?"

He goes back to the RCA and takes a seat.

"Okay," in a semirelaxed voice, "here's the problem. I don't want to lose my family. Pretty simply put, right? I'm not going to debate ideology. I'm not interested enough. I want one thing. I want to hold on to my past"—a hand gestures to Wallace—"and my future"—open palm out toward Hazel.

"So, you tell me, folks. Somebody find the balls to tell me.

How do I do that? How do I hold on to a family that doesn't want to exist anymore? 'Cause I'm owed at least that. I've held up my end. If you were part of *this place,*" voice rising to a yell and hand slapping down on top of the TV, "I gave you anything you asked for. Money. Time. Advice. More than one of you called me after midnight for bail. More than one of you have keys to my car in your pockets right now. If you decided you belonged here, that was enough for me.

"So, somebody tell me how I make it last."

He folds his arms across his chest and waits for a response.

Hazel takes a breath that everyone can hear and says, "Look, I'm not looking to break things up. It's just that some of us feel it's time to advance a little—"

"That means blowing up transmitters," Wallace yells.

"Hey," Flynn yells back, and points at him with his index finger like an annoyed traffic cop.

"You fucking hypocrite," Hazel yells. "There's not that big a jump between jamming the signal and dynamiting the tower."

"What we do is a joke," Wallace says, standing up. "It's for amusement. It's spirited mischievousness. What you want to do is terrorism."

"Stop it now," Flynn says, getting up to move between them.

"You're a joker, all right, you little freak—"

"You're street trash. I knew it the second I saw you—"

"Yeah, call the goddamn cops, you old fart. They'll cuff us together—"

"This is not a political gang. Why don't you and the rest of your uneducated ilk take your act down to South America and leave us—"

"What this group is or isn't doesn't get decided by you—"

"Dynamiting transmitters, vandalizing relay stations. This is ridiculous—"

Flynn stops the screaming with a reflex action, the only thing that occurs to him in the moment. He grabs a firecracker from his pants pocket, lights it behind his back, and tosses it onto the floor between them. The bang is given a boost by the size of the room. There's a scream from both parties and Hazel and Wallace are left dazed and crouching near the ground, backs turned to each other.

Flynn sits impassively with his head cocked down near his left shoulder.

Ferrie comes running up the stairs, yelling, "What the hell's the story?" in a cracked, high voice.

Flynn walks over to him, waving blue smoke out of his face. He claps Ferrie on the back, smiles, and says, "Just a little family argument. Nothing to worry about."

19.

Quinsigamond City Hall is a four-story rectangle of gray granite that stretches two hundred feet down the heart of Main Street. Its central entryway consists of an enclosed portico carved into an arch and capped by a two-hundred-foot Florentine tower that houses a huge and ornate eye-of-God clock and culminates in an open-air balcony.

Hannah stands on the first step of the enormous curving baroque staircase that leads to the City Council chambers. It's noon, but the street is practically deserted. In the glare that breaks through the cloud cover, Hannah can make out the enormous marble eagle that perches on the knob of the balcony's roof as if watching over the city. She can remember her father bringing her to City Hall when she was young, maybe to pay a tax bill, maybe to get a birth certificate. When they exited the building, he turned his daughter around and began to point things out—the red tile of the hip roof, the fanged gargoyles carved into the granite at each corner. He pointed out the balcony and began the story of Isaiah Timmons or Tomkins—what the hell was his name?—the first printer in America, how he stood on that balcony in July of 1776 and screamed out the Declaration of Independence for the crowd gathered below. But Hannah couldn't concentrate on the story of the rebel printer. Instead, she stared at the carved eagle at the top of the building, impressed by how lifelike it looked, and beyond that, how frightening it seemed, not really like an eagle at all, but more like a vulture, a bird of prey. It seemed as if the bird were perpetually looking out over the city for a new victim, an easy mark, a fresh carcass to swoop down on and cleave meat from bone.

And now, looking up at the marble bird almost twenty years later, Hannah still has this feeling. So she zips up her jacket and runs up the curve of the stairs.

Inside, the building is all quartered oak and mahogany. The ceilings are ridiculously high and the halls are lined with oversized oil portraits of the long line of Quinsigamond's mayors, each framed in heavy gilt. She wonders if this environment has any effect on the people who work in the city's offices each day. Would it give you a constant sense of history, of the progression of events that have shaped your home? Or do you quickly become immune to the out-of-date grandeur? Or is there another possible effect, a subconscious depression that results in watching decay chew on this structure with unbearable patience and persistence day after day?

The City Council chambers are on the third floor. Hannah opens a rear door and takes a seat on the last wooden bench just as Mayor Welby begins to call the meeting to order. It's not the normal time for a council meeting. The mayor's office announced the session yesterday morning with a brief press release sent to the *Spy*. It was a short statement informing "all concerned parties" that the matter of "unlicensed radio disruptions" would be addressed at an unscheduled session. Hannah, like the rest of the department, saw it as a grandstand play to appease the station owners and she had little intention of even reading the *Spy*'s coverage, let alone attending, until she got the message on her answering machine.

She can't imagine why G.T. Flynn would ask to meet her here. But she knows Flynn was connected to Lenore and that's enough to bring her downtown.

The room is packed. Welby is in position behind his raised

walnut desk, something like a judge's bench, which makes him tower over the city manager and the rest of the council. Though she doesn't make a hobby of studying local politics, Hannah has a native's grasp of the back-room alliances and infighting. Welby has Counselors Krieger and Lotman on his side and in his pocket respectively. Donaghue, Pfeil, and Campana line up with City Manager Kenner. And, at the moment anyway, the rest—Frye, Searle, Altier, Jardine, and Kurahashi—are in perpetual motion, always playing one side off the other, cutting deals and bartering votes as if the business of running the city were a never-ending swap meet.

The local cable access station has two television cameras mounted on small parapets at opposite sides of the chamber. The camera crew look like scruffy kids, fooling with their headsets and cranking knobs below their monitors, testing the focus on each of the councillors, who all seem to be leaning dangerously back in their seats and simultaneously using a hand to blanket their microphones as they whisper to their neighbors and make odd, squinty expressions.

Someone touches Hannah's shoulder and she flinches and turns to see a dark-haired guy who she'd nail at about thirty-five years, 165 pounds, maybe five eleven, with no visible facial markings.

It's G.T. Flynn. He's dressed in a deep gray double-breasted suit with a starched white shirt and a red-patterned tie knotted so tight at the neck that Hannah thinks he should be gasping. But gasping, she knows, is not Flynn's style.

She met him once before, about two years back. She was having lunch with Lenore at the Rib Room down in the Zone. Flynn slid into their booth with a run of smooth greetings and Hannah almost choked on her chicken salad to see Lenore actually stammer back her response. She thinks he was dropping off some insurance papers, maybe a life policy—she vaguely remembers some mention of Lenore's brother, Ike, as a beneficiary. Then he was gone, his exit as slick and abrupt as his entrance. It wasn't until they'd paid the check and were back on Rimbaud Way that Hannah asked her partner about Flynn.

Lenore said, "He's just a guy I know," in that definitive tone that sealed the topic forever. G.T. Flynn was never brought up again.

Now, he smiles and eye-motions for Hannah to slide in. She does and he takes a seat next to her, squeezed in, their thighs touching.

He leans back to her ear and says, "Thanks for coming," then sits forward and turns his attention to the meeting.

Hannah's not sure what to do. She has no desire to sit through a boring council meeting in order to find out what this guy wants. But there's a feeling that she may have to play things his way to satisfy her curiosity. She decides to sit back for ten minutes and see what develops.

Reverend Cotton of the Episcopal Church has his bald head bowed and his eyes squeezed shut and his hands clasped to his chest as he stands before the speaker's microphone and intones an invocation. The majority of the councillors look respectfully bored, except for Yuko Kurahashi. She's hunched over the conference table making notes on a legal pad, clearly annoyed with the traditional prayer that Welby refuses to eliminate despite her threats of court action.

The audience gathered on the benches behind a partitioning guardrail seems anxious to get things rolling. There are more suits and ties in the crowd than normal, but then, Hannah reminds herself, this isn't a normal meeting. These must be the station owners and managers, waiting to hear what the city is going to do to protect their interests.

As if on cue, Mayor Welby bends the accordion stem of his microphone until his lips almost touch the surface. He looks out over the council and the audience, then, ever the pro, locks his eyes on the TV camera with the red light on top, takes a deep breath, and says, in his slightly nasal but still-powerful baritone, "My fellow councillors, City Manager Kenner, our in-chamber audience, and all our city's taxpayers, I thank you for joining us tonight on such short notice. I've asked you all here to address the recent onslaught of the unlicensed and illegal disruption, or jamming, to use the current terminology, that has plagued many of our local radio broadcasters."

He pauses and picks his bifocals up off his desktop, slides them onto the tip of his nose, picks up a sheet of paper, and reads, in a more halting tone, "First and foremost, I want to assure everyone watching tonight that the Mayor's Office and the City Council and the local law enforcement agencies have been actively pursuing any and all avenues to end these disruptions, and any statement to the contrary is both untrue and provocative."

He drops the paper and takes a second to glower down at the audience. Hannah knows this is a reply to charges in yesterday's *Spy* that Welby was taking the jamming incidents lightly. Charles Federman, the owner of WQSG, had gone so far as to call Welby a "bought and paid-for hack."

Welby pulls his glasses off and seems to toss them down, emphasizing his annoyance. His voice raises slightly. "I want it made absolutely clear, right here and now, that my office will not tolerate this behavior. I've been in daily contact with Chief Bendix and the unit he's assigned to investigate these incidents. We've requested the necessary equipment needed to track the broadcasts and we're waiting to coordinate with an agent from the FCC."

The voice gets just a bit louder, more belligerent. "And if the private sector has any suggestions for further action, we welcome them with open ears."

Flynn leans into Hannah's side and whispers, "Here we go."

She turns to look at him but he's riveted on the speaker's microphone as a tall, bulky man with enormous shoulders walks to it. The guy's got a head of gray stubble and his face is shaved military-close to reveal red, almost-scarlet cheeks beneath a Nixonesque nose lined with a deep purple web of veins. He's wearing a navy suit and a maroon silk tie. And though he has the immediate bearing of a man who's never been infected with self-doubt, his forehead is gleaming with a wash of sweat.

He stands as if a steel pole has been attached to his spine, his hands clasped together behind his back, his legs spread slightly apart. He begins his oration as if in midspeech, voice already booming, making the sound system ring now and then.

"Our mayor has the standard politician's talent for soliloquy. But this is real life, not the debate club, and every day that goes by costs me money and the confidence of my advertisers. And I simply do not understand why this should be such a problem. Mr. Mayor, Councillors, you have a suspicious fire, you round up known arsonists. You have unlicensed radio transmissions, you round up the radio freaks. Is there an error in my thinking that you could point out to me, Mayor Welby?"

The bulk of the audience bursts out in spontaneous applause, fellow station owners, normally competitors, tonight ready to back their unofficial spokesman, Charles Federman.

Welby begins to bash away at his desktop with his gavel, saying, "I'd ask the viewing audience to control itself, please."

He says the word *please* like every harried schoolteacher Hannah has ever known. And it dawns on her, the way it must have just dawned on the mayor, that though he called this meeting to defuse an image problem, he could end up more sullied than vindicated. Charles Federman isn't Louis Lotman, cowed with a fast, harsh word or the threat of a review board. Federman is the real thing, a business animal with an instinct for determining weakness and manipulating image. Welby is going to have to scramble to turn this thing around.

And he does exactly the right thing. He dilutes the blame hanging in the air by calling up Chief Bendix and asking, with a bureaucrat's practiced weariness, to explain to the loud but ill-informed Mr. Federman the definition of "probable cause" and the difficulty of warrant attainment.

★　　★　　★

As the chief starts to speak in a raspy drone, Flynn slouches down a bit and says softly, "Do you remember me? We met down the Zone once? You were with Lenore Thomas."

Hannah says, "I remember you," in a noncommittal voice and continues to look at Bendix's neck as it bulges against his shirt collar.

"I was wondering," Flynn says, then hesitates and Hannah reads it as calculated. He swallows and starts again, "I was curious if you ever hear from Lenore anymore?"

She turns and gives him a look that she hopes says, *Cut the shit, pal.*

"Lenore moved away," she says. "As far as I know, she's never been back to the city."

"Not even to see her brother?"

Hannah's annoyed at the question. She says, "Why don't you ask Ike?"

Flynn nods, rubs a hand over his jaw, changes direction. "Look," he says, "I'm sorry if it was inconvenient for you to come down here. I didn't want to miss this meeting and I thought this might be a good place to get together."

"Nice and public," Hannah says. "Neutral territory."

His voice drops to a whisper. "Look, I don't know what you thought I—"

She interrupts, "*You* look, pal. I don't know what was between you and Lenore. But number one, I haven't heard from her. You want to get a message to her, you'll have to find someone else. And number two, I'll decide who I share information with—"

Now he interrupts, looking down at the bench beyond her as he speaks through semiclenched teeth. "Hey, Officer, I didn't come here to antagonize you, all right? I thought there might be some way we could help each other. There might be a few things we have in common."

Get up and leave, Hannah thinks. *Just get up and slide past him and go out the door.* But instinct keeps her seated. That and the mention of Lenore. *Everything keeps coming back to Lenore. It's like*

a bad Frankenstein movie: Lenore, the head-case scientist. And Hannah,
the misunderstood monster. But there's a twist to this new version of the
story. Lenore didn't take her body parts from fresh graves. She supplied
them herself. So, of course, the project was doomed from the start. The
more of herself that Lenore gave away, the more Lenore disappeared.
And when the creator did finally, literally vanish, the creation was left
incomplete.

Down on the chamber floor, Bendix is relinquishing the
public microphone to a walleyed little man who identifies himself as "Dr. Pasqual DeMango, tenured professor of postmodern
performance arts at St. Ignatius College."

The guy is dressed in this antique forest-green suede sports
coat with deep green leather elbow patches, a heavy, thick-
ribbed, cherry-red turtleneck sweater, black wool pants, and
unlaced Keds high-top sneakers. He has a broad nose that
dominates his face and a shock of jet-black wiry hair that shoots
over the top of his head and plunges down the opposite slope like
a frozen wave.

He touches the microphone hesitantly, as if testing to see if
he'll get a shock, but before he can speak, the mayor's assistant,
Mrs. Gilbert, rises to the mayor's mike and announces that since
the professor did not sign in with her prior to the invocation, the
rules of the council will not allow for his address. A wave of
audible dissension spreads through the room and immediately
the city manager, Maud Kenner, starts to make a statement,
without the benefit of her mike, about "high-handed nonsense,"
and someone else, Hannah can't tell who, calls out for a suspen-
sion of the rules.

And Welby goes into his gavel-banging mode.

Flynn touches Hannah's arm.

"Lenore and I had a mutual friend," he says.

Hannah gives him a shrug.

"A girl, a young woman, excuse me. Hung around the
Canal Zone. Hung with the punks down Rimbaud."

"She have a name?" Hannah asks.

"Her name's Hazel," Flynn says. "You know her?"

"Oh yeah," Hannah says, shaking her head and smiling. "I know Hazel."

Flynn takes a breath and says, "Lenore used to sort of check up on Hazel for me. You know what I'm saying? She used to keep me informed."

Hannah looks him in the eye and says, "And what did you do for Lenore?"

There's a long moment as they stare at each other until Flynn decides it's a standoff and says, "I took care of her business affairs. That's what I do for a living."

The council votes to allow DeMango to speak and the audience again begins to applaud, but their clapping dies out immediately as the professor, without any preamble, launches into a tirade against "a tyrannical and oppressive licensing system" and "the monopoly of the sound waves by fascist radio barons."

The radio people in the audience switch at once to a chorus of booing and catcalls as DeMango shakes a fist toward them and yells that the jamming incidents "represent a new and barely explored art form, and as such, should be given all possible tolerance."

At this suggestion, Charles Federman rises to his feet and begins calling for the microphone. DeMango pivots away from the council to face down Federman and screams, "To deny the new frequency poets their voice, to silence the visionary fever of this new wave of artists and thinkers, is tantamount to denying our cultural future."

Welby signals for the council police and DeMango grasps the microphone with both hands and rants, "You don't understand. This is a cutting-edge art form. Your attempts to infiltrate and crush the jammers are a walk down the road to barbarism and stagnation and—"

The rest of his words go unheard as two officers pull him

away from the mike and lead him, twisting and jerking, out of the chambers. Federman then grabs the mike, turns to Welby, and calls him a "monkey-boy with a pension." The chamber erupts with angry voices trying to yell over one another. And then the whole room is blasted by screeching feedback that seems to be coming from the cable TV equipment. The cable technicians tear their headsets off and cover their ears with their hands. Welby is up out of his seat, yelling at Bendix to get some cops in here. Maud Kenner is pounding on the council table with a flat palm.

Someone uncouples two electrical cables and the feedback ends. But the yelling and cursing continue. Federman's mouth is outlined with spittle. He's screaming, "Let go of me, Vinnie," to a small, round assistant who's trying to restrain him. Everyone's out of their seats and Hannah thinks punches could be thrown at any second.

Flynn says, "You want to get out of here?" and Hannah nods and follows him out of the chamber.

They don't talk till they're out on Main Street, standing in the shadow thrown by City Hall.

Flynn is lightly touching his left ear with his index finger.

"Jesus," he says, "I'm sorry I asked you down here."

Hannah ignores the apology. She's not sure what to feel about this guy and wonders how much that has to do with his connection to Lenore.

"Really, I'm sorry about this," Flynn says again, seeming genuinely flustered. "Would you like to go get a—"

Hannah cuts him off with a shake of her head. She starts to walk backward in the direction of her Mustang. After a couple steps she pauses and says, "I'll check up on Hazel. I'll call you in a couple days."

Flynn seems to be unsure what to say. After a few seconds he says, "Okay, I'm in the book."

She looks him up and down, from the pricy haircut to the imported loafers. And suddenly she's wondering if Lenore slept with this guy, and if maybe he was that one concealed, unspoken lover that she let her guard down for.

"I'm sure I can find you," Hannah says, then turns and starts to walk.

She knows he's still standing there, looking at her back, watching her walk. Or maybe she's feeling the eyes of the big marble vulture, resting up on the roof of City Hall, nested and waiting above Quinsigamond, looking down at her and sizing up an abundant meal of surprisingly tender meat.

20.

Ten miles outside of Quinsigamond, on a two-lane stretch on the outskirts of Whitney, Flynn pulls the Saab over onto the shoulder of the road and kills the engine.

Ronnie looks at him for a second, then says, "Well, Scooter, if you want to go parking don't you think we could get a more secluded spot?"

Flynn stares out of the window and says, "Pop the glove box."

"You used to love it when I was a wise-ass. You want a map or something?"

"Binoculars," Flynn says.

She reaches in and underneath a pile of small transistor radios, she touches a miniature pair of rubber sports binoculars. She pulls them out. They're army green and have a brand name, German she thinks, written on the side. She hands them over and Flynn grabs them and brings them up to his eyes without a word.

"A voyeur," she says. "Great. I'm an expert at this."

He hands the glasses over to her and says, "Take a look."

She puts her eyes to the rubber cups, focuses, takes in a large, weathered-shingle farmhouse. The building is three stories high, a mishmash of modified Victorian and French country styles. There's a wraparound porch moating the front entrance

188

and an attached barn off the back. The whole thing sits a good fifty yards back from the road, at the foot of a rising knoll. Planted in a side yard are volleyball nets and mounted on the barn below the hayloft door is a basketball backboard and hoop.

"The third floor is all open," Flynn says.

Ronnie continues to survey the property without responding.

"Like this big loft area. All unpartitioned. At least that's how it was, you know, twenty years ago."

He shifts in his seat. "They had two dozen steel-frame bunk beds. They were set up in rows. Like an army barracks. You had a locker that went underneath. You'd keep all your stuff in there. We'd be lined up alphabetically. We'd do everything alphabetically. Brush our teeth. Line up in the kitchen. Get in the bus. They used to park the bus in the barn. Can you see it?"

She tries to peer into the barn. The double doors are open, but the position of the sun makes it impossible to see anything inside. She shakes her head.

"They probably got rid of it. The thing was dying twenty year ago. This old Harvester monster. Sister Marietta's true love. She was a wizard, drove it like a goddamn tank. Always ready for battle."

Ronnie finally brings the glasses down. "This is where you grew up," she says in a flat, quiet voice.

"This is the place," Flynn says.

Ronnie thinks for a minute, then says, "Do you want to go in?"

He turns his head sideways toward her and squints his eyes like he's in pain. "Are you kidding?"

"Do you drive out here a lot?"

"Not a lot. I mean, what does a lot mean?"

"And you never go in?"

He doesn't answer.

"Do you stay in touch with anyone? Like any of the boys you knew here?"

He gives a slight shake of the head.

"So, why are we here?" she asks.

He opens his mouth, closes it, shrugs.

"You're a fountain of self-knowledge," she says.

He likes this. The easy tease, the playfulness. The throwaway intimacy. He wants to give it back and wishes he were as good at it.

He lets his head fall back onto the rest, keeping his eyes on the farmhouse. "It's a ploy," he says, "I bring all my dates out here. Women are nuts for orphans. Brings out all kinds of sympathies."

"I knew it," Ronnie says. "You reek of ulterior motive."

"Comes in a little bottle. Imported from Europe. Costs me a fortune. It's made from the spleens of just-dead lawyers."

"What about just-dead financial planners?"

"Nothing ulterior about our motives. We're right up front. Sign the check and try not to worry."

She smiles and nods, holds in the laugh. Then she changes the tone of her voice and says, "So, why are we here, Flynn?"

"Jesus, you're good at that," he says. "You could make some coin off that voice."

"So I've been told."

"I don't know. I just keep coming back."

"You know. Do you send money to this place?"

"Almost never."

"Almost never?"

"'I'm like that with money. I've got to beat myself up just to keep from dialing in to the TV preachers with my credit cards."

"Did they abuse you here?"

He makes a face. "It wasn't like that. I got hit in the head with a Bible once. Can't remember what for. Nun came upstairs before bed to apologize."

"Did you let her off the hook?"

"After I sold her a whole life policy."

"And got put on retainer to manage the sisters' savings account. Yeah, yeah, yeah."

"There you go," Flynn says. "You're on to me."

"No, but I'm working on it."

"I'm clear water, Ronnie. You can see right through me. There's not much here, I swear to God."

"Maybe you're not the best judge."

"Maybe there's no big mystery."

"Maybe there's a bunch of little ones. Like why you drive out here. Like why the yuppie biz-master hangs out with radio criminals."

"They're not criminals, Ronnie." An edge comes up in his voice.

"Yeah, well, I'm sorry, Flynn, but technically they are. It's a crime to jam licensed radio broadcasts—"

"And where I sit, it's a goddamn crime that some scumbag racist hatemonger like Ray Todd can fill the airwaves with fascist bullshit—"

"Go buy some licensing, Flynn. Go buy the station. Then pull Todd and pump your own grudges out at the public. That's the way it works. That's the system we've got."

"And if I don't like this particular system?"

"Seems to work well enough when you're hustling life policies and mutual funds."

"I provide a service, Ronnie. I don't put a gun to anyone's head—"

"And there's an off switch on every radio, Flynn. No one makes people listen to Ray Todd."

"There are reasons I do what I do—"

"Right," she says, indicating the farmhouse with a tilt of her head. "But you don't seem to know what they are."

He stops himself from blurting a comeback, waits a beat, then says, "Okay, maybe I'm just one more confused guy."

"And maybe you just don't trust me completely," Ronnie says. "Not yet. And maybe that's a smart move at this point. I can tell already, I'm more instinctual than you—"

"That right?"

"—and I think, maybe, you're sitting in the middle of this

awful paradox. And I think you tie yourself up in knots trying to make things logical."

"Paradox?"

"Yeah," Ronnie says. "I think maybe you've found that, through no fault of your own, by some quirk of nature, okay, the orphan boy moved pretty easily into the heart of the system. He ended up looking the part. The language came easy. He wore clothes well. He had a weird knack for sales and for saying the right words at the right time. He discovered this genius for subliminal manipulation."

"This is me, now, right? This is beautiful—"

"But the lousy thing was—the more Flynn moved into the heart of the system, the more he hated it. So here's the paradox. He stayed there and made good money off this system to finance the people who couldn't fit in. And who wanted to tear it down."

"You think I'm a man of huge responsibilities."

"You know why you hate Ray Todd so much—"

"Who says I hate Ray Todd?"

"It's because people with brains like Ray Todd are absolutely convinced they know what's best. Not only for themselves but for you. And they want to enact the knowledge. They want to make it as unconditional as nature. That's the heart of fascism, G.T. And what you can't stand, whether you know it or not, what you can't bear, is the fact that it's sleeping, to some degree, inside every one of us. It's like as a kid, you never figured that out. Or if you did, you just blocked it out completely."

"That's your take on human nature?" Flynn says. "Were your parents this cynical? Does this run in the genes?"

"I think maybe you come out here 'cause the nuns told you life was different. That if you cut into the human heart you'll find a sleeping Jesus. Not a sleeping fascist. And you want to figure out why they lied to you. And you sit in the car and never go up to the door 'cause you can't stand to finally give up their version."

He doesn't know what to say and this bothers him because

he knows that not speaking, not returning a quick rebuttal, validates what she's said. The car goes silent for a long awkward minute and when he does finally find his voice, it comes out different. There's no edge and no rhythm, no shading of an angry humor. And no sarcasm whatsoever.

He says, "I wish I could take you through that house."

More silence, and then, "There's this old dirt-floor cellar. Classic New England cellar. Mortared rough-stone foundation. Hottest day of summer, that place used to be cool as October."

There's a pause. He rubs his hand at his neck, touches his Adam's apple.

"Most of the others hated the cellar. It was dark. Musty. Shadows everywhere. But I loved it. I loved exactly those things. And way in the back, in the deepest corner of the cellar, was this little shaft area. I don't know, it might have originally been a potato bin or something. But when I was there it was filled with scrap wood. Just random pieces of plank and beams and I remember there was some hacked-up barn board. It was just this big pile of wood. Sat about four feet high. When it rained, when it really poured, the cellar would take in water. You ever smell wet wood? You know that smell? I'll never forget that smell."

He puts his hands on the steering wheel, the classic driving-school grip.

"I used to be missing a lot. The nuns would have something going on and they could never find me. By suppertime I'd show up. To this day no one ever knew where I was hiding. Drove them nuts. Maybe that's why I got hit with the Bible that time."

She watches his hands tighten slightly on the wheel.

"Probably not," he says.

"You were in the wood shaft," Ronnie says, flinching at her own voice.

He nods.

"I was in the wood shaft. I was in that little bin. Every time. I was sitting on top of the pile of wood. Really down in it. Kind of blanketed with scrap wood. It'd be covering my legs."

She gives him a few seconds to go on and when he doesn't, she pushes. "Why were you there?"

"I just wanted to be there. I just wanted to be alone. In the dark."

"What would you do?"

"I'd just sit. And then I'd listen to my own breath. And then I'd catch myself praying."

"Praying?"

"Act of Contrition." His voice breaks a little. She can hear stress in the short phrasing. Something's happening in his throat.

"You thought you'd done something wrong?"

"I must have. To be there. To have no one."

She brings her hand up to the side of his face, touches his cheek, and lets her fingers go into the hair above his ears. She's acting on instinct. She doesn't know what to say.

"That was a long time ago, Flynn," she tries.

His hand goes from the steering wheel to the shift. He pops the car into gear, lets out a staggered breath, and whispers, "Let's get the fuck out of here."

21.

Hazel is walking south on Rimbaud headed for the Rib Room. Hannah lets the Mustang hang a good two car lengths back, keeps her foot off the gas, and pulls to the curb whenever a car comes into the rearview. She takes a full block to study Hazel's walk and decides the girl has a genuine confidence, something innate, beyond a cultivated act. Beyond the sarcastic and impatient lip she uses on all her camp followers.

As they approach the diner, Hannah finds an open meter and parks. She has to jog to reach Hazel before she enters the Rib Room, but she manages to come up beside her and link their arms, just one more pair of lesbian artist punks out for coffee and small talk on a beautiful fall day.

Hazel freezes in place, gives away nothing in the second it takes her to get clear on who's latched onto her arm. Then her eyes tighten and her teeth clench and Hannah can almost hear her brain grinding for the most vicious greeting on file.

Hannah beats her to the punch, leans in and kisses her on the cheek with a rough, wet move, nods her head and puts on a mock smile and says, "Honey, why won't you return my calls?"

Hazel looks over her shoulder to the street and says, "You've just gotten too old for me, you narco bitch. You're really starting to look like that hag you used to hang with."

Hannah grabs some flesh between her thumb and forefinger, gives a pinch and a bruise that will be purple for weeks, and reaches with her free hand for the door. "You'll never change, you little brat. Let's have some espresso. You can show me your new tattoos."

Technically, the Rib Room does not serve lunch. The doors do not officially open until five. But for the past few years, Elmore Orsi has been brewing coffee for the select few who know enough to ignore the pulled shades and *Closed* sign. Usually a half dozen hung-over regulars will huddle in booths and silently browse the morning edition of the *Spy* until the aspirin kicks in and they can stand the thought of heading back out to the studios and clubs.

Hannah marches Hazel down the center aisle, holding her close, even at one point, as they pass Elmore at the cashier's station, pressing her head against Hazel's shoulder. Orsi gives a confused half-laugh, half-cough, and Hannah slides Hazel into a rear booth, then moves in on the same side.

"Jesus, have you gotten pushy," Hazel says, moving away from Hannah, leaning her back against the wall until she's sideways in the booth.

"I've been hearing the same thing about you, love," Hannah says, shrugging out of her suede jacket, exposing her holster and her Magnum.

"You wanted to talk to me, you could've just called."

Hannah gives her a long look through squinted eyes. "You don't have a goddamn residence, Hazel. You live out of a freaking car half the time."

Hazel looks down the aisle to Elmore, motions with her head, and says, "You could've called here."

Hannah reaches past her and takes a plastic menu from a metal-pronged salt and pepper holder.

"What happened to Wireless?" she asks. "They're not

taking your calls anymore? You and the radio freaks have a falling-out?"

Before Hazel can answer, Hannah yells out, too loud, "Can we get two coffees down here, please?"

Hazel rubs a hand hard over her left eye, which Hannah gets a kick out of.

"What is it in me," Hannah says, pretending to study the menu, "that gets such a big kick out of embarrassing you in front of the ultra-hip?"

Hazel doesn't say a word, just gives a bored, unblinking stare. Elmore comes down the aisle carrying two huge white porcelain mugs and a mini silver creamer, all atop a Day-Glo-orange serving tray. He holds the tray up on his fingertips, higher than his shoulders, performing, indulging Hannah with a mime's rendition of stiff, four-star service. He places the mugs in front of the women, positions the creamer between them, adjusts a bar towel over a rigid arm, and gives a solemn, theatrical waist-bow.

Hannah pushes the cream away and says, "You got to love that guy. He could charm the wallet off a dead man."

She takes a sip of the steaming coffee and adds, "So what's good in here? I haven't had Orsi's cooking in ages."

Hazel knows Hannah could hold out all day, keep her penned in the booth and numb her with hours of insulting small talk. So, she breaks easy, gives Hannah her full attention, and says, "Okay, what did I do?"

Hannah matches her new serious tone and says, "You tell me, little sister."

"I'm not your sister, Hannah. I honestly don't know what the Christ you want. Why don't you tell me and we can both get on with the day."

"Why don't you relax?" Hannah says, her voice slowing down and lowering to a level that makes Hazel buck a little. "If I want to sit here with you from now until summer, honey, that's exactly what we'll fucking do. And if I want to talk about goddamn makeup tips, that's exactly what we'll fucking discuss."

She reaches over, puts a hand on Hazel's leg just above the kneecap, and gives a long, hard squeeze. Hazel stays silent and motionless, but an ache starts up, not in her leg, but at the very back of her throat, a childhood kind of burning ache, more a prelude to tears than pain. Finally, she blinks a few times, looks into Hannah's eyes, and nods slightly.

Hannah lets go of her leg and shifts herself closer to Hazel. She starts to talk in a whisper, so intense and heavy with breath that Hazel starts to think she's going to draw the gun and pull back the hammer.

Instead she says, "Don't you ever, ever give me any attitude, Hazel."

Hazel nods again.

Hannah's nostrils expand as she exhales and she repeats, "I mean fucking never."

Hazel's nod increases in speed and Hannah continues.

"I've been hearing that you've been growing some balls since the last time we spoke. And that's fine. That's great. I kind of get a kick out of it, the thought of you putting some fear into the dorkwhites down here in the Zone. You want to terrorize your radio dinks, I think it's a riot."

She picks up Hazel's mug and takes a sip.

"But you never forget, from now till the day you fucking die, sister, that it was Lenore who hauled your seventeen-year-old ass out of Bangkok Park—"

"I didn't forget," Hazel starts, but Hannah cuts her off.

"Don't interrupt me. This is a story I like and one you seem to need to hear on a regular basis. You were one more little shithead with stupid parents who took a bus east and came into *my* fucking city. And that two-bit Cuban pimp, that greasy little Cardona, he was all ready to spike your little ass full of smack and add you to his stable. And for reasons that to this goddamn day I don't understand, Lenore Thomas stepped in."

"I know she did, Hannah—"

"Shut the hell up. A dozen little brats like you immigrate to Bangkok every goddamn week. It's not our job or habit to intervene. It costs favors and it's usually a useless, pathetic act. It's futile and everyone who knows me knows I hate futility."

Hannah looks away for a second, lifts her head to see Elmore staring at them from behind his register.

Hannah explodes. "Hey, Orsi, you old Italian fuck," she screams, "when's the last time the health board went through this dump?"

The Rib Room falls to absolute silence and Elmore turns on his heels and disappears into the storeroom.

Hannah waits a beat for the room to fall back to some degree of background noise, then continues.

"Lenore saw something in you, Hazel. Now, I've got no idea what it was. But she pulled you out of the Park before any damage was done. And she gave your name to her friend Flynn and told him to watch out for you in the Zone."

Hannah picks up Hazel's mug, sips, motions in a circle with it. "She hoped you'd do better than this. She hoped this would be a kind of way station while you grew up a little and figured out what you wanted to do." She pauses and says, "How old are you now, Hazel?"

Hazel has to gulp to lubricate her throat. "Twenty-three."

"Twenty-three," Hannah repeats.

They sit in silence for a few seconds, then Hannah says, "I know you do Elmore's books, Hazel. And I know you're good at it."

Hazel lets out a quivering, audible sigh, like a warning sign to a perpetual quarrel, a never-ending row with a disappointed parent, a frustrated mother who'll never understand an infinite number of facts.

"I don't understand why you still live this way, Hazel."

"It's my life, Detective," Hazel says, staring at the table.

"I don't see why you don't get a decent place to live. I know Flynn would help you. He helped Lenore and her brother when their parents kicked. He's good at his job, despite the radio shit."

"Please," Hazel says in a whisper, but Hannah keeps pushing.

"I don't get you. Why don't you buy some decent clothes? Why don't you grow up?"

The last question pushes Hazel over the limit and she finds some volume of her own and says, "It's my fucking life," suddenly unconcerned about the consequences of her outburst.

They stare at each other, both wondering if it's going to get physical, if punches will be thrown and steaming coffee tossed. But Hannah defuses the moment by bringing her hands together in a half dozen claps of applause.

"Still some piss left in the girl from Kansas, huh?" Hannah says. She pauses, drains the last of Hazel's coffee, pulls her own mug in front of her, and says, "Why don't we start this whole thing over, okay?"

Hazel lets her head fall back on her seat. Hannah thinks she looks tired and pale, that she could use a rare steak and a full day out in the sun, away from the noise of radios and self-righteous ideology.

"Last I heard," Hazel says, now kind of languid, maybe even, Hannah thinks, kind of sultry, "you were still a narc cop. I'm not dealing and I'm barely using and you guys are not known for your love of the Canal Zone. So, why this visit, Detective Shaw? Is there a reason for you harassing me and Elmore?"

"You're the eternal teenager, Hazel. Can't tell love from harassment. Normally people know when I'm harassing them."

"The contusions are always a giveaway."

"I'm not narcotics anymore. I'm homicide."

"Would that be a promotion or a demotion?"

Hannah gives a mock smile. "I just want to have a little talk with you, sweet one. Elmore was just being a nuisance. I think he's too interested in you, by the way."

"Is this where you make the pitch for the convent school?"

Hannah smiles and says, "No, this is where I ask you what the fuck you were doing at the Hyenas' clubhouse."

Bingo. The timing and delivery were perfect. Lenore would be proud. Now she needs to capitalize before Hazel can think up a convincing lie.

"You backsliding, little sister?" she snaps. "You bored with the art world here? You anxious to sell your ass for all the Cambodian fuckers over on Hip Sing Street?"

"Hannah—" Hazel begins, coming upright in the booth, but Hannah's not ready to let her explain, she wants to land a few more jabs.

"Nothing interesting happens in the Park that I don't hear about. And white-trash bohemian bitches putting out for jarheads is definitely considered interesting."

Hazel knows she's beat. Part of her knew it the minute Hannah took hold of her arm out on the street. She goes docile and simply says, "You going to bust me?"

Hannah cocks her head like this is the most stupid remark she's heard this season and says, "For what?"

"Oh," Hazel says weakly, "you people need a reason these days."

Hannah excises all the sarcasm and threat from her voice and speaks clearly and evenly. "The bantering part of this discussion is over, Hazel. Now sit quiet and listen to me. I'm a homicide cop. I'm also the department's unofficial liaison to the Park. That means I know as much gang shit as the gang squad. It means I still meet up with the vice people more often than they like. If it takes place in Bangkok Park, then very simply, I am involved. By this point, everyone on both sides of the legal fence has come to understand and accept that. I think you should too."

Hazel gives a single nod and Hannah goes on.

"Now, you probably heard about the priest who got torched in St. Brendan's. Somebody poured benzine all over this poor bastard's head and lit him up like a fucking rocket. Back in August, the Angkor Hyenas pulled the same stunt on a bodega that was under the protection of the Granada Street Popes. So either the Hyenas whacked the priest or somebody, maybe the Popes, maybe somebody else, wants me to think it was the Hyenas. Do you follow the story so far?"

Another nod.

"Now, we've had an idiot named Zarelli sitting watch over the Cambodians' little shop on Hip Sing. And he gives me a call the other day that some blond punk goddess just strolled in the front door of slopeland. And in the back of my brain, though I don't want to believe it, I've got a hunch who the Hyenas' visitor could be. So, I follow up my hunch, 'cause I want to confirm this news before I take any action. And goddamn if my hunch doesn't end up the truth. So, now you are going to sit there, little sister, and tell me in simple words what the fucking meeting was all about. And if it was to buy your way back into that cesspool that Lenore pulled you out of, you're going to wish you never put your seventeen-year-old ass on a Greyhound to Quinsigamond."

Hazel swallows, closes her eyes, rubs fingers over the bridge of her nose, opens her eyes, and looks at Hannah.

"It's not what you think," she says.

Hannah doesn't speak.

"We had heard, some people had heard—"

"What people?" Hannah asks.

"Some of the hackers," Hazel says, pleading slightly. "The little goofs with the keyboards and the modems. They kind of hang around the radio fringe. They think we're retro but hip. They—"

"What did they hear?"

"They heard there was a huge boost at this warehouse out near Boston Harbor."

"Go ahead," Hannah says.

"I don't know, you know, it was all rumor—"

"Tell me the rumor," Hannah says.

"Huge haul. Professional. Had to be. It would take semis to clear out this place. Drivers and muscle to move the shipping crates. And buy-offs. These places use real security. You boost a shipping warehouse, you know, you really piss off the big insurance companies. Last goddamn people you want to piss off."

"Come on, come on," Hannah says, intrigued but impatient.

"The rumor was that the haul, part of the haul anyway, was radio shit."

"Radio shit?"

"Yeah, quality stuff—Japan Radio, Sony, Otari."

"Go on," Hannah says, suddenly unsure of the conversation, feeling an annoying shift in the air as Hazel picks up pace and a little volume.

"Well, Jesus, you know, of course this would be merchandise my people would be interested in."

"The Wireless crowd," Hannah says, and Hazel nods and picks up Hannah's coffee mug.

"I mean we'd have to be talking forty percent off wholesale, even on minimum quantity."

Hannah shakes her head. "Back up. How does this rumor bring you down to the Hyenas?"

Hazel squints at her as if the question surprises her.

"Everyone in the Zone says the Hyenas are on the move now. Since Cortez left, the Popes are in disarray. This was a huge boost, Hannah. Even if it was strictly Providence-Italian, they'll need some distribution. We figured if the Italians shopped even part of it to Bangkok, it'd be through the Hyenas. We just wanted to be on the list to buy. You know, crap like this doesn't fall into your lap every week."

Hazel ends with a shrug and takes a long drink of coffee. She looks up to see Elmore back at the cashier's station, revising menus and stealing glances her way.

Hannah shifts her weight, looks down at Elmore but doesn't say a word. After a minute she slides back into her jacket and starts to get out of the booth.

She does a long stretch with her arms, cracks her knuckles out in front of her, and says, "First off, I'll be checking on a warehouse boost in Boston Harbor." She pushes her hands into her jacket pockets and says, "Then I'll be back down here to check on you again."

Hazel stays seated and raises her mug in a toast.

"Anytime, Detective. Next time let's make it dinner. It's always such a treat."

22.

A slow parade of moody regulars is starting to file into Elmore's Rib Room for the 5 P.M. early bird special—vegetarian chili and fresh brown bread. Elmore thinks it's some kind of crime to serve vegetarian chili in a joint that calls itself the Rib Room, but you've got to know your market and most of these kids put the kibosh on meat-eating.

Elmore's got the radio tuned in to WQSG and the place is filled with the sounds of *Grandslam Grab Bag,* a suppertime call-in sports show. Most of the Canal Zone crowd aren't big sports fans, but everyone's aching for the O'Zebedee Brothers to make a hit and QSG is the most likely target.

And sure enough, at about ten after five, as Elmore is pushing a plateful of diced scallions into his chili kettle, a furious argument about designated hitters is cut off in midholler and three high-pitched trumpet blasts announce the jam.

Bunt this, you bunheads. Yer outta the game. Suspended for the duration. Hit the showers running. O'ZBON clears the bases once again.

A spontaneous cheer explodes in the restaurant, followed by a wave of applause and whistles.

The broadcasting brothers of bedlam are back. The sibling spirit voices of subterranea are signal-sailing into your souls. Crank it up, Elmore, this dinner crowd is about to feast on fib-free fodder.

Enough, Brother John, with the asinine alliteration. God, it's infectious.

Which brings us to today's topic—infectious diseases. Like Doubt. I said it—the dreaded D-word. And I'm sorry, but keeping silent about our growing problem only makes everything worse. Our sources tell us that since we last spoke, more and more of you, who for the past five years pined for our return to Q-town, are walking around like some spike-haired minor league existentialists moaning, "O'Zbon is dead and anarchy is absurd." It's an interesting turn of events—in our absence, our cult grows and flourishes; upon our return, the number of true believers starts to dwindle. I guess faith is easy to maintain from a distance. But when the brothers' voice is heard on the home front, belief turns into a greased pig. Goddamn hard to hold onto.

Yeah, and it's weird 'cause this is the opposite of what we always thought. I guess absence does make the heart grow fonder and familiarity will sometimes breed a very hip contempt.

Now, there are two roads that Jimbo and I can navigate in this situation. We can pull up stakes tonight, get back on the interstate, and never give another thought to the hometown and the past. Or we can try to understand this backlash, do a biopsy on the locus of the doubt, work with the doubters, put ourselves at risk, and try to make you all certain that we are who we say we are.

Amen, bro. We am who is.

It's got to be one road or the other, 'cause like Elvis said—and I mean the dead one—we can't go on together, with suspicious minds.

I was thinking our problem over at about four A.M. and I started to wonder why we were such a hit last time 'round. Was it the freshness, the typical rush that greets any new idea or product? Yeah, it was that, but it was more than that. Since the collective we crawled out of the bubbling, primordial ooze, slapped on a bear-skin, and moved into a cave, we've been hooked on the one narcotic that never fails to fix. Absolutely addictive on initial contact. I'm speaking, of course, of the big M. Myth. That loop of an all-too-human story that was birthed in the slime and slop and salty blood of primeval consciousness. We listen to it waking and sleeping. We suck on it with each breath we pull in. We live it out in each minute step of our inconsequential lifetimes.

When we first passed Go with our initial broadcast, my brother and I put a new spin on a specific section of an old story and bounced it down to the playground where it would be most appreciated, sustained, enjoyed—Quinsigamond's little bohemia, the Canal Zone.

And you guys grabbed the ball and ran. What we thought was a harmless and onetime prank was entirely something else by the time it hit your unconventional ears. We were the classic rebel and madman visionary, the bad boys with the lineage that stretched from the nameless shamans of the foggy past down to St. Ti Jean and his misunderstood wanderlust. We called black white and up down and underscored the patter with a backbeat you could dance to. We were anonymous and that meant we could be anyone. We were unlicensed and that meant we were the enemies of authority.

And so, though we never planned it this way, we appealed to a wide variety of local subsets here in the city. Little groups, hybrids, cults. Small families that had nothing in common with one another, other than the fact that they felt excluded from the mainstream. And that *now* they had a voice that would speak for them.

Do I need to say that that kind of faith scared us as much as the Feds coming to town?

So, we ran. Picked up an AAA atlas and eased up the on-ramp. Injected ourselves into the interstate asphalt veins of this great land.

And an odd thing happened out there on the road. We started to miss being needed. That mantle of spokesman that was hung on our pirate signal started, in retrospect, to feel good and warm. So, after a time, we rolled back home.

But doesn't life have a way of stacking events into ironies? When we left, we were the Kings of Anarchy. When we returned, we were impostors to the throne.

But we never changed, folks. We never altered a thing. It's the same James. The same John. And, mostly, it's the same goddamn equipment.

You've got us rattled here, people. You're making our dreams chaotic. We're having historic nightmares—

Almost time, John-boy.

Now, the way I hear it, not only are you doubting the O'Z, but you're fighting among yourselves. I hear a little schism brewed up back at the ranch while we were on tour. Little bird tells me that some internal dissension is on the wax. I hear from the underground vine that some of the charter members who want "jam for the sake of jam" are butting heads with a cadre of liberation-technology greenhorns.

Time, Johnno.

Yeah, yeah, yeah. Let's not forget, people, that all the biggies, from Rome on down, tend to collapse from within. I'd like to say, "What the O'Zebedees have joined let no sibling savaging put asunder." But your future is not up to us. We could end up back on the road by tomorrow. One phone call could have us highway bound. We're commentators, not progenitors. You built up your family yourselves. And you can tear it apart from within if that's what you want to do. I know that right now it may seem like there's no solution to your dilemmas. That petty jealousies have turned into momentous ideologies. Simple squabbles into complex campaigns. All I can advise is to find an arbiter and latch onto any common ground, even the most craggy. Because if you sever the blood knots and burn down the family home, you walk alone. And what happened once will happen again. Your subgroups will divide into more subgroups. Community cancer, folks. Until each is just a group of one. And then you'll divide within yourself, within your heart.

Look, it's James again. One arm wants to carry on the tradition unchanged, keep things pure and on a completely artistic and comedic and symbolic level. The other arm wants to start lobbing bombs at antennas, injecting viruses into the stations' mainframes. I agree that those are pretty divergent goals. But you've got to look inward, find the common vein that flows back toward the brain. Now we've really got to run.

Okay, we've got to cut out. Listen, where I come from we used to have this trick. It went like this—when you lose faith, act like you still have it and it will come back. Don't try to figure the logic of that. Just give us a break here, huh?

C'mon, Juan, I'm cutting the signal.

Okay, okay. Flash to the orphaned entrepreneur. Something's rotten in Denmark. Our sources say to watch your step. Things aren't what they seem. Wish we could get more specific, but we're just giving it as we get it and—

John, for Christ sake.

All right already. We're out of here. You've got our future in your ears, friends. Believe in us as the one, true O'Zebedee Brothers Outlaw Network or be prepared for our demise.

The Choice is always yours.

Hic Calix.

23.

Ronnie has just started to doze when the alarm goes off. Flynn comes bolt upright with a surge of panic. Ronnie lowers the volume on the clock radio with one hand and with the other eases Flynn back down onto the pillows.

"Just the alarm," she says in her most soothing voice. "I've got to shower. I'm on in an hour."

Flynn watches her slide out of bed. "You could call in sick."

She stops in the doorway, turns back to him, covers her breasts with her arms, watches him roll his eyes.

"You want Ray Todd on the air for the rest of the night? We can't do that to the city."

"You're too public-spirited. Makes for a lousy hedonist."

"Yeah, well, even hedonists need a paycheck."

"Move in with me," Flynn says. "We'll set up a remote at my place. You can broadcast from the bed. Give the show a real edge."

"I think the show has enough of an edge already."

She turns and heads for the shower and yells back, "You want to join me in here?"

He swings his legs off the mattress and says, "And on top of everything else she's a mind reader."

Ronnie has one of those yellow plastic waterproof radios hanging by a black plastic strap from the neck of the shower nozzle. As Flynn climbs into the tub, she turns on WQSG. Flynn moves in and hugs her around the waist and they step under the spray of water. Ronnie takes an orange bar of soap from the dish and hands it over her shoulder to Flynn and he goes to work on her back. She closes her eyes, points her face up at the jet of water, and listens to the radio. Ray Todd is in standard form.

Hello, Quinsigamond, and welcome back to our final hour of *City Soapbox.* I am your host, of course, Raymond Todd, and God willing, we may just make it through an entire program without being assaulted and knocked into limbo by the lawless degenerates who've been trying so desperately to grab some headlines the past few weeks. If you've just joined us, please be advised that we're not taking any calls for the next thirty minutes. This is a memorial segment of sorts, an interview taped shortly before the tragic and violent demise of Father Andre Todorov. As will soon become apparent to you, I am not a supporter or follower of the late Father Todorov. At best, I would have to call him a sadly misguided figure, bamboozled by a misreading of history and an excessive ego. I'm afraid his horrid death cannot and will not alter my assessment. I broadcast this interview simply as a glaring warning, a piercingly clear example of the apocalyptic dangers inherent in the humanistic ideology. Whether the savage animals who hideously murdered this confused man will ever be apprehended matters very little in the end. Because, and hear me now, they are a minute manifestation of the coming evils. How ironic that Father Todorov contributed to the plague that caused his own demise. How pathetic. If the engineer will roll the tape, let's listen to the sounds of our own doom.

There's a second of air hiss and then a mechanical-sounding run of musical scales.

...My guest in the studio tonight is himself no stranger to local headlines. If you've been following the series of *Spy* articles over the past year or so, you're certainly familiar with Father Andre Todorov, associate pastor of St. Brendan's Cathedral in the heart of downtown. In the year since Father Todorov has been installed in his position at the cathedral, he's been relentless in his well-publicized dedication to what he calls "social action with the emphasis on action." The good father is the founder of the Calvary Peace Coalition and the Assisi Shelter down on LaBran Avenue. But the past few month have seen Father Todorov turn his energies to the growing gang problem that's descended on our city. Before the break, Father, you'd begun to correct some of my misconceptions about the gang menace. Let's explore the facts a bit, as I like to say. How many established gangs are there currently in the city?

That's difficult to say, Ray. We know, of course, about the top two. The Granada Street Popes, mainly from the Colombian community. And their growing rival, the Angkor Hyenas, comprised of Cambodian refugees. There are certainly three other smaller clubs that have emerged on the borders of Bangkok Park.

And they are?

The Tonton Loas, who seem to have a strong Haitian tradition, the Castlebar Road Boys, who define themselves as an Irish fraternal organization, and the Sal Mineos—

The Pecci family's errand boys.

Please, Mr. Todd—

'Scuse me, Father. Can you tell us, which have you had the most contact with?

I am equally available to all the rival factions. We're not here tonight to provoke any group by negating their importance in the overall peace.

Peace being the main objective in your ministry among these gangs?

Of course. I don't see—

Would you agree, Father, without delving into the requisite

sociological causes, that the main activity of these gangs, indeed, their very reason for being, is criminal—

Now, wait a minute, Mr. Todd. These are youths from a blighted landscape. They turn to the gang life as a matter of survival, a system for living where there is no other system.

But let's be clear and honest here, Father Todorov. That system is comprised of thievery, drug dealing, arms dealing, extortion, and the general, wholesale spreading of terror—

You're making very provocative remarks about an extremely complicated problem—

There was nothing complicated about the firebombing of the New Ponce Bodega last week—

That incident has not been proven to be gang-related, Mr. Todd.

I think what confuses most people, Father, is your insistence on devoting your time and effort to an element with very little respect for law and life—

We have to start somewhere. As Christ said, it's the sick man who needs the doctor. These young people have to be taught other skills—

Blame everything on ignorance, yes? Tell me, Father, what about these radio jammers who've begun to prey on us? Clearly these aren't ignorant savages.

I didn't say... I'm here to talk about the gang problem. I don't know anything about these jammers.

Just what you read in the papers, I'm sure.

I don't see—

I'm curious, when you venture down to Bangkok town, do you wear the collar, Father?

Not always, no. The idea is to first establish a rapport. And I've found if I dress in street clothes, it's a sign . . . I find it's the first step toward intimacy. It helps to remove the threat of my a priori role as an authority figure.

You do acknowledge, however, that you are, in fact, an authority figure. Correct, Father?

I'm perceived this way. The image of the adult, white, male priest. The force of the historical image is a powerful, stubborn symbol to overcome. I—

Do these gang members ever confess their crimes to you, Father?

Well, first, Ray, as you well know, we confess sins, not crimes. And secondly, most of the gangs are not Catholic.

Most?

Well, the Granada Street Popes are. And the new one out of Ireland—the Castlebar Road Boys.

And these two, they claim to be members of the Church?

What I mean is, they were raised in the tradition. Their native cultures are—

Could you briefly distinguish between crime and sin for me, Father?

Excuse me?

Crime versus sin. Please.

[*Pause*] Well, I mean, it appears obvious to me. A crime is a violation of a man-made law—

And a sin—

Would be an affront to, a disruption of, one's individual conscience. I don't see—

Now, last month there, when you and your little coalition drove down Route 63 to the industrial park and poured human blood all over the lobby of the Gibson Tech corporate office. Would that there be a sin or a crime?

I don't see how this concerns the gang issue. I thought we were here to discuss—

And so we are. Which brings me to my question, did one of those street scum gangboys supply you people with the blood? *"Lucky day, Father T. Got a big red barrel full of B negative from a little grandmother we just gutted."*

[*Yelling*] Mr. Todd, for God's sake—

[*Yelling*] And you've got a hell of a nerve invoking the name of God, you Marxist insult to Rome—

[*noise of microphone coming loose*]

. . . is ridiculous . . . despicable . . .

[*Yelling*] Keep walking, you liberal humanist fraud. Your days are numbered, you—

Ray is cut off, but not by a jammer. The WQSG theme music comes up and a prerecorded promo blurbs the station's virtues and then segues into an ad for a medical malpractice attorney.

Ronnie and Flynn are on the tub floor, gulping air and water spray, hearts pumping, leg muscles trembling. After a second,

Ronnie opens her eyes and looks at Flynn. A smile breaks out on his face. And then, at the same time, they both begin laughing.

"I guess Raymond gets to us both," Ronnie says over the blast of the water.

24.

Loke steps through his office door to find Detective Hannah Shaw seated behind his desk, her booted heels resting on his blotter, a thick leather-bound book open in her lap.

Though he's affronted by her display, Loke nods as if he's impressed, maybe a little amused, by the audacity, the sheer in-your-face disrespect. But Hannah's not even looking up to see his grin and his nod. She's running a finger along something of particular interest in the book. As she reads, she shifts in her seat, digs a hand into a pocket of her leather jacket, and lackadaisically pulls out a badge pinned in a custom leather wallet. She waves the badge around over her head like it was a flag or some kind of college pennant.

Finally she finishes reading, looks up, points to a chair, and in a put-on enthused voice says, "Loke, you little devil, why don't you have a seat?"

Loke stands still for a second trying to decide which way to play it, then remembers the lecture he's just had to endure at Uncle Chak's place. He slides into a chair before the teak desk and says, "You must be Detective Shaw. I am so honored. We finally get a chance to meet."

Hannah repockets her badge and says, "We'll both remember the day for years to come."

Loke widens his eyes and says, "No doubt," in some weird accent like William Buckley gone Asian.

Hannah lifts the book she's been reading from her lap and reshelves it in the case behind Loke's desk. "Quite a page turner there," she says. "Jesus, those Khmer Rouge are imaginative bastards. I never would have guessed there were so many uses for trash bags."

"You use what you have," Loke says, his hands tossed out to the side like a bored magician.

"And pragmatic," Hannah says. "You can suffocate the victim *and* dispose of the remains. Such clever little pricks."

Loke gives a smile that he thinks is modest, then says, "I must be one of the last players in Bangkok Park to meet Hannah Shaw."

Hannah comes forward to the desk and brings her back rigid. "Well, I don't usually get down to the errand-boy level—"

Loke cuts her off, still good-natured, and says, "'Warlord,' if you don't mind. I'm such a stickler when it comes to language."

Hannah nods and squints. "Whatever. You guys are all a little anal for me. For the record, though, you don't use my first name. I'm Detective Shaw to you, son. That's the first rule and it's a goddamned important one."

"Of course, Detective. I didn't mean to be rude—"

"I'm sure you didn't," Hannah says. "Just like you didn't mean to fry that hotshot priest down St. Brendan's."

Loke immediately starts shaking his head. He stands up and walks to the desk, plants his hands on the teak, and looks down at Hannah. "The Hyenas had nothing to do with that. You can talk to my uncle—"

Hannah stands up and matches his heat. "Your Uncle Chak doesn't cut any shit with me, you little jarhead bastard. Who the fuck do you think you're talking to? Uncle Chak is a loose wing nut with too few brains and too small balls. No Asian in this town has ever crossed Doc Cheng and lived out the year, you stupid bastard. Not even the Japanese. There's a system down here that works and it pisses me off when some dickhead slope who stepped off the boat Wednesday and moved some smack on Friday suddenly thinks he can fuck with the whole machine."

Loke stares at her, brings his voice back to friendly, and says, "Why are you here, Detective?"

"You sit back down, junior," she says, and he does, slowly. "I know the whole story about you and your family. Uncle Chak wouldn't even be breathing if the Latinos hadn't had a power vacuum at a crucial moment."

Loke makes an ugly grin at her. "Ah yes," he says. "Mr. Cortez. The King of Bangkok Park. My understanding is he had to leave town in a great hurry. I've heard rumors about Cortez. Wasn't he a close friend of your mentor? What was her name? Lee-Ann? Lorraine? Something . . ."

Hannah takes a second, steadies herself, and leers back. "That's it, friend. Show me the extent of your ignorance. Tip your whole hand. Jesus, it comes down in the genes."

"Again, Detective, I don't mean to offend. Like everyone in the Park, I simply hear rumors."

Hannah looks over to the floor-to-ceiling cabinets to her left and says, "Cortez would have gutted your fat uncle on a whim. Had him served as the weekend special at Chak's own noodle joint."

She looks back at Loke and head-motions to the cabinet. "What's in there?"

Loke loves the question. "The usual, Detective. Office supplies. Paper. Pens. Instant coffee."

Hannah rubs her eyes. "Decaf, I'm sure."

She gets up from the desk, turns her back to Loke, and studies the wall maps of Cambodia and Quinsigamond. Without turning back around, she says, "I believe that you didn't whack the priest."

"I appreciate the vote of confidence," Loke says.

Hannah shrugs, moves a fingertip up to follow a local street, and says, "You're not smart enough to grab a Yale diploma, even with Chak's big check to the endowment. But you're not stupid or ragged enough to make that public a hit for no reason."

"The Hyenas have enough to be concerned about. We have no need to murder an innocent civilian."

Hannah turns around.

"Then who did it?" she asks. "And why do they want us to think it's you?"

Loke shrugs and tries to look bored. "Maybe the Popes? We've been having our differences, as you know."

Hannah shrugs back at him. "Maybe."

"It could be anyone, Detective. Maybe the Castlebar Road Boys. Those Irish, they always have the religious hang-ups."

Hannah walks over to him, raises her right leg, and plants her boot on the cushion of Loke's chair, her pointed toe a half inch from his crotch.

Loke raises his eyebrows, looks from the boot up to Hannah, and says, "It would never work, Detective. The difference in our ages—"

Hannah cuts him off and in a low voice says, "You had a visitor in here recently, didn't you, asshole?"

"I don't know—"

The toe of her boot edges forward just a bit and she lowers it just enough to touch the inseam of Loke's pants.

"You answer my fucking question right now, you dickhead Ivy League scumbag. You've got no idea what kind of problems I can bring into your life. You already know I carry some kind of weight down here. You know that because Uncle Chak told you. But Uncle Chak is a lightweight jarhead who hasn't been playing the Park long enough to know who backs me or why. He doesn't know how I figure in the landscape. And he can't risk anyone in his family pissing me off until he finds out."

She applies some more pressure onto his crotch. His eyes stay fixed on her.

"That's a position I love to be in, junior. I love to be feared. So keep me happy. You shiver a little bit. And you tell me who came to visit you."

"Obviously," Loke says, a small catch in his throat as if he needed a sip of water, "you already know."

"I want to hear you say it, junior."

He takes a breath, puts his hands on the arms of the chair, smiles. "A young woman named Hazel. An artist type from down in the Canal Zone."

She stares at him for about thirty seconds, then puts her foot back on the floor and says, "Very good. What did she want? And if you make any kind of joke—any lewd reference or comment—I'll pick a bone in your face and break it."

He believes her. Even with six of his best muscle-boys shooting billiards outside, he knows she's telling the truth.

"She's looking to immigrate. Into the Park. She wants Hyena protection. She wants a franchise."

Hannah makes a long sigh in spite of herself. She gives Loke a single, long bow of the head.

"Is she connected to you?" Loke asks. "Is there a problem with this?"

"Did you touch her?"

"I didn't lay a hand on her," Loke says. "I don't touch white women."

Hannah stares at him, but somehow his comment defuses itself, drains her edge, and she decides it's time to leave. She takes a step to the door, stops, and says, "Wise policy, junior. That woman's a walking plague."

Loke's face gives nothing up.

"If you hear who lit up the priest," Hannah says, "be sure and give me a call."

Loke simply says, "Come again, Detective."

"Believe me," Hannah says, "I will."

25.

In the glass elevator, on the way up to the studio, Ronnie and Flynn neck like anxious teenagers, breathless and dizzy, mouths overly wet and heads bobbing and twitching in an imitation of panic. They're awkward, hands colliding in midgrope, feet stutter-stepping as they reposition. And they're both gleeful about their awkwardness, as if it was a sign of youth and unexplainable innocence.

Flynn especially finds the feeling a wonder drug, a therapy sent from God, unasked. Since their airport slow dance his body has started to believe he's seventeen again, bone and muscle still growing, every possibility untapped. There was no loginess or heaviness when he woke in the morning, no preoccupation and instinctual prioritizing. He feels like his vision is sharper, his teeth more rooted in his gums. He feels like his lungs have been stripped of some greasy film that caused them to work at minimal efficiency.

He moves his mouth to Ronnie's neck and sucks there and he can feel her shiver and push in against him. He entwines his legs between hers. He lets his hand fall from her breast to the waist of her skirt. His fingers hook over the edge, nab her shirt, and start to untuck it.

The elevator bell rings and she steps backward from him in a stumble and starts to straighten clothing and hair, staring at him the whole time, no words, but a lot of breathing and the wetting of her lips with her tongue. Flynn looks at her and shakes his head and says, "There's no way I'm going to make it till two A.M."

She tucks her shirt in slowly and says, "Maybe you won't have to."

They move out of the elevator and turn right toward the studio. He falls behind her and gooses her and she makes a playful, blind swat backward with her hand.

Through the huge plate glass they can see Ray in dim light, hovering behind the microphone in a cloud of cigarette smoke. The corridor speaker is shut off, but his mouth is moving. Ronnie stops for a second to watch him.

"Well, he didn't get bumped tonight. Your pals must be vacationing."

"Not my pals," Flynn says, surprised by her comment.

"Look at him," she says, "I wonder what the topic is now."

"Isn't it always the same?"

"It's weird. He's got a short menu. Strictly seventies rants. Fluoride. Interferon. The trilateral commission. Teddy Kennedy. Sun Myung Moon. It's like his buttons jammed in '75 and he's never moved on. I mean, he doesn't even slag the Japanese. Not a word about Latin America. I always figure even the other nuts must think he's a relic."

They move inside and Wayne waves to them from behind his board. Ronnie nods and then leads the way through a side door to a small break room. It's a little brighter inside. There's a green vinyl couch, a coffee table covered with trade magazines, a brown mini-refrigerator with a Mr. Coffee on top of it, and a few mismatched folding chairs.

"All the luxuries," Ronnie says.

The walls and the ceiling are all faded white acoustic squares with hundreds of tiny pinholes. One wall is dominated by a huge cork bulletin board that's plastered with pushpinned newspaper clippings, more than half of which have yellowed. It's a depressing sight. Ronnie gestures to the board with her head and says, "It's Ray's. News for the brain-dead. I don't know where he gets them."

Flynn spots a headline that reads, "Soviets Using Psychic Clone Moles Deep in Pentagon."

The other walls are filled with a few promotional posters from station advertisers and there's a large, wood-framed photograph of a red-faced barrel-chested middle-aged man wearing a charcoal suit with shoulders so square they look like they were fitted with two-by-fours. The man has a severe look on his face, like he's ignoring a migraine long enough to plot military strategy. He's posed, holding a pair of bifocals out away from his body.

"That's Federman," Ronnie says. "The station owner."

"Looks like a real pit bull."

Ronnie shrugs. "Never met him in my life."

She hands him a kelly-green coffee mug with *WQSG* in white block letters stamped on the side. She fills both their mugs halfway, then digs her mescal flask from her bag and fills the rest with booze.

"That's the beauty of this stuff," she says. "You can mix it with everything. It doesn't corrupt. I've tried."

"You're on the air in ten," Flynn says. "Isn't this illegal?"

She smiles and rolls her eyes. "You want to spend four hours unmedicated, talking to the sexually dysfunctional? Show some mercy."

Flynn sips at the mescal and Folgers, makes a face, and says, "I'm saving all the mercy for later."

Ronnie says, "Don't promise what you can't deliver."

He wants her to smile, but again she doesn't. She walks over to the mounted wall speaker and turns a knob on the bottom. The room fills with Ray's voice.

What is it you're trying to suggest to me, sir? What is it you want me to accept? What I'm asking, very simply, is, what is your agenda?

And if you'll give me a minute to—

Because perhaps we can save everyone some time and ag-
gravation. Because if what you want to poison us with—no, wait—
more to the point, if what you want to poison our *children* with is
more evolutionary claptrap from the camp of leftist atheistic homo-
sexual heathens, then I'm going to have to pull your plug, my
friend—

I'm sorry, but not everyone who sees the scientific inconsisten-
cies in creationism is gay or a socialist or an atheist. You want to
paint everyone—

Yes, honey, we know, it's a tough life. Are we going to have a
little tantrum now?

Can we stay on the point? Can we please just stick to the
topic—

Listen, darling, you have begun to bore me. Next call, Earl from
the north side.

"Creationism," Flynn says. "We've picked a good night."
"Not bad," Ronnie says: "Gun control is a good night.
Nixon is a good night. The Knights of Malta is a fantastic night.
He gets screaming. One time, Wayne and I had a bet about a
coronary. I think that was the night he said Klaus Barbie has
been misunderstood. Bad press and weak-minded historians.
You should've read the mail that week."
Flynn walks over to the bulletin board and starts to read
clippings.
"How much of Ray is gimmick and how much is from the
heart?"
Ronnie moves up next to him and he thinks he hears her
sigh.
"Radio's a weird business," she says. "I think Ray's like a
lot of people. It starts out as gimmick. You pick a schtick you're

pretty good at. Something that comes natural. Then a lot of late nights go by and you talk to more loons than most people see in a lifetime and at some point your voice sort of takes over. The words just slide out. You don't think about it a whole lot."

Without looking at her, Flynn asks, "What about with you?"

She doesn't say anything, gives out a quick brush-off laugh.

He pushes it. "I mean, you're this Zen master of the sensual, right? Authority on things erotic. How'd that end up your schtick?"

The door opens and Wayne sticks his head in.

"You're on in five," he says. "Ray is doing windup after the spot."

Ronnie nods, raises her mug up to him, and he disappears. She takes a long swallow from her mug, refills it, and starts out the door. Flynn follows her to the broadcast booth and they stand in the doorway staring at Ray's back, watching him sit rigid with one arm parallel next to the mike, a cigarette with a long head of ash jammed between his index and middle fingers. Over the booth speaker comes the close-out music for a mortuary ad. Ray twists his head from side to side as violins fade. Watching him, Flynn almost expects to hear an awful, high-pitched scraping noise escape from the guy's shirt collar. The sound of a rusted pipe being forced from a welded joint. Instead, there's a few moments of silence that become dramatic, almost uncomfortable. Flynn can feel anticipation blooming, a readiness or yearning in every set of ears tuned to QSG. Ray knows how to work the invisible audience. There's no need for eye contact or physical presence. All Ray needs is the sound of his voice, his ability to lower timbre and increase the richness of tone and construct a fullness in the vibrations emitting from his larynx. The man knows how to play the pauses, knows, instinctively, the power of timing.

If it wasn't for his lack of control, Flynn thinks, he could be captivating, a real aural commodity.

Ray takes in a last drag from the Camel, blows it out over the mike in a long vapory line, and begins his summation.

My friends, I think you know as well as I do that we barely scratched the surface here tonight. We've quoted scripture and shown the folly of man, the weakness of his science and his ego. We've let the crackpots have their say, within the limits of decency. Let the liberal-spewing eggheads and lovers of darkness vent their routine spleen. It's been over a century since Mr. Charles Darwin trotted his little simian sideshow across our path. And in that time his doctrine has infiltrated our schools, assaulted the minds of our children until they turned their backs on truth and righteousness. Perhaps those of us blessed with the knowledge of the divine wisdom haven't fought hard enough. Perhaps *our* weakness is the greatest outrage of all. I don't know.

[*Pause. Voice rising*]

But I do know that the Millenium is coming. It is racing down upon us like a blazing chariot. We're already starting to feel its flames on our mortal skin. Those are the flames of eternal damnation, the province of the dark one, the final home of the wicked and the cursed. The place where the seeds we have sown in this life will bear fruit forever after. There are choices to be made in the days ahead. Battles waged. The worst kind of battles. Civil wars. Blood struggles between kin. There are two mighty armies readying to clash. They carry the same blood in their hearts, but they've been divided by choices of the soul. There is a family of light.

[*Pause. Voice rising*]

And make no mistake, there is a family of darkness. We know these two clans by different names from time immemorial. The family of Righteousness and the family of Evil. The family of Truth and the family of Falsehood. The family of Order and the family of Chaos. They've clashed since the archangel Michael cast Lucifer downward. There can be no compromise between them. Only one family can prevail.

[*Pause*]

And so, I think our discussion tonight can be seen in the larger picture. Its implications are staggering. The question is nothing less than—Are we men, made in the image and likeness of God, or are we soulless animals, creatures of the flesh void of any chance for redemption? Darkness or Light? Order or Chaos? The days of tabling that question are over. Each of us must seize the truth and fight the enemy with a viciousness that won't allow defeat.

[*Pause, a long audible breath*]

Next time: Jane Fonda, the International Monetary Fund, and the Book of Revelation. I'm Raymond Todd. Good night and God speed.

He queues up his theme music—a weird, midspeed mix of something like organ and zither. It makes Flynn uncomfortable and he's grateful when Wayne fades into the top-of-the-hour network news feed.

Ronnie moves forward, reaches down, and mutes the lead report about an air crash at O'Hare. She leans over Ray's shoulder and says, "They let you alone tonight, big guy. How come?"

Ray doesn't seem to want to acknowledge her or relinquish his chair. He continues to draw on his cigarette and stare past the hanging microphone out the plate glass at the dim corridor beyond. Finally he wheels backward, collects his things, a pack of Camels and a clipboard fat with scrappy mismatched pieces of paper.

"Tide is turning, sister," he finally says, giving a look to Flynn, who nods.

"Smells that way," Ronnie says, sliding into the seat and adjusting the headphones over her ears.

"I'll leave you to your little orgy," Ray says to Flynn on the way out of the booth.

"Pleasure meeting you," Flynn says back.

"Get comfortable," Ronnie says, and Flynn settles down on a small stool behind her. Through a window to their left they can see Wayne on the phone in the engineer's booth, lining up Ronnie's first calls.

Ronnie brings up the volume on the news and they come in on the upbeat close-out story, really just a headline and a few words of follow-up on a young girl in Nova Scotia who found a classic message in a bottle. Then the network announcer signs off and the theme music comes up.

Wayne breaks in to ask, "All set?"

Ronnie takes a sip of coffee and nods while adjusting the position of her mike.

"I got a nonorgasmic twenty-eight-year-old female banker on line one," Wayne says, "an impotent gay musician with chronic nightmares about wild dogs on line two. Line three is standard bondage, male. And line four is a recent divorcee with a bad body image."

Ronnie hits a button on the board and says, "Gimme the wild dogs and tell the divorcee to hang on."

Flynn watches Wayne nod and slide on two different headsets—one heavy model around his neck, and another light, black plastic model over his ears. The ear set has a small tubelike mouthpiece that curves to the front of his lips. He looks like a NASA programmer. His hands are both on a mixing board that's below the level of the window. An ad for a real estate development fades and the theme music to Ronnie's show starts up—some low-key after-hours pseudo-jazz, alto sax, light brush drum, a little piano doodle. Flynn wonders who chose this theme and if they thought it appropriate to the show. And now, listening closely for the first time, instead of sitting in the darkness of his study, lying in the dentist's chair and anticipating the sound of Ronnie's voice, he decides it is appropriate, somehow it does convey the mood.

A pretaped announcer's voice slides on, female, very low, on the verge of raspy, suggestive. It says, "Live from downtown Quinsigamond, it's *Libido Liveline,* with your host Ronnie Wilcox."

Ronnie takes a sip from her mug, tilts her head back, and lets the coffee run down her throat in a slow trickle. Then she takes in some air, lets it out through rounded lips like she was blowing a smoke ring, and as Wayne brings the theme music down, she says, in a slightly breathless but confident voice:

How are we tonight? How is everyone feeling? The lights on my phone tell me there are some problems, some sadness or misunderstanding. It feels like a good night to banish some of those troubles, to start down the path toward self-realization. Self-intimacy. Because the better we understand ourselves and what gives us pleasure, the better we can pass that pleasure on to others.

[Pause. Sips coffee]

Ronnie's in a fine mood tonight, friends. Ronnie feels like anything could be possible tonight. She's dying to hear your voices. But before we begin, I'd like to pass on a general suggestion, a small idea that might spark the senses a little. Maybe heat things up. When the show finishes tonight and you're still wide awake and wondering what to do, give the great outdoors a try. I'm serious now, all right? We've got such gorgeous weather lately. Get outside. At night. Find a secluded park. Find a wooded grove. Bring your partner and dance. Tango, maybe. Under the stars, in the moon-light. I know.

[Deep breath]

Sounds a little retro, a little kitschy. Little Doris Day-ish. Sure. But trust me, ten minutes with the breeze moving in your hair and the sound of the leaves blowing past your feet . . . It's different. Anything can happen. The moon goes to work on the blood, you know. Try a little slow dance out in the night. See where it leads. Call me. Let me know.

[Pause]

Now, on to our first call. Hello, Carlo, you're with Ronnie. Relax and talk to me. My assistant tells me you've been having some bad dreams lately.

Flynn stares at her back and listens to the caller relay a nightmare of snapping, foaming Dobermans surrounding his naked body. It's an awful image and the person on the phone is articulate enough to make it detailed and vivid. The voice chokes up a little once or twice, but Ronnie has a knack for calming and reassuring. She leads the caller through to the end of the night-mare and then gently starts to probe for its cause, the real reason this man has called.

And as Flynn stares at her back, the slope of her shoulders, the mild sheen of light off her hair, he starts to think that possibly a turning point has already been reached, that the days ahead may have little resemblance to the ones past. The idea of this not only excites him but fills him with a kind of distracting pulse, a wave of energy that feels like a benign, enervating tension running down his spine. It makes him feel like he has to move, do something to release pressure.

So he gets off his stool and walks up to her, puts his hands on her shoulders, and starts a slow rubdown. For a second, he flinches, wondering if he's done something wrong that might disrupt the broadcast. But Ronnie's a pro. She places one of her hands over one of his and never stops talking.

Flynn leans down and kisses the top of her head and takes in the smell of coconut. Then he pulls away and walks out of the booth.

Wayne looks up from the board, startled, maybe even a little frightened. Flynn tries to put him at ease with a smile and a hands-in-his-pocket shuffle.

"Don't let me interrupt you," he says.

Wayne shakes his head too fast. "Once enough calls are lined up, the rest is cake. Ronnie does her own carts. I just keep an eye out for problems."

"G.T. Flynn," Flynn says, sticking a hand out and nodding.

Wayne shakes his hand and doesn't think to offer his own name. Instead he says, "You known Ronnie long?"

"Not too long, though I've been a listener from the start."

"Ever call in?"

Flynn smiles. "No, but I probably wouldn't tell you if I had."

"Oh yeah," is all Wayne can think of to say. "Right."

The guy's got some feelings for Ronnie, Flynn thinks. *The poor bastard has to work with her every night and will never give any indication, any sign of attraction or desire. He's probably furious that I'm here tonight.*

"Ronnie was telling me..." Flynn starts, looking down at

the board, appearing to study the banks of knobs and sliders and meters.

"Yeah?"

"She was saying how it usually goes during the show. How you two operate. Quite a team, huh?"

Wayne likes to hear this. He'll remember the exact words. He says, "We're pretty good. We work well together."

"You can tell," Flynn says, nodding and pulling down the corners of his mouth. "You can see the rhythm. That's why I had to come down here tonight. I didn't want to get in the way or anything, but I really wanted to see you two do it. After listening for so long. I'd hear her mention your name all the time. I always wondered what you two looked like."

"Now you know."

"Yeah. Now I know," Flynn repeats. "Tell me, is it always so natural? I mean between the announcer and the engineer. I mean, you two seem like you could do this with your eyes closed."

"Well, we're pretty good. Not everyone—"

"I mean does every night go this smooth? All the calls lined up, all the ads timed right."

"Well, we—"

"And when do you go out for the food?"

Wayne just stares at him, then finally says, "The food?"

Flynn smiles. "Yeah. Ronnie was telling me how the night goes and she was saying you know all the great takeout places. Chinese. Mexican. You can get them to hang around after closing till you pick up. She called you the King of Takeout."

"Oh yeah? The King of Takeout?"

"Yeah. I thought that was great. So, when do you go? 'Cause I insist, no argument now—I want to treat you two tonight. This is on me."

Wayne stares at him a little bewildered, then says, "Well, we really didn't discuss—"

Flynn cuts him off. "Ronnie said she was dying for some Tandoori. That Indian place down San Remo Ave—"

"She wanted Indian? We've never gotten—"

But Flynn has already pulled a fifty from his pants pocket and is tucking it into Wayne's hand.

"Yeah, we were driving down here tonight and she started going on about how she could go for some biryani and some Tandoori shrimp."

He puts an arm around Wayne's shoulder and starts to steer him toward the door.

"Usually we wait until—" Wayne begins, but Flynn talks him down, saying, "Looks like everything is under control here. All the lines are lit. You take your time, we'll be fine. And you know, if you could find a bottle of wine, your choice, that would be great."

Wayne stares at him, bewildered and cowed.

Flynn chucks him under the chin, gives him a small push out into the corridor, winks, and says, "I think there's a liquor store over on Seventh that stays open till midnight."

26.

Hazel and Eddie do a sweep around the block, then ease the van over the curbing and drive down a gravel and weed slope into the burned-out cavern of old Gompers Station. They drive in as far as they can and Eddie jockeys the van behind the remains of the marble stairway where it can't be seen from the street.

In its day, in the twenties and thirties, Gompers Station was Quinsigamond's answer to Grand Central. For decades it was the second largest train station in the state, a depot for every major line that passed through New England. Survivors from that era will tell you it had style. And a deceiving sense of permanence.

When the Gompers was opened in 1911, the public was let into a holy palace of the high industrial age: From atop a heavy granite base rose a white marble basilica consecrated to the religion of fast travel. Two symmetrical baroque towers shot up two hundred feet from street level. One hundred and sixty Ionic columns trimmed the exterior walls. The main waiting room was an elliptical vault that contained eighteen thousand square feet of space, capped by a domed ceiling in gilt frames.

Sometime after World War II, the railroads began the steady decline that led to the downfall of Gompers Station. By the early seventies, the last freight company pulled out and the worst of the erosion got under way. Anything of value was drilled or blasted out of place and carted away, and once the main ceiling was destroyed, the Quinsigamond winters began to go to work.

It might have been better if the station had been leveled and remanded to memory and museum photos, eternally new and forever whole. Instead, the place was left to rot into a bizarre modern ruin on the northeast corner of downtown. It looks like a chillingly realistic vision of a postnuclear landscape. The original flooring is gone, leaving uneven bedrock and gravelly dirt. Massive chunks of granite and marble are missing from the walls. The master stairway that led to the upper-level dining pavilion is more a gritty, crater-filled incline than anything else. The Ionic columns are crumbled and broken, and in some cases, lying on their sides. Indistinguishable rubble is strewn everywhere and the air is thick with grime and soot.

During the coldest months of the year, Gompers is an atom-smashed boardinghouse for dozens of homeless vagrants and drunks. From time to time it becomes popular with the growing pack of mental health cases deinstitutionalized from the Toth Care Facility. There are rumors that a group of wandering satanists celebrate Black Mass here on the Solstice.

And occasionally, like tonight, Gompers Station is a neutral meeting ground for gang rites and summits and unconventional transactions.

Eddie reaches for his door handle and Hazel shakes her head without looking at him. She's got a brown paper supermarket bag in her lap and her hands are inside it counting the money.

"No one tell you the days of big debt are over?" Eddie says, pleased with himself.

Hazel keeps counting and mouths the words *Shut up, asshole.*

Eddie ignores her. "What if they don't show?"

There's a second of quiet while Hazel finishes the tally, then she looks across at him and says, "They don't show up, we blow it all on smack and tattoos."

Eddie loves it when she talks like this. If he thought there was even a small chance of his meaning more to Hazel than muscle and handiwork, he'd drop Diane and steal a ring tomorrow.

"Who are we into for the wad?" he asks.

"This isn't *we*," Hazel says, emphasizing the last word. Then she continues, "I went to Elmore. And this dyke painter I know who's getting lucky at the Baldwin Gallery."

Eddie waits a beat, then can't help himself. "You go to Flynn?"

"No, I didn't go to Flynn," Hazel says, getting angry. "How the fuck could I go to Flynn? Use your goddamn brain for once."

"How do I know?" Eddie says, defensive. "You could tell him anything. You could say—"

"I don't lie to Flynn," Hazel says, almost yelling. Then she remembers where they are and forces some control.

"Look," she says, "we've got to do this clean. Okay? This is partly a small test, allright? We put up the coin, we take the merchandise, we glance, we just glance, okay, at the merchandise. And then we're out of here. We clear on that? No talk. No extra words. No 'goodbye, see you soon' crap. Okay?"

Eddie squints at her like he's insulted. He's about to tell her to save the instructions for the lightweights she's drafted, but then a knock sounds on Hazel's door and they both start in their seats.

"Shit," Eddie whispers. "I didn't even see the bastards come in."

Hazel mouths *Shut the fuck up* and pulls up on her door handle. They climb out of the van and Eddie comes around the back to stand behind her. There are three Hyenas, one out front and two others about two yards behind him. The front man is Loke and he's holding a small nylon duffel bag down by his side.

Hazel steps forward and hands him the grocery sack. He doesn't say a word. He simply nods and tosses the sack at the feet of one of his backup men, who picks it up and holds it under his arm.

"Not going to count it?" Hazel asks.

Loke shakes his head and tosses her the duffel. She follows his example by turning and handing it over to Eddie, who hefts it in his hand and seems to debate its weight.

No one says a word and Eddie moves to leave, but Hazel clears her throat suddenly and reaches into the pocket of her jeans. She hears a quick crush of gravel and looks up to see one of Loke's men has gone into a semicrouch and has a bead on her with a snub-barrel .38.

She hears Eddie whisper "Shit" and she stops moving, then slowly, with exaggerated care, she draws out a brass money clip with some bills pinched in it. Everyone stays rigid. There's a tension in the moment that's manifested in the lack of motion and the sound of Eddie's breath.

"I had asked you," Hazel says, "about another item." She extends the money clip out in the air toward Loke.

He stares at it for a while, then makes a quick hand gesture and his backup comes upright and stows his piece back wherever he drew it from. Loke reaches around to the rear waistband of his pants and brings forward his own handgun, a .44 automatic.

He shifts the gun in his hand and holds it out to Hazel grip-first. She takes the gun without looking at it and extends the money clip.

Loke shakes his head.

"I want you to have that," he says in a whispery voice. "It's a gift. Instead of roses."

Hazel opens her mouth, hesitates, then closes it again. She stares at Loke and pushes the clip back into her pocket, then she nods and starts to move for the van. Eddie follows her, climbs in behind the wheel, cranks the engine, and rolls the van back a few yards.

Hazel passes the gun from hand to hand, getting a feel for it, enjoying the coolness of the plating against her skin. When she turns to look out the window, Loke and his men are gone.

It's not until they're three blocks from Gompers Station that Eddie finally breaks the silence and says, "What the fuck is that for?"

Hazel's face stays expressionless, but she gives a small shake of her head like she's disappointed.

"We're in the Park now, Eddie," she says. "We're in Bangkok now."

They're quiet for another block and then Eddie says, "You gonna start popping liquor stores or something?"

They swing up an entrance ramp of the interstate. Hazel sighs and stares out at the lights of the oncoming cars. After a while she says, "No. No liquor stores, Eddie. You know, you're a sweetheart, but you got no feel for symbolism."

27.

Flynn watches Wayne standing before the glass elevator, staring up at the floor numbers, probably unaware of the fifty-dollar bill still crumpled in his fist.

Ronnie slides an ad cart into its slot and lowers the volume on a voice excited by a Volvo sale. She slides the headphones to her neck, swivels to face Flynn, and asks, "What the hell happened to Wayne?"

Flynn shrugs and says, "Sudden yearning for Tandoori. But don't worry, he said he'd bring back enough for all of us."

She squints at him and holds back a smile, and he says, "How long's the ad?"

"Not long enough."

He walks to her, swivels her back until she's facing the board, and begins to run his hands through her hair, then drops them down and starts in on her shoulders again. After a moment, he comes over the slopes of the shoulders and starts to unfasten the top button of her blouse.

"No way," she says. "I'm on in thirty seconds."

"Might take longer than that," he whispers, sliding a hand inside the blouse and fingering a nipple over the camisole. He can feel her lungs bring in air. She reaches up and back, touches the side of his face with her hand. The ad voice says, ". . . prices do not reflect dealer prep or tax," and without removing Flynn's hand, Ronnie leans forward, pulls the headphones back on, adjusts a volume knob, hits a button, and says, "Hello, caller from southern New Hampshire, you're on *Libido Liveline,* confide in Ronnie."

She gives no indication that anything unusual is happening. Flynn knew she'd be all control and it makes him want to push things further, make it a harder test. He switches to her left breast, this time sliding his fingers inside the camisole and squeezing a bit, leaning his head down at the same time to kiss her neck. Her head moves abruptly, but he's not convinced she wants him to stop.

Yes, hello. I'm a first-time caller.

Thank you. Thank you very much. For calling.

Flynn brings his tongue out and tastes her neck. The sharp, lingering sting of her perfume surprises him as much as the sudden change in her voice. He thinks she sounds like some female version of Elvis.

I'm not sure exactly how to start here. I'm just not . . . I've heard you in the past, you know, discuss my, discuss the type of problem I'm—

You're nonorgasmic, correct? This is what you told my assistant? You're not able to achieve orgasm?

The caller doesn't respond at first and Flynn thinks she might be a little put off by Ronnie's interruption and the abrupt manner she's taking. He agrees that it isn't her normal procedure and he wonders if his tongue and lips and hands are at all responsible. He hopes so and undoes another button on the blouse.

Are you still there, caller? Hello?

I'm here. I'm listening.

Have I identified your problem?

[*Pause*] Yes. You're correct.

All right, then, let's go to work. Now, I have to ask you a series of questions, and I need to know, before we get going here, if you're going to have difficulty answering. Because, as you can imagine, these are questions of a fairly intimate nature and I'm getting the sense that you're a bit apprehensive about being on the air.

Flynn pushes both his hands down inside her shirt, begins to squeeze both breasts and at the same time massage each nipple with his thumbs. Under the board, Ronnie kicks off her shoes.

It's just that, I've listened before and I never—

My manner surprised you. You thought I was abrupt with you. And I was. What you have to understand is that I don't have the luxury here of spending an hour with you, face-to-face, one-on-one, taking months to learn the personal history, to become versed in the childhood, review the traumas, hear all the details about the choice of lovers.

Yes, I understand.

I have to operate on instinct and the nature of the problem and the tone of the voice in my headphones. And I'm limited on time. Now, in the past you may have heard me take a more patient tack with another caller. But I'm sure we were dealing with a different problem. And certainly with a different person, correct?

Yes, yes, of course.

He brings his hands out and starts to unfasten all the buttons. He pulls the blouse out of the skirt and opens it wide, showing the silk, cream-colored teddy below.

Now, I'm going to need complete honesty from you if you want to accomplish anything tonight. And I'm going to need you to believe that, in fact, this one call, this next ten or fifteen minutes of talk, could change a very important part of your life. I'm asking for a good deal of faith on your part. Okay?

Yes, okay, I'm ready.

He pulls the tail of the camisole out of the skirt and when it snags for a second, he wonders if it's the kind that extends and snaps at the crotch. But Ronnie gives him a hand, shifting in her seat and pulling the hem free at her waist.

Let me start by asking you, is this a lifelong problem? Have you ever reached orgasm at any time in the past?

Well, you see, I'm not really sure. I don't—

Okay, fine, go no further. That's not a problem. Can you tell me, have you ever attempted self-stimulation? Have you ever tried to reach orgasm manually? [*Silence*] Come on now. Either with your hand or with a vibrator?

No. No, I haven't.

Flynn starts to roll the camisole upward, forcing himself to go slowly. When he comes to the bottom fold of her breast he tugs it in toward her body and pulls up even slower so she'll feel the silk rubbing past her nipples.

I sense that you have some reservations about attempting this?

It's just . . . I'm somewhat modest . . .

We're talking about the privacy of your own home. Close your shades. Turn on your answering machine.

I know what you're saying but I . . .

You've got to relax, learn to be more comfortable with your own body. Can I make some suggestions? Will you promise me you'll give them some thought?

He slides her chair back from the board just a bit and swivels it to the right. He starts to walk around to the side and can't help looking out the plate-glass window. The mall corridor is empty, but he wonders what will happen if Wayne changes his mind halfway to the Himalaya Express and returns. He's surprised to find the thought excites him a little.

Go ahead. I'm listening.

I don't hear a lot of commitment in your voice.

It's just awkward. You don't—

Yes, I do, my friend. You have no idea. Listen to me now. It's awkward at first, possibly, but you'll be shocked at how quickly your body will respond. Remember, you called here for a reason. The alternative is much more awkward. And more painful. Your subconscious is yearning for this change. You owe this to yourself. Doesn't it bother you, doesn't it drive you crazy, that there are feelings that you know exist and you know are tremendously powerful and yet you can't get to them? You can't ignite them. You don't know where to begin.

I don't—

No, you don't. And that's why you called. And that's what I'm here to give you tonight.

He goes down on his knees, reverent as an altar boy. He leans his torso into her, at first just laying his head sideways against her breasts, feeling the surprising coolness of her skin on his cheek. And then after just a second or two, he turns and brings his mouth to a breast, tongues the nipple a few times, very slowly, achingly slowly, time slowed down to an almost-frozen edging. Then he closes his mouth and starts to suck. He can see her chest rise and he knows how hard she's trying to stay in control. Then he closes his eyes and lodges in a rhythmic draw.

[*Breath audible*] Listen, tonight, before you go to sleep, I want you to put on some music. Forget the TV tonight. Put on some thing soft. Lush. You know what I mean. Something sensuous. You know what will work for you. Whether you think you do or not, trust me. You know. And if you have any wine in the house, I want you to pour yourself a cool glass of wine, maybe a nice merlot, that would be good. [*Deep breath*] Then I want you to draw a bath, fairly hot. And I want you to add some bath oil to the water. I want you to get some candles if you have any in. And I want you to place them around the tub and light them. Keep the regular lights off, okay? Understand? And leave some talcum out on the vanity if you think of it.

He switches to the other breast without opening his eyes. He kisses the skin between them as he moves. The skirt she's wearing zips up the side.

Now I want you to start to get undressed. But I want you to do it before the mirror, with the candlelight reflecting behind you. This might be difficult for you, but it's essential that you go slow and watch yourself. I need you to keep your eyes on yourself, keep your eyes on your body as it appears in the mirror. And tell yourself it's good, it's fine, you approve. Say the words aloud if you have to. Whisper them. Convince yourself if you're a doubter. Assure yourself. Compliment yourself. Let your clothing just drop to the floor. I don't want you to even think about it right now.

He starts to draw down the zipper and has to slide his hand under her and lift her slightly off the chair. She suddenly surprises him by reaching down and bringing her hand up into his crotch. He almost makes a noise, but stops in time, hunches inward, and stifles himself.

Now I need you to step into the water. Feel its warmth surround your legs. Feel the steaminess, the slickness of the water. Go down into it slowly, feel it lap up against your buttocks, then slide down, let it cover you totally, let it wash over you, come up over your sides and cover your belly and come up around your breasts. Can you picture what I'm saying to you?

Yes. Absolutely.

You and about fifty thousand listeners, Flynn thinks. He swivels the chair so she's lined up directly in front of him.

Do you know what I want you to do now?

Yes, I do.

He puts his hands on each of her knees. Her legs are already spread apart, but he pushes them outward till they touch the arms of the chair. She places her hand on his arm and he can't tell if it's a signal to stop or to keep going.

Okay, let's say it. I need you to touch yourself. Can you say it?

Touch myself.

Stimulate yourself. Arouse yourself. Love yourself.

Arouse.

That's right. You know what I'm saying here.

She's squeezing his arm, applying a tremendous amount of pressure. He suddenly realizes how strong she is. But he has no idea what she wants him to do. And he hesitates, does nothing.

[*Deep breath*] The big question is, can you do it?

So she takes control and starts to push his hand upward under the skirt. She guides him to the center and she's already wet and now the hesitation is gone and he knows what to do. He looks up and her shoulders are moving slightly up and down and she bites her bottom lip and releases it. He wants her to finish with the caller, go to an ad, get off the air. But it's clear that's not what she wants. He knows she wants to stay on the air to the end.

Yes, I can. I think I can.

You know you can.

Can they hear her? Does every listener know what's going on here? Is Wayne in his car, weeping, pounding the dash with the fist that holds the food money?

You do what I say now. Tonight.

Her voice is urgent and her words are interrupted slightly by grabs for air. It seems so obvious to Flynn. She's grabbing the arms of her chair and her knuckles are going white. He rotates his hand for better position.

I want to thank you—

You just do what I say. Promise me—

I do, I promise—

Then good luck, and we move on to our next caller.

Flynn looks up at her shocked, but he doesn't stop. He wants her to grab an ad cart and jam it in, fill up the studio with the promise of sales from the raspy language of pitchmen. But that's just not going to happen. She pulls a hand off the chair arm, punches down on a board button, brings her hand back to his head, and grabs a fistful of his hair.

Yes. You're on *Libido Liveline.*

She's overly loud and there's a catch to her voice at the end of her words as if she'd just emerged from below water.

Yes, Ronnie. Tremendous show tonight. A real classic.

He waits, but there's silence, so he stops and she yanks on his hair and then speaks.

Yes. Your question.

Is everything all right? Is there a problem?

Flynn begins to withdraw his hand and she shakes her head, both her lips pulled into her mouth. He makes a head gesture to the microphone and she nods rapidly, then unclenches her teeth and leans forward.

Not at all. Do you have a question?

I'm a first-time caller, Ronnie. First-time caller, but a longtime admirer.
[*Pause*] Thank you. And your question?

Flynn moves his hand to her thigh and leaves it there, motionless.

Well, it's more a comment than a question. A warning, you might say.

A warning?

Yes, that's right. I know your show is very popular among the Wireless crowd.

At the mention of the bar, Flynn straightens up slightly and turns his head to stare at the flashing lights of the board.

And I've got a feeling those O'Zebedee Brothers might be fans of yours also. And I feel a need to be open here, to inform the whole miserable cult of bastards of my intentions.

There's a minute of dead air as Ronnie catches her breath and stares down at Flynn. Then,

Ronnie, you there? Hello?

I'm afraid, sir, you've called the wrong show. We're here to discuss human sexuality. That's our topic here. I think maybe you want Ray Todd's—

They know who I'm talking to. They've been warned. The joke is over, okay? They're screwed. I'm in town and I won't be leaving till the job is done. They know what I mean.

I'm afraid you've got the wrong show, caller. I'm going to have to cut you off now—

I am in town, you little bastards. I know who you are—

She reaches out and kills the line.

We'll be right back after these messages.

She jams home a cart, and an announcement for a bluegrass festival starts up.

"Why did you stop?" she says, head back, looking up at the ceiling.

"You were losing it. You couldn't speak."

"You shouldn't have stopped," she says.

He doesn't know what to do. He feels foolish and inept. He starts to say, "I could still—"

But she cuts him off, smiles down at him, and removes his hand.

"I don't think so," she says.

She swivels until her back is to the board and then starts to get dressed.

"I don't get it," he says.

She tucks the last of her blouse into her skirt and says, "Relax. Food's here."

And he turns to see the doors of the glass elevator closing behind Wayne. The engineer starts to walk slowly toward the studio. He's got a brown paper bag in his arms. It's gone wet and dark near the bottom.

Ronnie stands up and runs her hands through her hair. She gives Flynn a soft punch to the shoulder.

"Better luck next time," she says. "God, I hope he brought some curried beef."

28.

Speer cuts the engine of the Ford and slouches a bit in his seat, but it's no longer possible to fall into the comfort of a standard surveillance posture. So he tries to ignore his twitching muscles and the rhythmic ache that pulses through his temples. He tries to concentrate instead on the landscape.

The Goulden Ave whores are smoking dusted joints, trading stories about the kink of the week and generally hanging out, waiting, squeezed into their Lycra and spandex, maybe mildly hoping for that one mythical all-night john who'll pop for a room in the Penumbra and a bottle of Johnnie Walker. There are probably thirty to forty of them spread down the two blocks of Goulden between Granada and Grassman, but there's one core group, a semilegendary clique of hustlers that congregate around the entrance of the Hotel Penumbra. They're sometimes called "the best and the brightest" by the bachelor-party yuppies who cruise in from the suburbs.

Just a year ago, the Penumbra was an improbable but absolutely gorgeous piece of work, a hundred-year-old, five-story arc that served as preposterous crib for Cortez, onetime neighborhood mayor for the Latinos. Cortez dumped an enormous percentage of his income into mutating the hotel into a surreal vision that spliced elements of spooky High Gothic with splashes of Euro-industrial. It never should have worked, but

249

Cortez willed it into being and shined a barrage of klieg lights on it so the city had to look.

Then Cortez disappeared. And the vision that took ten years to refine toward perfection took only twelve brutal months to decay into a darkened hulk of looted rooms, graffitied walls, and burned-out floors. No one knows for sure who owns the Penumbra today, though it's possible the city has been saddled with it. But in the absence of a resident landlord, a pimp named Bedoya has taken to renting out the uncharred rooms by the hour.

Speer grips the steering wheel, sweating, habitually moistening his lips and gums, wondering if the dozen women loitering in front of Cortez's desecrated monument realize the fierceness of this devolution, if they understand it as a simple and beautiful example of eternal laws, not the humanist babble about survival and extinction, but the most ancient stories, tales concerned with the expulsion of the unworthy, vignettes about vile, unfit creatures being cast downward.

He takes his notebook from the passenger seat, opens it, rereads the last few lines of rigid print, then picks up his pen and continues writing.

(Goulden Avenue)

My life continues, Margie. I'm involved in the meat of one of my most annoying investigations. You would say I found them all annoying and that I loved the annoyance. (Maybe in the same way that I used to love the static, what you thought to be blank noise, undefined, incapable of being interpreted.) I don't disagree with you out of hand. I'm just not sure "love" is the correct word in this instance. Rather, I would say that I am compelled to view "annoyance" as an opponent of complacency. Complacency can be equated with weakness. And weakness will always lead to disorder, confusion, an irreversible breakdown of progress and history.

In this vein, I'd like to attempt to explain my attention to seemingly meaningless static. Though I am still making progress in Dr. Helm's book (though, to be honest with you, I am having trouble accepting his contention that it is the *repression* of a "female sensibility," trapped, hidden, and degraded in every male, that is the cause for everything from harsh words to Cambodian genocide . . .), I took a look, yesterday, into another tome from the self-help library you had abandoned in our home. I happened to scavenge Dr. Rothstein's *Death Takes No Holiday* before moving to my current residence. The doctor goes in for the popular notion that casts Anger as one rung on the inevitable ladder up to an acceptance of Death as a natural (and constantly imminent) state.

Possibly, this is where we differed the most, Margie. I continue to see my anger as an assault on death, an affront to its peasant (communistic) power. And even if I'm forced to admit that, at some point, my defeat (and Death's victory) is certain, I still have the comfort of the knowledge that I did not bow down to a foe I cannot respect.

A pain begins behind his left eye. He rubs a hand over his face, takes some deep breaths, then slides the notebook and pen under his seat and looks down Goulden Ave He fixes on a dark-skinned girl, maybe seventeen. He watches her bend down to the window of a slowing low-rider and begin a full-bodied negotiation, a form of barter where suggestion is everything. And the ease of her movements and gestures, the lascivious way she runs her hand along the side of her own breast, tells him yes, these women may be the best and the brightest, but they haven't got a clue that there's a ton of granite metaphor easily within their grasp, waiting to be noticed and understood. Cortez's barren empire of signs flanking their backsides might as well be Notre Dame or Chartres.

Still, he's not without some degree of sympathy for these women. They're animals of commerce and at the very least he can understand the rules that drive their lives. There's an obscene order to their motivations and actions, a primal, logical capital-

ism played out in a carnal market. And the fact is they never had
the benefit of a Sister Bernadette, Speer's first-grade teacher,
with her rosary beads cloaked inside the flowing black habit and
transformed in an unseen instant into a flailing whip, a blessed
lash that could beat the commandments forever into a still-
forming skull.

He leans forward and pops the glove box and for a second
he stops and stares at his hand lit in the dim green glow that
emits from the band selector of the dash radio. His skin looks
gray and then almost translucent, as if, if he continued to stare,
he'd see through the skin to the muscle and bone below. He
blinks his eyes and pulls from the box a pint of Four Roses and a
warm can of Jolt. He pops open the soda and takes a long drink,
wedges it in his crotch, twists off the top of the bourbon, and
throws down a shooter's swallow.

The radio is tuned between stations, and the car is filled with
a low, consistent hiss of static. Speer has no idea what time it is.
On the drive to Goulden Ave, on impulse, he pulled up next to a
sewer grating, unstrapped his Bulova—the one Margie gave him,
inscribed *All My Love Always*—and dropped it down through the
slot into a pool beneath the street. He's not sure why he did this.
He could argue with himself that it was a symbolic attempt to
begin to move on, to eliminate reminders of his wife, of the
woman he long ago invested his soul with. But the truth is he
has no desire to forget Margie. To stop writing the letters. To
abandon his plans for reconstructing their life together.

There's a small silver crucifix dangling from the rearview
mirror in the center of the windshield. Speer lifts his hand to it,
recoils his index finger, then tweaks the cross lightly. It begins to
sway back and forth through his line of vision like a pendulum,
and with each arc Speer shifts his field of focus from the dying
Christ to the clan of whores jabbering a hundred yards away.
The process makes his head ache worse, but he keeps it up for a
time, and then, without really thinking, he begins to recite a
Bible verse drilled into him long ago by Sister Bernadette, words
pushed down into the densest meat of his brain, where they

could never evaporate.

Do not defile yourself by any of these things, for by all these the nations I am casting out before you defiled themselves; and the land became defiled, so that I punished its iniquity, and the land vomited out its inhabitants . . .

The words trail off, but he continues to move his lips for a while, a silent babble, an inaudible glossolalia, as if a mute tongue of purging fire had visited this Ford sedan parked at the side of Goulden Ave. When he finally brings his lips together, he restarts the car's engine and begins to roll toward the Penumbra.

Steam is rising from the sewer gratings along Goulden and it combines with a low layer of damp fog to give the whole street a different look, as if the block had been lifted out of Quinsigamond and transported to Berlin in 1931, all shadow and harsh electrical light against red brick and iron beams and whining, distant police sirens chronically sounding in the distance.

Mina is the first to approach Speer's car. She's small and a little wiry, dressed in a red vinyl miniskirt, sheer black stockings with a polka-dot design woven in, a shiny, royal-blue halter top under a ratty imitation-fur shoulder wrap. Her hair is a weird retro shag cut with the last traces of a burnt-red dye job growing out. She moves across the sidewalk at a slow pace, a true saunter, to the accompaniment of accented calls from her colleagues. Speer picks up a mention of *señorito blanquito*. He slides the passenger window down all the way and as Mina leans down on the door and smiles, he toasts her with his pint and says, "The kingdom of heaven approaches."

"Your lucky night," Mina says. "This kingdom has the discount for *un policía*."

Speer doesn't even try to protest.

"I'm off duty and very lonely," he says in a low and awkward voice, feeling a run of sweat slide down the middle of his back.

"Let's see how lonely," she says, rubbing her thumb and forefinger together in the classic cash sign and looking backward over her shoulder at the sisters who continue to hoot and laugh and sing.

Speer slides a wad of bills up slightly from his breast pocket and Mina says, "You have a date for the prom, *policía*," and climbs in the car next to him.

They enter the basement apartment and Speer flips on a light, then goes to the folding table and turns on the radio. As the sound of static plays from the speaker, he moves back to the door, locks the bolt, and secures the slide chain. Mina tosses her throw over the stool, walks to the tiny rectangular window in the far corner of the room, up near the ceiling, and says, "You get water in here?"

Speer ignores her, takes off his suitcoat, and throws it on the wicker rocking chair. He goes to the single kitchen cabinet, pulls down an unlabeled bottle, and begins pouring what looks like bourbon into a white coffee mug that says *One Day at a Time*. Mina walks over to the radio and begins to spin the tuner, looking for some music.

Speer wheels around immediately and says, "Don't touch the radio," in a flat, slow voice that makes Mina squint at him. He walks to the table and readjusts the tuner until the room is filled with static again.

"What are you doing?" Mina says. "This gives me the headache."

Speer cups her chin in his hands, tries to smile, and says, "Five minutes, you won't notice it."

As if this is some sort of cue, Mina steps into him, brings her mouth up to his neck, and begins to unbuckle his belt. Speer jerks away, but Mina's persistent, following the flow of his body, trying to unlatch the belt as she says, "It's okay, *papacito*. Mina take good care of you."

Speer gets his hands on her shoulders and holds her still, but he's breathing heavy and he stammers as he says, "Now, you slow down. You slow down and we'll do this right."

He takes a long breath, then moves over to the bed, gets

down on one knee, reaches underneath, and pulls out a worn and crumpled brown paper shopping bag. He reaches into the bag and for some reason the crinkling, rustling noise that his hand makes bothers Mina, tenses up her stomach like a sign of the flu coming on. Speer pulls from the bag a medium-length blond wig, done in sort of a bland style with a limp curl at the ends. He holds the wig out from his body with one hand and awkwardly tries to straighten the hair with the other.

He carries the wig across the dim room as if it were a chalice, kind of reverent, maybe a little bit scared, Mina thinks. He holds it out to her as if he were giving her a gift, an engagement ring that cost a year's salary.

"You want me to wear it?" Mina says.

Speer nods.

"You know, you could've just bought a blonde, saved us both the trouble."

But she takes it from him, fits it on her head, tucking her own hair underneath. Speer puts a hand on her shoulder and steers her toward the cloudy mirror hanging over his bureau. Mina adjusts and tucks a bit, rolling her eyes the whole time, but smiling as if this could be a fun game, or at least a good story for the girls when she gets back to Goulden Ave.

Speer stands behind her the whole time, hands lightly on her shoulder, looking at her reflection with devoted attention, adjusting his stance a bit, seeming to be looking for something he hasn't named. When Mina gets the wig as attractive as she thinks is possible, she holds her hands out at her sides for inspection. Speer nods back at her in the mirror, then turns her around, steps back, and begins to look her up and down, feet to wig and back to feet again.

"All right," he says. "Fine."

He takes the money from his shirt pocket and holds it up in the air for a second, eye-level, then tosses it on top of the bureau.

"What do you want me to do?" Mina asks, and follows the words with a long-practiced lick of her lips.

Speer moves around her, takes a seat in the rocker on top of his suitcoat, loosens his tie, and puts his hands down on the rocker's arms.

"Now you stand in front of me," he says, his voice barely audible. Mina positions herself before him.

"Now," he says, "you get those whore's clothes off you."

She nods, slides out of her heels, then, slowly, arching her body side to side, she begins to pull her top off over her head, saying, "You gonna love what Mina's got for you."

"No," Speer barks, surprising them both. Mina holds the loose halter against her chest for a second, then Speer starts rocking slowly, lowers his voice, and says, "Don't use that name. In this room, your name is Margie."

Mina nods and Speer says, "Say it."

"My name is Margie."

"Say it again."

Mina sighs a bit, but complies. "My name is Margie."

"All right," Speer says, "keep going."

She drops the halter to the ground, reaches around behind, and unzips the skirt, then pushes it down her legs. She unsnaps the garters on her thighs and does a very slow roll-down of the stockings. She can hear Speer's breathing get heavier and she sees him shift slightly in his seat. She bunches up one stocking and throws it into Speer's lap.

"I don't want that," he says, his voice a bit high, but there's no conviction in the words and he leaves the stocking where it's fallen.

Mina puts her hands on her hips, turns her waist slightly side to side, showing the customer all the vantages, letting him take in and cement the memories he'll call up weeks and months from now.

Speer repositions his feet and stops the rocker from moving. The only sound in the musty room is the dry catch of his swallow over the low static of the radio.

"Lie down on the bed," he says, and Mina smiles at him and stretches out on her side, her elbow bent and her arm propping her head as she looks at him.

"Lie on your back," he whispers, and she obeys.

He continues to sit in the rocker staring at her as she stares up at the ceiling.

"Close your eyes," he says, and she turns her head and glances at him, then heeds his request.

There's nothing but static for a full minute, then Mina hears the creak of the chair as he stands, but she keeps her eyes closed. The ritual johns will freak if you screw up the program at a crucial moment. But then they pay well when you follow the directions exactly. All in all, it balances out.

From across the room, she hears him say, "I'm very tired tonight, Margie. Do you have to hear the story again?"

She doesn't know what to do. She's not sure he wants her to speak. And if he does, she's not sure what the answer should be. So she says nothing, stays prone with her eyes squeezed shut.

Then he whispers, "Please tell me the story," the words muffled as if he were trying to keep his lips from moving, a bad ventriloquist or a kid cheating on a school exam.

"Please tell me the story," she repeats, and can tell immediately she's done the right thing, her instincts are on target.

She hears the sound of a zipper being opened.

"But Margie," he says softly, "you have no idea the day I've had, the things I've witnessed out there."

"I want to hear the story," she demands, her voice bolder, more adamant.

And as if her tone has energized him, she hears the rapid fumbling of clothes being shed, coins falling from pockets and clanging on the linoleum floor.

"Please, Margie," but his voice is already resigned, "I just want to lie down next to you. I just want to hold you and sleep."

"You tell it to me right now," she snaps, feeling in charge and liking it, sure he'll capitulate to any request.

He comes to the side of the bed, strokes her cheek gently, takes her by the wrist. Then she feels the coolness of the metal and at the same time hears the ratcheted-click sound and opens her eyes in time to see him securing the other end of the handcuff to the frame of the bed.

"What the fuck," she yells, and jerks her arm away, but she's already locked in. With her free hand she takes a futile swing at him, but he sidesteps it and holds a finger up to his mouth, saying, "Quiet down, Margie. Right now."

Mina shakes her head at him, controls herself enough to say, "I don't do this shit, asshole. You want this shit, you go down Hip Sing Street. Everyone knows that."

He's naked from the waist down, but he's still got his starched white shirt on and his tie is still pulled up to his throat. He's smiling and nodding, saying, "Relax, Margie. You've done this before. This is not a problem."

"Take this thing off or I'll start screaming—"

"Margie—"

"I mean it, asshole. Get it off now."

He holds the key up in the air for her to see and says, "Please, Margie. I'll let you go anytime you want. You know that. But I'll pay you double your rate if you relax and stay. I always have. I'm a man of my word."

He suddenly doesn't seem very dangerous to Mina, just an intricate kink with some cash to burn.

"Let me hold the key," she says.

He places it gently on her stomach. She picks it up and holds it in her free hand.

"I want triple time," she says. "These things are uncomfortable."

"My money is your money, Margie. Have I ever denied you anything?"

Mina slowly settles back on the bed and he stands over her, brushes her cheek again like a lover, and says, "Now close the eyes and ask me."

He starts to move to the foot of the bed and Mina realizes this could be over in three short minutes, so she closes her eyes and takes a breath and says, "Tell me the story again."

There's a pause. He gives a dry cough and says, "If you insist—"

She interrupts and says, "I insist. Right now. I want the story. Give it to me."

She hears him take a deep, halting breath and she spreads her legs, but he doesn't move from his spot at the foot of the bed. And then he begins.

"Mr. Hoover was born on January first, 1895, in Washington, D.C."

What the hell is this shit? Mina wonders, and starts to open one eye. But Speer yells, "Don't you dare, Margie. You asked and now you'll have to hear the whole story. You asked for this. You did."

With one hand, Speer is grabbing the foot bar at the end of the bed. And with the other, he's grabbing himself.

Mina closes her eyes before she bursts out laughing. She bites down on the inside of her cheeks to keep silent and thinks, *Rosalita won't believe this.*

"Mr. Hoover went to law school at night, attending George Washington University. He graduated in 1916 and went on to, to . . ."—there's some hesitation, some deep breathing, then he continues—"achieve a master of law degree the following year, whereupon he entered in service to the Department of Justice as a file reviewer"—the voice speeds up just a bit—"and within two years was appointed special assistant to the then Attorney General, A. Mitchell Palmer. In May of 1924 he was named acting director of the Bureau of Investigation"—a pause for breath, a swallow, the pitch gets higher. "Disgusted with the scandals of the Harding administration, Mr. Hoover devised his own rigorous methods of recruiting and regimenting new personnel." The end of the bed lifts off the floor slightly, then bangs back down, and Mina almost convulses with laughter, but manages to dig her nails into her thigh to short-circuit the attack. "Mr. Hoover established the world's largest fingerprint file, brought practicing scientists into the world of law enforcement and built, built"—the bed lifts and bangs again—"the National Academy where," and again the bed slams up and down, "officers from all over the country could come, come, and train and"—*this is it,* Mina thinks, *el fin grande*—"and he retained his post until his death at, his death, on May second, 1972, his death am-amid vicious rumors about his loyal and trusting, he brought order to, he brought, he saved, he ordered, hunted the agents of chaos and anarchy that, he, he...," and the rest turns into a groaning yell and the bed is shoved back against the wall and Mina opens her eyes to see only his hand still grasping the foot bar. The rest of him is crumbled down on the floor below her eye level.

Mina shakes her head, allows herself a small giggle, and starts to unlock the handcuff. At the sound of this, Speer climbs to his feet. His face is flushed and he's got a scowl on that tells Mina it's time to grab her money and leave. She swings her feet over the edge of the bed and says, "Listen, next time it's Hip Sing Street, okay? They got shit down there..."

She starts to gather her clothes together and Speer approaches her holding the One Day at a Time coffee mug and says, "I'm glad you've come home, Margie—"

Mina starts to pull the halter over her head and says, "Yeah, I'm glad too. Now you owe me a hundred and fifty. Let's go."

Speer acts as if he hasn't heard her. "But there has to be some penance for leaving."

Mina looks up at him and says, "Listen, dickhead, this is getting old. I'm done being Margie, okay? Now, get my money."

"There has to be some atonement," Speer says. "There has to be some regret. Some contrition. There must be some compunction. There has to be a balance, Margie. I've explained this before."

Mina says, "Look, asshole," and starts to stand up, but Speer shoves her back down on the bed and before she can move, he's on top of her, straddling her and pouring the contents of the coffee mug over her head. And as she smells the gasoline, Mina begins to scream.

Speer clamps one meaty hand over her mouth and uses the other to search his shirt pocket. Mina bucks, jerks her head enough to free her mouth, and instead of screaming, bites down on Speer's thumb, sinking teeth into skin and drawing a rush of blood. Speer screams and Mina manages to slide one leg up and rams a knee into his groin. His air cuts off and he falls sideways on the bed.

She jumps up, leaves the rest of her clothes on the floor, and is out the apartment door before Speer can get to his feet.

She runs two miles, her bare feet getting bruised and cut, through alleyways and between buildings, completely disoriented until she comes around a corner to Granada Street. She cuts down Voegelin and runs in a rear entrance to the Penumbra. She huddles inside the charred remains of Club 62, tries to catch her breath, tries to wipe the sting of the gasoline from her eyes.

She backs up against a wall, suddenly freezing in the cool November air. She squats down, hunches over her knees, thinks, *I'll get Bedoya and he'll get the Popes and they'll find the mother—*

And then the thought breaks off, derailed by her vision of her first glance at his face behind the wheel of that boxy car. The face that told her, in that first instant, *I'm a cop.*

A gust of wind blows through the broken windows of the nightclub, whistles into the burned-out and gutted cavern, begins to sound, in Mina's freezing ear, like a word. Like a name.

Margie.

29.

The bath is filled with steaming hot water and a generous dose of the French raspberry oil. Hannah sits on the edge of the bathtub, naked, the bathroom door locked, Lenore's notebook, once again, sitting in her lap like a small animal of some kind whose greatest asset is its deceptive coloration, the bland and boring outer skin that causes most predators to ignore it.

Hannah runs her hand down the spiral binding, then over the cardboard cover. *It isn't fair, Lenore,* she thinks, *and that's typical of you. This is a one-way conversation. A monologue. There's no way for me to object or maybe even agree. I don't even know where you are. Why did you do this to me? Why did you have to choose me?*

Given the chance, she wonders what she would say to Lenore.

She could just pivot, right now, right this second, turn on her behind and drop the notebook into the water. She could watch the pages start to turn to a mushy pulp, watch her mentor's rigid printing begin to dissolve, begin to bleed into a curling stream of thin blue waves, contaminating the water with all this scrawled craziness. What if she drowned the notebook, then she stepped into the bath, slid down and let the ink-infected water engulf her body, course up around every curve and bend of her anatomy, wash over her, this full-bodied, blue-tinged baptism? What would happen? Would the madness seep into her through her pores? Would Lenore's bent words penetrate through the skin, her lunatic worldview jump into the bloodstream and make a dash for the brain stem?

Without thinking, she opens the notebook randomly, looks down at the page, and reads:

Maybe the only reason I'm writing is to thank you for looking in on my brother. Don't ask how I know this. It could simply be a guess.

Like my guess that I must be the central joke down the division these days, Richmond gagging himself trying to come up with the new one-liner. "Why did Lenore cross the road?" It's all right. We always joke about things that terrify us. Things we're too stupid to fully comprehend.

In the midst of all the mockery, I can still claim my refusal to hold an ideology. I will not be raped by anything as limiting as a belief system. Because the nature of each and every one, from the dawn of that most hazardous of realities, human consciousness, all the way through to the milliseconds in which these words are being born, is predicated on the most primal and deceptive system of them all: language. And yet, I'm still trapped within it, still bound to make the slashes and circles, the lines and dots and waves, the pathetic icons accumulated throughout the nightmare, if I want to communicate with you, H.S. Your only approach at the moment is the eye scan, your brain decoding this hash of ink and pulp.

Remember this, Hannah: that once I was the queen of rational thought. I was the Mother Superior in the order of cause and effect. I was a loving concubine for ideas of pragmatism, logic, deduction, pure reason, and free will.

And then things began to change. And the changes began to come faster, until their speed began to increase geometrically. And my faith in the supremacy of our senses began to wobble. Because I could see the limitations of these organs—the eye, ear, nose, tongue, the skin itself. And it began to appear to me that while our environment perpetually evolves around us, our capacity for perceiving it is frozen. So, we end up terrified apes on a roller coaster whose engine has revved and gone out of control and started to build to a limitless speed.

And once an understanding like this violates you, Hannah, you can never go back. You can't help but be certain that every clove of garlic in the kitchen of Fiorello's Ristorante has an infinite number of tastes. Every drop of cold water that slips down your neck in a late-autumn rainstorm has an infinite number of sensations. Every gust of powder that drifts past you in the shooting bunker has an infinite number of fragrances. Every tone you hear on the radio has an infinite number of components.

And every gesture you witness, from every landscape you observe, has an infinite number of meanings.

It's like a cancer of analysis: malignant possibilities reproducing themselves without restriction.

If you're convinced I'm psychotic, Hannah, then you should have no fear taking up this challenge: Go down to Bangkok Park and look for evidence of the gangs. Just walk around and note what you see—things like the graffiti and the tattoos. Then go home. And in an hour more signs will come to your mind—the hand signals, the footwear dangling from the streetlamps, the color of their cars.

And in two hours, more signs will come to you—the earrings their whores wear, the sources of the brand names they hang on their smack, the specific day of the week they shake down the merchants, the peculiar patterns in the bandannas they wear around their smooth shaven skulls, the placement of the knife wounds on the bodies of informants.

Guess what happens after three hours, Hannah?

How does a woman go from being a detective with a methodology, a devotion to the clue and the motive and the conclusive solution, to . . .

She slaps the book closed and throws it against the bathroom door. It bounces down to the floor and lies there, like a taunt, like one of Lenore's perfect, stinging put-downs, a fast comment about cowardice or stupidity.

And finally, in that moment, Hannah realizes what she would say to Lenore. The words come to her brain without any effort or preparation. She'd say, "Go to hell, you bitch."

She'd say, "You're a goddamn loon. There's nothing you can show me anymore. You're over the top. I don't need you. I don't need anyone. And thank God, because there is no one. And it's a relief to finally understand that. Not just in my brain, but in my heart. In my stomach, where all the real understanding has to come from. There's no one left, Lenore. No one who could understand how badly, how desperately, I want to leave this city, how many people I'd be willing to hurt just for a chance to escape. And I have no place to escape to. No preplanned destination. No geographical goal. No resting place that I can aim for. I simply, only, want motion. Movement. Distance. From all these familiar streets and buildings and signs. From all these memorized faces. From all these voices playing over and over in my ear until I hear them in my sleep. I want distance from Quinsigamond. I want distance from my own life. From my past. All these years piling up with events and choices, decisions and random crap, until it's such a weight on the shoulders you feel the ground giving way under your feet. You feel you'll be pushed straight into the earth, buried alive and then buried dead by the weight of your accumulated past. I want out before this happens. I'm not as brave or smart or obsessed or committed as you, Lenore. I want out. I want movement. I want to be a solo pioneer. I want to head west, toward the next big ocean. I want to maneuver the Mustang onto a series of secondary highways, one leading into the next, roadsides painted with state boundaries and all of them blurring as I speed past. I want no more memory and I want no more prophecy. I want no newscasts or weather reports bleating from my radio. I just want to drive forward, sleep in my seat, buy fruit and crackers in anonymous convenience stores, and sit on my trunk at dusk, pulled into some overgrown field hundreds of miles from red brick, hundreds of days from my point of origin. I want to lie back and look up at the sky and not attempt to recognize and name constellations. I want some peace and I want a lifetime of quiet."

She starts to cry now, fighting against it and failing, a burning behind the eyeballs as she hunches down over her thighs and knees, her face falling into her hands as a childish sobbing begins to catch and her breathing goes rapid and shallow.

"So I reject you, Lenore. I don't want you. I don't want anything to do with you. Let the fucking cock crow, Lenore. Three times. Ten times. I don't care. I reject you. Just go away. Just leave me alone."

30.

Hazel put out the word to meet at midnight, but by eleven-thirty all her people have arrived at the old airport. They file into the abandoned terminal in groups of two and three and take their seats silently on the long-dead baggage claim conveyor belt.

Gabe has built a small campfire in the center of the semicircle formed by the belt. The fire is not an original idea. Gabe spotted the debris of several previous fires when he first arrived. He assumes the old airport is probably used by a number of transient groups, from homeless drunks and tramps to moody, horny teenagers. He hopes none of them decide to stop by tonight, but if they do, he's sure Hazel will handle the situation. He thinks there's not much Hazel couldn't handle. His walloping crush on this strange woman is growing daily.

As the group settles in around the fire, Gabe starts to think they look like a mock Indian tribe. Heavy-metal Apaches. Biker-punk Comanches. There are at least a half dozen Mohawk 'dos present, a lot of lampblack around the eyes, pounds of jagged silver jewelry—ear and nose rings and all kinds of symbolic neckwear—and tattoos. The whole crew is big on tattoos. It's not like it's a requirement. Hazel says there are *no* requirements. They just happen to share an intrinsic love of body design. So, underneath all the studded leather and torn denim is a wide variety of well-toned skin canvases exhibiting multicolored scenes of both natural and mythic art. But most of all, engraved across biceps and buttocks, are strange non sequiturs, clipped and illogical phrases, linked words and sometimes numbers whose meaning is a code known only to its bearer and his immediate circle.

There's a rumor that Hazel wears a male name, done in scarlet ink, on the bottom slope of her left breast. No one will admit to having seen the name and there have been a few drunken guesses as to what it might be. But Gabe doesn't believe it exists. He can picture Hazel with maybe an exploding microphone on her bottom, maybe even a standard *Question authority* down the back of one leg. But a man's name on her breast? That implies a branding of sorts. It's close to an ownership symbol and Gabe knows for certain that Hazel would have nothing to do with it.

He watches her as she sits up on the ticket counter, staring out the plate glass at the pocked runway in the moonlight. He'd love to know what she's thinking and then begins to imagine her as a pilot, a bomber pilot, looking so sharp in one of those classic, butter-smooth black leather jackets, maybe one with the fur trim around the collar. He adds himself into the picture as her copilot, maybe the bombardier, the two of them huddled in a tiny cockpit, air masks loose on their chests, talking back and forth in low, assuring voices, consulting maps and waiting for the moment, the instant, when they come down low, snap open the bay doors on the bomber's underside, dump their missiles, and then cruise upward, full throttle, away from the coming boom of heat and air.

He suddenly realizes Hazel has pivoted on her behind and is staring back at him. There's no way to read the expression on her face, so he drops his head and begins to tend the campfire.

Someone on the end of the belt sparks a joint and begins to pass it down the line. Gabe doesn't know how Hazel will react to this. Personally, he thinks the group should know the seriousness of this meeting and hold off partying till they adjourn. But, again, Hazel isn't here to make rules. She'll probably ignore the joint, impose seriousness with her voice and body movements.

She slides off the ticket counter now, a definition of ease and grace. She moves to the semicircle at a moderate pace, letting the heels of her secondhand ankle boots ignite an echoing click on the terminal's mustard tile floor. The sound is like a gavel that brings the meeting to order. There are seven of them in all, including Gabe and Hazel. The oldest, the construction greaser called Eddie G, is probably closing in on thirty. Gabe is the youngest. No one's really sure of Hazel's age.

She steps up onto the baggage belt. She looks tremendous. She's wearing stretch black pants with a huge maroon suede belt with big brass buckle, a zebra-striped tank top under an ancient, milky-blue jeans jacket with a barely visible zodiac wheel on the back. She pauses above them all and looks down at each face lit by the campfire, then steps down inside the semicircle and positions herself behind the fire. There's a small but constant breeze making its way into the terminal and it fans the flames toward Hazel's boots and makes a slight whispering sound.

"Okay," Hazel says, "we're here. I'm not going to stand here, like Browning or like Flynn, and say something asinine like 'Thanks for coming.' I don't owe you any thanks. You're all here 'cause you want to be. And every one of you knows that being here means something. Nobody here is stupid."

She pauses and then, after looking at them again, she goes slowly down on her knees, her behind resting on her heels, her thighs parted and the fire angled between them. She passes her left hand through the flames slowly, like she was trying to clear them away to see something on the floor below. She looks up again and lowers her voice a little

"We're not at Wireless tonight, are we? We're not at some futile negotiation upstairs in the Anarchy Museum. That's because negotiations are over, kids. Done. Wireless has nothing to offer us anymore. It's falling apart. From inside, the way these things always do. I don't have time to go into the details, but trust Hazel, the break has already happened. There's some very swinish behavior going on. Browning and all his old mothers have completely turned. There's nothing more to discuss. It was bound to happen. I saw it coming. I told you all what I saw. Okay."

She brings her hands together in a loud clap and stands back up.

"So, we are on our own and I don't know about any of you, but it feels great to me. This means there's nothing holding us back."

She walks over next to Gabe, crouches, and puts a hand on his shoulder. "That makes me very excited," she says. "Things get crazy from here on in. But we've got nothing against crazy, do we, Gabe?"

He looks into her firelit face, so thrilled to be singled out that he forgets to answer and one of the group laughs.

"No, we've got nothing against crazy, Hazel," she answers for him.

She stands up again and moves back behind the fire. "We've been waiting for things to heat up forever"—another pause—"so let's be clear about a few things. As good old Flynn used to say, let's review the agenda. 'Cause there aren't going to be a whole lot of these get-togethers from now on. This isn't a joke anymore. There's about to be some serious movement. Some serious relocation. As of tonight, this isn't a social club. We're not here for the secret handshakes and the passwords. What are we here for, Gabe?"

He's ready this time, thankful for a second chance. As if reading from a book, he says, in a nervous, explicit voice, "We're here to fuck up the normal modes of communication."

The words slide out without a stutter or a stammer and he knows if he could just be next to Hazel twenty-four hours a day, he'd never have a problem with his tongue again.

"That's right," Hazel says, unable to stop a smile. "Very good, Gabe."

She steps over to Eddie on the other side of the belt. He's

got the joint hanging from the corner of his lips. She puts a hand on Eddie's shoulder and Gabe flinches.

"And with that in mind, Eddie, why don't you tell everybody what we picked up tonight?"

He takes a hit off the joint and passes it to Diane, the redheaded cashier he lives with.

He stands up, though no one's asked him to, puts his hands on his hips, and says, "Genuine, top-of-the-line plastique. Courtesy of our new friends the Hyenas."

Hazel runs a hand through Eddie's semipompadour, then wipes it across the back of his jacket.

"Oh, Eddie, you sweetheart," she says, allowing herself just a little upbeat humor and enthusiasm.

She steps back to the center of the semicircle, squats down over her knees, and lets the fire illuminate her face.

"Flynn has asked for one more meeting, one more try at reconciliation, he says. I wasn't even going to mention it to you. I thought I'd let them sit there in their little playroom and just wait all night. But I've changed my mind. We'll go. We'll make the break official. We'll leave nothing to question."

She stands up.

"I'm going to want to see every one of you back here afterward. Once we've established ourselves, security will become a big factor. After this first time, we'll work in groups of two and three. But tonight I want everyone here."

She indulges them with a last smile.

"Think of it as an Independence Day party. And Eddie, you're in charge of the fireworks."

31.

Speer gives up trying to sleep after a half hour of tossing and turning. He pulls on a pair of pants, goes to the kitchen sink, and splashes several handfuls of cold water on his face. Then he moves to the refrigerator and takes out a half-empty can of Jolt soda. He takes a sip from the can, reaches into his pants pocket, and pulls out two white tablets. He blows a piece of lint off one of the pills, tosses them in his mouth, and washes them down with another hit of soda.

He moves to the metal stool at the kitchen table and takes a seat, flips on the plastic gooseneck lamp, and turns on the Kenwood. Static eases into the room. He opens his spiral notebook, glances at the wall clock, and starts to finger the tuning knob. Small, mostly unintelligible sounds make clipped entrances and exits as the indicator band slides down the range of frequencies. At 12,750 kHz, Speer stops and locks the tuner. He waits with his eyes closed and then a flutelike instrument sounds, something like a cheap penny whistle. It plays a simple, twenty-one-note melody, stops, then plays it again.

And then again. It's a loop, a continuous pattern. The repetition soothes Speer. It's like a forgotten childhood song that's been given back to him. And now he can go on with the night.

He uncaps his Paper Mate and turns to a clean notebook page.

3 A.M.

Dear Margie,

Perhaps, finally, when all, as they say, is said and done, my dearest hope is that you come to own this notebook. I will admit that the likelihood of this happening is probably not very great. I could take precautions—place the book, at some point, in a safe-deposit box, list it in a will, contact an attorney, and legally establish you as my beneficiary. (In fact, your name is, of course, still on my standard Bureau-issue policy.)

But it seems to me that this could be thought of as tantamount to forcing my thoughts on you. And that is the last thing I want.

No, the best thing is to place this pulpy volume on the wings of chance. Perhaps it will be burned by Corny, the building super, just hours after the incineration of my own tired and all-too-mortal bones. Why the mention of death? you might ask. Simply because a large, essential part of me feels dead, has felt this way since your departure.

What does it feel like to be dead? It feels like the hiss of static, Margie. Does that make any sense to you? Do you find this inept hyperbole? I'm being very honest here. I'm attempting to explain the nature of my mind to you. Do you recall the sound? In the dark, in the middle of the night, often in the summer, when I was sweating and suffering insomnia, and I would go into the next room and turn on the receiver?

You despised the noise. Do you remember the incident, years ago, that Fourth of July? Our own fireworks. You said, "If you'd only tune something in. Anything but that static." The next day I found the Koss headphones you'd left on my desk. But I have to admit, I still cannot wear them—that feeling of pressure over my ears.

Can you possibly see why I'm in such a void today, Margie?

Why your leaving has shorted many of the deepest relays of my brain.

Again, part of me feels DEAD, Margie. And, I'm sorry, but you must accept responsibility for this status.

My current plan is to feed my (in your words: "legendary") anger. I hope that this will resurrect me, lead me out of this cave of numbness. I feel that it's working already. Certain organs are humming—that needles-and-pins feeling of returning life. My eyes and ears and, maybe most important, my intuition are all coming awake. Soon, I'll be seeing things clearly again. Hearing all the sounds on all the bands.

THIS is why I used to listen to the static, Margie.

Recall, above, I referred to it as "seemingly" meaningless. All in the ear of the beholder, my once-loved. The truly angry man, the absolutely enraged man, can ferret out patterns and signs that all others will miss. His rage will bring him a hard-won purity with which to hear all the plans and plots and subversive information below the surface skin of this world. He will come to know his enemies. And he will triumph over them in his newfound wisdom.

To you, I'm sure, this doesn't appear to have proved the case in my own personal history. But like most people, I'm sorry to say, you look at circumstantial evidence and accept it at face value, already having placed a particular meaning and value on it. You would say that my superiors dismissed me because my "legendary anger" resulted in the torture-death of a suspect. You would say, like those well-intentioned colleagues, that had I simply gunned down Mr. Ruggles—a genuine subversive as heinous as any I've tracked—we could have built a case of self-defense. But, instead, I cuffed the man around a telephone pole, took the emergency gas can from the trunk of the car, baptized his full skull with cleansing petrol, then slowly smoked a Tiparillo down to the glowing nub as I paced circles around this pleading conspirator.

But let me explain to you, Margie, what I could not tell my coworkers or the ranking agents of the review committee that dismissed me and then buried the facts of my actions anyway: When you are striving to save the soul of this world from absolute chaos, you must do more than fight the good fight. You must display a savagery that knows no conclusion. You must prove your willingness to always take the next step. To always exceed the limits of the will *and* the imagination. We will have order. And we will stop at nothing to achieve it.

Ruggles's flaming head was a transmission to the agents of disorder.

But, I ramble.

I have much work to do now, sweet ex. I remain yours, with my ear to the ground.

32.

"I finally get to see the den of iniquity," Ronnie says as they climb up the stairs to Flynn's apartment.

"More like the den of indemnification," Flynn says.

Ronnie raises her eyebrows and Flynn shakes his head and says, "Insurance joke. Forget it."

He unbolts both locks on the steel door, swings it open, and extends an arm for Ronnie to enter. Then he steps in behind her, resecures the door, opens the small foyer closet, and punches buttons on the box mounted to the rear wall to deactivate the alarm.

Ronnie smiles at him as he slides out of his jacket. "Expecting the S.S., maybe?"

"Can't be too careful these days, right? I sleep easier knowing I'm wired."

She moves in and puts her arms around his neck and says, "We'll see about that."

They stand clenched in the entryway for a while, just kissing, like high school steadies desperate for the date not to end. Finally, Ronnie brings her mouth away and says, "What have you got to drink?"

"How 'bout a couple brandies."

"Sounds perfect."

He steers her into the living room, takes her suede coat from her shoulders, and hangs it on the hook of an antique brass post. He slides out of his leather jacket, tosses it on a couch, and moves around the corner to the den, yelling back, "Get comfortable. I'll just be a second."

"My God," Ronnie says, "you've got so much space."

She hears Flynn laugh from the next room. "That's the beauty of owning the building. This used to be three separate units. I knocked down some walls and spread out."

He comes back into the room holding two snifters filled halfway with a smoky auburn liquid. He hands her one, raises his glass, and says, "To Marconi."

"You romantic," she says, then she raises her own glass and says, "And to the diode rectifier tube."

"You tech-head," Flynn says. "I'm impressed."

They both take a small swallow. Flynn gestures to the couch and they sit. It's a slightly odd moment for them both—two people who've spent a good chunk of the past twenty-four hours groping each other with no restraint, suddenly sitting back for some quiet conversation. It feels a little planned, a little formal.

Ronnie takes another sip and says, "This is a great building."

Flynn tilts his head and smiles, pleased by the remark.

"Almost a hundred and twenty years old," he says. "Designed by Tuckerman Potter. It's on the historical register."

Ronnie shakes her head. "You get off on that stuff, huh?"

"Stuff?"

"I don't know, society stuff. You know what I mean."

Flynn takes a drink and shrugs.

Ronnie sits up a little and says, "Or at least you seem to."

"Meaning it's not true?"

"Meaning I'm not sure. But why would a guy so concerned about the historical register knock down walls in the building and alter the original design?"

Flynn can't help laughing. "You're good at what you do," he says, "figuring our motivations—"

"Any tenants upstairs?" Ronnie interrupts.

"Not anymore. I don't need the rent and I like my privacy."

He stands up and extends a hand toward her. "You want the tour?"

She gets up and says, "Absolutely."

Flynn takes her hand and walks to the other side of the living room, fooling around, playing the professional guide. He lets his free hand sweep out into the air as if presenting some circus act. Then he points to the fireplace and begins.

"Carved wood panels imported from Ahmedabad, India. Vermont marble repainted to match its original shade of oxblood and fitted with pierced brass panels from England."

He points to an ornamental clock on the mantel. "Picked it up in France. Dates to around 1900. Beaux Arts style."

He gestures to the couch. "An Abbotsford pseudo-Gothic sofa. You know the word comes from the Arabic *suffah*, meaning bench. Mahogany frame, stuffed with horsehair."

He nods to the odd chair next to the sofa. "Genuine George Jack easy chair covered in brocade."

Ronnie moves over to the chair, puts a hand on it, but turns her attention to a framed print on the wall. It's a matted piece of calligraphy, a poem inked in ornate lettering:

> You little box, held to me when escaping
> So that your valves should not break,
> Carried from house to ship from ship to train,
> So that my enemies might go on talking to me
> Near my bed, to my pain
> The last thing at night, the first thing in the morning,
> Of their victories and of my cares,
> Promise me not to go silent all of a sudden.
> —Bertolt Brecht

Flynn calls her attention from the wall and begins to point to cabinets and end tables. "A Vile-Cobb George III mahogany bombé commode. A James Lamb veneered mahogany sideboard out of Manchester, probably around 1875. And that there, that's a satinwood cabinet with ivory handles designed by E. W. Goodwin."

"E. W. himself?" Ronnie says, lifting up her eyebrows, playing a parody of some impressed tourist. But she loves the show. It's so unexpected, a real curveball. She would've expected Flynn to be all yuppie contemporary or franchise Scandinavian.

And he likes the fact she's kidding him. He finishes up by swirling some brandy around in his snifter and says, "The floors are pure maple, walls are covered in canvas with bas-relief borders, ceiling's Adams plaster."

Ronnie is shaking her head slowly and smiling. "And you know what all that crap means?" she says.

"More or less. Had to find out just enough to know when I was getting taken by the dealers."

"G.T. Flynn getting suckered," Ronnie says. "Tough to picture."

"You should see what they gouged me for a carved oak four-poster bed."

Ronnie steps up to him and runs a hand up into the hair over his ear. "Yeah, but I'm about to increase its value tremendously."

From a back room deep in the apartment a phone rings once and stops. Flynn leans in, kisses her forehead, and says, "Hold that thought. That's the business line in the study."

Ronnie squints at him. "You get business calls at three in the morning?"

He starts to move out of the room, saying, "That's part of the deal when you handle people's money for them."

He walks through the den and then through a small anteroom and stands before a pair of varnished-wood doors on tracks that slide into the wall. He unlocks the sliding doors, steps inside the study, rolls the doors closed again, and relocks them. He turns around a little hesitantly. The contrast between the Victorian decor of the rest of the apartment and the cool minimalism of the study always makes him a little queasy, like he's stepped off a carnival ride before it's completely stopped.

The study is so absolutely different from the rest of the

building that it might as well exist in another space and time. This is the way Flynn wants it. The study has a specific and definite purpose. It houses a distinct, unique vein of his life. He wanted the room to be a small world unto itself. He wanted it to feel like every time he rolled open the sliding doors and stepped inside, he was crossing an enormous threshold, darting through some cultural membrane and into a vault of secret, hidden yearnings.

He crosses over the soundproof carpeting to the end section of black metal shelving and grabs the cordless phone and says, "Hello."

"Flynn," a woman's voice says, "it's Hannah Shaw."

He'd expected Wallace or maybe Hazel. "Detective Shaw," he says, "it's a little late—"

She cuts him off, clearly annoyed. "Yeah, I'm not doing so good with time these days. And I figured you'd just be getting in from Wireless."

"I didn't make it to the bar tonight," he says. "I'm entertaining some guests here at home. What can I do for you, Ms. Shaw?"

There's a pause, then a sound that's part breath and part laugh. "Do for me? Look, Flynn, you're the one who asked for a favor. If I got you at a bad time—"

His sales instincts kick and he changes his voice and says, "No, no, I'm sorry. You're right. You're absolutely right. Sometimes the phone can just jangle you, you know? Especially at this time of night. You expect to hear there's been some sort of accident or—"

"Yeah, fine," Hannah says. "Look, I checked up on your little friend and it looks like she's trying to make a move."

"My little friend," Flynn repeats.

"The woman is not what she seems, Flynn. And her allegiances are definitely not to you. You're being set up. I'd have thought you were a better judge of character."

"Listen, Hannah—"

She makes it clear she doesn't like the familiarity. "In the future I'd be more careful who I associated with, Mr. Flynn. Man in your position should really take precautions. My advice at this stage of the game would be to get some distance from the woman. She's a disaster. She can't be trusted."

"Detective," Flynn says, "I wonder if we could get together tomorrow for—"

"It's late, Flynn, like you said. I did you a favor. Mainly because you were a friend of Lenore's. Now, I'm extremely busy right now. You can either take my advice or forget it. Really doesn't matter to me."

Before Flynn can speak he hears the click of her hang-up.

He stands still in the darkness for a minute, then brings the phone up to his mouth, taps it against his lips.

Okay, he thinks, *we've lost Hazel.*

He moves to put the phone back on the shelf and flinches. *She was talking about Hazel, right? Why didn't she mention the name? Why didn't she say "Hazel"?*

He tries to replay Shaw's words, wishes he'd taped the call, wishes he could just hit the toggle on his reel-to-reel and rehear everything that was said. But it's like the conversation mutated into a vague dream as soon as Shaw disconnected. And now all he can bring up, the only words that he feels sure he heard are *the woman is not what she seems.*

And then, from the living room, comes Ronnie's slightly muffled voice calling, "Hey, Flynnster, I'm getting lonely out here."

33.

The Tribal Drum Noodle House sits down on Watson Street, at the very border of Little Asia, one of the last outposts before the ways of the Orient dissolve into the glossy and sulky exhibitionism of the Canal Zone. As a matter of fact, the restaurant shares a common wall with a slick new hip-hop joint called Propa Gramma, run by a mulatto Casanova named Jerome LaCroix.

The Tribal Drum's proximity to the Zone has altered it a bit, set it far apart from the dozens of other Asian eateries in Bangkok. More often than not, the majority of the clientele come from over the line, semihungry artists and poseurs drifting from the red brick galleries and smoke-clogged cafés, slim books clutched in hands, looking for some decent wonton and maybe a communal plate of moo shu vegetables.

Because of this fact, the Drum's owners, a holding company called Sozhou Limited Trust, tried a faddish motif that clicked and held. Some regulars believe the invisible company stumbled on an unknown designer crazed enough to bring back seventies kitsch. An opposing faction maintains that the joint's owners are brand-new to the shore and their sense of American style, and maybe even language, was born while religiously studying seventies TV sitcoms day and night. A third, slightly cocky group holds that the decor has more to do with the fact that the holding company botched a warehouse job and somehow got saddled with a gross of pastel-colored Princess rotary telephones.

Whatever the case, having some Beijing ravioli at the Tribal Drum is like dining in a museum of the tacky and synthetic. There are Lava lamps on the tables and beanbag chairs in the lounge. The floors are covered with lime-colored, heavy shag carpeting. The bartenders dress in mint leisure suits and qiana shirts opened to the navel and equipped with long dagger collars. The waiters and waitresses wear zip-up velour jerseys and bell-bottom pants made from a shiny material that no one can put a name to. Lately, the manager has been pushing Thursdays as Polyester Night.

But it's the Princess telephones that have evolved into the real draw. Each booth is wired with one, but they're only workable inside the Drum. You can't dial out, but you can call any other table in the place. The Canal Zone crowd went crazy for this gimmick and the restaurant suddenly became a retro singles club. In one of the Zone's underground weeklies, an article came out detailing the benefits of this newfound playland: In this age of detachment, disease, and serial killers, mingling with horny strangers was a risk too great to take. We've entered a new epoch that demands what the author termed "The Death of the Date." The article eschewed physical contact "up to and including the actual witnessing of the romantic-other's face." But this doesn't have to mean the end of dating. Using the Tribal Drum's new methodology, we can continue to link up safely and secretly and solely electronically.

And now the Noodle House is a nest of chronic bell-ringing and choruses of mumbled, fabricated names whispered into powder-blue receivers by boothfuls of depressed, skinny, pale-faced sculptors and playwrights and lonely method actors.

Hannah can't believe this is where she's eating dinner. But this is where Dr. Cheng told her to be and she didn't push the issue. The doctor's voice seems more withdrawn and haunted each time they speak and Hannah senses that giving him an argument could sever their ties for good, explode a unique relationship that's taken a year to mold.

She's sitting in a rear booth, working on her fourth cup of tea, trying not to listen to the dodges and equivocations that issue from the hip young mouths surrounding her. All these odd words and vague phrases seem to rise and mix in the air with a heavy cover of smoke from a wide selection of European cigarettes. When she feels her annoyance increasing to a danger point, she reminds herself that all this phone babble has got to be better than the idea of these people mating and procreating.

Hannah personally detests the telephone. She acknowledges the machine as an instrument of progress, a timesaver—in some instances, a lifesaver. But her own experience has been that the phone has brought more bad news than good by an enormous margin. And though she's never told anyone this, on at least one occasion she's held the barrel of her Magnum up to her ringing bedroom touch-tone.

She glances to her watch. Dr. Cheng is only ten minutes late, but that's enough to signal a problem. The doctor is a fanatically punctual being. It's a concept tied into his notions of respect and order and efficiency. She understands that he doesn't want her coming to the Herbarium anymore, but if he was sick or another meeting ran late, he should have sent a messenger.

She swallows the last of her tea and slides from the booth as the phone rings. And she hesitates, knowing that right now, hearing a stupid word about love or sex could result in some quick and futile violence—some anonymous crotch scalded with boiling ginseng.

But she picks up the phone anyway and says a flat "Yeah?"

There's the sound of someone trying to breathe through a semiclogged throat, then a distant, weak cough, and then the soft voice. Dr. Cheng says, "I'm sorry to keep you waiting, Hannah."

She slides back into the booth, switches the phone to her opposite ear. "Is there a problem, Doc? Everything all right?"

Another attempt at a cough, then, "I apologize for my delay. I'm afraid I won't be able to see you tonight."

"Should I come by, Doc—"

"No, no," he says, adamant, the voice suddenly stronger. "This won't be necessary. I have some information for you. Something you might find useful."

As he speaks, it again occurs to Hannah that, supposedly, these phones are all internally wired. You can't dial out. They're not hooked to the street poles. They're not part of the normal city system.

"Doc, where are you?" Hannah blurts.

She hears a faint sigh that holds more resignation than annoyance and Hannah bucks, not exactly at being stood up, but more at the feeling that the doctor intends to make this a brief and one-sided conversation. Hannah is used to getting her questions answered.

Dr. Cheng says, "I had some of my people make some inquiries."

"Inquiries," Hannah repeats, in a voice that gives just a hint of impatience.

"We spoke with management at a selection of the major chemical distributors in the region."

This time Hannah stays quiet and the doctor knows he's got her full attention and cooperation.

"I felt that I might have certain avenues of persuasion not available to your people, Hannah."

He says "your people" like the department was her goddamn family. Like Zarelli and Richmond were her crude brothers, Miskewitz some bored and tired stepfather.

"We uncovered some information," the doctor continues, drawing out the last word, "that I felt I should share with you."

Hannah tries to keep her voice bland and says, "I'd appreciate anything you've got,"

"A company called Hofmann Chemtech. Out Route 77 in Whitney. Second-generation business. A midsized firm that picked up far too much debt during the boom. They swallowed some smaller competitors. Modernized the plant. Again, we see a lack of vision. The loans are tottering. The shylocks at the door."

She wants to say, *Can the analysis and give me the goddamn name, Doc,* but instead gives a mild, semi-interested, "It's a brutal market these days."

"I had once reviewed this particular firm for investment. Years ago. But even then, I didn't like the numbers."

Hannah simply says, "Ironic."

"Yes," the doctor says, and then there's a long moment when neither speaks.

Finally, Hannah breaks and says, "You spoke to some people?"

"As I said, a few of my aides have been making inquiries. Visiting plants in the region that supply benzine or benzine-based products."

A picture comes into Hannah's head that she can't immediately dismiss: a scene of Cheng's meat-boys beating a name from the lips of a broken, cash-strapped man who can't conceive of why his life continues to unravel. She would like to hope they didn't have to go too gangland, permanently harm the tongue or eyes or kneecaps. But she knows Cheng's "aides" walked away from Whitney with something. Or Cheng wouldn't have made this phone call.

She grabs tight on the phone, switches it back to her original ear, and says, "You've got something to tell me?"

Another pause, then the doctor says, "We assured the individual there would be no official consequences. There were violations of certain licensing and—"

She can't stand it anymore. She yells, "Just say it, for Christ sake," and then she immediately regrets her action.

In a dispassionate voice, Cheng says, "They sold a small amount of benzine to an unaffiliated Caucasian male six weeks ago. Cash transaction. Two meetings. All business conducted in the woods behind that Catholic orphanage in Whitney."

"A name?"

"No." He takes a shallow breath, then adds, "But at the initial meeting, the buyer produced a badge of some sort."

"A badge? You mean, like a police badge?"

There's no answer and for a second Hannah thinks Cheng has hung up, then, as if he's just recalled a punch line, the old man says, "A Federal badge."

Now it's Hannah that goes quiet for a second, then asks, "No name or number?"

"The seller says it happened very quickly. That it was likely intended as some kind of threat or motivation. Believe me, Detective, had there been more information, my people would have returned with it."

Hannah knows this is the truth.

From behind the facing wall of her booth, without any warning, horribly loud percussion suddenly revs up from Propa Gramma, the club next door. It's followed by the syncopated call of a mostly unintelligible rap sermon from what sounds like a female duo. The words *bastard, sisters,* and *payback* seem to be repeated like a funk-mantra backed by a strong bass line. Hannah covers her free ear with her palm and presses the receiver tighter against her head.

"I hope you'll find this story helpful," the doctor says.

Acting contrite isn't Hannah's strong suit, but she tries to put some humility behind her words and says, "I'm sure I will. Thanks for filling me in, Doc."

"You're welcome," Cheng says. "And I hope, should you learn anything more, you'll not hesitate in relaying your findings to Little Asia."

Hannah takes her palm from her ear, makes a fist, and futilely pummels the shared wall, as if this will lower the volume of the music.

"Since when is it necessary to say that, Doctor?"

There's no response.

"I've always worked the split with you," Hannah says, turning sideways away from the wall, her voice rising. "We've had an unspoken agreement. When have I not honored the deal?"

Finally Cheng says, "Our understanding has served us both."

"I'll bring you what I find," Hannah says, suddenly wanting to hang up.

"I'm sure you will," Cheng says. "But it would be better if I came to you—"

"Yeah, I understand. You don't want me down Verlin Ave anymore—"

"You don't understand, Hannah—"

She cuts him off and says, "Tell me something. You own part of this place, right? You own a piece of the Tribal Drum?"

He gives a wheezy laugh and says, "I'm simply a neighborhood doctor, Hannah—"

She interrupts again, "And I'm the Virgin Mary. Do yourself a favor and soundproof this dump."

"I'll check on you soon," Cheng says, and then, after a beat of silence, he hangs up.

Hannah sits for a second with the phone still pressed against her head. A waiter approaches carrying a fresh pot of steaming tea atop a red plastic tray. His neck is weighed down with a dozen ropes of gold chain. His hair blown dry into a perfectly curved helmet that covers any sign of his ears.

"Can I get you something?" he yells over the music.

Hannah can actually feel the pulse of it through the wall. She slides out of the booth and faces him and without thinking, she says, "I've been stood up."

He puts on an exaggerated frown as if he finds this impossible to believe. He gestures down to the phone and says, "Why don't you sit back down? I'll bring you a Mai Tai and you can see who calls."

Hannah stares at him, shakes her head, then moves for the exit, throwing her shoulder into the waiter's arm as she passes, sending the boiled tea into the air, splashing a shower over the next booth of jabbering regulars.

PART THREE

SUNDAY

34.

Flynn has no idea how to lose this edgy feeling that's lodged in his stomach since he took the call from Shaw. But he's convinced that attending the Todorov Memorial Parade down here in the Zone sure as hell won't help. Unfortunately, Ronnie insisted, so now they're shoulder-to-shoulder with the elite hip, trapped in a chic swarm roaming from display to event to performance down the length of Rimbaud Way.

It's not that Fr. Todorov had any solid connection with the Canal Zone clique. Mainly, he liked to be seen eating in the restaurant of the month with the poet of the week. But the Canalites have this weird passion for parades, and any occasion is usually suitable for a petition to block off the main drag and form a swaying convoy of disparate and stylish contingents, each equipped with makeshift costumes and floats and their own P.A. system for spreading one more unique manifesto.

The bulk of the Canal Zone is made up of mammoth brick mills and factories, the earliest of which ran off the current of the Benchley River. A few of the small factories still operate, but for the most part, the backbone of Quinsigamond industry has fled heating costs and union wages and vanished to places like Arizona and Malaysia.

Fanned out beyond the old sweatshops are the tenements that housed the immigrant labor. Flynn thinks that maybe the most interesting piece of Quinsigamond history is the half-forgotten fact that the Yankee bosses were adamant about housing each ethnic group separately. So there was an Irish block and an Italian block, a French block and Polish block. The unspoken idea was that if these dissimilar workers didn't learn each other's language, they'd never be able to organize and turn their collective power against the owners. Though the plan failed, Flynn can see there was this awful brilliance to it, this mad social-scientist flair. Keep the peasants suspicious of each other and they'll never notice their real enemy.

Generations later, those original mill-working families have battled their way up to middle class and beyond. The Yankee barons are long since dead. And the factories are the decayed remnants of an invisible war, settled by neither victory nor negotiation, but rather, simple and vicious obsolescence. The buildings are used as everything from theaters and warehouses and biker clubs to subdivided office spaces, a roller-skating rink, a bowling alley.

And the tenements for the workers are now tenements for the art crowd. The cheap rent and gritty ambience have pulled in bohemians from all over New England and they slouch up and down McJacob and Dupin and, especially, Rimbaud Way—the Zone within the Zone—day and night, looking for imagery, free coffee, semi-soft drugs, pseudo-safe sex, and bitingly hip conversation. There appear to be laws about dressing in black, avoiding the sunlight, suppressing visible emotion, and the proper use of hair products.

During an average day, the Canal Zone streets are crowded and busy. Today the place is a bobbing sea of skinny bodies. There are people everywhere and they're all feeding off each other, communally crazed on this buzz running through the air, this shared conception that some major incident is about to take place. Flynn has never been to New Orleans during Mardi Gras, but he'd bet this might be a close approximation. It's like a spontaneous unorganized circus has gotten lost on the road and come to an unexpected stop in some outdoor museum of the middle industrial age. It's like a ragtag carnival has mutated and grown to an unreasonable proportion.

This is their idea, Flynn thinks, *of a memorial for a murder victim?*

The idea down in the Zone seems to be to invert everything, toward the end of finding some other, hidden level of meaning. It's as if all the residents have agreed that, no matter what else they might do to turn a coin or relieve the pressure, *this* is the real job, this hunt for codes and messages is the only genuine occupation. Their environment practically demands it. There's so much input. There's no way to avoid all the signals and symbols and markings that scream from every direction. They move through a constant sea of obscure bulletins, an ongoing blitz of never-quite-clear communiqués. The graffiti alone is blinding. Every individual red brick in the Zone seems to be partially splashed with paint. The residents will tell you that no one ever sees the artist in the act. You simply walk down the street one day and notice a picture or a word or a series of words that wasn't there before. Supposedly, there's an acquired thrill in trying to discern different styles, in attempting to guess who created what.

Flynn looks down at the long side of the old Seward typewriter factory. The wall is covered, right up to the roof, thirty feet off the ground. He wonders if you flew over the Zone in a plane, would you find signs on the roof itself? The artwork is striking. There's real talent down here, people with actual ability. Do they really prefer mill walls as their canvases? Is this the medium they most want to work in? He stares at the Seward and tries to take everything in: pictures of fire rings, photo-real crucifixes, naked bodies copulating, silver B-movie flying saucers, still lifes of orchids and small dead birds, a ram's head, a pentagram. And then there are the words, sentence fragments mostly—

O'ZBON RULES
the boys are back in town
Jammers do it on the run
"...night is the cathedral where we recognize the sign..."—Vega

A sheet of white paper catches a breeze and blows against his legs. Flynn picks it up and reads. It's a flier, an ad for a free concert following the parade:

Today Only
From the roof of "St. Anthony's Temptation"
Q-town's own
SEVERED ARTERY
plays a *free* "Open Channel Jam" Jam
from their soon to be released album
Chug the Hemlock on Visigoth Temple Records

Flynn lets the flier fall to the street and he and Ronnie continue to move slowly down Rimbaud. They start to spot dozens of pockets of sideshows, little circles of performance artists, huckster games, Grand Guignol puppet shows, and, surprisingly, corny little novelty schticks. But this being the Canal Zone, even the standard carny bit has an edge and a weirdness to it.

On the corner of Goulden Ave there's this bearded transvestite shill running a Guess Your Neurosis booth. Out in front of Bella C's Tavern there's a trio of sad-faced doo-wop singers trying to croon harmony out of these old Workers' Party folk tunes. Next to them, a teenage girl is working a cardboard monte table using a Tarot pack. But the hottest attraction of all seems to be a Dunk the Mime tank in front of Orsi's Rib Room. People are lined up before the diner, waiting to toss baseballs at a round target. The current patron is hurling speed balls like he's furious and on his second pitch he nails a bull's-eye and the white-faced, black leotard-clad Marcel Marceau wannabe plummets from his perch into a tub of water.

Halfway down Rimbaud, a carousel has been planted in the center of the street, but instead of horses the wooden animals are all myth creatures—griffin, hydra, basilisk, sphinx, bunyip, harpies, various dragons, all with open, fanged, predatory mouths. Next to the carousel is a revival exhibition of classic late-seventies slam dancing. Skinheads lined up in rows at opposite gutters seem to wait for some obscure signal, maybe some crude octave buried in the Hüsker-Du bootleg that's blasting from Marshall lamps mounted on the closest tenement rooftop. At the right moment they charge at full run to midstreet where they collide with an opposing punk, smash knees, chests, skulls, ricochet off each other and enjoy lesser, secondary collisions with other flying bodies.

Flynn and Ronnie pass through a charge, somehow untouched, and move along past a row of slick trench-coated hipsters, eyes hidden behind black lenses in 1950s Steve Allen frames. Each ranter is up on his own fruit crate and that small elevation gives them some credibility, Flynn thinks. They gesticulate as they ramble, all throaty, scatological babble, a dozen different bent ideologies to sample and take or leave.

None of this craziness is amusing Flynn and he fears that the levels of both his anxiety and the street weirdness are increasing as they walk. Ronnie senses the tension. She pulls him up onto the sidewalk and yells near his ear, "You want to head back to the Rib Room and get a coffee? It's still a while before the parade comes by."

Flynn can't help himself. He says, "The Memorial, you mean."

Ronnie takes his arm and pulls him down another block where the music is slightly muted. She shrugs and says, "What?"

He shrugs back at her. "Don't you think this is a little, I don't know . . . disrespectful?"

"Disrespectful?" Ronnie says. "That word doesn't get used very often down here. God, Flynn, you sure know how to surprise me. It's a celebration. Jeez, Mr. Catholic here. You never heard of celebrating the sacrifice?"

"You mean the Mass?" Flynn says. "You never heard of 'for the greater good'? What good comes out of Todorov being fried? Where's the redemption?"

"Maybe that remains to be seen."

"Yeah," Flynn says. "Maybe."

She looks at him a second, as if debating whether or not to keep talking, then she makes a decision and starts to move again. He goes after her, takes her arm, and pulls her next to him. He wishes he could find a way to tell her what's going on, but he's not sure himself. He wants to shake this feeling. He wants to find a way back to that first night at the old airport, that feeling of ignition, of being conscious of the excitement and the possibility, the chance at a long-shot renewal. But the harder he works at shrugging off this virus of paranoia and suspicion and general unease, the more it seems to integrate itself within his system, honestly like a cancer, these haunting cells of distrust multiplying, jumping from organ to organ, forming pathways to further infection, toward a near future of... what? Where does this kind of virus leave you? In the shadow of a degrading psychosis? With a spleen full of perfect intolerance, aged beyond recognition, but still alive enough to feel the waves of panic and impotence and persecution?

It's that goddamn call from Lenore's little clone. *You're being set up.* By who, for Christ sake? If it's Ronnie, then where's her margin? The jammers don't touch her. She's the goddess of the radio freaks. Why come after them? Unless her allegiance is to the station in general. Unless she simply believes in this system, this program of licensing and control and commerce. Unless she's a *believer*, a zealot, a reverse picture, a mirror image of Hazel who can't accept the disorder the jammers create, can't allow for a world where anarchy is the goal, rather than harmony. Where chaos is honored and yearned for over discipline and regularity.

Flynn needs to put some food in his stomach. He grabs Ronnie's hand and starts to maneuver the two of them faster through the throng of revelers. But before he can spot an open café, Ronnie squeezes his hand, gives a quick squeal, and points across the street. Between two identical red brick tenements, someone's erected an ancient wooden Ferris wheel. It just barely fits into the alley between the buildings and it rises just as high as the seven-storied apartment houses. Each carriage is painted a different color and the spokes of the wheel are trimmed with ropes of multicolored lights. Tenants sit in the open windows of the top-floor apartments on either side of the alley and when the wheel halts to let the occupants of the bottom carriage exit, the tenants lean out and touch fingertips with the riders stranded up top.

As Flynn stops to watch this display, Ronnie grabs his arm and starts to run for the wheel, yelling like a kid, "We've *got* to go up."

She buys two tickets from a large black woman wearing an old cotton housedress covered by an ankle-length leather coat with huge flaplike lapels and metal-studded epaulets. Ronnie's excitement is genuine and Flynn thinks that if he can just catch a bit of it, he can turn the day around. He can kill the haunting in his stomach and end the night slow-dancing in front of an abandoned runway.

They climb into a sky-blue carriage with the name *Ghost Rider* stenciled in glitter paint on the front, buckle the heavy safety straps across their laps, and the carny woman latches the metal crossbar, then yanks down a lever behind her and they start to rise. It's a slow climb—they stop briefly every few minutes as someone below exits a carriage and new riders get on. But then it's a full ride and the continuous loops begin. For some reason the wheel is running backward and though Flynn has never been afraid of heights, he hopes Ronnie won't get funny and start rocking their rig.

She huddles into him like some midwestern teen surprised by love at a church fair. She lowers her head onto his shoulder. She's trying, he knows. She wants some fun, a little romance. She wants some possibilities. Why can't he give her that? It should be simple, as natural as the movement of his feet on the cracked tarmac the first night, or the progressions of the saxophone that guided their hips and arms.

Something's lacking now. Something's fallen away. He simply doesn't know how to restore trust. And though Ronnie can't know the cause of his discomfort, she knows something's wrong.

They come to the crest of the wheel's arc, maybe sixty feet up, and the tenement witnesses smile out on them. Flynn thinks he and Ronnie must look like some kind of icon for love or courtship, some sort of current definition of the first stages of mating. Something in him wants to yell to the people in the windows—two paint-spattered young men on his side, a trio of college-age women, all dressed in green camouflage garb, on Ronnie's side—*Don't believe it yet, the facts aren't all in.*

As they linger at the top of the arc, the lights that line the spokes start to flicker and then die out all at once. The sputter noises of the wheel's generator cease and a gust of greasy-smelling smoke blows up past them. From the ground, the French-Haitian accent of the woman in the leather storm coat starts to bellow a string of bilingual curses. Flynn looks at Ronnie, then peers out over the side of the carriage to see the attendant pounding on the generator.

Flynn shakes his head and Ronnie says, "What?"

"I think we're stuck up here."

Ronnie seems more excited than anxious and says, "Tremendous."

"You're kidding," Flynn says, again annoyed.

"This is fantastic," Ronnie says, leaning forward and tilting the carriage a bit. "Look at the view."

"This isn't funny, Ronnie," Flynn says. He looks down again and yells, "Hey, move this thing."

Now Ronnie pulls away from him and in an equally annoyed voice says, "What the hell is wrong with you?"

"Nothing."

"Like hell."

Flynn runs a hand over his face, exasperated, and says, "You know, I tried to tell you I didn't want to come to this thing."

Ronnie sighs. "Well, I'm sorry. I didn't think it was that big a deal."

Flynn looks to the window and the painters give him a smug pair of smiles.

He looks away and says, "It's not a big deal. I'm just...Just a bad day."

Ronnie lets her feet stretch out into the air, stares at them, and says, "Am I keeping you from Wireless?"

"For Christ sake—"

"I just don't get it. You're like night and day. What, do your radio friends disapprove—"

"Don't be sarcastic," Flynn says.

"Have you broken some club rule?" she asks. "Is your heart reserved for the jammers?"

He lowers his voice and says, "I wish you wouldn't use that word."

She can't let it go. "Does it have some connotation I'm not aware of?"

"For one thing, it's illegal. And for another, like I've already told you, it's got nothing to do with me."

There are a few beats of silence as they both pretend to study the street below. Then Ronnie ignores her instincts and says, "Sounds like I'm pushing a button here, G.T."

Flynn turns sideways to face her and says, "And it sounds to me like maybe your interest in this thing is greater than I thought."

She tries to keep a smile on her face and says, "Which means?"

"I'm not sure what it means. That's what worries me."

"You're questioning my motives, G.T."

"You're giving me reason to."

"You think I want you to lead me to the people who are knocking QSG off the air? You think that's why we're together?"

He stares at her a long time before saying, "Hey, Ronnie. We've known each other about forty-eight hours. Okay?"

She cocks her head in a way that makes him think she's about to start rocking the carriage. Instead she says, "So how much time has to go by before I can ask you questions?"

"I'll let you know," he says, trying to sound like he's joking.

"My curiosity is piqued. I want to hear the life story. Birth to our meeting at Wireless."

"Never invite that kind of boredom on yourself."

"What's the matter, Flynn? Am I suspect for wanting to know about you?"

"You'll notice *I* haven't asked any questions."

"Yeah. And I'm starting to take it as a sign of disinterest."

"Wrong. Incorrect. Couldn't be more wrong."

"Isn't there anything you want to know about me?"

Flynn shrugs. "I just figure we'll come to it as we go, you know. I figure we'll just naturally run into things. We take a walk, we see a dog, you say, 'I had a dog like that when I was little.' Okay, now I know you owned a retriever."

"I never had a dog," Ronnie says.

"Okay. There you go. Now I know that."

"What? Is every discussion an interrogation to you? I mean, you sell life insurance for a living, for God's sake. You've got to be good at small talk."

"Now, that's different," Flynn says. "That's a device. Tool of the trade."

"Funny, we both talk for a living."

"Well, we both get paid for talking. Big difference."

"You're disagreeable today, Flynn."

"You wanted to know something about me. There you go—I'm pretty discerning about the choice of words."

"A word fetish, huh?" Ronnie says. "A little anal retentive in that department—"

"I didn't say that, did I?"

"Did I do something to put you in a bad mood?"

He looks at her, gives her his best Whole-Life-with-Decreasing-Premium smile. Then he catches himself, kills the smile, shakes his head in frustration, and says, "No. You haven't done anything. There's just a hell of a lot on my mind. I should have left work problems behind."

She looks down to his Ballys and slowly back up till she's focused on his face. Then she brings out her best heckler-squelching voice and says, "I'm not buying."

"Pardon?"

She takes her hands from the pockets of her jacket and folds her arms across her chest. "I'm not buying it," she says. "I've got a different theory on what's happening here."

He doesn't like the tone or the direction she's heading. "Want to fill me in?" he says, though he's not sure he wants to hear the rest.

"I think we're intrigued by each other. I think there's some real infatuation between us. I think we want to follow it, give in and see where we end up. I think we know the sexual possibilities look very good. Neither one of us can stop thinking about the studio the other night—"

"So, where's the problem?" he asks, getting nervous with the buildup.

"The problem is we're not sure of each other's motives or intentions."

"Who is," Flynn says, "when you first meet some—"

"No, no. This is a little different from your standard new romance. Okay? This is something else, beyond the normal doubts like has this person got some dark side I won't see for six months? This has to do with different kinds of questions."

He thinks she wants him to say *such as,* but he stays silent.

Ronnie goes on. "Questions like—is this person, maybe, setting me up? Using me to get information? I mean, I'll admit you've got some reason to be suspicious. I came to the bar to find you. Specifically, to see what you knew about who was jamming the station."

He stays quiet for another minute, then says, "Okay, you're sure you want to get into this?"

She nods. "Got to happen sooner or later and now's as good a time as any."

"I'm not so sure about that," he mutters, glancing down to the ground.

"It's not that far a fall," she says. "Odds are one of us would survive."

He doesn't like the comment, but he lets it go.

"Okay," he says, "first of all, it's a fact that I have other things on my mind lately. There's a lot of pressure at work. Sales are down. The competition is brutal."

"You just didn't strike me as a guy who worried a lot about competition."

"Everyone worries about competition, Ronnie."

"Especially radio stations."

"I know that you think that, at very least, I know something about the jamming. You think I know who's knocking Ray down. You tapped into some fringe adolescent somewhere who heard of my name and passed it on. Okay, the fact is I *do* hang out at Wireless quite a bit. I know the owners. I handle some money for them. I spend quite a few nights there. So you've got guilt by association. You sure you're comfortable with that?"

She lowers her voice. "Look, Flynn, what we've done in the past two days should tip you off to the fact that I'm, you know, a little quirky. Unconventional. Let's say unconventional. I'm kind of intrigued by anything that's a little different, a little off balance, okay? So the jamming interested me. I wanted to know more. So I called some horny fans, some kids who listen to the show and try to picture what I look like. And, yes, they gave me Wireless and they gave me your name. And a bunch of other names—"

"What names?"

"What does it matter? Let me finish here. So I went the other night. And I asked some people, some women, who you were—"

"Which women?"

"And they pointed you out. And I liked what I saw. Where's the crime? My point is I don't know exactly why I went to Wireless the other night. I just wanted to take a look. I wanted to start something new. I didn't have a specific motive—"

"Like hell. You started asking questions as soon as we met—"

"And it worked," she says, her voice rising enough for the people in the tenement windows to stare. "It got you interested. It started things rolling. That's what I *do*, for Christ sake. That's why I'm so good on the air. It's instinct. I just feel where someone's buttons are. And then I push. I like to dive into new water all the time, G.T. What's the problem? It keeps life interesting. Jamming is something I know next to nothing about. And the jammers seem interested in me, remember? I'm the one they leave alone. I'd like to know why."

"I'll bet the people you work for would like to know why."

"You're really starting to annoy me," Ronnie says. "You know that?"

"Just reassure me. Just say to my face that no one asked you to check things out."

"The other night in the studio. You think I did that at someone's request?"

"I'm just saying—" Flynn begins, but she cuts him off and he can see the anger flooding her face.

"You've got two choices, Flynn. You can think we stumbled into each other and something interesting is about to happen. Or you can think I'm using you to get the jammers."

"Now, wait—"

But she cuts him off again and he knows he went with the wrong response. His instincts are failing him.

"Well, screw you. You bastard. You think I rent my body out so the management can cut losses?"

"No, Ronnie, look—"

"You look. You little scumbag—"

"Please. I didn't mean—"

"What? Tell me." She's yelling now.

"I loved last night. I didn't mean to say—"

"I don't know what you mean, Flynn. I don't know any-thing about you."

"Just let me explain, give me a second here."

She lowers her voice again, but brings her face up close to his. "You blew it. You're a schmuck."

There's a burst of applause from the women in the window. One of them yells, "Give him hell, sister," and balls her hand into a radical fist.

Ronnie turns and starts to unbuckle her safety belt. She turns and gestures to her newfound comrades. "Move over, I'm coming in."

Flynn reaches over and takes hold of her arm. She bucks, flails her arm out of his grip, enraged.

She says, "Let go of me," loud enough for the whole street to hear.

"Hey, people," one of the painters yells from his window, "you're going to get hurt."

"Jesus, c'mon, Ronnie," Flynn rasps with his molars clenched together.

She glares at him and starts to climb up onto the seat. The carriage rocks forward and Flynn screams, "Jesus Christ, sit down."

Ronnie braces herself with a hand on a strut and starts to raise her leg. Flynn reaches out and grabs the back of her jacket and without any thought she pivots on one foot and puts a quick, sharp boot into his ribs. He lets go of the jacket and doubles up over his lap and Ronnie starts edging out of the carriage and reaching for the windowsill.

Voices start to yell from every angle, riders in other car-riages, people in the lower tenement windows, the crowd in line below. Flynn starts to unbelt his strap as the generator starts a run of coughs. And then it catches and the wheel bucks and starts to turn again. Ronnie's hand falls from the sill and she yells out and grabs onto the wheel's wooden spoke. She starts to lose balance, then swings her legs out of the carriage and wraps them farther down the strut.

"Shit," Flynn yells. "Ronnie."

He gets on his knees, faces backward, trying to look into the big central gears, but he only gets seconds before his carriage reaches the ground. And then the attendant is in front of him, furious, ripping open the guard bar, barking, "What the fuck you think you doin' up there?"

Flynn jumps out of the car and pushes past her. He sees Ronnie running across the street, into the swarm of the crowd. He starts to push people out of the way and some start to push back. But when he gets to the curb, he's lost sight of her and now, finally, the Todorov Memorial Parade is moving through Rimbaud Way. The lead float, an antique hearse trimmed with twirled black crepe paper, is weaving from curb to opposite curb, followed by a long procession of dozens of Zone insiders, all of them dressed up in heavy black robes with cowled hoods pulled over their heads, each carrying their own, tiny, individual pine box up on their shoulders and chanting in singsong, made-up Latinish babble to the accompaniment of a squad of high-stepping saxophonists wearing rubber death heads and decked out in deep purple zoot suits, blowing a frenetic version of "When the Saints Go Marching In."

Flynn runs out into the midst of the parade, knocking into several faux monks, sending their symbolic coffins to the street. The crowd starts to make a communal *boo* and a couple of the bigger monks throw a few punches Flynn's way, but he absorbs them running, makes it to the far side of Rimbaud, and tries to break through the new wall of bodies. People poke and jab and spit on him, but he keeps ducking and moving and twisting his way deeper into the mob.

But there's no sign of Ronnie.

He looks to his left and sees a small service alley blocked off by a blue metal garbage Dumpster. He heads for it, hoists himself up on top, and looks out over the waves of human skulls. She's long gone by now.

He studies the parade for a few minutes, thinking this will tell him what to do, give him a clue toward a course of action.

Instead, the sight just brings on more confusion. It's as if the long line of bohemian marchers and raunchy floats and graphic novelty acts were a tribute, not to Fr. Andre Todorov, but to bedlam itself. As if the only way to truth, or even to the simple expression of loss, were through the maverick and gaudy display.

As the tail end of the parade—an authentic-looking confessional booth, all ablaze within a small orange and silver low-bed U-Haul trailer—swings around the corner onto Aragon Ave, an overamplified voice shrieks down at the crowd, "Are you ready for a kick in the ear?"

The communal attention of the street shifts back down Rimbaud and up to the roof of a renovated old church that's now a club known as St. Anthony's Temptation. Four young men are standing at the lip of a parapet that's centered between two spires. They're all wearing white dinner jackets over their bare chests and black bow ties around their throats. They've all got enormous boom-box radios strapped around their shoulders like guitars and behind them is an unbroken row of black amplifiers stacked a good ten feet high.

Flynn watches as they extend arms and join hands and, in unison, take a long, low bow as if their performance had just ended. Their boom boxes hang down and sway before the trunks of their bodies and Flynn thinks for a second they might be having trouble coming upright because of the weight of their equipment. But they rise in a practiced, graceful sequence and then the spokesman lifts a hand-held microphone to his lips and says, "We are Severed Artery and welcome to our free Open Channel Jam jam block party."

Then one by one they lift a theatrical arm to their dangling radios and turn their knobs and the street is walloped with a blast of screeching feedback. The whole crowd brings their hands to their ears and a slew of people actually drop to their knees. Three Artery players look at each other with some degree of alarm, but the apparent leader of the group is sporting a huge smile, as if this were exactly the audience reaction he'd been aiming for. He raises his arms up, Bela Lugosi style, and his bandmates hesitantly follow suit. Then, again in unison, they drop their hands to their radios and attack the tuning knobs.

A bizarre and nauseating mix of unintelligible noise washes down over Rimbaud as the titanic amps howl this awful, deafening amalgam of competing sounds from up and down the band waves. There's static and pop songs and the spoken voice, emergency broadcast tones, bebop horns, speed readers screaming car deals, a radio Mass, a radio swap meet, a high school football game, speed metal riffs, a Spanish speech with delayed translation, stock reports, Mozart's *Magic Flute,* and much more static.

The group seems to be spinning their knobs in three-second intervals, one tuning randomly on the heels of the next, like some twisted camp song rounds. The volume is excruciating. And it seems to be increasing.

A wave of panic starts to break out. The mob in the street starts to disperse, but no one knows where to escape and bodies begin to collide and fall. Flynn spots a trio of skinheads trample over the back of a young girl who's fallen. He jumps down from the Dumpster and tries to push his way toward her, but he gets knocked down himself. He takes a boot in the face and blood starts to flow from his upper lip. Another boot comes down on his hand, and fingers break. He heaves upward with his shoulder, finds an opening, gets to his feet, tucks the crushed hand under his opposite arm, and begins to run. He cuts through an alley, ends up on McJacob, and keeps moving, heading toward Bangkok Park. Away from the noise.

He runs till he's on Grassman and he realizes the din has faded a bit, receded enough so he can stop and catch his breath. He sits down on the curb outside a small Oriental storefront. He takes his hand out and looks at the fingers, bent in unnatural directions and already swelling to the size of breakfast sausages. Blood is still flowing from his mouth and he reaches to a back pocket with his good hand, pulls free a handkerchief, and applies pressure to his lip.

His lungs are heaving and his ears are ringing a horrible, nonstop, low-toned gong. He wonders if there will be any lasting damage, if the eardrum itself has bruised or even ruptured. If he'll be left trying to read lips and make hand gestures with his newly mangled fingers.

But on the heels of that concern, he thinks of Ronnie. And his heart gives a fresh double punch. Did she make it out all right?

And was the last thing she heard the sound of his miserable doubt?

35.

V. U. Gomi Scrap and Salvage, up on Cornell Hill, is the biggest junkyard in the city. It might also be the oldest. It's a family business, currently run by Vern Gomi, master scrapman and third-generation eccentric. Hannah has been here half a dozen times before, either haggling over parts for the Mustang or tagging along with the digging crew from the Medical Examiner's Office. Gomi S&S used to be a favorite burial spot of the Pecci family. Don Gennaro utilized the yard as a geographic signature, a standard general warning, broadcast via the graphic *Spy* photos—pick and axe crew gagging, holding handkerchiefs to noses. The message was always the same and easy to understand: *Do not welch when the vigorish comes due down San Remo Ave.*

Hannah is sitting on the side of a doorless, overturned refrigerator, a mammoth old Frigidaire like the one she grew up with. She's dressed in a charcoal cotton turtleneck, her black jeans, and an old navy P-coat she bought last year in a second-hand store. She's got her department .38 out and she's drawing a bead on various-sized rats darting in and out of piles of rusted bale wire, rushing over the black hulks of torched Chevys and Buicks. The hoods of the burned-out cars are littered with old wine bottles, probably one of Vern's halfhearted collections. Every now and then a rat knocks a Yago sangría container to the

309

ground. She'd like to let a round or two fly, see what kind of accuracy she can count on in this glare. But she doesn't want to give the wrong impression to her date, the heir apparent to the newly founded Iguaran dynasty.

She closes an eye and sights down on a fat albino mother gnawing a corncob on top of a tubeless television set. She's almost certain she could whack the rodent and she stays with it for a while, continuing to squint, following its small movements and readjusting her arms accordingly.

Then Nabo steps into her line of fire and stands frozen, not frightened, the picture of control and composure. His arms are down at his side and his posture is so erect he looks artificial, almost like one of these heavy metal appliances scattered around them. The kid is a Colombian Gary Cooper, only more threatening, more predatory, not necessarily just a protector. His huge brown eyes stare at Hannah, waiting for her to make a move, initiate contact. He's dressed in jeans and a light leather blazer over a navy-blue T-shirt. Hannah would bet her car that he's carrying at least two pieces under the coat, automatics, and probably extra clips in his pockets.

A young woman moves up near him, stands slightly behind him and holds onto his arm. She's as dark as Nabo and for a second it occurs to Hannah that they could be brother and sister. But her manner of dress is pure hooker—spandex and satin and plenty of skin-piercing. She has the frightened look of a confused teenager. It's clear she's not used to being awake in daylight. She keeps blinking and holding a hand up over her eyes. Nabo lets her hold onto his arm, but beyond that he ignores her.

Hannah holsters her gun and thinks about starting off with a line. That's what Lenore would do. Something like, "So this is the other woman," or, "I knew you'd be the kind of guy to bring his secretary on a date."

But Nabo's eyes kill off the impulse to imitate her mentor and Hannah simply says, "You wanted to see me?"

He nods and starts to move forward, dragging the girl along

like a pull toy. When he's opposite Hannah, he positions the girl on a turned-over washing machine but stays standing.

"My father sends his regards," he says, and gives a small head-nod without breaking eye contact. The kid has more of an accent than his old man and Hannah finds this unsettling for some reason.

She matches his formality, but it makes her feel out of balance. "Tell your father I'm grateful for any help he can offer me."

Another nod, then he motions to the girl. "This is Mina. She works down Goulden. Out of Bedoya's stable."

Hannah dips her head toward Mina, but the girl looks away. "Mina has some information for me?"

Nabo inhales and moves his hands up to his hips. "She has a story," he says softly. "It may or may not be of use. My father said you should decide for yourself."

Hannah looks to the girl, not sure how to play this. She doesn't want to insult Iguaran by offering Mina cash or connections. At the same time, she doesn't want to stray into rudeness, fail to acknowledge the gesture. What's frustrating about this situation is how common it's becoming, the ever-increasing subtlety of customs and traditions. It's like the ways of the Park are changing weekly. What's ironic is that she should feel like a native, but she never has. She works on the streets in the city where she was born and yet, since Lenore disappeared, at some point every day she feels like she's the most obtuse tourist in the most volatile foreign land on the planet.

She turns her head and tries to study Nabo's face for tips, but there's nothing there. The kid isn't vacant, it's just the opposite—he's so savvy at such a young age that he could already be a player. He's not like Loke or any of the other junior lieutenants who all wear their ambition like fat gold jewelry. If she had to bet today, she'd put money on the Iguaran family to fill the power void in Bangkok. And she realizes it's not the king who's convinced her of this. It's the prince.

Hannah clears her throat and says, "Let me hear the story and then we'll talk."

Nabo and Mina speak in Spanish for a minute, a hushed, clipped exchange. Then Nabo starts to tell about the bad john, the basement apartment, the handcuffs, the make-believe name, the history lesson. And finally, the awful baptism with *la gasolina*. Now and then, Mina breaks in with some clarification or additional information. She speaks in English, but only to Nabo.

Hannah stays calm and attentive, but stares at the girl through Nabo's whole spiel. When he finishes, she asks, "Could you describe the man?"

Mina nods her head rapidly.

"Could she find the apartment? Does she remember where it was?"

This time the girl squints her eyes and gives a slow, moody shrug. Without waiting for Hannah to comment, Nabo turns to Mina and says, *"Espérame en el carro,"* and the girl immediately slides off the washer and runs away, disappearing behind a mountain of half-demolished TV sets.

There's a full quiet minute as they stare at each other, then Nabo says, "It could be nothing."

Hannah decides to be direct. "You know it isn't."

Nabo mimics Mina's shrug.

"Okay," Hannah says, "what do we do now?"

"My father would like to cement our relationship."

"What happened to taking our time? Getting to know each other a little better?"

Nabo folds his arms across his chest. He's more comfortable staring than talking, but he's confident and he's completely clear about his old man's objectives. "My father wants to make a deal now. Tomorrow could be too late—"

"For who?" Hannah interrupts.

"We have information, Detective. We have people who . . ." He lowers his voice, starts again. "Bangkok is about to explode, Detective Shaw." His voice is completely polite, almost rehearsed. "Every day that passes is crucial. You need to make sure your alliances are in place before the explosion happens."

She doesn't want to say it, but something forces it out.

"I'm *aligned*," overemphasizing the word, "with Dr. Cheng."

Nabo clams up at the name, looks from side to side as if surveying the value of the debris all around him, as if there were a way to get wealthy off the discarded mess of Quinsigamond's biggest dumping ground.

Finally, he looks back to Hannah and allows what almost looks like a smile to spread on his dark lips.

"My father said you were too smart to be foolish."

Hannah just shrugs, already regretting the mention of Cheng.

"My father said to tell you, you are smarter than your predecessor."

She keeps her voice even and says, "Your father never knew Lenore Thomas."

In the distance, a hundred yards away at the biodegradable mountains of rotted food, Vern Gomi's beat old bulldozer starts making its way over the hill and begins to push multicolored piles of garbage into one large, steaming heap. Nabo and Hannah both watch in silence as Gomi grinds back and forth, sinking now and then into the muck, mashing gears as he extricates himself.

Without looking away from the hill, Nabo says, "What's it going to be, Detective?"

Hannah gets up off the Frigidaire and rolls her head around her neck. She blocks Lenore's voice from her head and says, "Let's go talk to Mina about that address."

36.

Wallace moves down Paterson Ave, fiddling with the keys to Flynn's office and trying to remember the code to shut down the alarm. Flynn gave him the keys over a month ago, but until now, Wallace has always considered this more a gesture than an invitation, a way of signifying allegiance to the surrogate father.

The keys are attached to what looks like a small suction cup, a round, slightly curved and ribbed piece of green rubber with the words

G.T. Flynn
Financial Services
You Are Protected

stamped in white lettering on the surface. When he first saw the key chain, Wallace asked what it was supposed to be. Flynn looked disappointed and told him to guess. Wallace stared at the circle of rubber and asked if it was a drink coaster and Flynn shook his head and said, "You've got to think symbolically. It's a safety net. You know, like the firemen catch people in. A safety net. Get it?"

Wallace runs his fingers over the rubber "net" and shakes his head. He doesn't like "thinking symbolically." It doesn't come naturally. He wishes it did, because ideas and signs and symbols seem to mean so much to all the new people. And the fact that he

314

finds them so bothersome and, frankly, unimportant is one more unwanted hint that his era is fading out.

He stops in front of the Victorian and looks up at it for a second. Then he climbs up the stairs and across the front porch and up to the huge front door. He unlocks the three dead bolts and steps into the darkness of the office. He brings his hand to the wall, feels for the light switch, and flips it, but the room remains dark. He steps over to the alarm box and sees the red "armed" light is off, the system is down.

Wallace closes the door behind him and relocks a single dead bolt, then starts to feel his way through the outer reception room toward Flynn's office. He'll sack out on the couch till G.T. gets home and they can talk. *Flynn was raised a Catholic and he'll understand the need for confession. He'll feel compelled to forgive the sins of a fallen dwarf, fall into the role he plays so well—the gracious benefactor.* Wallace doesn't like this kind of cold analysis, but he's spent a lifetime sizing people up in this way, looking for the telling inflection in the voice, the pattern in small, unimportant behaviors. There's a way to find hidden motivations. It's a method Wallace has honed for so long that now it's simply reflex. He couldn't shut it down if he wanted to. *Who needs who more? Does the father require the son or is it the other way around?* And suddenly he flashes on that image of Flynn as the runaway orphan, fifteen years old and gobbling down Olga's meatballs like he hadn't eaten in weeks, like he was some skeletal refugee, a displaced person from a vague and distant borderland, desperate not only for the spätzle and the rye bread but for the words of the deformed missionary, the dwarf in the cardigan, this mutated mirror image of the shining television dad dispensing the words of a new religion called jamming.

It's not even a contest, Wallace thinks. *The boy'll be weeping the tears of absolution before morning. And then he can find a way to eliminate our new problem.*

He steps into what Flynn calls the deal room, the place where he sells all the papers that fund the family. Wallace starts to move for the desk when he hears a small whine, the sound of a tight hinge, and he squints and stares forward to see the swivel chair behind the desk begin to turn.

"Jesus, G.T.," he says, "you scared the crap out of me."

There's no response for a second. And then there's a small, rumbling laugh, and Wallace knows it's not Flynn.

A voice says, "Sit down," and Wallace stays motionless in the doorway. A flashlight beam clicks on and shines in his face, runs down the length of his body. After a second, it reverses itself and shines up into the face of the speaker. Wallace wants to run, but he's terrified to make a sudden move. It's like having a wasp land on your arm and not knowing whether to slap it or to freeze and wait for it to fly.

Speer turns off the flashlight and comes forward in the chair, plants his forearms on the desk, and leans on them. In this new position, patches of his face become visible from the dim light outside the window. But his eyes are kept in shadow. Speer takes a clogged breath in through his nose and says, "You're late for my dance lesson, Mr. Browning."

Wallace stays silent, but his heart launches into its most violent pulse, as if it were hurtling toward an imminent and horrific car crash, as if it were being lanced with the longest and fattest hatpin in the world.

Speer begins to barely rock in the swivel chair, his body just slightly tilting back and forth.

"I think," he says, "you came here to tell Mr. Flynn about me."

Wallace shakes his head in the darkness and feels the trembling begin along his jawline.

"You need to know," Speer says, the voice overly controlled, like a bad actor always aware of his own deficiencies, "that even if you were to be rid of me, there are others. Your kind of behavior..." He fades as the anger builds, begins again. "The disorder won't be tolerated. Anarchy is regression. It's weakness. We will not tolerate it..."

There's the sound of fingers being drummed on the desktop, a rolling beat. Then Speer says, "Why don't you sit down there on the couch and we'll both wait for Mr. Flynn? How would that be?"

Wallace moves one foot a step backward.

There's the sound of a long, dry swallow, then the voice is lower, more threatening. "Sit down on the couch."

Wallace pivots and bolts. He bangs an elbow into the secretary's desk but keeps moving, gets to the front door, turns the knob and pulls, but he's forgotten about the dead bolt. And then Speer is behind him, grabbing him by the collar of his shirt, throwing a jab into the small of his back that drives him down on his knees.

Wallace falls on his side, tries to cover up, but Speer has a blackjack out and begins whipping it across his arms and side, and then he rolls Wallace onto his stomach, plants a knee on his back, and begins to pummel the back of the head until it's clear the dwarf has lost consciousness.

Speer stands up and repockets the sap. He's breathing hard and he takes a second to hunch down, hands on his knees, head lowered like he's just finished a set of wind sprints. He sucks air for a full minute until his lungs quiet, then he reaches down and grabs Wallace by the wrists and drags his body back into Flynn's inner office. He lifts him onto the couch, holds on to one wrist, feels for and finds a racing pulse. Then he drops down on one knee and the trunk of his body hangs over Wallace.

Speer reaches into a back pocket and pulls out the silver flask, hesitates, then brings the curved metal of the container up to his cheek and touches it to his skin for a few seconds, as if trying to cool himself down.

He puts the cap end of the flask in his mouth, bites down with his teeth, and begins to rotate the bottom slowly with his left hand. As he turns, he blesses himself, makes the sign of the cross, his right hand reverently touching his forehead, breast-bone, left and right shoulders. Then he spits the cap to the floor, places his thumb over the mouth of the flask, and tips it slightly until his thumb is wetted with the contents.

He sets the flask on the floor carefully, leans in closer over the body, brings his thumb to Wallace's forehead, and, again, traces the sign of the cross. As he moves his thumb, he mumbles, ancient and foreign words, sounds from the past.

"*Memento, homo, quia pulvis es et in pulverem reverteris.*"

He brings his hand behind Wallace's head, gently cups the neck, and lifts the head to an angle. He reaches to the floor, picks up the flask, brings it to Wallace's mouth, and pours a long swallow of benzine down the open, sleeping throat.

37.

Flynn does something he's never done before. He shows up at the mediation drunk. He's killed most of a bottle of Glenlivet, not entirely to ward off the pain in his hand. He thinks he looks the part of a drunk, a classic white-collar Scotch man from the last generation. A guy with a regular after-work hangout, a place where you could eat a blood-red steak at the bar. A place with heavy wood and some brass.

He's dressed for the part, a good example of the word *disheveled*. His shirt won't stay completely tucked in his pants. His tie seems to be unraveling on its own. His hair, the showcase of his grooming habits, is winging out behind his ears, strands uniting into tufts that follow no plan of parting.

He's playing with the TV-chassis diorama in the middle of the Anarchy Museum. No one is speaking to him. In fact, the whole room is held in a field of silence. Wallace's old boys sit on their crates and folding chairs. They act like the place was a lazy barbershop, that they've assembled simply for the free copies of *True Detective*. Their leader has absented himself from the proceedings and Flynn takes this as a personal slap in the face and the biggest and best sign of how total a fool he's become.

Flynn doesn't completely understand why the old boys bothered to show up. It's the reverse of what he expected. He assumed Hazel and the gang would come, just for the sake of one last argument, one final blast of adrenaline and name-calling and polemic.

But when he entered the museum, there was the old guard, a dozen or so decaying statues, plus Billy, the one young member of Wallace's gang. They were all sitting quiet like they were waiting for a very late bus. And, except for Gabe, Hazel and company were nowhere to be seen. Flynn decided to wait a half hour simply because it seemed easier to sit on the floor and toy with the contents of the old RCA cabinet than to attempt the drive back home.

The fact is he doesn't really want to be back home. He wants to be someplace different. He wants to be with Ronnie.

So why did you drive her away?

Throughout his life, Flynn has wished he could pick up a guidebook, a text, that would clearly explain his motivations, show a route from sparks in the brain all the way through speech, movement, physical activity. He wants a field guide to his own mind and desires, a primer that would treat him as an object, or better, an idea, something a method can be applied to or layered over. Like an instructional transparency. Like those Mylar illustrations in the *Britannica* that show the interior of the body, one sheet lying over the next, respiratory system, circulatory system, nerve pathways, connection of the bones, until a whole is formed, an entire unit, a complete body.

Halfway through his third Scotch, Flynn became aware of a simple truth that was so obvious and so pathetic that he now feels embarrassed by both its presence and his long ignorance of it. But it's there and it's not going away and it was Ronnie who induced its birth in his conscious, if raving, brain:

It's not the jam. You stupid bastard. It has never once been the jam. You don't care about the jam. You're heir apparent to Wallace and you couldn't care less about jamming. You could go either way. Take it or leave it. You dumb, pathetic fuck. It's the jammers. It's the family. The connection. You want to belong. Look at yourself. You're the mediator, the father confessor, the counselor, banker, errand boy, historian. You want to keep them together. You want to be at the heart of the home, the

center of their lives. The idea has nothing to do with it. You're a
political idiot. You've lied to yourself that you're some provocateur. But
you want to be Abraham. You want to be Big Daddy. You want unity
and you want blood-love.

And the biggest question is: Why couldn't you make a normal
family?

Now Gabe crosses the space between them, eyes on the
floor, hands pushed into his pockets. He's dressed in the standard
black T-shirt, ripped blue jeans, and high-top sneakers. Flynn
watches the boy walk toward him and remembers being fifteen.

Flynn has always thought of his own childhood as a classic,
if nonunique, tragedy: a compilation of archetypal images, as
automatically known as that black-and-white film portrayal of
the helpless widow at the mercy of the black-caped, handlebar-
mustached banker/landlord/robber baron. He tends to recall his
first decade in terms of snapshots: the nuns of the orphanage
grouped around the head dining table, the dingy kitchen of the
first foster home.

But now he feels that, even as an orphan, a displaced,
exiled child, he probably had an easier time than Gabe. Because
Flynn knew instinctively, reflexively, how to act the part of the
integrated when necessary. And Gabe is one of those people who
never will, who'll go a lifetime just missing the markings of the
franchised. He's been betrayed by a hesitant tongue that will
always recoil at the first pulses of nervousness or fear. Flynn may
always feel isolated, but Gabe is a truly marked individual. His
isolation is visible outside the skin, like a defective infant whose
stomach developed outside the epidermis. Gabe will never be
able to fake integration the way Flynn can. And they both know
this.

So when Gabe comes to a stop next to Flynn's shoulder,
Flynn makes it easy for him. He pivots toward the kid and
extends a hand and says, "Looks like your people have really cut
and run this time."

Gabe simply gives a sad nod.

Flynn shrugs. "Why don't we tell the gang here to head home? It's all over. Nothing's going to happen here tonight."

Gabe sits down on the floor next to Flynn and pretends to look into the diorama.

Flynn puts a sloppy hand on his shoulder. "Want to thank you for coming out here tonight, Gabe. I know it was an awful choice. And to be honest, I'm surprised. I mean, it's no secret how you feel about Hazel."

"You're la-la-loaded, G.T."

"Can't disagree with you. But it's medicinal. Broke some fingers."

"I da-da-don't think I've ever s-seen you loaded."

"Well, consider it another first. We're breaking records all over the place tonight."

Gabe gives him a weak smile. "Na-none of this is your fault, G.T."

Flynn shakes his head. "I didn't exert enough force. I tried to appease everyone. I couldn't bring the whole thing into focus."

"What do you ma-ma-mean?"

Flynn puts a hand on his shoulder, but then lets it fall away. "I mean," he says, louding up on the last word, "that I couldn't make the big picture clear enough. That the reason we all end up here doesn't have much to do with jamming."

Gabe stares at him like he's segued into a lost language.

"Forget it," Flynn says, looking back at the diorama.

"Why don't we ga-get out of here, G.T. Okay? La-let me take you out. I know a new place down in the za-zone."

"I've had quite a few already, right?"

Gabe shrugs. "Sa-so one more won't hurt. La-let me—"

And his sentence is broken off by the sound of Hazel and her group throwing open the museum's doors and stomping into the room. It sounds like they're all wearing jackboots. They halt into a phalanx behind their leader and she stands with her hands on her hips and surveys the room, a punk Patton juiced up on attitude, certainty, and probably a hit or two of speed.

"Son of a bitch," Flynn yells in a voice of delighted surprise. "I knew it."

He struggles up to his feet and yells, "The kids have come home."

He starts to walk toward Hazel and says, "Daughter of mine, I knew you wouldn't let me down."

She looks surprised, cranes her neck out slightly, and says, "Jesus Christ, Flynn. You're shit-faced."

"It's a new look," he says. "I was due for a change."

Hazel looks past him at Gabe and says, "You get lost, sport?"

Gabe opens his mouth to speak, but Hazel cuts him off with a disgusted shake of her head and says, "I nailed you as a lightweight from the start."

Flynn steps directly in front of her, face-to-face. He drops his voice, plants a kiss on her cheek that she tries not to react to, and says, "I knew you'd come, Hazel. I knew you'd remember."

She turns her face away from him and says, "Go sit down, Flynn."

No one makes a move. It's like the whole room is waiting for some delayed performance to begin. There's an edginess that's apparent without any manifestation in sound or motion.

Finally Flynn says, "What? You're running the show tonight, Hazel?"

She stares at him and there's no meaning he can put to the look on her face. He hopes the booze is responsible for this. But he'd bet against it. He's about to lose her, he knows. He's about to lose this whole pathetic family. She's come to make it official. There's nothing he can do. Any impressions of control he once felt are gone. And the infuriating and heart-crushing frustration comes most of all from the fact that he doesn't know what he did wrong. He's always felt that at a basic, cellular level, this was a cause-and-effect world. But now something in his intestines, rather than his brain, tells him he's been wrong. Logic and patterns and inviolable rules of force and reaction are just imposed explanations, convenient fables that comfort us if we don't fuck with them too much.

All he can think to say is, "What did I do wrong, Hazel?"

"Knock it off, Flynn," she says. "Don't embarrass yourself here—"

"Embarrass myself?" he screams, and the room sits up at the volume and the echo. He's suddenly furious. "Where the fuck do you come off talking to me like that?"

She's trying to keep any emotion off her face. "Please, G.T.," she says through a tiny mouth, "I have to do this."

"Do what?" he yells, his voice elevated to the borders of a child's tantrum. "I took care of you," his arm actually extended and pointing a finger at Hazel. He yells the words separately, as if they were written on cue cards that aren't being manipulated quickly enough.

"Ja-Ja-G.T.," Gabe begins, but Flynn waves him away with his spare hand.

"Look," Hazel says, her own volume increasing to match him, "I know everything you did for me. And that doesn't change anything. We're out, G.T. We're already gone. This isn't a game to us anymore."

He takes a few shaky steps toward her, puts his hands on her shoulders. Eddie steps up from the background and Hazel snaps, "Take it easy, Ed."

"This is crazy, Hazel," Flynn says, trying to bring his voice down. "What do you do now? You start throwing rocks? You start buying weapons? This is ridiculous. What are you telling us here? You're terrorists now? Against who?"

Hazel actually smiles, a slight, weak turning of her mouth. "Against the liars," she says.

Flynn lets his hands fall from her shoulders. "We're all fucking liars, Hazel."

She shakes her head at him, a small tail of braided hair swings out and drops to her chest. She steps around Flynn and looks out at the old guard.

"The divorce is official, tell the dwarf for me."

Billy J stands up, folds his arms across his chest and says, "If what you do sprays back at us, you'll regret it."

"You just remember, Bilbo, my friend Eddie would love a chance to see how far he could throw you."

Flynn leans his butt against the television chassis. "So that's it," he says to Hazel's whole group. "No meeting. No mediation. All bonds are severed. Good luck and the next time we hear about any of you it's in the *Spy*. 'QSG Studio Firebombed in Early Morning Attack.'"

Hazel shrugs.

"I could rat you out," Flynn says, looking down to his feet, his voice on the edge of a slur.

"No you can't," Hazel says quietly, embarrassed for him. "And no you won't."

There's a calmness and certainty in her voice that preclude a rebuttal. So, Flynn pushes his hands into his pockets and says, in a lower voice, without thinking, "What did I do wrong?"

"I'll see you around, Flynn," Hazel says, and doesn't wait for a response. She turns and heads for the door and the others follow her out in a tight-knit formation, a little cluster of whispering leather. The last to squeeze out the exit is Eddie the meat-boy. Flynn notices a small old-fashioned vacuum tube hung from a belt loop of his jeans by a lancet. It bounces off his ass as he walks.

Then they're all gone and Flynn is left with Gabe and the old guard. He wobbles to the front of them, and all he can think to say is, "Go home."

Billy J moves to his side and takes over, saying, "I'll call you all tomorrow. We'll talk to Wallace. C'mon. It'll be okay."

They all climb off their fruit crates and folding chairs, but they move slowly, they linger a bit. It's clear they want some explanation and assurance, a few words that things will be all right, that by morning Flynn will be sober and rational. That by afternoon he'll start picking up the pieces.

But Gabe knows Flynn can't give them that.

"Go ahead," Billy says, "I promise. Wallace'll call you all tomorrow. Everything will be fine."

Billy leads them out of the museum and when the door bangs shut, Gabe sits down on the floor next to Flynn. The room seems enormous around them.

"Let's ga-ga-get out of here," Gabe says.

Flynn doesn't move for a while. Then he brings his damaged hand up near his face and turns it from side to side slowly, inspecting the palm and then the knuckles. He lets out a low, rumbling belch, looks up at Gabe with squinted eyes, and says, "The thing is, I thought I could really hold it together. You know? I thought I had some, you know, hold over them, over all of you. The son who made good or something. Like my presence would have been enough. Like I was some kind of fucking symbol."

"Ca-c'mon, Fa-Fa-Flynn."

"I thought it would just go on and on. For some reason. It seemed . . . I thought, like, Wallace brought me in, and I brought Hazel in, and Hazel brought you in—"

"Let's go. La-lemme help you up."

Gabe stands and puts a hand under Flynn's arm and Flynn gets up, seemingly unaware his body's moving, lost in thought, wetting his lips.

"Jesus," he mutters. "When you're this wrong . . ."

Gabe fishes through Flynn's suitcoat pockets and comes out with the keys to the museum. "I na-know, G.T.," he says.

They start a sloppy waltz toward the exit, Flynn letting himself lean down onto Gabe's shoulder, Gabe struggling under the weight in a stuttering shuffle.

"About everything," Flynn says.

Gabe nods as he pulls forward. "We'll go da-downstairs and pa-pa-pour some drinks," he says. "We'll ta-ta-talk all night."

38.

The only things left in the apartment's mini-refrigerator are half a mug of day-old instant coffee and his last three hits of crank. Speer mixes them together and tosses them down the gullet with a hard, awkward swallow. Then he sets himself up on the stool, opens his notebook, uncaps his writing pen, and turns on the Kenwood. He rolls the band indicator up to the desired frequency, then very gingerly begins to up the volume.

The room slowly fills with the sound of barking dogs, high-pitched yaps, like puppies, small-boned breeds—dachshunds, Chihuahuas, toy poodles. The broadcast seems to alternate between miking the whole dissonant chorus of barks and howls, and then spotlighting a single star, a brokenhearted crooner of untranslatable canine woes.

Speer's head pounds. He feels like his temples have taken on a rubbery, elastic quality, that cold air is being pumped into his cranium from some unseen port. And no one's aware of or concerned about the skull cavity's maximum capacity of air volume. He feels like explosion is imminent. Like he could break the strongest sphygmomanometer without flexing his biceps.

But he forces himself to turn to a blank sheet of paper and write. He's afraid the letters will blur before his eyes, but when he prints *Margie,* it's completely legible.

Dear Margie,

I've kept my word now, haven't I? Have you been molested? Have I tracked down your address and telephone line? Taped your conversations and photographed your comings and goings? Have men in second-rate gray suits come to your door, looked through your suitcase, asked questions about the men you see?

I don't understand you. If you could see what you've done to me, if you could see how I've deteriorated, the thoughts that come to me now. You know what I'm capable of. Why do you want to bring this on yourself?

I've been patient. I've allowed you time. Each night I've returned to this apartment to find it empty. Can you possibly imagine the silence of this room when it's four A.M. and the radio is off and I can no longer even hear myself breathe and start to think that I've gone deaf?

I could snap the pen I hold in two. I could picture it as your long, sleek neck and I could grope for the long line of the jugular and the rear rope of the spinal cord.

I know that when all is said and done, the papers will attempt to distort the truth in their inimitable way. I am prepared for this. There may be mentions of Oswald and Ray, Sirhan and Ali Agca. But we both know I am nothing like these pawns. I know who holds my strings. I know their purposes and so, for the moment, I allow us to use one another. But I always hold the scissors. I am more than myself now, my love. Remember how I once told you that I loved holding my weapon because it made my hand feel better than it was?

Do you?

This feeling is like that feeling. I performed a baptism tonight, darling. And I have heard the call of a new Gabriel. But this one announces death rather than life. The storm before the calm. The rapture before a divine infinity.

I will finish up my business soon, Margie. And then I will come for you.

39.

"You sure this place will hold our weight?" Diane says to Eddie as she awkwardly climbs up an old rope ladder to the roof of the airport terminal.

Eddie follows her, one hand reaching up to goose her behind. "It'll hold everyone," he says. "Trust me."

They're the last to arrive. Hazel and the rest have been sitting on the roof for almost a half hour, huddling against the drizzle, whispering predictions and gossip, trying to control their excitement like greed-crazed kids on Christmas Eve.

Hazel gives Diane a hand until she gets both feet planted and gains her balance. The roof pitches at a mild angle and the asphalt shingles are coming loose from the nails in a few places. Eddie hoists himself to the top with more strength than grace. He takes a few hesitant steps up the slope, then seats himself next to Hazel. He shakes water from his hair like a clumsy but perpetually happy dog.

Hazel has an old pair of Bushnell binoculars up to her eyes. She's looking to the west of the city, fiddling with the focus ring. They're Gabe's binoculars and she doesn't think the focus ring works anymore.

"You sure this is the best spot to be?" Eddie asks, pulling a can of Colt .45 from his jacket pocket, popping the top, and letting a line of foam bubble over the can, over his hands and down the rooftop in a mini-river.

"Great view," Hazel says. "Nothing blocking us from this angle."

"Yeah," Eddie says. "It's not the view I'm talking about."

Hazel lets the binoculars drop and dangle on a black strap around her neck.

"I'm saying we're not hidden at all," Eddie says. "We're wide open here."

"Little fear is good for us," Hazel says, like she's not very interested in the topic. "It'll keep us careful right from the start."

"You call this careful?" Eddie asks.

She brings the binoculars back up to her eyes, turns her head slowly to the side, and says, "You're going to have to trust me tonight, okay, Eddie? It's real important that we see everything from up here tonight. We're elevated. We're away from the major part of the city lights. We're under the stars. Vision'll be at its best up here. It'll make a real impression. Something everyone'll remember. I promise."

She hands the binoculars to Eddie and looks at her watch. "And there's no chance of something blocking our signal," she says. "Speaking of which..."

Eddie stares at her for a second, then catches on and wedges his Colt can in his crotch while he digs in his pocket. He pulls out a small rectangle of gray plastic that has a square red button protruding from its side and a silver antenna knob mounted at its top. There are little silver lightning bolts raised on its face below a round mesh speaker.

It's a standard kid's play walkie-talkie, the kind you'd buy in any mall electronics shop. It had belonged to Gabe. Like the binoculars, he was thrilled to have donated it to Hazel and the group. Hazel's more than a little bothered by Gabe's absence. It was clear that the kid was in love with her. What could possibly have caused him to bolt on her biggest night? She knows he felt some respect for Flynn, that he trusted him and maybe looked at him as a weird kind of father figure. But Hazel knows Gabe had it bad for her and he would've been the last person she'd have picked for defector.

Eddie hands the walkie-talkie to Hazel and she pulls the antenna out to full extension, then she stretches her arm out and points westward. Eddie thinks it looks like she's pointing a magician's wand and the feeling on the roof is weird enough so that he can imagine a cloud of smoke swarming into view with a classic fire-burst sound and a rabbit or a dove appearing in the air at the end of the antenna. But instead, Hazel just points and bites down on a growing smile.

"You have any problems I should know about?" she asks Eddie.

"This time it was cake," he answers. "I'm not even thinking about what it'll be like next time."

"And no one saw you?"

"There's nothing out there but raccoons and squirrels."

"And driving back?"

"I was just driving. Like everyone else."

"Okay." Hazel nods, then leans over and puts a hand on Eddie's shoulder, brings her head across, and kisses him on the mouth. The can of Colt drops from its wedge, rolls down the roof, and explodes onto the cement below.

"Hey," Diane says, and Hazel looks up at her and says, "Good job. Both of you."

She gets up on her knee, pivots slightly till she's facing Diane, then cuffs her behind the neck, pulls her forward, and lands a second, identical kiss. Diane jerks away and Eddie can see Hazel holding down a laugh.

Hazel stands up, looks from face to face while using the antenna to scratch at the back of her neck.

"Tonight," she says, in a voice that sounds like she's reading from a prepared script, "we make our first big blow against the order of things. We're about to make some pretty big confusion. And confusion is life. Confusion is antistagnation. Anarchy," and she draws out the word, "has become a word in the dictionary. But in about ten seconds, we're going to define it, right out loud, right up against the sky where it can't be missed, for the whole freaking city of Quinsigamond—"

"And a few towns beyond," Eddie says, and his mouth spreads with a weird, proud smile.

Eddie can tell Hazel doesn't like being interrupted, that she hates having a joke spliced into this important moment. But to stop and smack him with an insult would only compound the disruption, so she nods and keeps going.

"I know you're all clear that once the shit hits the fan tonight, it's a new situation. There's going to be some real consequences here. But no one forced you to come up here and sit on this roof. You're here 'cause you've made a decision. And I congratulate you on it."

She pauses, again looks at each individual face, slightly blue in the moonlight. Then, in a low, dramatic voice, she says, "So, I guess it's showtime."

She turns her head and extends her arm and points the walkie-talkie antenna out toward Devlin Hill, a mile west, where WQSG's broadcast tower stands like an enormous museum piece, a classic example of industrial ego and the power of metal and height.

Everyone on the terminal rooftop stares out at it. It rises up like some enormous iron age pseudo-crucifix or the skeleton of some gigantic but primitive missile, nothing streamlined, all harsh corners and crisscrossing support struts. To Hazel, the longer she looks, it starts to seem like something more than a radio antenna. It starts to take on the feel of an icon, something with an aura of historical or even religious importance. She wonders if anyone else feels this way.

"Everybody have a clear view?" Hazel asks.

A few people adjust themselves slightly and everyone else just nods.

"Okay, then," she mouths. "Let's shake things up."

Her thumb squeezes the walkie-talkie's talk button flush to the side of the unit. About one, awful, aching second hangs. And then another. And another. The tower continues to stand tall and

complete. A murmur starts to spread around the roof, a communal voice of surprise and embarrassment and confusion. Hazel
looks down at the plastic box, trying to control both panic and
outrage. She extends her arm out again, the magician now frantic
to get the trick right, to redeem himself before the audience
heads for the lobby. She thumbs the red button again and again,
but the result is the same. The tower stays erect and untouched, a
stubborn wall of resistance.

"Eddie," she says, in a seething, about-to-explode voice,
"what the fuck did you do wrong?"

Eddie's behind her, shaking his head, wiping his mouth over
and over with the back of his arm.

There's a crackle of static from the walkie-talkie and then a
run of distant, forced laughter from the small mesh speaker.
Hazel closes her eyes and bites down on her upper lip.

"Are you there?" Loke asks.

The murmur from the rest of the group increases and Hazel
keeps her back to them.

"Hazel, my love?" Loke says. "Are you there?"

Hazel stares down at the speaker and mouths the words
please and *no*. She looks out at the tower, brings the walkie-talkie
up to her mouth, presses the red button, and whispers, "Why
did you do this to me?"

Then she thumbs down the volume and brings the speaker
up next to her ear so no one else can hear.

"I'm afraid," Loke says, "your request to immigrate has
been denied, Hazel. I'm so sorry. But this does happen to the
best of us. There are quotas to be maintained."

Hazel jams in the red talk button like she was crushing an
insect and says, "What did I buy? It sure as hell wasn't plastique."

"You bought shit, Hazel. That alone should show you how
out of your depth you are. You should take your little party
there and swim home fast."

"I can't go back," Hazel says, and is shocked to find her
eyes starting to sting and water. "There's nowhere to go."

Loke transmits a small snort, then says, "Life's a bitch, isn't it? You should come back down Bangkok and thank me, Hazel. I've given you a memorable lesson. You'll take this one to the grave. This wasn't a swindle, this was an education. Your own little MBA. Take the gang out and celebrate. On me. And if you get lonely, later on—"

She clicks off the box and heaves it. It sails in an arc like a weak pop-up, then comes down out on the runway and shatters into a pile of plastic shards and wire and aluminum. She brings a hand up to her eyes, presses hard, takes a breath, then begins to turn around to face her people. But before she can see their faces, before she can record the looks that have to signal something like pity, she moves to the edge of the roof and starts to climb down the rope ladder.

40.

Ronnie had wanted to call it an early night, to take advantage of her one night off, maybe eat some lo mein from a takeout carton and watch the Weather Channel until she fell asleep. Instead, she forced herself to sit at a scarred and battered table at the public library and page through the more recent issues of *Chronicle of Modern Media* and *Wavelength: The Radio Industry Weekly*. She opened a notebook and copied down about two dozen possible employment prospects, then moved into the audio room, donned a pair of heavy, archaic headphones, and listened to *Lulu's Greatest Hits* for about an hour.

Now, crossing Main Street and staring up at Solitary, she's convinced she brought this feeling on herself, this sense of almost-adolescent sadness, of a kind of nostalgic ache for a city and a life she's only known for a little over a year. She's never been one who enjoyed playing martyr, who secretly relished her own misfortunes. But tonight she wishes she were. Like her mother. Or maybe like Flynn. Or like the callers she ministers to six goddamn nights a week, people who've allowed fear to strip them of pleasure and sensuality and even, sometimes, of movement. Right now, she wants to scold herself in the same unflinching manner that she scolds her faceless callers: *It's old but it still works, boys and girls, face the truth and the truth will set you free.*

335

And the truth is that for all its griminess and decay, for all its disorder and regression and violence, she's come to love Quinsigamond. She's come to care for this city in a way that's never happened to her before. She's felt a naturalness here, a sense of not exactly contentment, but more like correctness, this Zen-like assurance that these are the streets she was meant to move through, that the air hanging over this city was destined to be filled with the ring of her voice.

And on top of that foundation came G.T. Flynn. More than anything, she'd love to be able to say that it was simply Flynn's doubt that ended everything. Or that he meant nothing more than Yves back in Toronto, a warm body and a shared laugh, a way to pass the time during one more extended stopover. But the truth, the magic bullet of her career, the freeing agent of all repressions, the truth is that in a matter of hours she let Flynn become something else. In the glow of her own headlights, in the sway of some retro slow-dancing, like an overprivileged teenager with too much time on her hands, she let Flynn enter the realm of a possible future.

Why? She wishes there were at least some theories, some ideas about the effect of the city's drinking water on her brain functions. Or about some chemical kicked free in her bloodstream on her last birthday. But what she hasn't wanted to acknowledge until just now is that she sensed something about Flynn almost at once. She picked it up in the form of a pure signal, an uninterrupted line of energy, like the crazed bleating of a spastic Geiger counter stumbling onto a pile of virgin uranium.

She sensed the need, the vacuum, the total force of *want*. Not the simpering cravings of the average emotional cripple, but the wantings of a pro, the black hole yearning for connection that subsumes every other desire. Like her mother, Flynn's a creature of binding, an absolute copulator, a high priest of the drive for communion. His doubt was never the product of disinterest. Just the opposite. He needs complete coupling, seamless unification. He wants to be twinned in the way other people want money or immortality. And that kind of raw, ongoing *want* can bring someone to the edge and then nudge them over.

Just like my mother, Ronnie thinks.

She steps into the elevator and presses for the seventeenth floor. *If I felt the signal,* she thinks, *if I remembered the consequences, why didn't I run out of Wireless?* The truth is: *I let this happen.*

She lightly slaps herself in the head with the notebook that holds the names of twenty-five radio stations, all of them thousands of miles from Quinsigamond. A couple of them in Europe. One in Jerusalem.

The elevator deposits her on her floor and she digs out her keys and lets herself into the apartment. She'll have to talk Vinnie into an extra night off this week. He can give Ray a double slot, her going-away present to the most amusing fascist she hopes she'll ever meet. There are dozens of things to do. Get the updated résumé and stat sheets reprinted. Set up a rush job with a modeling agency and photographer—she thinks she'll be a blonde this time out, design her next face in the form of a neo–Marilyn Monroe type. The furniture rental company will have to be called. And then there's the ritual sorting of the cassettes, the junking of the disposable sound crap, and the trunk storage of the tapes she'll take out of Quinsigamond. She'll make lists, slide into her organization mode.

But not tonight. Tonight she wants one more round of balcony hedonism. So she changes into her kimono, grabs the mescal and the last of the gourmet Swiss almond fudge ice cream, and moves out onto the lounge chair, determined not to think about Flynn. Or her mother. Or the odd and annoying attachment she's somehow developed for this dying factory town. Tonight she wants simplistic input, the taste and texture of the liquor, the fudge, the ice cream. The feel of the cool fall breeze over her legs.

She opens the sliders, moves out on the balcony, eases down into the lounge, and immediately feels something beneath her.

She reaches around and pulls up a notebook—a generic, spiral-bound school model. It's opened and the covers are folded back on themselves. The exposed pages are filled with writing, heavily inked block letters done with a felt marker. For a second she thinks Elaine, the cleaning lady, must have left it out here. But Elaine normally comes on Tuesdays and Fridays. And the handwriting doesn't strike her as female.

Ronnie brings her legs up, positions the notebook against her knees, and starts reading from the open page:

... Here's the intersection where you meet these jammers, Margie. You're both aberrations of nature. Do you recall the nature shows I used to watch? *Untamed World* and the others? You'd never watch with me. But what I saw might have helped you, Margie. The images I took in might well have saved you from the awful path you now find yourself walking. At some point in all of those shows there would be a dramatic, often slow-motion scene of a predator and his prey—let's say a jackal and an antelope. And we could see the toned, bulging muscles of the jackal as it darted down some dusty slope. And we could see the antelope buck and panic and run. But the antelope never gets away, Margie. And eventually we must see the inevitable scene of the jackal's jagged teeth slicing into the antelope's soft neck, tearing open the throat, holding tight like a reinforced vise until the antelope slumps into a pile of its own weak death.

The jackal did nothing "wrong," Margie. You do realize this? The jackal was simply stronger than the antelope in a variety of ways. His reward for his strength is, first, sustenance, and second, but maybe most important, the sustained order of things.

My job, Margie, is to keep order. It's what I've been put here to do. How could you spend almost twenty years with me and not be aware of that?

The problem with you and these radio criminals is that you

opt for chaos in the desperate, mistaken hope that you can topple the natural order of things. You hope that somehow you can confuse people into calling weakness strength and vice versa. Your goal is to reduce all of history to some pathetic and abstract linguistic argument.

I am here, very simply, to see that this does not happen.

Ronnie moves the notebook off her knees and lets it drop to the floor. Her brain is starting to race a bit and she absentmindedly takes a long swallow from the mescal.

Could belong to the handyman, the maintenance guy, what's his name, Dave something? But what the hell was he doing in the apartment? I didn't call in for any repairs.

She gets up suddenly and moves to the railing. And as she looks down to the street she spots all the normal clusters, all the separate night groups that have made up the landscape this past year—the Dumpster scavengers, the gay hustlers, the hooker twins, and the corner dealers. But tonight, this time, for the first time, they all seem to be looking up at her, unblinking, totally focused on the seventeenth floor of Solitary, as if some vision had corralled their collective attention, as if God's own drive-in movie were showing on the face of the building.

Ronnie turns and runs inside to the phone. There's no in-building security, but the bank that's holding the note provided her with a twenty-four-hour number to call in case of emergencies. And though she doesn't know what she'll say when her call is picked up, it's starting to feel like an emergency is coming on, like she's just felt a warning tremor that could signal the big quake.

She fumbles with her address book, presses the phone to her ear, and starts to dial the first numbers, then stops, presses the hang-up button, listens, presses again, then again. The phone is dead.

She grabs the Jeep keys off the kitchen counter, runs to the hallway, and thumbs the elevator button. She's peppering to herself the standard *C'mon, C'mon,* when the hallway's ceiling speakers come alive, not with the slow, narcotic Muzak they were designed for, but with a voice, a low, slightly raspy male voice. A classic radio voice, someone who could speak with authority and anger in the middle of a sleepless night.

The voice says, "Veronica."

She cringes and wheels around, but the hallway is empty. Her heart starts to feel like a massive and endless bee sting.

The voice says, "Veronica, it's time to wipe the face of your savior."

She starts to run, moving south, turning corners and zagging with the curves of the hallway.

"Veronica," the voice says, following her, coming at her from above, "I'm here to absolve you, show you the error of your thoughts. Take the chaos from your heart."

On impulse, she turns to a door and grabs at the knob, but it's locked. She continues down the hall, which seems longer and more angled than she's ever remembered, like a maze, a futile labyrinth without an exit.

"Veronica," now a yell, a harsh rebuke.

She grabs another random doorknob and turns and this one opens. She steps into a dark, bare unit of blueboard walls with unfinished electrical wiring jutting from small square holes and hanging limp like dying, atrophied arms. She runs through the living room into a rear bedroom. She goes straight for the closet, steps inside, pulls the door closed behind her, and sinks to the floor.

She knows this is exactly the wrong thing to do, but she doesn't move. She pulls her body in, shoulders hunched up to the knees and arms wrapped tight around her legs. She starts to rock slightly on her behind, as if she can't control the movement. Her breathing starts to go wrong, too much air coming in, no exhalations. She starts to feel both dizzy and nauseated, starts to wish she could make the closet smaller, pull the closet down on top of herself.

Muffled, as if the words were being spoken into a pillow,

she can barely hear the ceiling voice out in the hall. She can't make out any words beyond her own name, but the voice is booming, ranting, elevating into some kind of apocalyptic tirade, an anger of limitless proportions.

And it starts to sound like her mother's keening in the middle of the night, her mother's wrenching sobs and grunts, her mother's air overloaded with the helpless misery of the insane. And all Ronnie can see is the dark wall of a trailer in Gainesville, Florida. Twelve years old and folded in on herself, lying fetal on a skinny bunk in the dark. Pretending to be Anne Frank. Pretending the monsters, the voices, are going to storm through the attic door and end the waiting.

And then there's silence. The muted bellowing has stopped. She waits for what seems like hours, tries to calm the breathing, tries to hold off the nausea and the waves of absolute panic. She strains, listens for the bark of her name.

But there's nothing.

She comes up into a sitting position, presses her palms against her forehead for a long minute, stays still, and counts her breaths. She stares down at the bottom lip of the closet door, thinks about staying here, silent, rigid, just breathing, until she can see morning light under the lip.

Then, without thinking, she rises and pushes open the door. And screams at the sight of his face.

His skin seems tinged yellow and his eyes seem enormous, the whites a horrible pattern of red branching lines against a bleached-yellow backing. There's an oily skim-coat on his forehead and his lips are pale and tightened across the run of his teeth.

She tries to bolt around him, but he grabs her by the wrist. Immediately, she swings her free hand up to hit him in the face, but he catches that wrist as well. And they stand there like petrified dance partners.

She holds herself rigid and he brings his face up close to hers and whispers, "Don't fuck around here, Veronica."

She tries to prevent a huge, gulping swallow, but it happens, anyway. Speer doesn't try to move her or hurt her, he just holds her in place by her wrists, his tongue darting out of his mouth a few times, moistening the patch of skin below his nose.

She could scream again, but she knows there's no one to hear her. And it's likely both her wrists could be snapped in one movement.

"I know he was at the station with you the other night," Speer says, clearly having difficulty keeping his voice in control. "I know he was right there next to you while you did your filthy show. You don't know what you're involved in here. You've got no idea. You picked the wrong side of the fence. And that's not my fault. Your stupidity is not my fault. Sooner or later you're going to have to realize that."

He takes a stuttering breath and then his head drops to her neck and he begins to kiss her with a wet, open mouth and too much pressure. And then she feels his teeth and this controlled, limited biting begins. It hurts, but she stays silent, eyes closed.

A phrase comes to her that she hasn't heard since high school. *Love bruise.*

And then he's finished. She knows in the morning, on her body, warm or cold, there'll be a round, brown mark on her neck, a sign that the night really happened.

He steps backward. His face is shining with sweat. There's a foolish, limp grin on his mouth. He waits a moment, looks her up and down, and then in a movement that's so fast it seems at odds with the man's bulk, he steps to the side, releases one of her wrists, bends the other behind her back, pulls a set of handcuffs off his belt, manipulates her down to her knees, and cuffs her wrists together.

Then he pulls his revolver from a holster inside his windbreaker and holds it up in front of her face, sideways, not pointing the muzzle at her, more like it was a visual aid, an advanced show-and-tell item. He grabs a handful of her hair at the back of her neck, gives a sharp tug until her head is aimed at the ceiling.

He bends down, brings his face next to the side of her head, pushes the tip of his tongue into her ear, and then swallows and whispers, "We're going to see Flynn now. And if you give me any problems, I'll put this gun in that filthy mouth of yours and turn you into a goddamn bonfire."

41.

Hannah takes the china teacup from her lips, swallows, and says, "There's no way to tell someone what ginseng tastes like. They've got to try it themselves."

Dr. Cheng nods to her and smiles, then places his cup back on the saucer that rests on his bony knee. "You give your friend Ike the recipe for the kelp soup with ginger. Two weeks, you'll both feel like new people."

They're sitting in the living room of Cheng's apartment above his herbarium. It's a tiny place where he's resided for over fifty years. The apartment is laid out like a modified bungalow or railroad flat, with three rooms running front to back. There's a small galley kitchen at the head of the building, followed by the living room and a tiny bedroom with grass-cloth walls that contains only a bamboo trunk filled with coolie gowns and a thin straw mat that the doctor has used as a bed since the day he moved in.

In contrast with the bedroom, the living room is cramped and filled with all Cheng's worldly possessions. The walls are lined with shelving on which rest hundreds of old, threadbare books, moldy leather and vellum and snakeskin volumes, their spines lined with Oriental characters. Alongside the books are various-sized mason jars filled with cloudy liquids and vague vegetablelike forms, things pickled and pruned and toxic-looking.

There are no labels on any of the jars and Hannah wonders if the doctor has ever made a fatal mistake, dispensed a poison instead of a remedy, ended a life rather than saved one. She decides this is probably unlikely. Or at least it's never happened by accident.

Hannah has never deceived herself about Dr. Cheng. This kindly old man serving her tea and inquiring about her friend's health is still one of the deadly crime lords of the city. This humble-looking man has amassed a lifetime fortune off the opium trade, gambling, extortion, prostitution, political fixing, and very likely, murder for hire. She also knows that if their purposes crossed and a mutual resolution looked unlikely, neither one would flinch while going after the other. Cheng could have her neck snapped as easily as he serves her ginseng. And Hannah knows, if her back were against a wall, she could pull her Magnum and whack the old man with little or no hesitation.

And yet, they genuinely like each other. They find one another's company pleasant and informative and beneficial. Hannah thinks that Cheng views this contradiction the same way she does. They're both players in a machine that neither can completely understand. And they know that machine runs on the brutal and rigid laws of both business and nature. If those laws conspire to pit Hannah against Dr. Cheng, they'll act accordingly and not waste time debating the nature of fate and free will. In the meantime, they'll enjoy ginseng tea and quiet, often enlightening conversation.

The building is quiet. Downstairs, in the front of the shop, two of the doctor's muscle-boys are playing a dice game at a small folding table. They nodded to Hannah as she came in the rear entrance and went up the wooden spiral stairwell to Cheng's apartment. Unlike the doctor, the muscle-boys were dressed in double-breasted silk suits. She has a feeling that Cheng might order his staff to dress this way, a pointed contrast to his peasant attire.

Hannah is dressed in pleated black woolen slacks and a black leather blazer over a red silk blouse that she knows the doctor loves. Sometimes, when they're sitting like this, talking quietly, segueing easily from subject to subject, roots and bark and herb medicine giving way to money movement and new players in and out of the Park, Hannah wishes she'd known Cheng fifty years ago, in his prime. Even then he was a committed bachelor, a weird Triad monk, married only to his vision and his plotting. At night, at home in her apartment, Hannah has caught herself once or twice wondering what it might have been like if she and the doctor were contemporaries. Could they have become lovers? Could she have seduced the lord of Little Asia into a very different kind of partnership, something beyond the bonds of importation fees and opium distribution? And if she did, whose world would they have moved into? Could she have made the crossover into full-blown Bangkok residency, no longer just a semi-untouchable envoy, not the one cop with the knowledge and connections that translate into a permanent visitor's visa, but a woman with Park citizenship, an official denizen of Quinsigamond's underbelly?

The fact that she's not sure of her answer is what makes it difficult to broach the subject she came here to discuss—what to do with Fr. Todorov's murderer. Hannah doesn't want to clash with the old man. She knows that for all his pleasantries and hospitality, he's uneasy with her presence here. She doesn't want them to have to walk opposite sides of the street. But she knows Dr. Cheng has ideas about tradition and consistency. And she knows those ideas could conflict with her own plans.

She takes a breath and says quietly, "I owe you for tracking down the benzine, Doc. I hope it didn't cost you too many favors."

Cheng takes a dull silver coin out of the loose sleeve of his gown and begins to roll it around his fingers with the skill of a carnival pro. Hannah knows this is his lucky quarter and that the sight of it usually means a serious and possibly not-pleasant discussion is about to begin.

"I'm long on favors, Hannah. And please remember that identifying the priest's killer was in my best interest. Little Asia functions best outside the glare of the spotlight. The last thing we needed was more ranting and raving from the Brothers Grimm."

Hannah laughs. "The Brothers Grimm" is Dr. Cheng's pet name for Mayor Welby and Chief Bendix.

"It seems to me, though," Cheng continues, "that we both still have a problem. When dealing with insects, identification is never a substitute for extermination."

Hannah's smile fades. She tries to make herself speak slowly and maintain a friendly demeanor.

"Then we *do* have a problem, Doctor. I've got a source that says this guy was a Fed. Now, he was bounced eighteen months ago. But I still can't let you pop a Fed—"

Cheng interrupts with an even, low voice. "You saw the remains of the priest, Hannah—"

Hannah knows where he's heading and cuts him off. "That's exactly right. That's why we need him breathing. We need him squirming on the courthouse steps, sweating for the *Spy* cameras. Everybody needs closure on this. I swear, it's best for business to do this my way."

"This Speer," Cheng says, pursing his lips and hesitating as if the name had caused a sour taste to form on his tongue, "attempted to incriminate my people—"

"Doc, this is the Hyenas we're talking about. *My people?* Back at the cathedral, you were the one who said Uncle Chak was trying to squeeze out from under your thumb. For six months you've been telling me the Cambodians want to splinter."

"Certain traditions are never ignored, Hannah. You know this."

"Doc," Hannah says, trying to cover her exasperation, "you're contradicting yourself here. This bastard was a Federal cop. You whack him Asian style, you'll have the press down here for a decade. This is *exactly* what the Colombians want. Don't give it to them."

"The Colombians are the least of my concerns, my dear."

The words *my dear* have an odd ring, somehow more

threatening than endearing, but still a mix of both. She ignores the tone and presses on.

"I need to make myself clear here. I'm not sure you understand me. I need to speak with the man. I need to sit on him for a while. I need to do things to him in order to know what he knows. I need to know exactly what happened at St. Brendan's. Why this guy popped the priest. And why he did it the way he did it. What's his bitch with the Hyenas? How is he tied into Bangkok? Did he have a connection with Uncle Chak that hasn't come clear yet?"

Cheng opens his thin lips to speak, then appears to change his mind. The coin disappears back into the folds of his gown. He clears his throat and in a brand new tone he says, "Would you care for any more tea, my friend?"

There's no threat now, but also no intimacy. It's suddenly as if she's some tourist who wandered into the wrong noodle shop. The discussion has ended and the patriarch, at least in his own mind, has won out.

Hannah shakes her head slowly for a long moment and then whispers, "No more tea."

They start to rise from their seats. And from downstairs comes the sound of glass shattering. Instinctively, Hannah draws out her gun and turns toward the spiral stairs.

She glances back to see a slightly confused look on Cheng's face.

"It could just be a glass," he says, and she's shocked at his words.

Call them, she mouths.

Cheng composes himself, then cranes his head toward the staircase and yells, "Kuhn, Lui, are you all right?"

They wait for an answer and when none comes Hannah crosses into the kitchen, her Magnum up parallel with her head. She steps slowly onto the ancient tile floor and leans until she can barely get a view out the window in front of the sink.

It's the landscape she had feared and expected: Across the street from the Herbarium, sitting on the roofs and hoods and trunks of their Trans Ams and Shelby Mustangs and customized Firebirds, she counts eighteen Angkor Hyenas. Pulled prominently in front of all of them is a metallic-blue Corvette convertible. Loke leans against the passenger door. In the moonlight, his face seems to glisten a bit, as if he were overheating in the cool of this November night.

Hannah thinks the whole scene resembles some glossy, stagy performance piece, more suited to the Canal than Bangkok, some baby-boomer dream of ethnic, urban thuggery, all ready to be set to music. She turns back to the doctor and says softly, "Looks like Uncle Chak is making his move, Doc. He's got a dozen and a half boy scouts outside."

He nods to her, his face showing nothing.

She wants to say, *I'm sorry,* but settles for, "You've got a piece in here?"

Dr. Cheng can't help but smile. The warmth and feeling flow back into his voice and he says, "Fifty years, Hannah. I never had to carry a gun."

Before she can stop herself she blurts out, "The myth has lost some power, Doc."

With her free hand she reaches down to her belt, grabs her backup piece, and extends it toward him butt-first. Cheng is shocked and wildly amused. He waves the weapon away and says, "Will you never learn a sense of tradition, daughter?"

Hannah's touched by the term, but annoyed by his passivity.

"I'm not going to just hand you over to these dicks. They're errand boys. They're wet punks, for Christ sake. They're not worthy of sweeping your walk."

Cheng is looking at all the books and herbs that line his walls. He says, "Remember, Hannah, in the end, it's always your own that come for you."

She despises his acceptance of the situation.

"These bastards aren't your own, Doc. I knew Chak was scum the first time I saw the little shit. I should've popped him then."

"Go now," Cheng says.

"Like hell."

"They know who you are. They'll let you leave."

"If they know me, they know I'll never let them whack you. They know they'll have to go through me."

Cheng shakes his head. "I tried to tell you not to come. I tried to—"

"I can't believe you don't have some shooters on standby. Just those two downstairs?"

Cheng crosses to her and puts an arm on her shoulder and she realizes the old man has not only been expecting this but maybe even imagining how it would take place, what the schematic of the assault would look like, which direction his enemy would come from, what time of the night they'd choose to visit.

More glass shatters on the floor below. Hannah tucks her .38 in her rear waistband, shakes her head at Cheng, slips out from under his arm, and moves for the stairs. She keeps her back to the curve of the rail going down. Before she reaches the bottom she can see the two meat-boys on the floor, sprawled at awful angles, their heads both wrapped in green trash bags, suffocated just like it spells out in the Tuol Sleng torture manual. The bodies are covered with broken glass. The front display window and the glass pane in the front door have been shattered, broken inward, and in the midst of the splinters and shards covering the shop floor, Hannah sees two silver ball bearings, slightly larger than gum balls. It's a favorite Hyena signature, normally used as a warning flare to shopkeepers slow to pay their protection fees.

Outside, the street is sickeningly quiet and motionless. The Hyenas stand rigid, staring at the storefront as if posing for some painfully slow sculptor, as if caught by some Canal Zone artist's Hasselblad, a full-color frozen epic on the nature of looming threat. Hannah would like to toss off some demeaning comment about how they resemble bony-faced male models, beef for hire recruited for a retro music video, ready to prance and sneer and insinuate ideas of teenage sexuality and ego and half-understood romance. But the fact is that the figures momentarily paralyzed in the artificially deserted street are the real creatures, true gangster meat, more than capable in the ways of murder and vengeance, sadism and power. They're the advance guard, Uncle Chak's psychotic marines, proud and honored to strike the first blow against the old order of Little Asia, replaying in their born-cynical brains every promise Loke has made to them concerning status and money and their place in the future of Bangkok Park.

Hannah holsters her Magnum, steps over the Glad-bagged head of one of Cheng's failed shooters, and moves to the front doorway. She knows Loke can see her and that it's a fairly good sign he's allowing her to advance. She takes a breath, opens the door, and steps out onto the sidewalk. On the far side of the Firebird, she sees three Hyenas, arms braced against the roof of the car holding what look like Vz58 assault rifles. She knows she's already lined up in their sights.

She takes two slow steps to get off the sidewalk and onto the street, keeping her hands and arms raised slightly like a priest at a key moment of consecration. As she moves, she keeps her head faced straight toward Loke, but her eyes do a quick sweep of the whole picture and she sees these bastards are loaded. They came for the old man with their best hardware and it now looks like a detailed illustration of overkill. She spots a set of four Hyenas behind the Trans Am drawing down on her with a string of semiautomatic pistols, probably Tokarevs smuggled from back home.

Four more little shits, a couple who look to be about fifteen years old, are kneeling at the rear of a Mustang, absolutely stiff and sweating over the shafts of their light machine guns, maybe RPDs. Nosed in near the front of the Mustang is a customized El Camino whose bed is filled with five Hyenas carrying various small arms—pistols, rifles, and shotguns.

Stationed in front of this semicircle battalion is Loke's Corvette. Standing uncrouched at the trunk of the car is Loke's lieutenant, a simple .38 Colt Diamondback protruding from his belt line, a lesson in subtlety compared with the rest of this crowd.

And then, on the other side of the car, out front, in line with the shop entrance, no barriers dividing him from Hannah, is Loke. It's his big night, the graduation and diploma he never managed to extract from Yale. He's slightly looser than his charges. He's completely motionless, but his spine is a bit slack and he's got his ass leaning against the car's hood. His arms are folded across his chest and Hannah can't spot any weaponry, but she does notice a new tattoo that she knows he didn't have when she visited the arcade. Though it's November, Loke is dressed in a stretch white tank top and on his pumped left arm, in black ink, is an intricate picture. From this distance, about seven feet, Hannah sees what looks like a big black patch, like a latent birthmark that's suddenly come to the epidermal surface with a fury. But if she were closer, if she could hold and examine the arm the way a lover or a doctor might, she'd see an exquisitely detailed depiction of some obscure, primal architecture—a re-creation of a wonder from Loke's homeland, a carving of a grinning Bodhisattva. A god's face as it looks upon violent death and random destruction. A face that can only grin at some ongoing spectacle of human suffering.

As Hannah studies Loke, she comes to see him as a changed man. It's clear he genuinely believes that tonight is the beginning of a position, a career, a life he's been dreaming of and waiting for. His posture alone reveals a message. She thinks he looks like a cross between an Oriental cowboy and a method actor with maybe a little post–James Dean rockabilly hood thrown in. He's actually greased his hair back like an early-Elvis Brylcreem model. Hannah thinks he should have dangled a hand-rolled cigarette from his lips and parked a backup behind his right ear. She can see Loke understands that image is half the battle. That he knows power and position and sex and a hundred lesser commodities are first and foremost a condition in the brain, an ability to create an agreed-upon atmosphere. What she wishes this kid could see is that Dr. Cheng understood the same thing fifty years ago. And the fact that this understanding can't alter your demise when the fated time arrives.

Hannah takes a few steps until she and Loke are about a yard apart and he barks, "Enough."

She stops moving and says, "I'm impressed you managed to clear the street. These buildings are filled with his people."

Loke can't help a small smile as he says, "They used to be his people."

She stares into his face. "You really think Chak can pull this off?"

"It's a foregone conclusion, Hannah."

It's clear he enjoys using her first name and she smiles to acknowledge his pettiness.

"I know your car is parked in the alley," he continues. "You can walk to it unmolested. Some of my uncle's people will be contacting you in a few days."

"I've got a better idea," Hannah begins, but Loke cuts her off with an even voice and says, "Just shut up and leave now. You look back here and one of my people will cut you in half."

Hannah keeps herself from spitting out some smart-ass insult. Instead she matches his control and says, "How would Uncle Chak feel about that? First days of any administration are tough at best. You and your uncle both know I'm connected with most of the other neighborhood mayors. You whack me in tandem with the old man and they're all going to wonder what kind of family has taken over Little Asia. They might even sit down and discuss Chak's résumé—"

"You've got an inflated sense of self-worth," Loke says, but Hannah knows what she's said is more truth than bluff and Loke can't risk making a stupid move tonight.

They look at each other for a few seconds and Loke says, "Go bring out the old man. We'll make it painless."

Hannah lets a laughing breath out her nose and says, "No, you won't. You'll take his head off his neck while he's still alive and you'll put it on a spike for everyone to see. You can't pass up a signal like that. It solidifies the grab in everyone's mind. It's the first and best sign of the new order."

Loke rises up off the car and says quietly, "Give me your gun, Hannah."

She holds an unblinking stare as she pulls free the Magnum and surrenders it.

Loke accepts the weapon, then in the same low voice says, "Go get the old fucker, Hannah."

She shakes her head slightly and says, "I can't do that."

But now Loke is looking past her, smiling again, and he mumbles, "It seems you don't have to."

Hannah turns her head to see Dr. Cheng standing in the doorway of the Herbarium, looking out on the street with a gray, now-ancient face, looking, more than anything else, small and stooped.

"Oh, Doc," Hannah says to no one, and her voice surprises her by coming out as something of a whine.

Loke yells across the distance to the doctor, "I'm glad you've decided to join us. I promise no one will harm you."

Hannah considers a grab for the Magnum. It's possible she could drop the lieutenant at the rear of the Corvette, maybe even get Loke in front of her as a shield. But she knows these kids are so pumped and tense they'd probably squeeze off a barrage before their leader could call them off and she and Loke and the doctor would all be an indiscriminate pile of shredded flesh and lead-shattered bone in seconds.

Cheng starts to move off the sidewalk in this awful shuffle step, looking down at his slippered feet and saying, "You go now, daughter," in a loud rasp that sounds nothing like his voice.

Hannah turns slowly, making sure she doesn't move her arms from their raised position. She bites off the words that come from her mouth: "Get back inside, you stupid bastard," but he keeps coming toward his death as if he hasn't heard her, as if her body didn't exist here in the street, the only force between himself and the certainty of a bloody and somehow embarrassing death.

The old doctor comes up next to her and stops moving, looks Loke over from boots to skull, then looks past him to this teen death squad overloaded with imported weapons, a few probably juiced on a quick premassacre crack-smoke, some seeing the legendary Dr. Cheng for the first time.

They look back on him with neither reverence nor contempt, but something like bewilderment. *This* is the man their uncles and grandfathers spoke of? This little toad is the man they spoke of, in whispers, at the markets and during the domino games? *This* man, in the ridiculous old robe, the hands and face so lined and wrinkled, the feet in slippers, for Christ's sake?

And for the first time, Hannah can't believe it either. And in that instant it becomes clear to her—the absence of any defense, the absence of that small army of loyal shooters ready to sacrifice their own lives and rip up the entire Park before letting any harm come to the doctor, the absence of a presumptive hit on Chak when he missed the monthly summit. At some point, she knows now, the doctor looked in a mirror and saw what the Hyenas are seeing now—a small, very old, very tired man who's been condemned to a rare and awful fate: Dr. Cheng has outlasted his era.

And Hannah is suddenly overwhelmed with the weight of the old man's self-knowledge. It's a heinous destiny—to outlive your relevance to the environment, to overstay your welcome in the life of your street.

It's as if a raging flu virus has infiltrated her body in a passing second. Her stomach goes and her joints seem to swell and her knees and neck weaken and she's engulfed with a spasm of nausea and dizziness, as if she only now understood that this *scene*, this *event*, was happening around her. A moment ago it was a movie or a math problem, all instant calculation and clockwork deduction, the summing-up of distances and the assessment of firepower and the varying rates of probable speed. Now she understands why Cheng is walking into the mouth of the dragon. Now she remembers that she has never been a citizen of either the Park or the city proper, but a woman always in orbit, an eternal exile chronically passing through.

A run of bile starts to rise up in her throat and she gulps air and forces it back down. She stares at Loke and feels Cheng's hand on her arm, actually pushing her away, trying to shove her off the site.

A horrible smile spreads on Loke's face and then there's Cheng's voice near her ear, repeating in a softer croak, "Go now, daughter."

And she decides to pull the .38. To blow that miserable fucking smile off Loke's face. In that instant, it's worth her life to plant a bullet in the center of his mouth, to explode the lips into minute scraps of pulp, to shatter the teeth into calcium dust, tear the pathetic tongue free, sever tonsils, rupture infinite capillaries, dynamite an exit crater through the rear of the skull that will obliterate forever that smug, ego-soaked, self-satisfied grin.

But as her arm begins to move, the street erupts with the sounds of shrieking tires and crack-stoked war cries and the pop and bang of an incoming blitz, a ground-level strafing, cruising in from the south. And suddenly the Hyenas are bailing off their cars, leaping to the ground, scrambling for new positions, screaming the whole time in Khmer and releasing their own barrage of gunfire.

Hannah butts Dr. Cheng to the ground, rolls and draws the backup gun, and faces the oncoming assault. It's a platoon of Granada Street Popes barreling down Verlin Ave in candy-apple red Jeeps and wide-body fat-wheel pickups and a single beat and blown-out low-rider Chevy, all of them loaded with every gaudy option they can steal. And the Popes are pumped for blood and mayhem. This isn't a hit-and-run drive-by. There are too many of them. Hannah spots six vehicles, each with a driver and three shooters in the bed. They're here for elimination. They're here for a last gamble on exterminating the Hyenas.

It's a genocide carnival. The Popes sling their vehicles into a V-shaped wedge, then roll out to the ground on the far side, a flashy bunker to shoot from. It's clear this isn't a spur-of-the-moment offensive. Their moves seem integrated. There's no suicide charge and no friendly fire. They've been trained and outfitted by the new mayor of the Latinos. Iguaran.

The Hyenas were ready to waste a ninety-year-old herbalist, not fight a do-or-die campaign. All they've got now is adrenaline jolt and the fact that Little Asia is home field. It's not enough. The Popes begin lobbing smoke grenades and one lands in the Corvette and as a gray fog gets into the air, a long run of syncopated assault fire tears across the Hyenas' front.

Hannah rolls back on her stomach, does an awkward lifeguard's grab around Cheng's chest, and drags him inside the doorway of the Herbarium. The old man is choking on smoke, but he seems unharmed. Hannah comes up into a sitting position and looks out the shattered storefront window. Through the smoke she can see that the three kids in the Firebird have bought it—their bodies pushed onto their backs by the barrage, their weapons useless on top of them. One kid's hand is blown off.

The rest of Loke's soldiers are trying to hold the line, returning blasts that pock the sides of the Jeep wall, but do nothing to reduce or even contain the enemy fire. They jump up from behind their cars in random spurts like pinballs popped from an electrified cup. They're screaming the whole time, seemingly at some unseen force above them in the air. Their heads do a stutter-shake as they scream and fire. Their unified howl is both furious and horrified. More than anything else, they seem to be yelling for help or instruction, their heads whiplashing toward Loke and back to the fire line, as if their high-pitched, terror-clogged yelps in Khmer translated to *do something, save me*.

Hannah grabs the front of Cheng's gown and pulls him close to her face.

"My car's around the corner. At the head of the alley. We can make it out."

She knows she'll need the doctor's cooperation. They won't get two feet out the door if he balks or squirms in any way. But the old man seems beyond assent or objection. Hannah's not even sure he's following her words. He seems to be looking past her, out at the smoky fireworks in the street, like he was trying to memorize, permanently implant, the shrieks and roars of agony and panic and disbelief that make it around the muzzle blast and now, suddenly, the blast of music from what must be the Popes' car stereos. They've got their stereos synchronized to a single station or tape. And Hannah understands at once that they're mind-fucking the Hyenas, showing their Cambodian victims that this is more a party than a war, a bad-ass blood dance to savor and celebrate.

The music is some kind of south-of-the-border post-salsa tune, all spliced up with machine-gun percussion machines and weird jungle-bird sounds that mutate into screeching, Gillespie-ish, bebop horns. Almost Tito Puente, but crossed by John Cage. It's like a new-world, multiethnic cacophony. Tribal, but juiced with electricity. And it's absolutely appropriate as the sound track to this bloodbath. The Popes are tearing into the Trans Am brigade, almost as if they don't want to kill the poor bastards just yet but make them linger on the border of death, anticipating each bullet that infiltrates the hull of the car and the asphalt around their feet.

Hannah reaches down and takes Cheng's hand, brings it straight to her mouth, and bites into his flesh. The doctor screams with as much surprise as pain, jerks the hand away, and Hannah sees the trickle of blood rising up to the surface. Before the old man can recover his thoughts, she grabs him by the gown, locks his arm inside her own, pulls out her gun, and lunges out the doorway in a crouched run.

It's only about five steps around the corner to the alley and her momentum brings Cheng along without any hindrance. But as they turn into the alley, there's Loke seated on the hood of her Mustang with Hannah's Magnum in his hands, arms extended out from the line of his body, drawing down on them. Loke has taken at least one hit in his left thigh and his pants leg is saturated. The kid's eyes look glassy and after a second his arms start to waver a bit. Hannah takes sight on him, center chest, but as she squeezes the trigger, Cheng bucks suddenly and brings his shoulder up into her shooting arm. Her bullet sails high and impacts off brick. She loses her balance, goes down on a knee. It happens in an instant: she tries to step around Cheng and resight the gun, but Loke opens his mouth, lets out a yell, and squeezes off rounds, a run of discharge, four shots. Four bullets from Hannah's own Magnum. And she watches the old man knocked onto his back by the blast, his black gown spurting red, a hole exploding in his neck.

She jerks her head back toward Loke, swings her gun up as two more shots sound, but this time from behind her. The upper half of Loke's head explodes, the body lifts and flies backward onto the car, then slides off the hood and crumbles downward.

Hannah turns to see Nabo, Iguaran's son, still posed in a weird, profile shooter's stance with his right arm fully extended and his hand gripping a customized sawed-off.

Behind him, where the alley empties back to the street, a half dozen pools of fire have erupted and the combined glow backlights the shooter. It takes a second for Hannah's eyes to adjust and by the time she can get a bead on him, she knows there's no need to. If he wanted to kill her she'd be dead already.

She watches him slowly lower the stub of a shotgun until it rests against his leg. He's wearing a dark oilcloth raincoat and it gives him the look of some silent and foreign cowboy sucked out of his time frame, transported from the pampas to Bangkok Park for the sole purpose of a mass bloodletting.

Hannah tenses as Nabo reaches to his belt and pulls out a fat buck knife. He brings the knife to his mouth and opens out the blade with his teeth. Then he begins to walk down the alley, sawed-off still next to his leg. Hannah keeps her weapon up, ready to fire. But he moves past her and kneels down next to the half-headless body of Loke. He lifts the slack right arm by the wrist and for an instant Hannah thinks he's actually feeling for a pulse. Then his intentions are vividly clear: he takes a grip on Loke's dead hand, brings down the buck knife, and cleaves away the thumb. He puts the thumb in a pocket of his raincoat. The proof and the reward. The Park equivalent of the scalp. The ear of the bull.

As he wipes his blade on Loke's pants, he stares at Hannah and from this new angle she can make out his features. He's even younger than she'd thought and there's almost a softness around his eyes.

"The Hyenas," she says, and flinches at her own voice. "Are they all dead?"

He pauses for a second, and she thinks he's unsure of whether or not he should speak with her. Then he gives a single nod and says, "Just about."

She looks away from him, down to Cheng. She reaches out and pulls his head into her lap, can't think of what more to do, and so simply covers the blackening hole in his neck with her hand.

Nabo stands up and angles himself away from Loke's body. He says, "You're free to go."

Hannah sits still for a minute, continues to stare down at Cheng's head, uses her free hand to fully close his eyes. Without looking up, she says, "The old man knew it was coming. He saw everything about to give way. A lifetime of work."

Nabo walks to her and extends a hand to help her up. She ignores it.

She says, "Save your strength, boy. All fucking hell is about to break loose. Everybody splinters now. Everyone's on their own. Every shithead with a gun or a bomb makes his move now—"

Nabo clears his throat, spits on the ground, and says, "Once Cortez left, war was inevitable—"

And Hannah cuts him off without raising her voice. "This isn't war, dickhead. This is chaos. This is regression."

Nabo reaches down, grabs her arm roughly, and pulls her to her feet. Cheng's body rolls to the ground, lands facedown, displaying the gaps of his exit wounds. Hannah breaks the grip and gives Nabo a hard shove. He bounces back a step, lifts both his hands to shoulder height, lets a smile come over his face. In a low voice he says, "Easy, *chica*. I know who you are. Everything's all right here."

Hannah spits in his face, but he continues to smile. He brings a sleeve of his coat across his cheek and says, "You come down to the abattoir in a month. The Park will be back in order. Iguaran will put things right."

Hannah shrugs out of her jacket and places it over Cheng's head and back, covering up the wounds. She comes upright and says, "His people will want the body. You make sure it's here for them."

His smile fades and he swings his sawed-off up onto a shoulder. Hannah thinks he looks like some old cigarette advertisement, an image from a fading billboard. A static picture from some forgotten fable of the West.

She turns away from him and starts walking out of the alley, toward the smoky gleam of the street fires and the stench of gasoline and freshly slaughtered Hyenas.

42.

Gabe takes Flynn's keys and locks up the Anarchy Museum, then leads the way downstairs to Wireless. The place is in darkness. Ferrie and Most have gone home for the night. Gabe steers Flynn into a side booth, turns on a single blue-tinged light, grabs a bottle of Jack Daniel's and two water glasses from the bar, plants a twenty in the register keys, and moves back to his friend.

The booth is a big wooden monster with a black, worn-down gloss and what looks like fifty years' worth of names and numbers carved into the table. Gabe pours some bourbon and watches Flynn work a small maroon penknife. Flynn goes about inscribing with the care of a diamond splitter. He's hunched over the table, his face close, down near the wood, his free hand pressed flat for balance and his writing hand moving deliberately with steady pressure, the blade cutting in deeper than the average carving. The problem is, he's too drunk for the task. The knife keeps slipping out of the working ridge. Gabe sees this as a little dangerous, but he knows that suggesting Flynn stop would only prod him to bear down more.

Gabe doesn't know what Flynn is writing. He doesn't want to ask. If Flynn wants to reveal the inscription on his own, then fine. Otherwise, Gabe will stay in the dark. He's never seen Flynn drunk before and it disturbs him more than he would have expected. He's seen him a little relaxed, a little loose, making his way through a weekend Wireless crowd, buying rounds and tossing back a few himself. But in those instances there was always a feeling that Flynn was holding more control than he let on, that his conviviality was planned, something close to a method, a practiced technique for putting others at ease, for creating a clannish, bonded atmosphere.

Flynn lets the penknife fall from his hand as if he's instantly grown bored. He sits back in the booth with a little too much force and his head bangs against wood. He doesn't seem to notice. His eyes are fixed upward staring at the old tin ceiling. He goes a long time without blinking, then, when the eyes finally do close, they stay that way and he begins to talk.

"When I was in the Galilee Home. When I was a kid. Long goddamn time back, like, twenty-five years now, okay? Twenty-five years. Quarter century, right?"

"Long ta-ta-time," Gabe says.

"Goddamn right. Long time. I had the nuns. They ran the home, you know. Old nuns. You couldn't guess how old. I'd try to guess. No way. You'd just go blank. You'd just sit there. Every number you'd think of, you'd go—unh-uh, older than that."

He goes quiet for a second. The eyes open but stay fixed on the ceiling. He licks around his lips.

"They had this old, this ancient projector. Movie projector. Big gray monster. Bell and Howell. Weighed a ton. I used to carry it. Well, I tried to lift it once. Must have been, you know, I think now, must have been an old eight-millimeter. The big sprocket holes on the side. Every year at Christmastime, they'd haul out the projector. Put it down on its old rubber stub legs there, you know. This is after dinner maybe, still at the tables in the dining room. Always dark in the dining room. Guess they thought it was good for movies. So they'd put a big screen up in front of the room and they'd run this movie. Same freaking movie every year I was there. This cheap *Life of Jesus* movie. Practically a filmstrip thing. All narration. People on the screen, these actors, who were these people? These actors dressed up in these kind of robelike clothes, you know, rope belts and all. Sandals. They'd be playing, like, Mary and Joseph and Jesus. Well, Jesus is on the way, right? She's expecting. She's pregnant with God and all. And it's the old story, right? Heading for the census, looking for a hotel, no room at the inn. The whole thing. Some guy with this Boris Karloff voice narrates the whole thing. Standard Christmas pageant thing. Holy family in the manger. I used to watch it. Every year, okay, same time. 'Bout a week before Christmas, bang, the old nuns in black haul out the projector and there's Mary and Joe knocking on doors, no vacancy, the water's about to break, hit the barn, lie down in the straw, the animals all around. I always expected the Karloff voice to do a cow. Give us a big *mooo*, Boris. Never happened.''

He brings a hand up to his forehead, leaves it there a second, then brings it down over the eyes, nose, mouth. It comes to rest, flat on his chest, like he was ready to say the pledge of allegiance.

"So one year I'm watching the movie. And something hits me. Something different. Little light flashes on in the brain. What do they call it? Kick in the eye, you know? Little epiphany. I'm watching it this one year, just like every other year before and, for some reason, this time something goes snap inside and I realize, for the first time, I realize—I am pissed. I'm angry. I'm furious. This kid being born in the barn, he's got your standard mother and father. He's got your basic family. And I'm in this dark dining room with these half-nuts old women in black who have us on our knees first thing in the freaking freezing morning. And I got no mother. And I got no father. And I reach down on the table and grab hold of my vanilla pudding dessert and I throw the fucking pudding up against the screen. I mean I haul off and pitch the goddamn pudding. I hurl it, okay? I pelt it. Fastball. Freaking bullet. And it splatters all over the movie, all over the wrapping in swaddling clothing and the shepherds all kneeling around on straw and the big freaking light from the star in the corner of the screen. And some of the pudding hangs there on the screen and some of it sort of rolls down in little, rubbery jumps, down the screen and falls to the floor.''

They sit silent until Gabe can bring himself to ask, "Wa-what'd they da-do to you?"

Flynn finally looks down from the ceiling and stares at him like he can't understand the question. Then he says, "What do you think they did? The closest one grabs hold and beats the piss out of me."

There's a few more seconds of silence, then Flynn adds, "Tell you something, though. They never showed that god-damn movie again."

Gabe nods slowly and sips at his bourbon. Flynn turns sideways in the booth, brings his feet up onto the seat, and lets his head loll back into the corner till it looks like he's getting ready to take a nap. He folds his arms across his chest and tucks his hands up under his armpits and says slowly, "You're not a lightweight kid. Bitch never should have said that."

Gabe stares into his glass and just as slowly says, "Pa-please don't ca-ca-call her that."

Flynn shrugs but he can't help but press. "Why'd you stay with me, Gabe? You're out of your mind about her. Why'd you stay with me?"

Gabe meets Flynn's eyes, swallows, and says, "'Ca-cause we bu-bu-both wanted the sa-same tha-tha-thing."

Flynn seems to think about this for a second, then brings his hands up to his face and rubs at his eyes. He talks as he rubs. "I've been thinking lately, okay? About all of us. About every-one at Wireless. All the jammers. I was thinking, it looks to me like we're all missing something, or we're all slightly, you know, off. We're all marked a little."

"Sa-sa-'cept for ya-you."

Gabe doesn't know why he's said this. All he wants is for this awful night to end the only way it can. He wants simply to finish the drink, turn off his brain, and walk away. But some-thing opened his mouth. Something pulled the words out.

"I'm not marked, Gabe?"

Flynn's voice is a little high and rough.

Gabe shakes his head. "Not outside, na-na-no."

"And that's what counts?"

"Makes a big da-difference."

"Maybe not." The voice lower now, even threatening, the preamble of an argumentative drunk rolling toward a sloppy fight.

But Gabe can't stop it. He can't get past the fact that there's something completely wrong with this moment, that the roles are being played totally wrong. That it's Flynn who should be doing some consoling and showing some strength. And he can't help knowing that for all her faults, at least Hazel had strength. Especially at the end. When it counted.

So he says, "Maybe not? How can you la-look at me, ta-ta-tell me it doesn't ma-ma-make a difference? Ja-Ja-Jesus, Flynn. *You are normal*," his own voice raising now and he doesn't care. "La-look at yourself, the way you live and dress and act. The ca-ca-color of your skin, the shape of your bu-bones, the money in your pa-pa-pocket. Wireless. The j-jammers, it's all a fucking ch-choice for you. It's a fucking j-j-joke."

Flynn sits rigid, his lips pulled so tight together they begin to turn a bluish purple shade. And then out of nowhere his hand comes up from his lap, grabs his water glass, tosses his bourbon into Gabe's face, lets the glass fall to the table. He grabs Gabe's T-shirt and yanks the boy into the table's edge. Flynn pulls back a fist, but instead of letting it fly, he hesitates, takes a breath, lets go of Gabe's shirt, and sinks back in the booth.

Gabe sits dripping, still shocked by the speed of both the outburst and its termination. Finally, he takes a paper napkin from the dispenser and begins to dab at his face.

"It wasn't a joke," Flynn says in a shaky voice. "Don't ever say it was a joke."

Gabe shrugs, shaken, maybe even ready to cry. He refuses to make eye contact. He looks at the wall clock and says, "Ma-maybe we should sa-say ga-good night."

"We're saying more than good night."

Gabe shrugs again, but makes no effort to respond.

"Don't try to tell me how I feel, Gabe." The voice is low

and taut as if the sudden burst of anger has killed off some of the booze.

Gabe reaches for another napkin and says, "I think ma-maybe you d–d–didn't understand—"

"Shut up. Right now. Just shut the hell up. Don't you dare presume to tell me how I feel. I didn't misunderstand a thing. You don't know me, Gabe. You don't know how I feel or why I do what I do. And I never knew that until just now. And it's a shitty thing to learn. But once it's clear, once you see it—"

Gabe starts to slide out of the booth, but Flynn grabs hold of his arm.

"You're sca–sca–scaring me here."

"Good. Perfect. That's what I want. You stay scared, Gabe. You stay fucking petrified—"

"I gotta ga–ga–go."

"'Cause I made up a picture where none of us were ever scared and that was bullshit. And I made up a picture of Hazel where she was always grateful and always needed me. And I think tonight I've got to clear up all these misconceptions. I want to stop lying to myself, you know, Gabe. I made up this myth. I'm such a mother of a salesman. I sold myself. Like I plunked myself down into my imported leather customer chair and gave myself a Class A spiel. Top-shelf hustle. I should bronze my freaking tongue. And I bought into it. Completely. Whole package. I was signing the check before the last pieces were in place. That's the funniest part, okay, that's the rim shot, right there. I was as good a customer as I was salesman. I climbed into the palm of my own hand."

"Pa–please," Gabe says, straining to get free, but Flynn has both his wrists pinned down on the tabletop.

"I'd made it up. It was a simple goddamn lie. Well, not simple. Complicated. Really intricate. Lots of pieces, all fit together, from a lot of different directions. That's a myth, right? That's what I did. That's what I'm trained to do. What I've practiced at all these years. I sell people the myth of security. Talk to me. Talk with Flynn. Or let Flynn talk to you. You pay me and your world cannot fall apart. It's in the contract. Guaranteed. Like that Cajun chef says, you know. *I guarantee.* See, son, Daddy bought long on the myth of the family. Myth of belonging. Myth of the clan. I took all these random stories and put them together. Like train cars. Linked them up, car after car, one long line, all coupled together."

Gabe suddenly stops struggling. Instead he gives a long, bored sigh and says, "Sta-sta-stories?"

Flynn wobbles a bit in his seat and loosens his grip.

"Yeah. Absolutely. You got your story of Flynn meeting Wallace Browning. Little kid meets this fascinating character. And he's a dwarf, okay, could it get more perfect, straight out of a fable, you know. And the dwarf has got a secret. Enter and sign in, please. And the dwarf will share the secret with the boy. Show him how big it is. A whole world. The jammer's world. And the dwarf teaches the kid, right, you got the apprentice story there. The kid is chosen so the craft gets passed on. Down the line. Like the train cars."

He lets go of Gabe's wrists and sinks back in the booth. They stare at each other. Flynn clears his throat and waits to see if the boy will run. But Gabe just continues to stare at him, so he lowers his voice and continues.

"So, time comes, roles start to change, Flynn has to pick a kid. Continue the line. Keep the story going. And he doesn't have a kid of his own. So, one night he meets Hazel. And bang—the story rolls on."

He lifts up his glass to his mouth, then realizes it's empty and puts it down.

"But here's where the story twists. Where the surprise ending starts to explode. Ready? Flynn has one of those satoris. An epiphany. One of those instant enlightenments. It happens just when all the train cars start to uncouple and the fucking thing is ready to derail."

Gabe stares at him, waiting for the story to finish.

"He figures out, too late, there's the irony, he figures out that the craft never really mattered to him. It was immaterial.

Moot point. The jamming was just a by-product, just this excuse. The politics behind it were meaningless to him. The philosophy behind it. He just loved the connection. The binding. Just wanted the feel."

Gabe slides out of the booth, stands in front of the table rubbing his wrists, and seems to look past Flynn.

"I'm the original idiot, Gabe. Took me over twenty years to figure out something that simple."

In a bored voice, Gabe says, "There are a lot of ways to have a fa-family, Flynn."

Flynn closes his eyes and gives a small laugh. "Jesus, did Hazel train you. Made you into a big free-will man, huh? Will it hurt too much if I tell you Hazel's a deluded little bitch?"

"Fa-fa-fuck you," Gabe says, without much force behind it. "I never should have ca-come here tonight."

He turns and starts for the exit, but Flynn keeps talking after him.

"You fall into things. They take hold of you," he starts to yell after the boy. "Things take hold of you, Gabe. Things come after you."

The last words are a whiny rasp and Flynn brings a hand up to cover his face, then at once he brings his hand down, picks up the bourbon bottle and pulls a long draw from the mouth. He turns his head and looks for a long time at the radio mounted at the end of the table against the brick wall. He stares hard, trying not to blink, as if sooner or later he'll notice something about the machine that he's never seen before.

He puts his hand on top of it, then reaches to the side knob and turns on the power. A dull yellowish glow lights from behind the dials and band selector. It's a soothing light, dim but warm. He keeps the volume low and starts to turn through the AM frequencies until he comes to WQSG.

There's a moment of static, but he's neither disappointed nor worried. He puts his hand back on top of the radio and waits.

Then the static starts to cut in and out, to splice itself with flashes of dead air and then with flashes of high-pitched squeal. And then the brothers start to speak to him:

Showtime, brothers and sisters. And in the beginning was the word. And the word was made into electromagnetic signals that could fly through the air. And the word was brought to live in the box. And the word was interrupted by a message from your sponsor.

We're back for one last curtain call, friends. As you probably know by now, things haven't exactly worked out as we had hoped. Live and learn, right? It just takes some of us quite a while to figure out the simplest lessons. Like old Saint Ti Jean's role model used to say—You can't go home again. I don't know why that is exactly, but it doesn't matter. The point is, don't try to screw with a modern proverb. This is brother John O'Zebedee broadcasting a little mission of mercy. As everyone in earshot knows, a lot of big dominoes fell tonight. The karmic wheel was busy as a Benzedrine beaver, and the O'Z boys aren't real enthused about the slot she came to rest in. But that's the thing about the wheel and where she stops. You can't buy her off with money or good intentions or human sacrifice.

You know, gang, about five years back, Jimbo and I got a little bored one night and took a shot at a radio-play production of *Rebel Without a License*. Neither one of us does a very good Dean, but we did learn a hell of a lot about the medium. The biggest thing we learned was that there was a pretty good-sized group of individuals out there that for one reason or another felt very left out. And they seemed to tune into us by instant instinct. And just that act of listening to us, all at the same time, linked them up a little, made them part of something bigger than themselves. And there's a real charge in that idea, a real flash, a real feeling of union and maybe even transcendence.

But this life doesn't like transcendence a whole goddamn lot. And five fucking years can be a long goddamn time when you're living in a car in the Mexican desert and the nights get colder than a well digger's ass, excuse me, Mr. Waits. From where I sit now, everything that happened five years ago seems like some undertaker's bad dream.

Shit and onions, boys and girls, and about ten tons of it

appears ready to hit the industrial fan tonight. We understand things didn't work out quite as planned for our gal Hazel. And I guess my brother and I have a little disagreement over her plight. See, I say what Ms. H wanted to do was just another round of infantile violence that changes nothing but our capacity for humor. But James says that there's always a little blood shed and bone shred and metal bent during the course of a revolution, that more than one redcoat took a farmer's musket blast so that you and I could live free in the land of the brave.

I don't know who's right tonight, folks. I just know this: the saddest salesman since Willy Loman is watching his myth deconstruct right before his ears.

I don't know what to tell you, G.T. I'm just the voice in the box, the ghost in the machine. I've got no more answers than you do and I'm not even half the salesman. 'Cause I could never believe the way you always could. I still can't force that kind of surety on myself. My brain won't allow it. Maybe it's a genetic problem. Who knows?

All I can do is pass on information. And there's really no gauging what that's worth. You be the judge: the eternal agent of enforced order has finally made his way to our fair city. And he's classic madman material, G.T. Grade A nut case. His name is Speer, he's leaking paranoia juice everywhere he walks, and he's got the rage levels of a career speed-head. Hair-trigger temper. Sadistic imagination that would make Sade envious. But that's not the big news, Mr. F. The latest intelligence is that the psycho is also a fraud. He was retired from the Federales over eighteen months ago. They gave this demon a fifty percent pension and told him to walk. Which is just what you want to do with an agent who's got twenty-five years of shooting bunker and interrogation skills and now faces the gates of hell every morning and prays to Genghis Khan.

I wish I could give you better news, my CFP/CLU hombre. But better warned than happy. No one on-line seems to know where Mr. S is tonight. But he's a pro when it comes to tailing a wanted man. And you fit that description for him. He seems to think you're the end-all and be-all of the jamming movement. The messiah of microphone mischief. The glue that holds the communication anarchists together. We may know better, but sometimes there's no talking with a delusional fascist. All night, I've been chewing on the question of why he didn't come after James and me. And I think I've got a possible answer. We're not of his world. He can't even see us. But you, Mr. F, you dress the part. You walk and talk and function like an integrated citizen, a franchised model of belonging. And I don't think he can live with the fact, the paradox, that you turn your back on the franchise every night and strike pranksterish little blows against the order. The order you seem to embrace by day, the order that seems to be set up to make it easy for someone like you. We're not here to slag you, G.T., but I guess I've got to say, I'm sort of forced here to say, that I see how the agent's mind works. He sees the picture of you, granted it's all external, but it's an external world, G.T. We make judgments and carry out the consequences every freaking day based on nothing more than what our eyes flash on. And that first flash says you're a white, upper-middle-class, attractive, educated, assimilated, nonhandicapped, hail-fellow-well-met. If the system we've been calling Quinsigamond, or hell, even America, is set up for anyone, honey, it's set up for you. What the agent can't see is that, obviously, something inside is different or broken. It has to be. Why else Wireless and the sound-effects clowns? Why else bite the hand that feeds you? So, what's the internal difference, G.T.? If it were just anger, from whatever long-ago reasons of powerlessness, I think you'd have been with Hazel tonight, singing that old Drifters tune. We can't help thinking it's more a need than anything else. A Want with a capital *W*. That inside the Armani suits, you're as hollow as the St. Louis banker in his green face paint.

What are you thinking right now, G.T.? Are you thinking—none of this two-bit pop analysis is helping me any right now? You are correct, G.T. So maybe it's time for us to fade out. You have our last message. This Agent Speer is on his way. Anyone with half a brain would know where you could be found. So, forewarned is forearmed, I guess. And to some extent, the rest of this story is up to you. You're not the only one listening tonight. There might even be a *radio professional* or two tuned in. Maybe a woman of grace and wit and humor and strength. Maybe someone like that could save your yuppie ass. I dunno.

See, the trick is, you've got to place faith in someone like that.

You've got to go outside of yourself. And experience tells all of us that when you do that, nine out of ten times, you get screwed in a way that lingers. But the alternative is absolute self-reliance, and with some apologies to Mr. Emerson, that's a system that, taken to the limit, has its own kind of side effects. You don't have to be a lawyer to know the law of diminishing returns and being completely alone can suck every bit as much as betrayal. I think, anyway.

So, dig in, G.T. You've got some advantages. You know the lay of the land. You're on home court, so to speak. Remember the Jimi Hendrix theorem: *Feedback can be an art, too.* We'd love to stay and see the credits roll, but time is short and windows narrow. If you walk away intact, drop us a line by Tristero. And if you happen to dharma-bum it out onto the road with a lascivious navigator, listen for our signal. Here's a big hint: grab a copy of Ti Jean's *Flashes of Moriarty* and read close when you get near the end—just after where the Saint places a bet on Blue Foam . . . Who knows, G.T., we could meet again. I'm outta here. And brother James wants to say goodbye.

I'll make it short and semisweet. No man's a prophet in his own town. And in Quinsigamond, he's a regular outlaw. I can't blame the men in blue or the station owners. They were just playing their parts. But you guys, the so-called faithful, you let me down. You needed a voiceprint to believe in O'ZBON. And that takes all of the magic out of it. I guess doubt is like a bell: once you've rung it, you can't call back the chime. It runs off, vibrates outward, touches more than it should.

So, now the heat is on. And as soon as I finish changing the plugs and oil, we're gone again. I guess maybe we were more than a little naive to think we could come back to the plains of former glory. It's just a bitch that our last night in the old hometown had to be such a family feud. Personally, I disagree with John-boy. I think Hazel's heart was in the right place, even if her planning was a little shortsighted. If I know anything, Hazel, it's that you've got to sink your pilings deeper into the ground if you want your house to stand for the long haul. But who am I to judge? My brother and I are coasting on discount gas and prayers to Marconi. Like all parties in bohemia, this one was swell while it lasted. Unfortunately, I've got a feeling the big broom is being taken from the utility closet as we speak. And we want to be mobile before the janitor spots our debris.

Remember this, gang. There'll be other parties. The pendulum will swing back one of these days. In the meantime, play the blues and prop each other up. And to you, G.T., I guess you're going to have to go for the balls. Sometimes you're left with no other option. That's the thing about this life. Your options almost always narrow down.

When you're young, there's always someone warning don't burn your bridges. What they fail to tell you is that those bridges are going to catch the spark anyway, spontaneously combust, and the light that inferno throws off will only illuminate your failures and dead dreams. And you go on kidding yourself there'll be other ways back home, other ways to start again. For Christ sake, we live in the land of the remake. Head west. Change your name. Find the frontier and a new life. It's supposed to be a metaphysical Homestead Act. But at some point you come to understand, in one of those blinding flashes of satori, that there just is no way back. That the landscape has changed and warped and eroded so much that not only are there no bridges but there are no goddamn roads, there's not even a way to turn around and have a clear vision, to get a fix on where it was you came from.

I think that when we were bunked down in Baja and Juan got the yearning to head back this way, I think even then I knew better. But you know us local boys, suckers for a good story and a long shot. Fine. Call me a cynic. But what does that make all of you out there who doubted us, called us frauds and weak imitations? Even old Uncle Elmore had to go thumbs down. Well, the truth is, we are the real thing. And I don't give much of a damn tonight who believes what. But, like the original vagabond said, folks, don't think twice, you know. Here's the mike, bro, let's hoover some petrol and see if we can't make the northern border by nightfall.

Well, friends, it's that time. We're wandering bhikkus, once again. Hometown boys make bad. But like I always knew in my soul, what's the sense of being from Quinsigamond if you don't know that sooner or later it's going to break your heart? *Hic Calix.*

43.

The radio falls back to a blast of whiny static for a good ten seconds, then it turns to dead air. Flynn just stares at it, tries to concentrate, as if he can will himself toward sober. Within seconds, he's unclear on a lot of what was said. He knows the O'Zebedee Brothers addressed him directly, but he doesn't find this unusual or alarming. These guys know their audience. They know Wireless and they know all the main players. He's sure they mentioned Hazel. He knows they mentioned the name Speer. And he thinks they may have made reference to Ronnie.

But even this drunk, Flynn isn't enthused about taking life advice from radio ghosts. And besides, whoever the O'Zebedee Brothers are, they're leaving town. One more myth that the city will have to live without. It's possible these boys have the right idea, that now is exactly the correct time to cut losses and run, pull the money out of the bank, gas up the Saab, spend some time in transit. Flynn can suddenly picture it, checking in and out of Ramadas and Holiday Inns, identical franchised rooms, always set off the interstate, their signs visible at night from the shoulder of the highway. He can imagine spending his days in the dim seal of mall cinemas, tiny cement boxes with bad sound and miniature screens, all identical, all showing the same features. Spending his nights back at the hotel lounge, learning to love generic vermouth, teaching his body how to sustain itself on a diet of olives and bar nuts. Experimenting with a new form of small talk, boozy gab time with farm-belt tractor salesmen and local divorcees, corn-fed women with good teeth and a flinty reserve of pride, adamant not to show their disappointment in this life.

But then, interrupting this picture, without warning or reason, comes the image, the real memory, of dancing with Ronnie. He can see that night at the airport, everything set in the smoky-blue beams of the Jeep's headlights, the lights of Quinsigamond down the hill like an endless pattern of connections, the sound of that late-thirties saxophone just on the eve of bebop, still melodic and moody. And the feel of Ronnie's hair against his neck, the feel of her arms weighted on his shoulders, the smell he can't completely define, maybe coconut or vanilla. And the feel of her mouth, the movement, first the softness and then the wetness. And finally, her body pushed into his, so achingly slowly, still aligning its movements with the music from the radio, but just barely, just an imitation of the slow dance now, building into something else, the embrace that involves more than the arms, that draws both their full bodies to each other through their clothes and constructs a rare, flushing heat, a warmth that somehow avoids the idea of temperature, of measurement, and instead becomes a binding force, like magnetism or electricity. And there is an ache to it, but no pain, a deepness that persistently vibrates, that floods into the subconscious in pulses and tells the brain to sublet its functions, to give over to a primal, prerational sensation. The feel of Ronnie, this entire presence, against his body, moving.

Why is that feeling so important?

Because it means something so far beyond the immediate sensation. Because it suggests something that Flynn can only vaguely name, a general, imperfect word like *possibility.*

And what is it that's possible?

First, the desire to be absolute flesh. And then, everything else—*union, communion, community*. The possibility is that words like these can take on meaning in the here and now, can evolve beyond vague and ghostlike icons, beyond the juiceless drone of dry, cold theory. The possibility is that these sounds can become observable action: he and Ronnie, for example, one example, bound into each other and the world.

Flynn's dizzy with the thought. He feels unreal and light-headed, on the threshold of trance or dream or nausea. He looks around at the dull glint of the hundreds of curios and knick-knacks mounted on walls and shelves and bartops, all these jigsaw pieces that make up this bizarre world of Wireless like the topography of a stubbornly elusive dream. And he hears his own voice, his unique noise, out loud, from his own throat, ask, "What the fuck is it I want?"

And from the speaker of the table radio comes the whisper, "You want to avoid me."

And Flynn comes out of the logy dream state and into a wave of terror that breaks on his body in the form of a classic, unstoppable shudder. There's a beat, the vague sound of wind, then the voice goes on. "But that's not going to happen, Mr. Flynn."

He climbs out of the booth and does a stumbling run for the men's room. He pushes open the door, slides onto the tile of the bathroom floor, and catches a look at himself in the mirror. He turns to the row of green metal stalls, sees a pair of loafer-clad feet protruding from the last toilet. He steps forward, his stomach seizing up, his head flushing with a rush of heat.

He looks and sees a stunted body propped against the porcelain bowl. Lifeless, the head unrecognizable, that horrid, everlasting image of burned flesh—all hair gone, the skin seared away in uneven layers, the lower, remaining tissue left a shocking, unforgettable, somehow violent pattern of shadings, mainly deep purples and reds gone the tone of medium-rare steak.

Oddly, the rest of the dwarf's body looks unburned. It's just the head that's been torched.

Flynn stares a woozy second and says, "Wallace."

Then he falls backward, his shoulder slamming against a sink. He rolls on his side as all the Scotch and bourbon in his gut comes jetting upward, and he begins to vomit and heave. When his stomach empties, he pulls himself to his feet and runs from the john back into Wireless.

The radio in his booth has come alive again. But this time, the voice is familiar. Ronnie is yelling, "Flynn, get out."

Then there's a bleat of squealing static, a bite of sound track for a moment of implied violence, and the first voice returns, a bit out of breath, saying, "Yes, Flynn, come out of that dark barroom and get some fresh air. It's a gorgeous night. Wonderful air. You come join us. Up here on the roof."

Flynn does a sprint for the stairway, turns the corner past the entrance to the Anarchy Museum, and bolts up the dark enclosure that leads to the roof of Wireless. He shoulders open the tin door and comes out into the night.

He stands still and looks to the opposite edge of the roof. There's a large, meat-faced man with a slicked, modified crew cut plastered away from his face. The hair is a pepperish color. He's dressed in a zip-up windbreaker with a fleece collar that's turned up around his neck. He's wearing black slacks that end too high on his legs, exposing white tube socks and low-cut discount-looking sneakers. The man is a classic barrel-chested type, like some midwestern football coach who built his body tossing hay bales and swimming in always-freezing creeks.

His left hand is dangling at his side. It grips a large white plastic microphone with an enormous red-foam head, a domed top like a clown's nose. The microphone looks like a child's toy or a forgotten prop from a cheap old movie farce, some slapstick where people are constantly colliding and falling down stairs.

The man's right arm is bent and resting on Ronnie's shoulder. His right hand grips a gun that's pushed against Ronnie's throat. She seems wet, her clothes dripping, saturated, as if she'd been caught far from shelter, in some expansive field, as the sky opened and a torrent of water poured down. But Flynn knows it's not water. From ten, fifteen feet away, he can smell the fumes of gasoline.

Between them, in the center of the roof, there's a full puddle of oily liquid, a miniature shiny lake glinting slightly in the moonlight. Flynn looks up from the puddle to Ronnie, watches as the man chucks Ronnie under the chin with the gun barrel a few times. There's a minute of silence except for the sound of wind cutting across the roof, broken by chimneys and a smokestack.

"You're Speer," Flynn shouts.

Speer gives an exaggerated nod. "Thanks for joining us, Mr. Flynn. We won't be needing this anymore," and he throws the white microphone off the roof.

"So take me," Flynn says. "Let her go."

Speer ignores the suggestion with a mock-amused turn of his head.

"Move out of the doorway," Speer yells, and points with the gun to the edge of the roof.

Flynn keeps his eyes on Ronnie and moves toward the small parapet of brick and capstones.

Speer starts to poke around in his windbreaker pocket with his newly freed hand. Ronnie squirms a bit, gets jabbed in the neck with the gun barrel, and goes quiet again. Speer pivots and pushes Ronnie down to her knees. He's holding her by a clump of her wet hair balled in his fist and he uses his grip to start pushing and prodding her toward the gas puddle. Ronnie starts to scream and Speer releases her hair and shoves her forward into the puddle. He plants a foot on the small of her back, stares across the roof to Flynn and pulls from his pocket a small silver cigarette lighter that he proceeds to hold up, out in the air, away from his body.

"Terrible about the midget. Or, I'm sorry, the dwarf. Browning was a dwarf, right? They're so sensitive about those things. You all are. That semantic shit."

Ronnie stares out at Flynn but doesn't say a word.

"I hope I'll be able to bring the news to the widow," Speer says. "You know, once she's out of that hospital, she'll need some consoling. Don't you think, Mr. Flynn?"

"What do you want me to do?" Flynn asks.

Speer seems to ignore him. He gives a tug on Ronnie's hair

and says, "Going to put an end to all this jamming nonsense today, Mr. Flynn."

Ronnie's head jerks with the movement of Speer's hand. He rolls her skull in a slow circle, manipulating her like a puppet and seemingly enjoying the action to the point where Flynn can see him biting off a huge grin.

"You know how we're going to do that, Mr. Flynn? Same way you kill a snake. You cut off the head. You separate the head from the body, that snake is dead. I know. I've killed a good many snakes, Mr. Flynn. How 'bout you, now? You ever kill a snake, Mr. Flynn?

"You want this to be a one-sided conversation, son? That's not like you, is it? You're known for your way with words, aren't you there, son?"

Speer's voice has taken on this strange southern accent, almost a bad Lyndon Johnson imitation. He goes on without waiting for an answer. "I want to mention again what a beautiful office you got there, Mr. Flynn. I got a look at it the other day when the midget and I got together. Really something. I'd think a man like you, with your beautiful office and your beautiful suits and your beautiful girlfriend, I'd think you'd have enough to keep you busy."

They stare at each other and for a long moment the only sound is the wind cutting across the rooftop.

"But I guess the fact is," says Speer, the voice now void of any play, all edgy and horribly slow, "you're just one more stupid little prick. One more insolent little fucker who thinks he can screw with the natural order of things. What a fucking ego you must have, Flynn. You little anarchist scumbag"—the voice in full yell now—"you filthy little subversive." And now a scream. "You pathetic little son of a bitch, thinking you can fuck around with the law, with the natural order of things," and he throws Ronnie down to the asphalt and plants a foot on her back.

"Ronnie," Flynn yells, absolutely helpless, the back of his

throat burning. "For Christ sake, let her go. She hasn't done anything."

Speer bites in on his bottom lip, snorts air through a clogged nose, brings his voice back down a bit.

"Hasn't done anything? First of all, Mr. Flynn, she's got a filthy goddamned mouth. And second, she's got your stench all over her."

"Ronnie," Flynn says, the word detached from anything but panic.

"You know, Wallace and the others, your friend Hazel there and the rest, when you take a good look, they're really pretty pathetic creatures. Look at those lives. You know what I'm saying. Even Wallace, who tried so damn hard to fit in and get with the program. I mean he couldn't change his stature, could he? In the end he was always going to be this low-to-the-ground dwarf. And the rest of them barely even tried to be normal. They just cashed it in at the start. Lived for this goddamn place. But you, you're not pathetic, Mr. Flynn. You're not pitiable. No, sir. You're despicable. There's a huge difference. The reason you're despicable is that it didn't have to be this way for you. You made it this way. You chose this way. You weren't a dwarf. You weren't some goddamn punk woman. I'll bet your little friend Wallace would have given anything to be like you. But there's no way to ask him now."

He stops for a second to rub a hand over the bristle of his skull. "You're a real piece of work, Flynn. Classic smart-ass troublemaker. Guys like you"—there's movement, some pressure is applied to Ronnie's back and she yelps and squirms—"you're not stupid. That's never the trouble with assholes like you. You're just deviant. You use your goddamn, God-given intelligence for aberrant behavior. And you always rope other people in."

Speer flips the hinged cover of the lighter open with a toss and uses his thumb to strike up a flame. Flynn flinches badly and his heart punches inside his chest.

"And now it's time to put things right. First you're going to watch this filthy bitch burn, Flynn. And then I'm going to tear you in half."

Then there's gunfire. Two shots. One knocks Speer backward and Ronnie, screaming, starts to crawl, kicking out legs, pulling with her arms, hysterical noises barking from her throat. Flynn runs to her, goes to the ground, pulls her into him, touching her back and head, unsure if she's hit.

Speer rolls on one side and fires toward the doorway. Flynn looks to see Hannah Shaw squatting down, her arms extended in a shooter's stance, returning fire. Speer takes a hit in the chest, another in the neck. He heaves and rolls on his back and his arm jerks upward but falls back on top of himself. Blood starts to erupt from the neck wound. Flynn watches his mouth go into spasm, jerking open and closed but emitting no sound.

He turns to see Hannah running toward him, her gun still trained on Speer. She looks odd, like some younger version of a face Flynn used to know. She gives a quick look at him, turns her attention back to Speer, and brings the gun down again, sighting in on the head. Speer is making horrible gurgling sounds now, dying too slowly. Hannah walks forward, a slow arcing line, side steps. She goes in slowly, brings a knee down on Speer's darkening chest, releases one hand from the gun grip, still pointing the gun to the forehead. She reaches in delicately to the throat, extends fingers looking for a sign of pulse, waits several beats, then rises up off the chest and pulls the gun from the dying hands.

Ronnie has stopped screaming but she's quaking in Flynn's arms.

Hannah looks at the two of them, compressed into a vibrating pile. She swallows and says, "You take her down to your car and you drive out of here."

Flynn doesn't move or speak, just stares at her and shakes his head, first *yes* then *no*.

In the same even, horribly restrained tone, Hannah says, "Just get out. We have a mutual friend who would want it this way."

She watches as her words sink in. Then Flynn is pulling up to his feet, hauling Ronnie with him, steering to the doorway.

Hannah waits until they're out of sight.

Then she begins to do everything wrong. She wants to believe she's acting on instinct, but what's compelling her is a force with an unknown name, a motivation so new or so buried that it has no common label, no definition in the average heart.

She holsters her gun, then takes Speer by his long arms and drags him into the center of the gasoline puddle. She deposits him there, his belly wading in an inch of liquid, then she manipulates his wrists and awkwardly rolls him from stomach to back to stomach. She lets the arms drop to the ground, takes a breath, and looks out over the city, a hilly skyline of highway, a few modest high-rises, and dozens of pockets of man-made light.

Then she squats back down, reaches into Speer's back pants pocket, and extracts a starched white handkerchief, perfectly folded and creased. She shakes it loose, soaks it in gasoline, brings it up to the head, and wipes furiously, a new mother dedicated to cleansing every inch of soiled skin on her over-grown, mutant child.

She wishes the gurgling noise would stop or the eyes would close. She turns the head to the side slightly, opens the mouth with her fingers, and jams the sopping rag inside until only a few stray corners protrude, little flags of futile surrender.

Hannah stands up and walks a circle around Speer. His eyes look up at her, blink once. She feels dizzy with the smell of the gasoline. She reaches into her jacket and pulls out a book of matches. She looks at them for a second, a cheap green-covered pack with a line drawing of a lunch car on the front flap and the words *Uncle Elmore's Rib Room* beneath it.

She pulls free a stubby match with a small, crusty white head. She closes the book, tucks the front flap, turns the book over. She strikes the match and nothing happens. She strikes again. A small flame lights and grows and flickers. She cups it from the wind, squats again, drops it on the head, and steps back.

There's an elongated second of pure waiting. Then the catching, the spurt of flame, the furious run of heat and light.

She stands and stares as the fire continues to grow and feed on the chemical-soaked bundle. It's a funeral pyre. Like something out of history. Like something imported from an ancient, foreign culture. From a community with a love of cleansing and ritual and finality. From a clan with no confusion or doubt in the persistence of mortality and decay.

From some distant people who always know when the end has arrived.

44.

Hazel sits in the very last seat of the bus, her army duffel bag filled to bursting with every secondhand possession she's ever owned. She's got the bag propped up against the window and is using it as both a pillow and insulation from the wind that's blowing through a crack in the pane. She's trying too hard to sleep and not succeeding. She's trying not to think about the slight motion sickness that keeps loitering around the edges of her stomach.

She's an hour outside of Quinsigamond and headed west, she thinks, in the general direction of Chicago. Three hours ago, she was sitting in her usual booth in the Rib Room, drinking the last coffee she'll ever share with Elmore Orsi. Neither one of them spoke, but when Hazel drained her mug, Elmore handed her a white envelope that contained three thousand dollars and an all-route, coast-to-coast bus pass that doesn't expire for a year.

She tried to push it back at him, but Elmore shook his head and gave a smile and said simply, "It's not from me. I found it in one of the back booths after I locked up."

There was no postmark on the envelope, just Hazel's name typed in capital letters. She's surprised how little she cares about knowing who sent the money and the pass. She could name some likely candidates, but she chooses not to. She had planned on leaving at dawn anyway and the envelope simply steered her toward the Greyhound station.

She pulls her feet up onto her seat, pulls her knees up into her chest, and wraps her arms around herself. With one hand, she reaches up to her ear and secures the small pink earphone that's plugged into the old transistor radio in her jacket pocket. Of course it's tuned to WQSG. But it's only a matter of time and distance until she loses the signal and has to pull in something new.

From the sound of things, the Rib Room is buzzing, filled with people and noise and equipment. Ray Todd is broadcasting a special edition of *City Soapbox* on location from the diner. "Behind the lines, in the heart of enemy territory," as he calls it. Ray is in rare form, as if the tension of being surrounded by all this mutual hatred and suspicion has elevated his talents to new heights, given him abilities he'd never known before. Even his voice has mutated a bit, taken on this Cronkite-style low rumble which infuses his subject matter with more importance than it deserves. *After all,* Hazel thinks, *this wasn't a moon walk or a presidential assassination. It was simply a lesson in stupidity and vanity. In the cost of having a family.*

She closes her eyes, lets her body rock with the motion of the bus, and, in spite of herself, begins to listen and picture the scene.

If you've just joined us, we're broadcasting live from the Canal Zone in a special report concerning the events of the last twenty-four hours. As most of you know, an anonymous telephone call early yesterday morning led a team of explosives specialists to the WQSG transmitting antenna and support tower. The tower, located on Devlin Hill at the northern border of the city, was apparently wired with what at first appeared to be plastique explosive. An unnamed officer on the scene later acknowledged, however, that the substance and device found on the radio tower "couldn't have blown a gym locker. Either," he said, "it was a bad prank or these people are genuine idiots." Sources within the police department confirmed an anonymous telephone call from an individual who said that "a blow is about to be struck by the forces of anarchy. We're through joking." Police refused to disclose whether the caller was male or female...

Hazel can picture Ray, his studio set up in the extra-large "family" booth at the front of the lunch car and a host of slightly confused but intrigued Zone regulars crowding around the table, jockeying for position with Ray's fans and assorted QSG staff. In the middle of it all, Elmore Orsi is bringing mugs of coffee and platters of Danish, whistling and bantering as he runs a gauntlet of bodies and power cables.

Apparently, Ray has a three-way phone hookup going. He's interviewing both Chief Bendix and City Manager Kenner, prodding them both, trying to invoke a little name-calling and character-bashing.

CHIEF BENDIX: I want to be clear that we're treating this as a genuine bombing attempt, an act of wanton terrorism, if you will. Due to the grace of God and the talent of our Commonwealth's elite bomb squad, we were able to avert hundreds of thousands of dollars' worth of destruction. It wouldn't be prudent to disclose anything more at this point, until we've had a chance to assimilate all the information ourselves—

MANAGER KENNER [interrupting]: For God's sake, Chief, people within your own department say the tower was never in any danger. One of my sources called the incident "Mickey Mouse shenanigans"—

RAY [interrupting]: Chief, isn't it true the attempted bombing is rumored to be the work of a splinter group recently separated from local "jammers" who congregate right here, in this bohemian collective they call the Canal Zone?

[A chorus of boos and hisses from the crowd]

CHIEF BENDIX: Let me say that we already have people in this general neighborhood, yes. At this stage they're just asking questions, talking to the locals. This should not be construed as any centralized harassment. We're operating on information that's been supplied to us by reliable sources—

["Nazi scum," someone in the crowd yells, and is drowned out by cheers]

RAY: Oh, the artistes are restless today. Nothing like a little criminal anarchy to get their thirst for chaos up. Get your hand off that cable, lady jane. Go ahead and scream, you spoiled little heathens. I want this once-great city to know the sound of its coming demise. I want the people to hear what the harvest of their complacency and apathy sounds like. I want them to hear the spawns of their own weak loins.

["Up yours, Raymie," another voice yells, followed by an explosion of laughter and whistles]

RAY: I'm surprised you're all so jovial in light of the fact that your craven leaders have turned tail and run off. I should mention, again for our uninformed listeners, sometime after that anonymous phone call to the police, a "jamming" broadcast was picked up in the frequency range normally used by WQSG. Again, the jammers claimed to be the now legendary O'ZBON, or O'Zebedee Brothers Outlaw Network. In an odd and somewhat disjointed broadcast, the jammers lashed out at their once-loyal supporters, claiming their authenticity had been questioned since their return to Quinsigamond and stating that an abundance of inner squabbling had grown within the jamming community. After expressing their disappointment, the alleged brothers, who refer to themselves as James and John, stated their intention to leave the city once again. Let me ask you, Chief Bendix, do you believe these O'ZBON people are responsible for the attempted destruction of the WQSG tower?

CHIEF BENDIX: I think it's just too early to tell. Remember, we've been after these O'ZBON characters for a while now on the broadcast disruption charges. It's possible we're entering a whole new ball game now. This may signal a whole new level of crime. We've all crossed into new territory...

Isn't that the goddamned truth, Chief. Hazel opens her eyes and stares out the window at the blast-cut granite mounds that line the sides of the interstate. As she shifts in her seat, Gabe, sleeping like a puppy, falls sideways until his head is nuzzled on her chest. Hazel lifts her hand to push him off, then hesitates, instead softly runs her fingers through the hair on the crown of his head. *What the hell,* she thinks, leans forward, and kisses the boy without waking him.

New goddamn territory. Real frontier. I should've headed south. Someplace warm. Like the desert. No people. Just the sun and all those hard-ass reptiles. Snakes and lizards...

Goddamn you, Flynn. I didn't want to be your daughter. You incestuous bastard. You ignorant fuck. I wanted you in ways you never considered.

And goddamn you, Gabe. I didn't want to be your mother.

And now I just want to be alone for a long time. I just want to stay dry and quiet. Sink into the sand somewhere and let the sun bake me. No people. No bodies. Just the sound of the dry wind at night. No voices.

The QSG transmission starts to break up a little, the first cracks of static start to erupt in her ear. But she leaves the earpiece plugged in, and in the intermittent clarity she can make out some commotion back at the Rib Room. There's a disruption, a lot of background voices yelling until one makes its way to the microphone and becomes distinct.

...I'm sorry, I can't keep quiet any longer. Don't give me that look, you buffone. I haven't even charged you for the coffee. Now, let's be sane about this, people, huh, okay? James and John would not pull this kind of stunt. It's not their style. I know the brothers, okay, all right? I know what I'm talking about here. They're broadcasters, not dynamiters. They want the noise of words, not bombs. This isn't their signature. It's not the way they do business.

Excuse me, ladies and gentlemen, the voice you're hearing belongs to the proprietor of the Rib Room, Mr. Elmore Orsi. And just what is it you want to tell us, Mr. Orsi? That the attempted sabotaging of some very expensive property owned by my station was a joke? Little prank, perhaps? Is that it?

Well, yeah, maybe it was all a joke and maybe not. I just think the whole jamming gig is over. And it's all a godawful shame, really.

[*in a mocking tone*] A shame, is it?

Things were exciting there, for a time. A real festive feel for a while there. Seemed like new things were happening. But you can't change human nature. Everyone's bound to take things one step over their particular line. And then the whole party's over before you even know you're wet. What the hell. Now even the brothers, or whoever they were, now they're gone too. Everyone moves on sooner or later. But it was juice for a while there. A little secret family moving in the shadows, pulling their little pranks. The shame is, I think it was all just a swing against boredom more than anything else. But hell, like they say, it's time to call it a day. Change is a staple no matter what circle you run in. I've seen a lot happen, okay, I've seen quite a few come and go. The O'ZBON boys were special. It's just something you feel. It's too bad the comeback didn't work out. But something's either meant to be or it isn't, you know? And in the end, you just move on. It's like that singer said—that English kid with the glasses—he said, *radio is a sad salvation.*

45.

Hannah sits in the rear of Propa Gramma and runs her fingers lightly along her temples. The club is dark and crowded. The walls look as if they're hung with tar paper. The ceiling feels too low and Hannah doubts there's an adequate fire exit.

Up on a miniature stage, a trio of women, two black and one Latin-looking, all just slightly younger than Hannah, are performing. They call their group Simone's Demōns and they all wear these black-on-black wigs that are swirled and pinned down in a modified mini-bun near the back of their skulls. They dress in black wool turtleneck sweaters, matching black pleated skirts that hang below their knees, and white felt berets with tiny wicklike stems jutting out on the top.

They aren't playing any instruments. There appears to be a prerecorded sound track and one of the women stands behind a mixing board and alters the music, slows it down, speeds it up, makes it jump and skip and fluctuate in volume.

The other two women are the singers, but to Hannah they look more like some art-world parody of the old film clips that show Hitler addressing huge rallies, screaming propaganda until it looks as if his voice will rupture.

The women raise their arms in a series of strange, aggressive salutes. Occasionally they do a synchronized dance step. Mostly, they yell a barrage of hard-to-hear, one-tone invectives, little blasts of rhyme, mostly verbs, an occasional noun.

The harder Hannah tries to follow the message, the more lost she becomes. So after a minute, she just lets it wash over her, like rough water. Usually, she can pick out the last word of each phrase, the word they put all their emphasis and accents on—*protect, respect, reject, neglect, correct, suspect, detect, aspect, reflect, direct, deflect, insect*...

She knows she needs to call in and request assistance from Lieutenant Miskewitz. She knows she needs to make a simple physical move, to grasp a phone and dial a number. To bring in air and emit sound and let common words fall off her tongue.

Instead, she reaches to her lap and pulls up the brown padded mailing envelope. She reaches inside and withdraws Lenore Thomas's notebook, this bible of madness, transcribed by the strongest casualty Hannah will ever know.

She knows she shouldn't read it. She knows the worst thing she can do is finish the letter, that her only hope is to burn the notebook in one more fire. But there's a point in every common human life where the will runs dry and even the faintest vestige of strength has been depleted. We give that moment names of justification. But our naming will never stop us from hitting bottom and losing ourselves, losing the conception of hope, the imagined idea of what life could become.

I'm not myself anymore. But I'm not quite you either, Lenore. I'm left in between. Ready to fade.

She opens the notebook and picks up where she left off.

How does a woman go from being a detective with a methodology, a devotion to the clue and the motive and the conclusive solution...

...to being a mystic so deluged with undercurrent and

chaotic input that paranoia evolves from neurosis to cosmology?

Be patient. Like me, you'll start to lose that righteous grip on rationality, my young sister. My sweet Hannah. And you'll start to dwell on that opaque, other realm—Mystery. (And by this I do not mean the occult.) I mean that dogma where the only pattern appears to be chaos. Where the only consistency appears to be randomness. Where everything is secret and where the connections come apart as soon as they are known.

I mean the place where I live now, Hannah.

Let's guess what's going through your head just now. You're thinking I've hopped lanes, traded one rush for another, swapped my much-loved crank for antique acid. Sorry, that would be one more easy solution. And we both know, I pray, no, I trust, no, no, I guess, by now, we all know that life just won't work that way. The fact is, my new addiction isn't chemical at all. My new monkey is something so much stronger than meth or dust. Are you ready, Hannah? I'm mainlining Hidden Signs. Buried Signals. Coded Messages. I'm completely dominated by that whole subsurface reality that the brutal majority will not acknowledge, where every billboard is an endless bible of interpretations, where every lunch menu is a heinous political creed, where every boring phone conversation is a rape of multiple meanings, and always, always, malignant intent. There is a world beneath Quinsigamond, Hannah. And probably a world beneath that world. The year you've spent down Bangkok has to have changed you and hinted at this fact. I suspect you are beginning to think of yourself as a bar of iron. But even iron will melt at some ridiculously high temperature. Are your dreams starting to trouble you? Do you feel like there's something radically wrong with your digestive process? Has your period been irregular for the past six months or so? You can ignore the symptoms if you choose, little sister. This virus will not go away. As an infected patient, I can attest to its persistence. And there's worse to come. Your actions become uncontrolled—last summer I found myself mailing long letters, like this one, addressed only to:

General Delivery
The Andes Mountains
Argentina, South America

But so what? So my gospel sits in some dead-letter office, in some tiny valley village at the foot of a massive mountainside. There are some things we simply need to do. Movement for movement's sake. It's a way of advancing toward a resolution, a way of killing time until the Aliens show their faces. Already, I'm getting better.

But if you still choose to think I've lost touch, little sister, the loss, of course, is yours. Because, please, make no mistake in this one regard: things are falling apart at every possible seam. And into this breach of disorder and chaos, another putrid god is slouching for Q-town. But you have this promise, Hannah, when the beast comes, Lenore will be back to greet the little shit.

Hannah's head begins to throb and she closes the notebook. And then someone is sliding a shot glass in front of her. It's filled with a clear liquid. Hannah looks up to see Jerome LaCroix in his white silk shirt, opened to his navel, in his toreador pants with the gold brocade down the sides, up high on his two-inch heels, hands elegantly on his hips and a trace of a smile playing on his mouth.

"Girl, you just looked like you could use something," he says.

Hannah picks up the shooter and holds it near her eye, looking through it as if it were some tool of science. She sniffs at it, but there's no distinct odor, or rather there's an abundance of odors, but none she can specify and put a name to.

She looks up at Jerome and manages to say, "I really shouldn't. I might be pregnant."

Jerome brings a flat hand up to his mouth to convey a mock sense of shock. Then he shakes his head and says, "Might do the child all sorts of good. It's medicinal, you know. My own mother took it, in moderation of course, all the while she was carrying me."

Hannah nods at him, not listening, then raises the glass slightly, clears her throat, brings the shooter to her lips, and says, "To my sister, who recently passed on."

THREE
WEEKS
LATER

46.

"What's the sign say?" Ronnie yells from the car.

Flynn hunches over, cocks his head. "Says, 'Open 8 A.M. to midnight.' Want to wait?"

"It's only five-thirty. We've got two and a half hours."

"So you want to keep driving?"

Ronnie's silent, thinking. Finally she says, "Let's wait."

She pushes open the car door, steps outside, and goes through a long run of stretching and bending that Flynn finds both amusing and lovable.

He starts to walk over to her. "Your back hurting?"

"Just a little stiff," she says, and they hug and let both their bodies lean up against the side of the Jeep.

"We've got to take more breaks," Flynn says. "Switch off more often."

"Yeah, but you're not much of a navigator. And you're lousy with the radio."

He holds onto her and digs a finger into her side and she squirms and laughs.

"The funny part is, that's the truth," Flynn says. "I'm no longer a big fan of irony."

"It's only partly your fault. That last two hundred miles it was illegal to play anything but Elvis."

"The King always makes me hungry. You got anything left from the 7-Eleven?"

"We got licorice and nacho crumbs," Ronnie says. "And the beef jerky."

"Why did I buy that? I've got to be more careful with the money."

"It'll go a lot further down here."

They stand and look out over the desert, quiet for a while. They're fifty miles from the nearest collection of people and buildings called Sotela Village. They're parked in front of a small, transplanted lunch car, a 1940s diner that sits like a deco mirage fifty feet off the side of this secondary road. The Gothic lettering on the front of the diner tells them they've reached the Duluoz Cafe. They almost rolled past it, thinking it was just an abandoned mistake, a long-closed-down gas stop left to bake and recede in the sand. But as they went by, Flynn recognized the architecture as native Quinsigamond and yelled for Ronnie to pull in. He jumped from the Jeep and looked in the window and wasn't sure whether it was a good or bad omen. But it was a genuine, functional diner. And probably their best bet for breakfast if they stayed on this road.

"What do you want to do till they open?" Ronnie asks.

"Want to tilt the seats back? See if we can snooze awhile?"

She nods and they climb back inside and try to get comfortable. Flynn's behind the wheel and he turns the ignition key backward and hits the power button on the radio. A growly Texas voice rumbles into the jeep.

> ...And in conclusion, brothers and sisters, let me just reiterate that the Millennium is upon us and the time is short. The signs are already beginning to appear and we must not be blind to them...

"For God's sake," Ronnie says with her eyes closed, her voice midway between a laugh and a moan, "does every region get issued its own Ray Todd?"

Flynn doesn't find the preacher funny, but he bluffs and says,

"Absolutely. It's a requirement. You set up a country, you need a militia, a post office, and a guy to interpret the Book of Revelation."

A new voice comes on the radio with a light, melodic Mexican accent.

Thank you, Brother Baker, for your words of inspiration and welcome to *Borderland Broadcasts*. I'm your host, Sancho "el Coyote" Panza. It's going to be another gorgeous day, so let's get things started with a classic as we watch the sun rise together.

A scratchy rendition of this old tune from *West Side Story* comes on. Flynn can't place the singer. Possibly he's never heard this version before. He hears Ronnie start to hum along with the tune and opens his eyes to find her staring at him.

Before he can say anything, she cranks up the volume, tilts her head sideways toward the door, and says, "C'mon."

They get out and walk around the front of the Jeep. She puts both her arms around his neck, starts to sway, brings her lips to his ear, and says, "I'll lead," her voice low and on the verge of a laugh.

Flynn looks up at the lightening sky, tries for just a second to think of something to say, then abandons the impulse and turns his attention to the music and the slight motion of Ronnie's legs and hips against him.

And they slow-dance that way for a few moments, eyes closed, heads resting on each other's shoulder, palms of their hands rubbing slowly in circles on their backs. Flynn starts to kiss her neck, softly, more tender than exciting. He feels like he should whisper something, but he knows silence is better than an inexact, imperfect phrase. He wishes that what he's feeling right now could be channeled, like a strong, unbroken electrical current, and passed through his hands, into Ronnie's back, her spine, patched straight into her nervous system, unobstructed by language and air. He'd give anything for a connection that pure and direct, that free from interpretation and the need for translation. He knows he's not the first person to have this exact desire, but he's certain he's feeling it as powerfully as anyone ever has.

This moment, this instant, slow-dancing in the desert parking lot of a transplanted diner, is as close to his idea of perfection as he's ever likely to come. He wants his memory to make it eternal, but that's one more impossibility he'll have to accept. Everything starts to fade after a while. Decay is simply a matter of time. That's a given, a rule of nature, the thing that's left at the end. And in light of that, he knows, the best thing to do, maybe the only thing to do, is live in the warmth of this moment as it crests and peaks.

Hazel's probably right about order being an illusion. But where's the value in that knowledge? How is life improved by knowing this?

The unknown singer continues.

. . . somewhere, we'll find a new way of. . .

Then comes a blast of static that knocks "Somewhere" into oblivion.

They stop dancing, but remain in a tight embrace. They look at each other and then at the Jeep.

And of course, there's the sound of a mouthful of air being blown out over a microphone, a fresh breath, and an American voice:

Buenos días, amigos y amigas. We are back in the fellaheen fairgrounds. Come one, come all, and dance the day away with the d.j.'s of the dispossessed. Say *hola* once ag'in to Los Hermanos O'Zebedee and their Sistema Rebelde. *El caos continua,* kids, the chaos does continue.